FEET WITH NO NOSE
BY DAVID BUTLER

krest
PUBLISHERS

KREST PUBLISHERS

Copyright © David Butler 2024

First edition

Cover Design by Monique Hayes

ISBN: 978-0-7961-1466-2 (eBook)

ISBN: 978-0-7961-1465-5 (Print)

First published by KREST Publishers 2024

www.krestpublishers.co.za
Durban, South Africa

CONTENTS

DISCLAIMER

This book contains themes of historical racism and thus contains derogatory language for the intent of accurately conveying the time period in which this book is set only. The thoughts, actions, speech, and beliefs of characters in this book do not portray the views and beliefs of the author or the publishing company.

All italicised text is to be understood as dialogue spoken in Zulu, unless indicated otherwise (e.g., in the use of certain character thoughts, poetry extracts/book titles/film titles/quotes).

This book is for my children, Nicola and Tavis and my grandchildren, Oliver and Darcy; Oscar, Arabella, Pandora, and Sasha.

It commemorates the memory of Peter and Nester Hawkins who, dear friends, were the inspiration for Jack and Mavis McIntyre. It could not have been written without the love and support of my wife Sonja who, through thick and thin, has been my rock, supporting and encouraging me, right to the very end.

I would like to thank Tessa Sangster and Amanda Terblanche for their assistance and advice, and I would like to take this opportunity to thank the team at KREST Publishers - especially my tireless editor Chanel Pillay - they took me onboard, wrapped their arms around me and deftly steered this book to a successful conclusion.

CHAPTER ONE:

1914

Precisely at noon, the hooter sounded, not just to announce that the sun was in its zenith, but more importantly on this occasion, to warn the visitors on board that the ship was about to sail. It was a loud, resonating sound that seemed to come from the belly of the ship and made everything vibrate. The woman holding the pram bent forward to shield her two babies and only straightened up when the hooter stopped.

"What an awful noise! I'm surprised the children weren't scared stiff." Dot turned to the woman beside her, "I've been dreading this moment, Jess, but it's time to say goodbye."

They embraced and held onto each other as if this simple affirmation of friendship would be enough to stave off the sadness of parting. While they whispered their goodbyes and dabbed their eyes, the two men beside them stepped back, out of the shade, and made their way across the sun-bleached deck to the nearby port rail. There, side by side, and each marshalling his own thoughts, they watched with narrowed eyes the people on the deck below who, like funnelled sheep, began to bunch up around the gangplank's open mouth.

"Well, Arthur, time's up," the man with the clerical collar said, mopping his brow. "All good things come to an end, sooner or later, don't they, eh? I wonder if I'll ever be back. Durban grows on one, I think. We've always enjoyed our visits here – such a melting pot you know, so much promise of what could be." He broke off, chiding himself, and placed his hand on Arthur Barclay's shoulder. "Forgive me, I'm rambling. I just want to thank you and Jess once again –"

"Oh, don't mention it, Don. Jess was absolutely insistent. Besides, we are old friends. You married us, you know, so –"

"I know, I know. But you've been very generous." Don McIntyre paused and looked out over the bay. The sky belonged to the wheeling seagulls and far off across the still, flat water, the Bluff rose up into it, smudged blue-green and impenetrable.

"Dorothy and I were … what can I say … flabbergasted." Don's voice was low and measured. "When we came on board, the purser said that we had been upgraded. I knew straight away that it was because of you. We have a bigger cabin now. It will be a lot easier with the twins. You didn't have to do that, Art, you really didn't. But thank you. That's very kind of you, very kind indeed. You asked me not to say a word to a soul about who had paid for our tickets, and I have honoured that, though I feel that others should know."

"Don, what you and Dotty are doing for those two little tykes is amazing. It's the least –"

"Well, not all the congregation would agree with you, would it? I got the distinct feeling at the last parish meeting, many people who remained silent actually agreed with Mrs Arbuthnot when she said words to the effect that taking these babies back to England with us may be noble in principle but is cruel in practice. You know, one or two have even told Dotty that we are going against the natural order of things, and Brigadier Willkie-Scott, believe it or not, told her that we'd been in Africa long enough to know while one can teach a monkey new tricks, one cannot teach it to speak."

"Oh, I wouldn't worry what people say," said Arthur, "you know that's nonsense."

"Granted, but it was said all the same. Art, I have a favour to ask. They have not been baptised. I will attend to that when we get back to England. I would like you to be their godfather. More than that, will you stand surety for them? I mean, if anything were to happen to Dotty or me, I'd like you to be listed as next of kin. I would like to know that they will be taken care of, that they will have someone to turn to, even if that someone is way off in South Africa. Am I asking too much?"

Arthur reached out and took Don's hand in both of his.

"I'd be honoured, Don. I really would."

"Then that's settled. It's a heavy weight off my mind. Thank you. So now you'll have to come and see us next time you're in England – you'll have to come and see the twins! And they'll want to see their godfather, I'm sure."

"What are their names? My godchildren, I mean."

"It might sound a bit trite, but we're calling them Jack and Jill – can't get more English than that, can you? Now, we'd better get back to our wives – time to go. We'll come down and see you off."

They walked back across the deck and joined the ladies. As Arthur and Jess joined the queue, a lady in front of them turned around and, seeing Dot and the pram standing close by, stood aside to make room for them. She smiled and waved them in with an exaggerated sweep of her arm.

"Please, there's plenty of time."

"Oh no," said Dotty, pulling back on the pram, "we're not leaving – we're passengers. Just seeing our friends off. But thank you anyway."

"That's alright then." The woman bent forward. "Do you mind? Can I have a look?" She ducked down and peered inside the pram. Almost immediately, her head bobbed up – gasping for air like someone who can't swim. "Two babies – twins?" She spluttered, "Dear little things, aren't they?"

She turned on her heel and resumed her place in the queue. Her companion must have asked her what the matter was because Arthur, standing behind them, heard the woman say, "Don't look now, Muriel, but there are two black babies in that pram. A white woman with black babies! Fancy that!"

Arthur and Jess paused before stepping onto the gangplank. One last goodbye, and then with their backs hunched and heads pointed down, they began their descent, step by careful step. When at last they stepped onto the wharf, Arthur drew his wife into his armpit and steered her through the milling crowd. They looked up. The ship towered above them and the sun, now behind the ship's funnel, etched the upper decks as though with an indelible pencil. Arthur's eyes took a while to adjust to the shadows, and even longer to see what he was looking for. Then he found them, towards the stern, Don and Dotty, waving their farewell.

"Over there, Jess – at the back. Can you see them?"

"Yes, I see them." Jess waved furiously. "God speed!" she called out, two or three times, but her words, though high-pitched and fervent, attracted little attention and drifted away like flotsam on an ebbing tide, soon lost and bereft of meaning.

CHAPTER TWO:

1937

1

The Annex was not strictly speaking an annex in that it stood on a separate block of land and was connected to the hospital by nothing more than a secluded gravel path that passed beneath a wrought iron gate. For all intents and purposes, it was a drab, nondescript little house that had let itself go – it sat with sunken shoulders under the wing of the much larger and more imposing hospital that nestled on top of the hill, much like a brooding hen. But it was to the Annex that many of Bristol's unmarried mothers went, formless shadows flittering into the night. The service in this establishment was discreet and provided by midwives who also served as nurses in the adjacent hospital. It was to this unprepossessing place that two expectant mothers arrived to have their babies on not just the same rainy day in October 1937 but, coincidentally, at almost the same time.

Rosie Dunn had come all the way from Durban in South Africa to have her baby born on English soil. Her father, Frankie, had brought her over on the RMS Arundel Castle, a vessel which, he proudly told her, only that year had been transformed from a coal-burning four-funnelled passenger liner into a new, two-funnelled, oil-fired vessel that was now sleeker, and more than three knots faster than she had been in the past. Every day on the long voyage from the southern tip of Africa to the bottom of England, they had enjoyed fine weather and their excitement grew in proportion, the closer they came to their destination.

Rosie's mother had died while she was giving birth to her. Frankie too, died a little that day, and would forever hold her memory sacred. He swore at her graveside that he would never marry again. One thing he had learned from the war was that life was as capricious as it was ephemeral – a flickering candle, that could be snuffed out by the curling of an indifferent finger far, far away. Each moment, therefore, was precious and should be clutched to the bosom and cherished. From the moment of his wife's death, Rosie became the centre of his universe and could do no wrong. Even when she became pregnant, the result of a casual affair with a local barman who was married and had three children, he had not uttered a single word of censure, nor had he even so much as raised his eyebrows.

"What has happened, has happened," he told her in that typically sunny and upbeat manner of his. "Just think, I'm going to be a grandfather! If only your mother were here! She'd be so proud!"

The voyage itself was a giddy experience, for they wandered around the ship without restriction. This was a novel experience for them – they were Coloured, born and bred in South Africa, and were unaccustomed to fraternising with white folk. They mingled freely with more than a thousand other passengers, none of whom seemed to take the slightest notice of who they were. At Southampton, they were met by Frankie's wartime friend, Sergeant Joe Wilson, who told anyone who had time to listen that Frankie Dunn had saved his life on the Nairn Ridge in Palestine, at the Battle of Megiddo. He was pleased to be reunited with his South African friend – they had been apart for nearly twenty years – and he was determined to make him feel welcome. On the train, all the way back to Bristol, he entertained them with a constant flow of recollections and anecdotes that made them laugh. The Wilsons treated them like long-lost members of their family and allowed them unfettered use of the tiny, third-floor attic in their own home. Here, Frankie and Rosie spent the last two months of Rosie's confinement in happy co-habitation with this English family, as they counted down the hours to that imminent event.

2

Elsa Duncan, on the other hand, was a local – she came from Clifton, one of the oldest and most affluent suburbs in Bristol. Her father, Patrick Duncan, was an inner-city banker who, by the grace of a huge mortgage that he was able to successfully negotiate with his own bank, had recently managed to move his family to one of the smaller though still highly regarded houses on the prestigious Royal York Crescent. He was therefore a man who placed great importance not just on material well-being, but on social standing as well.

Elsa, his second daughter, was blessed with sultry good looks and a coquettish manner that turned heads wherever she went. He was proud

5

of her, and more so of the attention she attracted, as though it had more to do with him than it did with her. So, it came as a great shock – indeed, he was utterly aghast – when his wife told him that Elsa was pregnant. His outrage was only matched by his sense of betrayal – he took it personally and deemed it an insidious assault on respectability in general and his standing in the community in particular. For him, the odium of this embarrassment was compounded by an even greater sin – the perpetrator of this outrage was, he had just learned, a black man. This smudging of the bloodlines, as he would call it, was something Patrick Duncan knew in his bones to be morally wrong. He was firmly of the view that miscegenation contravened the laws of nature – that had God wanted sheep to inter-breed with goats, he would have made shoats. No self-respecting Englishman in his right mind could ever contemplate such depravity.

So, from the outset, he made it absolutely clear that Elsa could only remain under his roof on three, inviolable conditions. Firstly, she would renounce the man – she would never see him again, nor would she ever mention his name. Secondly, she should never allow anyone to suspect that she was pregnant – or as he said, driving a knife deep into her heart, a fallen woman. Her shame would not be allowed to contaminate his good name, nor would he allow it to besmirch the enviable reputation that he believed he had accrued with pain-staking devotion over many years for his family. Thirdly, and on this point he was most emphatic, when it was time, she would go off to a discreet place, have her baby in unobtrusive seclusion, and then would immediately give it up for adoption.

She, who had flitted through life as the apple of his eye, had never for a moment anticipated the dire consequences of her indiscretion – never had she comprehended the wretchedness and sense of alienation that would befall her should she ever wander from the warm glow of his adulation. So, fearful of the consequences that might befall her should she do otherwise, she accepted her fate with a meek shrug of the shoulders and did what she was told.

Though she renounced Jack and promised never to see him again, it took her a long time to expunge him from her mind. He, the unwitting architect of her downfall, lingered there, bold and finely etched, as though refusing to fade. She had met Jack McIntyre one night at a local dance hall. He was different, not because he was a corporal in a tank regiment, or even because he was good looking and all the girls fancied him – he was different because he was black, and she had never spoken to a black man before. And when he spoke, he sounded refined and genteel – more like an English country squire than one of those West Indians she sometimes encountered on her tram rides into the city.

Jack asked her to dance. And then he asked her again. And again. She was flattered. They danced all night. She had never had such a good time; he was fun, it was madly exciting, and he made her feel special. They met again the following night and the night after that – soon they were inseparable, meeting whenever they could. In the three brief months of their togetherness, she never once took him home and only told her family that she had met someone. One night he told her that he had been born in South Africa, that he had been adopted when he was a baby and had been brought up in England – he also told her that he had a twin sister Jill, who lived in Edinburgh and taught music. Often, behind the closed shutters of her mind, she would relive their clandestine assignations and the throb of passion that engulfed them whenever they found themselves alone – she would replay in excruciating detail the molten sensuousness that his long, sensitive fingers aroused in her and the spine-tingling feeling of loving and being loved.

The only way that she could cope was to persuade herself repeatedly that their brief affair had been a horrible mistake, that it could not possibly have worked out, and that what had originally attracted her – that he was different and came from a different world – would, in the end, tear them apart. No, she told herself a thousand times, I will not see him again, not even to tell him that I am pregnant. Overnight, she simply vanished from his life and with stoic determination prepared herself for a baby she did not want. She tried to plan for the time after her confinement when she could start life afresh, alone, and unencumbered by the flotsam of her past, but it was hard – very hard.

<h1 style="text-align:center">3</h1>

It so happened that the two young ladies arrived at the Annex within an hour of each other but under very different circumstances. Rosie, apprehensive but smiling gaily nonetheless, arrived with Frankie. They burst in through the door and shook themselves like dogs – droplets of flying water, catching the afternoon light, splashed on the floor like tossed confetti. The baby was not moving as often as it had nor with the same amount of vigour. It worried Rosie, but she decided not to say anything until she saw the midwife. Frankie rang the bell on the desk and almost immediately a nurse came into the room. She helped them fill in a handful of forms and then escorted Rosie into the labour ward which smelled strongly of disinfectant.

Elsa arrived shortly afterwards, wooden-faced, and ill at ease. Accompanied by her grim, thin-lipped mother, she was driven to the door in a taxi and was quickly ushered inside.

"Can we get some service here?" asked Mrs Duncan, looking around impatiently.

"Ring the bell, Madam – that's it on the desk," Frankie called out, "the nurse will come."

She did not bother to acknowledge Frankie's presence, not even with so much as a sideways glance. He tip-toed away to the bay windows where he stared with hooded eyes at people scurrying along the pavements in the street below. Mrs Duncan rang the bell, spoke tersely to the nurse when she appeared, and then filled in the forms. Elsa kissed her mother goodbye. Not a word passed between them, though acknowledgement flittered across their faces.

4

Frankie Dunn craved a smoke. It would have been unthinkable for him to have come this far only to miss the birth of his grandchild, but after six tense hours, pacing up and down outside the labour ward, the unrelenting urge to have a smoke had eventually become too much – his self-control, which all the while had kept him tethered to the porthole window, suddenly snapped and before he knew it, he had bounded out the door. Unleashed as it were, he had chased his craving all the way down to the corner store. There, to his great satisfaction, he found what he was looking for – packets of cigarettes lined up behind the counter, resplendent in their regimental colours, all gleaming enticingly in their cellophane overcoats.

"I'll have a packet of Army Club, please." As he approached the counter, the aroma of tobacco became stronger, and he sniffed the air hungrily.

"These ones?" asked the woman behind the counter, reaching up and twisting her head over her shoulder to see him, "Is this what you're after?"

"That's right," he nodded and pointed to the ones that she was reaching for. "Can you make that two packets please?" He caught her eye and smiled sheepishly, "I haven't had one of those since the war."

"Oh, you were in the war, were you?"

"Yes, I was with the Cape Corps – I'm from South Africa – we fought in Palestine."

"Didn't know that. Horrible things wars, you know. From South Africa hey, you came all that way to fight for us?"

"Yes, for king and country. Sorry, ma'am, I'm in a hurry –"

"Lost my boy on the Western Front, I did – cannon fodder he was. Them German guns mowed our lads down in the thousands. On the Somme it was, 1916. Poor dears never had a chance." Her eyes were moist, and he could feel her anguish. "That'll be two bob, love. Sure you don't want a packet of fifty for half a crown? No? Okay. So, you're from the colonies, did I hear you say? Fancy that! What brings you here now?"

"Well, my daughter is having a baby in the hospital up the road – I just came out to get some smokes. She came with me to visit a friend of mine from the war. He and his wife live here in Bristol. We're staying with them, you know. If you'll excuse me, I really must run. Rosie, my daughter, doesn't know that I'm here and I'd hate to miss it."

"That's all right, off you go! And the best of British luck!"

It was still raining when Frankie stepped outside, and gusts of wind blew wetly down the street. He stepped into a recessed doorway and turned his back momentarily into the wind to protect the flickering flame in his cupped hands. He lit a cigarette and drew smoke deep into his lungs. He exhaled, and tension drained from his body like bathwater once the plug has been pulled. There was nothing like a good smoke to settle the nerves and he smiled contentedly. He indulged himself with two more lungsful and winced ever so slightly as the raw smoke caught the back of his throat. Then, recalling that he had been away longer than he had intended, he ground out the half-smoked cigarette with his heel and scurried back up the street, as fast as his leather-soled boots on the slippery pavement would allow.

The moment Frankie returned to the waiting room, he hurried over to the labour ward door and peered through the glass window. He cursed under his breath. *I knew I should not have left her – what the hell is happening?* Frankie stared at Rosie's empty bed. The sheet that had been covering her enlarged belly like a reaching spinnaker was now tossed aside, carelessly it seemed, and now hung towards the floor like a collapsed sail. He twisted his head and could just see the end of the bed in the ward across the passage, the one that had been occupied by the English girl. It too was empty. Damn it, he thought, the minute I go for a fag, the action starts. At that moment a nurse-aid with her arms full of clean white linen came through the swing doors at the other end of the labour ward and hurried over towards Rosie's bed. Frankie took a deep breath and opened the door. He edged his body into the crack.

"Is everything all right?" he asked. "I mean, is Rosie – my daughter – the one that was in that bed – is she alright?"

"Hey, you're not supposed to be in here," said the nurse-aid, rather brusquely. "Can't tell you anything – the midwife is with her now. Now, out you go. I have to get these beds ready." She turned her back on him and began to remake the bed, fluffing the pillows and tucking in new clean sheets.

"Can you just tell me if she's had the baby?"

"You still here? Not born yet. Funny how things work out, isn't it – two births at once." She jerked her thumb over her shoulder, pointing at the other bed in the corner, "She's also in delivery –"

"You mean the one who was in the other cubicle over there?"

"Yup, we've got her in the second birthing room. Lucky for her, Sister is able to nip back and forth between them. So far, so good. Now, if you don't mind, I really can't talk – I have to make the other bed as well and I'm in a hurry. Please go back into the waiting room."

Like a boxer being waved to a neutral corner, Frankie let the door swing shut and tip-toed across the waiting room to the bay windows where he stopped and stared with unseeing eyes at the rain splattering onto the pavement below. For a moment he had a premonition that something might go wrong, that something awful might happen to Rosie or the baby. After all, his own wife Grace had died giving birth to Rosie. He shivered and reached into his pocket for a calming cigarette but then, with a muffled curse, realised where he was. *Take a grip of yourself! Rosie's strong, she's got wide hips – wider than her mother's. This is England and she's in a good hospital – so stop worrying.*

5

"Keep pushing," the midwife's words reached Rosie as though from a great distance, "push, push, push – it's better to get in two or three short pushes with each contraction, better than one long push. Alright, take a breather and we'll try again. Next time, instead of holding your breath for short periods, try blowing out steadily, you might find it easier. And don't be shy – make as much noise as you like."

Rosie was worried. She had no qualms about what the midwife, Libby, was doing. No, her concern was internal. She hadn't felt any movement from the baby for some time and was fearful that something might be wrong. And the pain – oh God, what she would give to make it go away!

Libby turned to her assistant, "Pass me the syringe please, Dora. Thank you." She held it to the light for a moment, flicked it with her forefinger a couple of times and then gave Rosie an injection in her upper arm.

"There," she said, rubbing the spot with a wad of cotton wool, "that's for the pain. It'll make you feel quite drowsy, but it's perfectly safe – nothing to worry about."

"The horn, please." Dora took the Pinard Horn that lay on the tray of instruments beside her and placed it in Libby's outstretched hand. She watched anxiously as Libby once again placed the wide end of the foetal stethoscope on Rosie's belly. Dora read Libby's face like a book; she knew without being told that something was wrong.

Libby, with her ear glued to the Pinard Horn, could not hear the one sound that she so desperately needed to hear – the foetal heartbeat. Initially, it had been there – whispered, as though from another room. But now she could not detect it. Stay calm, she told herself, stay calm. In her three years as a midwife, she had not experienced anything like this, so she decided to go and see Jessie. Jessie was a nursing sister and a midwife with years of experience – she would know what to do.

"Rosie, just hold on for a minute, will you. I won't be long – just going to see what's happening next door. Dora here will keep an eye on things."

Rosie, now very drowsy, nodded and raised herself up onto her elbows to mouth a question, but Libby had left the room before she could get the words out of her mouth. She looked at Dora, but Dora merely shrugged. Rosie sighed and settled back on her pillow. She stared at the ceiling. Even when Dora took her hand and held it in both of hers, Rosie did not look around. After a while, she began to rub her belly with her other hand, round, and round, and, as she did so, she recited the Lord's Prayer. Her lips barely moved, but Dora, still holding her hand, heard every word.

6

In the next-door birthing room, Jessie Wainwright was feeling pleased, but not enough to smile. She was pleased that everything was going well, but not pleased with her patient. A birth never failed to fill her with wonder, so it irked her to see Elsa's tight lips and deadpan indifference. She had seen mothers before who didn't want to have their babies, but not one quite like this. Time and again, in between the contractions, she had tried to lift Elsa's spirits with words of encouragement and bright smiles, but to no avail. Elsa listened with a blank face; she did what she was told, pushed when she was asked to push, but never once did a flicker of animation crease her pretty face. It was as though she just did not want to be there – as though, in a macabre sort of way, she would perform this bodily function only because she had to and once it was over, she would simply get up and go away.

Jessie looked across the bed to her assistant Phoebe and raised her shoulders, as though Phoebe might have an answer to this odd behaviour. But Phoebe merely spread her palms outward and raised her eyebrows. The sullen look on Elsa's face eroded whatever sympathy she might have had for her – there was no excuse, as far as she was concerned, for bad manners. On the other hand, Phoebe didn't really care. She was in a hurry to get back to the surgical ward in the main building where she was supposed to be – she had only come across to the maternity section to help because the nurse who should have been on duty that day to assist Jessie had called in sick. They heard the urgent squish of Libby's rubber shoes. Jessie straightened up and turned around to greet her colleague.

"Hi, Lib, what's up? Something wrong?"

Libby took Jessie's elbow and led her away from the bed so that they could not be overheard. "You'd better come quickly, Jess. I am worried. I can't hear the foetal heartbeat. What do you think I should do?"

"How's the patient? That's what I want to know. Any bleeding ... more than usual, I mean? Any increase in pain?"

"Name's Rosie. Some blood, but not enough to worry about. She's in a lot of pain."

"Have you given her anything for it – scopolamine perhaps?"

"Yes, about ten minutes ago. She's drowsy now, and calmer. I'm worried, Jess, I've got a horrible feeling that the child might be stillborn."

They walked abreast to the door and then Jessie paused. "I won't be long," she said over her shoulder to Elsa, "you'll be okay with Phoebe – she'll look after you while I'm gone."

When they were in the passage, alone and out of sight, Jessie held onto Libby's arm, detaining her. "Does she know – your patient, I mean – does she know there's a problem? How long ago did she last feel the baby move?"

"She went into labour shortly after she arrived. She told me that she was worried about the baby because it wasn't moving like it had before. I checked. There was movement, not strong, and there was a heartbeat, also not strong, but regular. She'll be shattered – she's so looking forward to this child."

"And this one," said Jessie, jerking her thumb backwards in the direction of Elsa's room, "doesn't want hers at all. Funny world, isn't it?"

By the time they reached her bedside, Rosie was no longer praying; and the languid way she turned her head and stared at them with vacant eyes told Jessie that the drug had taken effect. A rancid odour of stale urine, vaginal discharge, and sweat assailed Jessie's nostrils, making her wince involuntarily. She nodded to Dora and took the Pinard Horn from her. She listened to Rosie's stomach, moving it from place to place. There was no foetal heartbeat.

"Look," she said as she led Libby away from the bedside and out of hearing, "I think I'd better stay here with Dora. You go to mine – Elsa Duncan is her name. She's okay and it'll be a straightforward delivery. If you need my help, then send Phoebe to fetch me."

She saw Libby hesitate. "No, no – it's fine. Now, off you go," Jessie said, halting any further protest from Libby.

Jessie Wainwright had been a midwife for more than twenty years and was highly regarded in the profession. She loved her work and those who knew her would all agree that she was never happier than when she was aiding mothers to bring new life into the world.

Suddenly Rosie's contractions commenced again. They were close together and intense. Jessie signalled to Dora to get ready. The head presented. Another huge effort on Rosie's part, and the baby slid into Jessie's hands. It was a boy. His skin was blue. He had purple lips and floppy limbs. Ominous, tell-tale signs. Jessie flipped him over quickly and expertly began to rub his body, hoping for a colour change. Oh God, she said to herself, not this. She glanced at Rosie and noticed that her eyes were closed. Jessie could hear her own heart thumping loudly in her ears – there was no time to lose.

"Quick, Dora, cut the cord." As soon as it was done, she hurried out.

At the door she shouted instructions back over her shoulder, "Dora, the placenta. Get it out for me, please. Watch for bleeding. Tidy up and watch her closely. I won't be long."

In the nursery, she bumped into Libby who had arrived seconds earlier. They exchanged looks of surprise and then glanced down, examining the baby in each other's arms. Both were boys. One was beginning to turn pink, the other was still blue. One stretched and cried out, the other was limp and silent. Jessie knew the signs. Then, almost without realising what she was doing, she held up the lifeless baby and passed it over to Libby.

"Here, you take this one. I'll take yours."

"For God's sake, Jess, what are you doing?" Libby could feel her hackles rising.

"We're swapping them around, that's what. Don't you see – one of them wants a baby, wants it badly – she'll be a good mother. The other doesn't and won't. She'll give it up anyway."

She looked at Libby with bright, luminous eyes, "What about Elsa – how is she? How did she react?"

"She's fine, but suffering from post-birth daze, I think. You know, when it was all over, she just sort of fell back and rolled over. Strange one that. Like she's just blocking everything out, like nothing at all has happened. Very strange. Ask Phoebe. She'll tell you. Bet Elsa's already asleep."

"Didn't she ask for the baby?"

"No, not a word. As I say, she sort of turned her back on it."

"And Phoebe – how much does Phoebe know?"

"Well, she wasn't there when it happened – she was in here. I asked her to fetch more hot water and fresh towels. It all happened quickly, Jess. Before I knew it, the baby was in my hands. I cut the cord myself and came straight over here. Phoebe heard me call out, but it was all over by the time she got back to me. We met in the passage. I simply told her to take care of the afterbirth – you know, the usual procedure."

"Well, there you are! See what I mean? Come on, Lib! Let's do this little chap a favour! Let's give him the best chance we can. See, they are both dark, both boys – only difference is that one of them is dead."

She took the baby's hand gently with her little finger. "Think about it, Lib, if you were this little chap, what would you like to happen to you?"

"But we can't really do it, can we? What would people say? I mean, what are you going to tell Dora? She saw how blue the baby was – she knows the signs – she'll smell a rat, I'm quite sure."

"Who is going to ask? This is the last place where people ask questions, you know that. I'm not going to tell anybody anything. Don't worry, Libby – leave it to me. If Dora asks, tell her to come and see me. And if it makes you feel better, I'll sign the papers. And please tell Phoebe that she can go back now. There's not much more she can do

13

here – thank her for coming over to help us out. She's keen to get back to her surgical ward, I think."

7

Rosie was overjoyed that her fears had proved groundless – she had a healthy baby! And a boy at that! Frankie would be over the moon! She wasn't fussed about names; she knew that if it was a boy, Frankie wanted him to be called Isaac, after the Reverend Isaac Dyobha. She'd heard the story many times, how this brave man had rallied his comrades on the sinking SS Mendi, a troopship that was taking 823 members of the fifth Battalion, South African Labour Corp to fight in France in 1917. In the pre-dawn hours of a foggy February morning, just off the Isle of Wight, the Mendi collided with the SS Darro, an empty meat ship bound for Argentina. She was almost sliced in half, pitching the luckless men into the sea. Most of them could not swim and the Darro did not stop. Less than 200 of those poor souls survived the tragedy and when Frankie met some of them in London shortly afterwards, he heard about the death dance – how this man, all the way from Pondoland, had exhorted his comrades to remove their boots and join him in a dance on the listing deck of that stricken vessel. They danced and danced until they died. Frankie, moved to tears by this tragic tale, felt a profound sense of obligation to honour the heroic Reverend Isaac Dyobha and said that if God ever granted him a grandson, his name would be Isaac.

So, when Libby came into the waiting room to tell him the good news, that he had a grandson, he rushed over and hugged her.

"Oh my, that's wonderful! A boy! Tell my Rosie I am so proud of her!"

"She told me to tell you that his name is Isaac. Said you'd understand. Goodness, she was so excited – babbled on about a priest on a sinking ship in the war – said you'd know."

Frankie couldn't wait to get back to South Africa to show off not just his grandson but, more importantly, the English Birth Certificate that would accompany him. He had fought for Britain in the war, had seen first-hand how the British strode across the landscape like Romans, certain of their own omnipotence and carefree in what they said and did. He had tasted what it meant to be British and now he hungered for some of it – not in a gluttonous way, but enough to satisfy the smouldering discontent and the aroused sense of injustice that soldiering in foreign lands had inculcated in him. When he returned from the war, it was not as a conquering hero, but simply as a coloured man, returning home without fanfare or fuss – like a donkey being led back to its stable, he used to say. By insisting that Isaac should be born in England, Frankie had made his grandson British, something that gave him access to British citizenship – a lifeline that nobody could ever take away from him.

8

Libby had prepared her answer – if Elsa asked, she would say that there had been complications with the umbilical cord, that it had wrapped around the baby's neck, suffocating it. But when she came back to the bedside and reached for Elsa's hand, she had been pushed away. Undaunted, she drew her chair closer and leaned over.

"Elsa. Your baby. It was stillborn. There was nothing we could do. I'm sorry – so, so sorry."

Elsa turned her face towards Libby, turned it into the pillow and clutched the sheet so tightly that her fingernails dug deeply into the flesh of her palms. Jessie saw this and let out a long slow breath. She reached out a comforting hand, struggling within herself to find appropriate words of commiseration, but once again, before she could find them, Elsa pushed her away and rolled over and faced the other way.

"Go away. Just leave me alone."

Libby got up. She straightened the bedclothes without thinking and left the room. Elsa lay on her side and stared out the window. Sullen clouds bustled past, each one a Levite feigning not to stop for her plight. With the cutting of the umbilical cord, she had also severed whatever ties she still had to Jack. Stark, crisp images of their time together floated into view, momentarily blocking the clouds out. Like dead leaves falling from a tree, each one held her attention briefly before it eddied out of sight, only to be replaced by another. Lying there, in the rumpled bedclothes, she had an urge to reach out and try to catch them, but her body was numb and would not budge. So, she watched them twist and twirl, falling past her in no particular order. She willed herself to sleep, but the dead leaves kept falling and fell long after she had drawn the curtains over her tired eyes.

She went home. She had dared to hope that she would be received if not with open arms, then at least with smiles enough to ease her pain – enough to bring to her own life that semblance of normality that they all aspired to. But she quickly discovered the truth of the old adage that the past is with us, late and soon – she could not escape it. She realised to her chagrin that it could never be swept away or papered over, especially not in her own home where reality was never allowed to outstrip the preconceived and strongly held convictions that were championed around the dinner table, especially by her father. Though everyone was very civil to her and treated her agreeably, there remained a tension, an archness of attitude that was conveyed in so many sideway glances and back-of-hand whispers. Elsa soon concluded that she was spoken about more often than she was spoken to, and that, for all intents and purposes, nothing would ever change – she remained an outcast in her own home. By day, she managed to suffer this humiliation – which she regarded to be both cruel and unfair – pretending that it did not exist, but at night, alone in her bed, with one hand reaching furtively for a solace that was not there, she allowed the tears to flow, unhindered.

All thoughts of Jack were banished, but her mind would often wander to those forbidden places where his memory still lingered, especially when sleep evaded her. He wouldn't want me, not now, she told herself again and again, and I have no idea where he is or how to contact him, even if I wanted to. Besides, Daddy would be sure to find out.

Finally, months later, she made up her mind. She went to her father and told him that she wanted to make a clean break, and that she wanted to put her old life behind her and start all over again. If he would help her, she would like to visit her aunt in South Africa and, if things worked out well, she might even stay there and start a new life. For Patrick Duncan, his strait-laced sister was the perfect answer to a troubling dilemma. He wrote to her immediately and, without saying why, asked if Elsa could visit her. When the reply came, he called his wife into his study.

"My dear, I have just received the best possible news. Hilda has agreed to have Elsa. What do you think?"

"Me? What do I think? Lord knows what I think. You tell me."

"Well, I think Elsa needs to get out of here, at least for a while – it will do her the world of good. I'm told that Durban is a delightful place – just what she needs."

"But Hilda is single. And you know, a lot older. You … you think … I mean, is this really such a good idea? We always said that Hilda was a bit odd –"

"No, don't worry. From what I can gather, she's living a pretty good life out there. I think she'll be a perfect chaperone for Elsa – she'll keep her on the straight and narrow all right, just you wait and see. Now, leave it to me."

On the day of Elsa's twenty-first birthday, her father gifted her a specially reduced return ticket to South Africa for £50. Her mother, behind his back, gave her an envelope that contained £25 in well-worn, single pound notes. Three weeks later, as the shortening days and leaden skies announced the onset of winter, Elsa boarded the Edinburgh Castle and sailed for Durban. On board she transformed herself; she entered the on-board salon as a not inconspicuous caterpillar with long dark hair and emerged, dazzlingly bedecked, a golden-winged butterfly. The hairdresser shortened her hair for her, curling it in at the nape of her neck, and she dyed it a fashionable blond colour. To complete her metamorphosis, she applied liberal amounts of eyeshadow and changed the colour of her lipstick. Then, to finally rid herself of her chrysalis state, she changed her name. From now on, she would be Anna Duncan, her middle name that she had inherited from her grandmother. Elsa was the past; Anna was the future.

Waiting for her at the docks, was her Aunt Hilda. The two of them, both feeling hard done by and worn smooth by the vagaries of a blighted and unfair past, took to each other with a spontaneity and warmth that surprised them both. In no time at all and at her aunt's behest, Anna blended into her new surroundings – she became invisible, just another pebble in the detritus that was washed up onto Durban's golden beaches. She couldn't recall when she had last been so happy, so much so, that in her first letters home, she told her parents that she had cashed in the return portion of her ticket and was not coming back – indeed, she went on to say that she now regarded her previous misfortune as a stroke of good luck. She told them that Elsa no longer existed – she was Anna from now on. Her life in Bristol rapidly faded, and so did the people who had shaped it – they became blended into a hazy past. Jack just seemed to disappear; in her mind he was like a dropped penny, never to be retrieved, and seemingly lost forever.

***

Two months later, Frankie, Rosie, and Isaac disembarked from the mail ship when it docked in Durban. They had been away nearly six months which was the amount of time off that Frankie had arranged with his employer, Arthur Barclay. He had missed his work on the farm, missed looking after all the farm vehicles that were so essential to the smooth running of the farm – and he missed the creative side, making things that the farm needed with his trusty welding apparatus. He had a good job; Arthur more or less gave him a free rein with the mechanical side of the farm, and he had a nice house close to the workshops which Arthur had allowed him to connect to the farm generator, thus providing him with electricity – something that not many of his peers had. When at last the car broke free of Durban's cluttered industrial sprawl and began to nose its way north towards Zululand – only then did Frankie really feel like he was going home. He sat in the back seat with Rosie and young Isaac between them, and stared out the window, suffused with a feeling of immense contentment; the familiar fields of sugar cane, rolling like a green sea to the horizon, gave him that uplifting happiness which a man has when he knows he is coming home, home to his hearth and his kin, and all that he holds dear.

CHAPTER THREE:

1949

1

Shortly after Richard Barclay commenced his schooling at the local government school, an event occurred that brought him into unexpected prominence with his peers and, more specifically, to the attention of Andre Celliers, a strongly built, dark-haired boy who Richard idolized. Andre stood at least half a head taller than the rest of the boys in the class and had a nonchalant confidence that was more likely predicated upon his physical strength than any other defining quality – it certainly allowed him to assume command whenever the boys were at play.

On that particular day, the school bell had no sooner sounded the end of the last lesson when the prefabricated classrooms burst open, scattering children far and wide. One group of boys, satchels in tow and ahead of the rest, honked and hooted as they raced out through the school gates and fanned out across the tarred road, much as pent up geese do, with madly flapping wings, when they are let out of their coop. They ran helter-skelter onto a dirt side-road that veered off into a plantation of unkempt pine trees. Andre ran in front, Richard at the back. Unlike the others, Richard kept himself in check – he ran with his jaws clenched tight and a high-stepping gait, like a horse held on a tight rein. Andre had something that he was going to show them, something he had snuck from his father's bedside table. Richard, like the others, was dying to find out what it was.

Once they were around the bend and hidden from view, the boys stopped running and bunched around Andre, who knelt down to open his satchel. With a great flourish and an upturned, triumphant grin, he produced a catapult. They stared at it, mesmerised. Richard could feel his breath starting to quicken. This was a far cry from the catapults that the herd boys on his grandfather's farm carried around their necks to shoot birds; this was a weapon. It was heavy, gnarled, and well-worn, with thick, rubber tubing. There was something ominous about it, lethal even, that made them draw back. They watched Andre, arch-eyed, not sure what he was going to do next. He stood up and heaved the rubbers, pulling the leather cup right back to his chin. His extended left arm quivered and shook. Then, knuckles white with strain, he paused, as though holding an arrow tight on a bowstring. Richard would never forget that vision – it conjured up images of Robin Hood, resplendent in his green tunic, at once heroic and grand. He stared at Andre, envy throbbing at his temples.

Someone asked Andre if his father used it to shoot birds. He replied with a scornful laugh and tossed his head.

"Hell no! My dad uses it to shoot stray dogs that come and crap on our lawn. Or *kaffirs*, when they come into the orchard and steal fruit. He can stand on the veranda and hit just about any tree he wants to. You should see the *umfaans* jump out of the mango trees and run like hell when he lets loose with a couple of shots. But you must use marbles or ball bearings. Dad says they are more accurate and sting like hell!"

Andre's words thrilled Richard and his heart leapt. They excited him, not because of their unfamiliar earthiness or even their brazen implication about ends and means, but much more because in their verbalisation, they awoke him to a new awareness: Whites were superior to Blacks and could do no wrong. But they also worried him. Because he never heard them at home.

"Anyone see any birds? No crows or doves? No? Anything that I can shoot at?"

"Hey, Andre," someone called out, "can't see any birds, but I see something better. Reckon you can hit them from here?"

Andre's eyes lit up at the sight, and he licked his lips. This was better than birds. "*Umfaans* looking for golf balls – good stuff! My dad says they are cheeky buggers because they can't find lost golf balls when they are caddying, but they sure as hell can find them afterwards. They think they are clever."

"You're not going to shoot at them, are you?" asked Willie Simpson, a slightly built boy with wire-rimmed glasses that made him squint as he peered down the slope. "I mean, they don't look like they are doing anything wrong, are they? We can't really shoot at people, can we?"

"You aren't scared are you, Will?" Though the words were not directed at him, their mocking, accusatory tone made Richard's stomach tighten. The other boys turned on Willie, assailing him with a barrage of jeers.

"Course I'm not scared." Willie adjusted his glasses and spread his palms, "But why shoot at the caddies? Why not something else?"

"Because this is designed to shoot things, like dogs, cats, those *umfaans* – to teach them a lesson. And I didn't sneak it out of my dad's drawer just to muck around doing target practice."

Through all this, Richard remained in the background, silent and still. But apprehension flared his nostrils and made his heart pound. A tiny red light flickered deep in his head, warning him that this was unfamiliar territory.

"What about you, Rich? What do you think? You haven't said anything yet – you aren't chicken as well, are you?"

All eyes turned to Richard and skewered him. He was taken aback, helplessly pinned by the question. His ears were burning, and blood thumped in his temples. Tiny bubbles of sweat broke out on his upper lip. In that instant he knew alienation and in a corner of his mind, the tiny incessant voice shrilled louder and louder, telling him to just walk away and leave them to it. But the thought of being regarded as a scaredy-cat was intolerable. He squared his shoulders and faced Andre with a bravado he wore like a coat that was a size too small.

"Don't be silly," he said, stepping to the front. "Me, scared? Not at all! Look, if you think you can shoot as far as that, then go on, have a go."

Richard would have preferred not to have said anything – would have preferred to remain blended into his surroundings, to see without being seen. All his life he had enjoyed an almost voyeuristic fascination in what others did, especially if the things they did were illicit. While he had a deep-seated need to be liked and accepted by his peers, he shrank back from participation in activities that he suspected would raise eyebrows. Non-participation, he consoled himself, exonerated him from the burden of complicity and even guilt.

Andre stared at Richard for a long moment, then smiled as if something long lost had been found. He bent his head to examine the stone that he held in the catapult. Then, hunched forward and cat-like, one tentative foot in front of the other, he tip-toed into the bushes and peered through the branches at the clearing below.

"Over there! They're sitting down, in the shade. Have a go!"

The catapult rose up, stretched, held for a few shaky seconds, and then hurled the stone upwards in a high, graceful arc. For a moment it hung there in the sky, a speck of dirt on a blue canvas, before it fell slowly back towards the treeline and was lost from sight. They all ducked down and held their breath. Nothing happened. Far away they could hear the cars on the tar road and, closer by, the breeze whispering in the trees. But nothing else. They looked at one another, then at Andre. But he, bold and unperturbed, was already fixing a second stone into the sling. This time there was a reaction – a chorus of voices rose up from the bush below them.

A third stone crashed through the trees and scattered the caddies in all directions. This brought squeals of supressed laughter from the boys and they regrouped around Andre, watching him closely as he pulled more stones from his pocket.

"Good shot, Andre! See them run!"

"Boy! That was close!"

"I'll let rip a couple more. Hey, Rich, you got a stone for me?"

This startled Richard. Before he could reply, Andre dug a couple of stones out of his own pocket and fired them in quick succession. Shouts, loud and clear in the gentle breeze, wafted up to where they stood on dancing feet, laughing. Andre was bent over, rummaging in his pocket for another stone, when a tall dark figure stepped silently from behind a tree and made its way towards them. It was one of the caddies. He was cross. And he carried a stick. That made their laughter stop abruptly, as though an electric switch had been flicked by an invisible hand.

"What are you doing? There are people down there. Didn't you hear us call out?"

Andre looked up, startled. He loaded the catapult with quick, nimble fingers and raised it waist high. His body slipped into a menacing crouch, and he watched the caddy with narrowed eyes.

"No, no! Nkosana, stop!"

The caddie wasn't scared. He moved directly in front of Andre and raised his stick.

"Don't do that! There are people down there," he said, his voice loud and firm, *"you'll hurt someone if you do that. Go and play somewhere else."*

"Does anyone know what this bugger is saying?" asked Andre over his shoulder, "I don't speak Zulu, but I don't like the tone of his voice. He could be swearing at us for all I know."

"He's not swearing. He's asking us not to shoot stones or someone will get hurt."

All eyes turned to Richard; they stripped him bare, seeing him as though for the first time. He had spoken without thinking. The words just came out. If only he had kept his mouth shut.

"What do you mean someone will get hurt – he's not threatening us, is he? If you can speak the lingo, then you tell him to mind his own bloody business and not to be cheeky or else he'll get one of these in his mush."

Richard felt ten feet tall. He licked his lips with the tip of his tongue, revelling in the moment. Elation surged through him, washing away the impotence that only moments before had tormented him. The realisation that he could speak better Zulu than any of the others was like dropping a huge stone into a deep pond – it sent waves of self-awareness rippling to the furthest shores of his being and, in the giddiness of that exquisite moment, he felt transformed. That language could deliver such an effortless victory! Who would have thought it? And then, as though at the falling of a second stone, he realised that he could interpret the caddy's words any way he liked. Nobody would be any the wiser. He stepped round Andre and stood in front of him, facing the caddie.

"He says he is very sorry," he said calmly, looking straight at the black face. At the same time, he pointed over his shoulder to Andre, who crouched behind him, low and tense as a coiled spring.

"He says he didn't know anyone was down there. He was not trying to hit anyone either. It won't happen again."

The others looked at one another. It wasn't just the words, but the way they rolled off his tongue that made them regard him with unbridled curiosity. Richard heard Andre click his tongue noisily.

"Tell him to piss off, Richard. No *munt* is going to tell us what to do."

"I already did. Don't worry."

Richard kept his eyes fixed on the caddy. He noticed the whites of his eyes; saw that he had no shoes; that his pants must have been hand-me-downs because they were much too big for him and were held up by a thick fake leather belt; he noticed that instead of a shirt, he wore a grubby woollen jersey which a long time ago had lost its shape and now hung from his shoulders in shabby disarray – all this he noticed without looking.

"My friend says he did not mean it and he won't do it again. You can go and tell the others that everything is all right. Go well, my brother."

The caddy hesitated. He looked each boy up and down, then slowly lowered his stick.

"All right," he said at last, *"tell him to be careful next time. Stay well."*

Within seconds he was swallowed up by the bush. Not so much as a single leaf moved to mark where he had gone. A limp stillness hung about them like a shroud. No one moved. Silence crashed about them in breaking waves.

"Phew! Good thing you were here, Rich," Willie's voice sounded scratchy and far away, like a gramophone playing in another room. "He was a big bugger. For a moment I thought he was going to have a go at you, Andre."

"Like hell! He knew I'd have let him have it with this. That's why he buggered off."

They looked at one another, eyebrows raised. Then, without a word, they turned and walked back towards the road. Andre held Richard back for a moment, gripping his arm.

"Thanks," he said, leaning close to Richard's ear, "bit tricky, wasn't it? You like to come round to my place, sometime? Tomorrow maybe, or the next day?"

Richard laughed, a brittle little laugh. This was brotherhood, much stronger and infinitely more desirable than mere acceptance. He laughed again, his eyes bright and dancing.

"Sure," he said, nodding his head, "I'll check with my mum." Then, like a pilgrim at a shrine, he found the voice he was looking for. "Can't let a cheeky bugger like that spoil good fun, can we?"

At that moment a bicycle came down the road. Richard recognised the rider and waved. It was Mpango, cook and major factotum in the Barclay household. Richard patted Andre on his shoulder, affirming what had not been said, and ran out onto the road.

"Sorry, guys," he shouted over his shoulder, "my mum wants me. See you tomorrow."

He climbed up onto the crossbar of the bicycle and settled himself side-saddle between Mpango's braced arms. The bike wobbled, steadied, then straightened, and picked up speed. Andre walked a few paces after it and then stopped; he stared up the road, long after it had disappeared. The others were discussing Richard. He stood with his hands clasped behind his head, listening to them.

"He speaks Zulu like one of them," said one, rolling his eyes. "I didn't know he could speak like that – sounded just like one."

Someone snorted. "Yah, he's a *kaffir-boetie*, that's for sure."

"A *kaffir-boetie* – what's that?"

"Don't know," said Willie, cleaning his glasses. "Doesn't *boet* mean brother in Afrikaans?"

"It's a black lover, stupid. That's what it means. Except, my dad doesn't like black lovers."

"Neither does mine," said Willie. "But Rich seems a nice bloke –"

"Yah, but to speak Zulu like that means he must spend a lot of time with *munts* and that's not good. *Munts* aren't like us, they're different. My mom says I can't play with them – they are dirty and can give you stuff."

"My dad told me you can't trust the Blacks; they'll cut your throat for sixpence."

"Yah, that's right. My dad has a gun next to his bed – just in case."

Andre walked back to the others and waved his arms, herding them up the road.

"Cut it out, guys. Leave Rich alone, okay? I don't like them either. But if he does, that's his business. That's fine by me."

2

For a while, Richard basked in the warm glow that his new-found friendship with Andre provided and, with artless innocence, aped his every move and utterance. Molly noticed the change, saw the puff of his chest as new-found words spilled from his mouth, and she worried about him – worried about the company her son was keeping at school.

Suddenly, he wanted a catapult, and he kept badgering Amidu, their gardener, to make one for him. And, after much pleading on his part, she at last conceded and arranged for Richard to visit the Celliers' house. So, one afternoon after school, he accompanied Andre to his home at the Magistracy on the understanding that when Mpango came to fetch him at 5:00 pm, he would stop doing whatever they were doing and would come home right away.

No sooner had they arrived, then Magda, Andre's sister, sidled up. She had lovely brown eyes that danced all over Richard's face. When she tried to tag along, hoping to play with them, Andre shooed her away, saying, "No, this is boys' stuff – girls aren't allowed."

He then took Richard into the inner sanctum of his parents' house, to their bedroom, cavernous and still. It reminded Richard of a time when he had accompanied his mother to church; while she was doing the flowers in the vestry, he had wandered up the isle and had walked around the altar, all by himself. He remembered the eerie stillness there; it made him feel as though he was being watched by an unseen presence. The large bed in the middle of the room was like an altar. Richard wasn't keen to approach it; nevertheless, he followed Andre, treading lightly on his toes.

When Andre reached the bed, he beckoned Richard to come closer. Then, without turning around, he bent down and opened the bedside drawer. There was the catapult. The one that Andre's father used to shoot people with. It lay coiled up like a snake under a rock. Andre stuck his hand in and pulled out an old tobacco tin. He looked around, then opened it, and thrust it at Richard who recoiled – he was still thinking of snakes. When he saw the marbles and ball bearings piled on top of each other like miniature cannon balls, Richard felt his stomach tighten and he quickly looked away. Outside, through the curtained window and across the yard, were the mango trees, mostly dark green but splashes of yellow revealed an abundance of pendulous fruit. For a moment Richard pictured himself sitting in one of those trees, juice dribbling down his chin as he sank his teeth into the plump flesh of a nice ripe mango. That image was immediately replaced by another – he visualised volleys of round shots, fired with unerring accuracy from the catapult in Mr Celliers' steady hand, crashing through the leaves and finding his flesh. He shivered and turned away from the window. Andre closed the drawer and went over to the wardrobe that stood nearby. It had brass fittings and a mirror in the middle.

"Now, see this, Rich – promise you won't tell I ever showed you this?" He opened both doors carefully and then pulled back the clothes hanging inside. There, gleaming dully in the darkness and leaning obediently against the back wall, were several guns.

"You sure this is okay?"

"Course. Why not? We're only looking and –"

"What if someone sees us?"

"Rich, don't be a scaredy-cat. Now, see this –"

"I'm not scared. Just don't think we should be playing in here, that's all."

"I'm telling you, we're not playing. We're only looking."

Richard took a deep breath and reached in and held back the hanging clothes that blocked his view. "My dad doesn't shoot, but my grandpa has buck horns on the wall in his office. He must have guns, but I've never seen them."

"Careful. Don't touch. Never touch the metal, especially the barrel – fingerprints cause rust. Yah, my dad shoots a lot of buck – they make the best *biltong*. We've got some hanging in the garage – I'll ask Mom if you can have some. Now, see that box there? In the corner? That's where Dad keeps his revolver. I'm not allowed to open it – he'll kill me if he finds out that I've been near it. What's it for? It's a police gun. For protection – in case *coons* try to break into our house and rob us."

Andre closed the wardrobe, and they walked outside to stand together in the warm sunshine. Richard heaved a huge sigh of relief to be outdoors. The swathes of manicured lawn, bright in the sun and stretching all the way down to a shrubbery at the bottom of the garden, and the vaulted high blue sky soothed him and made him feel comfortable again.

They played a game of cops and robbers. Magda was the robber and Andre was the police captain. Richard was his sergeant. Heroic Andre, always in command, always on the winning side, told them what to do. Richard was thrilled; here he was, shoulder to shoulder with his hero, and also on the winning side. He played his subordinate role with unrestrained glee. Every time they caught Magda, they tied her up and took her to the coal shed which Andre said was the jail. Richard noticed that when she spoke to Andre, she spoke in *Afrikaans*, but when she spoke to Richard, she switched to English.

"Why do you speak Afrikaans to Andre?"

"Because my dad is *Afrikaans*," said Andre, speaking for his sister. "You're a *Rooinek*, like my mom – she's born in England. But we all speak both. Dad says everyone in this country should."

Richard mulled that over but said nothing. He'd never heard that term before. The notion that both languages should be spoken by everyone was novel and caught him by surprise. He very seldom heard *Afrikaans* being spoken – occasionally down at the rail or in some government office or other, but never in his home. Come to think of it, he wasn't sure if his parents could speak *Afrikaans*, even if they wanted to.

They went inside to the bathroom to wash their hands before tea. The sound of African voices, soft and compliant, drifted in through the open window. Richard went to the window and listened.

"Is that the servants I can hear? Are they in the kitchen? How many do you have?"

"Two. A cook and a girl. Well, we also have a garden boy, but he only comes twice a week. Rich, we're not rich like you."

"Like me? I'm not rich."

Andre laughed. "Not you, silly. Your family. My dad says your family is loaded."

"Loaded? Really? I don't think so. My dad never talks about –"

"Well, my dad says that the Barclays have just about everything that opens and shuts – he says they have a fancy big house, the only swimming pool in the village, three cars, a house at the Bay, and more servants than they know what to do with. Says your dad is a doctor – he makes lots of *mali*."

They walked out of the bathroom. "Hey, Rich, you go and have a chat with our cook if you like. I told him you were coming – said you could speak good Zulu. I'm just going to fetch Magda – it's teatime."

The kitchen was small but neat and tidy. The cook was cutting up vegetables and the girl, really a middle-aged, large-breasted woman, was fussing over the tea tray. They looked up, their faces as blank as old newspaper, but soon became alive when they heard Richard talk. They marvelled at his intonation and his easy use of idiom; white people, especially ones so young, seldom expressed themselves with such fluency. They nodded and chuckled to each other when he spoke. For his part, he revelled in being taken seriously by them – they listened and responded as though he was their equal.

When they asked him how it was that he spoke Zulu so well, he replied, "*Ngancelisa ebelini 'kama!*" and they threw their heads back and roared with laughter. They were still laughing when the door opened, and Andre's mother came in.

"What's going on? What are you doing in here?"

"I'm sorry, Mrs Celliers. Andre said –"

"You don't go into other people's kitchens without asking, do you hear? If you want anything from my kitchen you ask me, not Andre. And anyway, you shouldn't be speaking to these people – it's not proper. Now, Josephine, is the tea tray ready? Good. Stop mucking around and take it through to the *stoep*. What about the biscuits – hold on a minute …"

She went over to the pantry cupboard and unlocked the door with a key that dangled from her belt on a piece of string. She opened a tin and removed several round flat biscuits which she placed on a plate. Then, with her index finger bobbing up and down as it moved around the plate, she counted them, carefully. She closed the tin and relocked the pantry door.

"There you are. You can take them out now."

Richard was intrigued. He'd never seen a pantry door locked before. Mrs Celliers must have seen the look on his face. "Have to lock everything these days. Things have a habit of disappearing. If you're not careful, they just walk out the door. Now, come with me."

She took Richard by the hand and led him out of her kitchen.

At 5:00 pm sharp, Molly arrived instead of Mpango. When she got out of the car, Richard ran to her and threw his arms around her. She ruffled his hair then eased him away, but he held onto her hand and looked at her with moist shining eyes.

"I thought you said that Mpango was going to fetch me?"

"Yes, I did. But I decided to come. I had to go into the village, so I thought I'd pick you up on the way home. Did you have a good time, dear? Don't forget your manners – say goodbye nicely."

"Andre promised me some *biltong*. I won't be long."

Molly met Mrs Celliers at the front door but did not go in. They stood there, on the *stoep* with the sun going down behind them, and appraised each other with quick up-and-down looks that took in all the salient details they needed to form their opinions. Mrs Celliers offered Molly her hand.

"I'm Anna. Sorry, Molly, did you say? Pleased to meet you. My husband, Kobie, plays golf with your husband at the club. Would you like to come in for a quick cup of tea?"

"Perhaps another time. I'm afraid I'm in a bit of a rush. Thanks so much for having Richard, Anna. Is that an English accent I can hear? Very faint, but it's still there."

"Yes," Molly heard the barely concealed irritation in Anna's voice, "I'm from England – Bristol actually. I don't hide it, you know. But I also have no intention of ever going back. This is my home, and I am very –"

"Sorry, Anna," Molly reached out and wrapped her fingers around Anna's forearm, "I didn't mean to pry. I was just interested, that's all. I'm also from England. Bristol, did you say? Funnily enough, I was in Bristol during the war. That's where I met my husband."

"In Bristol? Really? What was he doing there?"

"We met in a hospital. I was in the Women's Royal Navy Service, stationed in Bristol – shared digs with my cousin in the old part of the city – quaint, we had a jolly time there. She was – is – a nurse. Trained in midwifery and orthopaedics –"

"She was a midwife in a Bristol hospital. Which one?"

"Well, I'm not sure how much midwifery she did – her heart was always in surgery. I do know that she nursed war casualties in the Emergency Hospital at Winford, just outside Bristol, because that's where I met my Bill. Do you know it? Out along Bridgewater Road? Anyway, she nursed him – he was a war casualty. One day I met her at the hospital for lunch. She introduced me to this tall, handsome South African soldier with a smashed leg and one thing led to another – here I am, Mrs Barclay!"

Richard appeared at her side. He looked up at Anna with wary eyes. "Mrs Celliers, Andre gave me this piece of *biltong*. Is it okay if I take it home with me?"

"Of course, my boy – take some more." She switched into *Afrikaans* and called into the house, "Andre, go and get more pieces of *biltong* for me. Richard is going to take them home with him."

Anna relished this display of bilingual fluency – it evened the scoreboard and offset the slight she had felt earlier. She switched effortlessly back into English, "Sorry, Molly, I didn't mean to be rude. It's just that we speak more *Afrikaans* than English in this house. Andre will bring more *biltong* for you – it's *kudu*. Kobie says that's the best meat you can get for *biltong*. I hope you like it."

Andre came onto the veranda, carrying a packet of *biltong*. "Here, Rich, give some to your sister – to Mary." Molly ruffled his hair. "That's nice of you, Andre. See that you give her some, Richy. Come along now, we really must be going. Nice meeting you, Anna. Say goodbye, Rich."

They drove off and when they paused at the end of the drive to turn onto Pearce's Crescent, Molly said, more to herself than to Richard as she looked first to her right then to her left, "Mrs Celliers seems touchy about being English, I wonder why? Seems determined to be taken for South African. Could have sworn that she blanched when I mentioned hospitals in Bristol – perhaps it reminded her of something. All rather strange, don't you think?"

Richard couldn't imagine why it would be strange, so he did not comment; he sat hunched down beside her, gnawing on a piece of *biltong*. He was pleased to be going home; he wasn't sure that he liked Andre's mother that much – she was scary.

"Mum, can you or Dad speak *Afrikaans*?"

"No, I'm afraid I can't. Daddy may be able to get by. But we don't need to, somehow."

"Andre's father says everyone should."

"Does he now? Well, I speak French – school French, but enough to get by. That's what I learned when I was growing up."

Richard thought about that. He sensed that Andre's father would not have been satisfied with that answer. He let it go.

"Mum, are we rich?"

"Why, dear, what on earth made you ask that?"

Richard looked up, "Andre said his father says we are rich. Are we?"

"Andre's father again. He has a lot to say, doesn't he? Are we rich? I don't know. Richer than some. Less than others. Money isn't everything. Not by a long chalk. Having lots doesn't mean you'll be better off. Or that you'll be happier than someone with less."

Invariably when topics of this nature came to the fore in Molly's presence, she would launch into a long and passionate philosophical discourse that would be as much for her own edification as it would be for that of her listeners, but today her comments were unusually brief and said with such staccato abruptness that Richard twisted around and looked at her, quizzically. Molly was preoccupied. She couldn't get Anna out of her mind. Why had she been so sensitive?

3

A few days later, just before his eighth birthday, Richard accompanied his mother into town. Molly parked the Land Rover and stepped onto the pavement. She turned around and called out to Richard who was fiddling with the passenger-side car door.

"Come, Richard, leave that alone. We haven't got all day. Please get a jerk on."

She didn't wait for him to join her, but strode off up the street, feeling a little like she was swimming against the tide. Streams of people were meandering in the opposite direction. Town is unusually full, she thought, then she realised that it was the end of the month. Pay day. She glanced at her watch and noted it was nearly noon. They were in a hurry, she reminded herself, off to catch the midday buses that would take them to their homes in the reserves. As if to verify this, she paused and looked back over her shoulder. People were pouring out of shops – especially from the trading stores at the bottom end of town where, she noted dryly, Blacks did most of their shopping and where there were none of those demeaning signs above the doors that irritated her so much, the ones that so tactlessly said, "Whites/*Blankes*" or "Non -Whites/*Nie Blankes*." Even from where she was standing, way up the hill, she could see people milling around, many of the womenfolk weighed down with luggage that they balanced on their heads. Boxes and bags of all sizes and descriptions were being loaded onto the roof racks that had been welded onto the top of the buses. Gentle eddies of a faint breeze drifted downwind, engulfing her with an array of smells that her English nose still found strange.

Out of the corner of her eye, she saw Richard gawking into a shop window down the street. She cupped a hand around her mouth and called out to him.

"Don't dawdle, Richard. Daddy has a busy day at his surgery, and we can't keep him waiting." She turned on her heel and zig-zagged her way up the street.

Richard heard her but did not look up. He shuffled along sideways, lost in thought. Then, unexpectedly, he bumped into someone. Startled and momentarily disorientated, he stumbled and would have fallen, but a strong hand reached out and gripped his upper arm, steadying him. Richard looked up. A black face stared down at him – flared nostrils, big black eyes, inquiring eyebrows, cheeks edged with straggling wisps of white hair, lips pulled back in surprise to reveal large, even teeth and, on top of his balding head, a well-oiled head ring, or *isicoco* as he knew it to be – all this he observed in the little time it took him to regain his feet. He did not like being held by a native and he tried to wrestle his arm free.

"*Let go!*" He tried to prise away the fingers that held him tight. "*Let me go, I said.*"

"*You walked into me. You should watch where you are going.*"

Richard struggled harder. "*Let me go – it was your fault – let go!*"

It was then that he noticed that the man was wearing a *bheshu* instead of European trousers. He had an old khaki shirt, wore *nxambalela* shoes, and carried a large *knobkerrie* in his left hand. He became aware of the man's musky odour. It reminded him vaguely of smoke from damp firewood. He's an old bugger from the reserves – nobody to worry about. But he could feel his world fragmenting around him, and he teetered, as though poised on the brink of a yawning abyss.

"*Let me go, you bloody fool – let me go!*"

He clicked his tongue in the native fashion and shouted, "*You are hurting me! You bloody kaffir! Let me go! I'll call my mother.*"

With those words, the thin thread of caution, usually so reliable for one who feared so much, snapped and he tumbled into the void.

"*Hey, don't you swear at me!*" The man lowered his head and pointed deliberately at his *isicoco* on his head, "*See this, can you see this? It says I am an elder. You should know to respect your elders. And you should apologise.*"

The indignity of being held like this by someone whom he considered to be of no consequence goaded Richard's resentment, and he renewed his struggle with increased vigour. He did everything he could to pry the man's fingers off his arm. Nothing like this had ever happened to him before. He almost broke free. Passers-by began to gather around – much like floating leaves whose downstream progress is arrested by some protuberance or other, they bunched up and began to enquire among themselves, asking what all the fuss was about.

Just then, Molly appeared. She hesitated, then pushed through the crowd and stood protectively behind her son.

"What's going on?"

She was acutely aware of difference right then – aware, quite simply, of her whiteness and all that it conferred. A vein in her neck stood out. She would not show fear ... or inflame the situation. So, when she spoke, in English, she chose her words carefully and made sure that her tone was flat and quite devoid of emotion.

"What is going on?" she asked again. "Why are you holding him?"

Richard's relief was instantaneous, and he twisted his head around with a cheeky grin. His world was coming together again; his feet were once more on firm, familiar ground. He jabbed his finger at the man who was still holding him by the arm.

"He walked into me, Mum. And he won't let me go. Tell him to let me go."

The man could not speak English, but he understood what was being said.

"*He walked into me,*" he said shaking his head, "*then he swore at me – called me a bloody kaffir. I am old enough to be his grandfather. He should say sorry.*"

The alien words leapt out from the couching Zulu words and struck her, as surely as she had been slapped. She recoiled and shook her head. A bright smudge of pink crept up her neck and stained her ears. Molly searched the man's face. Since she had been brought up in England and had only been a few years in South Africa as Bill Barclay's wife, her Zulu was rudimentary and her pronunciation hesitant and clumsy. She did not understand every word, but she gathered enough to piece together what had happened. Despite his angry face, she saw before her a man of dignified stature – he was so upright and restrained, so self-assured, somehow so devoid of malice that she immediately made up her mind.

"Is that right, Richy? Did you swear at him?"

"No, I just said –"

"Did you, or did you not swear at him?"

"Yes, but I didn't mean it. Honest – it just came out."

Molly closed her eyes. She could feel her toes gripping the soles of her shoes. Her own flesh and blood, she thought, how could he? Where did he get this from? She took a deep breath.

"Please let him go." Her voice was calm, so eviscerated of emotion that she hardly recognised it. She saw the man stiffen and raise his eyebrows.

"It is all right, just let him go and I'll handle this."

He did not understand a word she said, but he knew. He saw in her clear bright eyes what he was unable to hear, and he relaxed his hold. Richard pulled free and gleefully wrapped his arms around his mother's waist.

"Thank you, Mummy. I was getting so scared."

But Molly wasn't done. She took off her shiny leather belt and hefted it, gripping it by the buckle. Richard looked up and to his mortification saw that his mother's face was implacable, distant, utterly devoid of warmth. He panicked. The tectonic plates of his world drifted apart again, and he found himself marooned, alone on a tiny island of certainty in a widening sea of doubt. Fearful of what might come, he scampered away from her, wide-eyed and pleading.

"No, Mummy, it wasn't my fault – true, it wasn't, I promise you it wasn't."

But to no avail. She went after him and caught him firmly by the arm. He did not struggle – her grip was tight, like a tourniquet. She leaned down, bringing her face so close to his that even then, in the moment of panic, he was able to detect the fragrance of her perfume, something ordinarily so familiar and intimate that images of her sitting before her dressing table, dabbing the precious liquid behind her ears and onto her wrists, immediately flashed before his eyes.

She bent him over and struck him with her belt. Richard shrieked.

She swung the belt twice more, striking him across the back of his legs. He heard the revulsion in her voice and saw the contorted ugliness of her face – he had never known her like this before. Her words, spat at him one by one, hit him like hailstones and he cowered beside her, hands above his head.

"You have never heard your father or me speak that way, so why do you think you can? You don't call people names, do you hear me? Especially horrible names like that. Never again – do you understand? Good. Now, say sorry."

She pulled him round by the scruff of the neck so that he could face the man. Richard averted his eyes, whimpering piteously.

"Say it."

He said that he was sorry, but the words were barely audible through his tears.

"Say it loudly, Richard. He did not hear you. Say it again and look him in the face."

He looked up and repeated it, louder this time. A feeling that he had somehow been betrayed and unfairly treated hurt him to the core. It was so unfair – Andre, his hero and now his friend, used words like these all the time. So did the others at school. They didn't get into trouble, so why should he? He did not understand. How could his mother take this man's side and spank him in public, in front of so many black people? How could she do this to him? Were those words really so bad?

Molly straightened up and addressed the man.

"Is that all right? He won't do it again."

All at once she became aware of the people standing around and the hush that had suddenly fallen over them – it was as though her rising and falling arm had activated a giant set of bellows that had sucked the sound out of their round, open mouths. Had she been a conjurer then, and had just pulled a rabbit from her hat, they would not have been more surprised.

The man standing before her took a moment to find his voice. He wondered how a white woman, a mere slip of a thing at that, could do that for him, a black man. A slow smile crept across his face, rolling back the tension that had been stretched across it and loosening his tongue. He offered her his hand, the other respectfully touching his elbow.

"*Thank you, Inkosikazi,*" he said, touching her fingers briefly, "*I am grateful. Stay well.*"

With that, the man saluted and walked away. She stared after him, watching him go with his head held high. Her heart was beating loudly in her chest and all at once she felt utterly spent, like a runner who has crossed the line and then feels like vomiting from exhaustion. She steadied herself and turned to her son. This time her words were soft and gentle – now they were to his wounded self-esteem as oil balm would have been to the raised welts on the back of his legs.

"Now, Richy, let that be a lesson to you. Never be rude and always respect your elders. Now, hold my hand, and let's go and find Daddy. He'll be wondering where we are."

<h1 style="text-align:center">4</h1>

At the end of the month, Busisiwe Dlamini arrived at the Barclay residence mid-afternoon and immediately set about preparing the evening meal. She had come from the reserve on an old, rickety bus that even with its windows wound right up, leaked so much dust that the passengers were constantly reaching for their handkerchiefs and blowing their noses. She had come with her young son Gordon, dressed in his best clothes, and Thandi, her younger daughter.

Busisiwe came on the last day of every month, and always brought the children with her so they could visit their father, Amidu, who was the gardener and general factotum in the Barclay homestead. That may have been the given reason for the regularity of her visits. In reality, she came because the last weekday of the month was pay day. She needed to be there to wheedle whatever money she could from Amidu before he frittered it away. She always came in hope – hopeful that he would, at last, acknowledge his responsibility and would settle the issue of *lobola* with her father, once and for all. It never happened. After each visit, she would return home feeling belittled, as though she had been squeezed through the interstices of a *hluzo*, and try as she might, she could never hide the sad, haunted look that took possession of her eyes and told her father all he needed to know without ever once asking the question.

She placed her things in Amidu's room and turned to Gordon, urging him to go down to the big house to see if Richard was there.

"Go, my son, go and play with Nkosana Lichad – see if he is there. He should be back from school now. I am going next door to say hello to my friend Ntokozo – she should have time off now. If I am not here when you get back, you'll find me in her room."

"Ma, you want to see Nto – you sure that you don't mean Umfundisi Mkhize? Isn't he the reason you want to go next door?"

The boy is growing up, she thought, he's beginning to see things. She lunged at him playfully, pretending to spank him on his bottom. *"Now, Gordon, enough of that. I have no idea if the Umfundisi will be here, but I do know that Ntokozo will be. Now, run along. And change – put your old clothes on. I don't want you to get your good clothes dirty. You hear me?"*

Then, with Thandi on her back, she walked through the gap in the hedge that divided the Barclay property from that owned by the Methodist church and which, currently, was occupied by the Reverend Jim Dingley, newly arrived from Manchester. The native quarters for both properties were, according to age-old custom that separated servant from master, tucked away at the same end of the properties. They were located as far as possible from the main house and in this instance were adjacent to each other. The gap in the hedge thus gave the servants of each house easy access to one another. Busisiwe was hoping for news of her friend, Reverend Mkhize who, when he came to town for church meetings, would stay in the spare room that Reverend Jim had set aside in the native quarters for just such occasions. Long ago, when she had been working for Molly Barclay, she had met the Reverend Mkhize and over time they had become friends. He was older, balding, and wore black-rimmed glasses that made his eyes seem too big for his head. He listened. He would hear what she had to say without interrupting. It was as though what she had to say was important, as though each word had meaning and was worthy of dissection on its own accord. She found herself telling him things that ordinarily she would have kept to herself – things said with sad, downcast eyes that were, in her opinion, inextricably linked to the discordant relationship she had with the *amadlozi*.

But Ntokozo had not been in her room, so Busisiwe had turned away, a little irritated. She was making her way back through the gap in the hedge when she saw three crows flying overhead, straight and low. She squinted at them and clicked her tongue. If only they had been eagles; eagles flying in line were regarded as a good omen – a sign even, that the spirits were pleased. The sound of voices approaching from the path that led down to the big house made her turn around. Gordon and Lichad, she said to herself, they must be coming here to play. She waited for them. Richard still had his school shirt on, and she noticed that the boys were carrying toy cars with them.

"*Sawubona, Nkosana, how are you?*"

"Hello, Busisiwe. I am well, thank you. It is good that you have come – I can play with Gordi. Ma will be pleased to see you as well." Richard watched Busisiwe bend forward at the waist to more easily reach Thandi who sat perched on her back, watching him with large, solemn eyes. Busisiwe gripped Thandi's arm and swung her down to the ground.

"*Hawu, Thandi, you mustn't be frightened.*" Richard squatted down and put his arms out, "*Come and say hello.*" Thandi rubbed the back of her hand against her mouth, sizing Richard up. Then she smiled and toddled over to him, and he hugged her. She had always like Richard; he was always nice to her. Busisiwe laughed. Then she went inside, leaving them to play.

5

The boys had spent some time creating for themselves a labyrinth of tunnels and bridges, all intricately connected by a maze of roads. Now, faithfully reproducing the sounds of gear changes and tight cornering, they sat in the shadows and pushed their toy vehicles around those earthen roads. After a while, Richard sat back on his heels and, with growing interest, watched what his friend was doing. Absent-mindedly, he used the back of a muddy hand to brush aside the fringe of blond hair that hung over his eyes. He was fascinated by his companion's deft use of opposite lock in reversing as a method of negotiating a lorry and trailer around a series of sharp bends. He had to try it.

"Hey, Gordi," he said, crawling forward and grabbing hold of the protruding trailer, *"let me have a go. It's my turn now with that one."* Gordon tightened his grip, knowing that if it were simply a matter of strength, he could easily retain possession of the lorry. *"Gordi,"* said Richard, loading each word with borrowed authority, *"I said let go."*

Gordon stiffened with annoyance and for a moment a primitive urge to defend what he possessed seemed to hold sway – he held on, thrusting his jaw forward while sparks of angry defiance flashed in his dark eyes. It was only for a moment. The realization that he was staring into a white face hit him with the unexpected suddenness of a striking snake. Of course, he said to himself, he's a *mlungu*. Poisonous understanding, released by the recognition and implications of that single fact alone, coursed through his veins like a neurotoxin, relaxing his muscles and clouding his eyes. He felt suddenly listless, as if overcome with tiredness, and he let go, no longer interested in their game.

Without uttering a word, he stood up and straightened his clothes. Impassive and disinterested, he watched Richard playing with the lorry and trailer. Gordon had changed his clothes. A silver safety pin, vainly holding together the sides of his button-less shirt, gleamed brightly against the dark expanse of his prepubescent ribcage. He shivered, noticing that the sun was now balanced precariously on the edge of the corrugated roof of the *khaya* behind him. Next door a gramophone was blaring out some penny-whistle music and down by the main house he could hear Mpango calling, *"Lichad! Lichad!"*

It's late, he said to himself, *I must go – it's getting close to my bath-time.*

"Gordi, look here! See, I can do it too!" said Richard, his voice shrill with excitement.

Hearing no reply, he twisted around but remained seated on one knee that he kept tucked under him. The sight of his friend standing there, now slump-shouldered and blank-faced, shocked him. It reminded him of something, but he couldn't remember what. A twinge of conscience shrivelled his scrotum and prickled its way up his spine.

He scrambled to his feet, his mind struggling for answers. Did I really do that, he asked himself, did I say something so bad? Then he remembered – he had seen that submissive look on the face of Bruno, their younger dog when Rusty, the dominant male, challenged him for his bones and he would slink away with his head down and his tail curled up between his legs. But we are not dogs, he thought, surely not.

"Gordi, I'm sorry," said Richard, struggling for words of restoration, *"here, you take it. I'll play with this one."*

And he stretched across the divide, holding out the lorry by its trailer so that it dangled forward diffidently, as though it were an offering to an animal that might bite. But in his heart of hearts, he knew that the spell was broken, that their game of make-believe was over; he knew that there was nothing he could do now to recapture the blissful contentment that all afternoon since his return from school, had covered them like a blanket and, for him, had helped to expunge the horrors of the school playground from his mind. Oh no, he said to himself, his heartbeat quickening, go away – I don't want to even think about it. But that unpleasant memory would not go away – now released, like an escaped balloon in a confined space, it swirled around in his mind, tormenting him mercilessly.

"It's all right," said Gordon gently, acutely aware of Richard's embarrassment. He reached out for the proffered plaything but did not take it. Instead, he stroked it briefly with his index finger. *"It's all right, Nkosana. But it's getting late now."* His words were like a gently wagging tail. *"Maybe we can play again tomorrow. See, Mpango is calling."*

They stood still and listened. Mpango was the Barclays' no-nonsense cook and Richard was rather frightened of him. His loud calls of *"Lichad,"* *"Lichad,"* shouted over the bottom half of the kitchen door, were becoming louder and more impatient. For Richard, they suddenly became a blessing in disguise.

"You are right, Gordi. I had better go. Let's play again tomorrow." With that, he turned and raced off towards the main house. His nearly overlooked *"Stay well, Gordi,"* was flung over his fleeing shoulder and it seemed to bounce slowly back up the earthen path and only reached the silently staring Gordon, long after he had rounded the bend and had disappeared from view.

6

The room was hot and fetid, almost oppressive as if all the air had been sucked from it. Above her, the single-sheeted corrugated iron roof racked across rough-hewn timber trusses had begun with pitiful creaks and groans to settle itself into a more comfortable position as evening approached. The heat was exacerbated by a small brass Primus stove, which hissed and spluttered under the burden of a large, aluminium pot, and no matter how many times Busisiwe wiped her brow, a mosaic of beaded sweat would instantly reappear. From time to time, she would take up a wooden spoon and, with quick circular motions, would stir the *impupu* bubbling inside the pot. At last, the mixture began to thicken, and with a sigh of relief, she trimmed the flame down to a simmering heat. She sat down heavily on the bed, glad to have a few moments of peace and quiet.

If only she could find the courage to tell Amidu one last time. Things could not go on like this. Unless he accepted his responsibility and restored her honour, she would leave him for good. She had no job and wouldn't have one until the children were old enough to be left in the reserve – she didn't even know if Molly Barclay would take her back. She had no prospects at all. Meanwhile, she was obliged to live in the reserve at her family's *kraal* – she had no home of her own, no cattle to sustain her, and no status to resurrect either her self-esteem or her father's regard. Worse though, was the certain knowledge that she was out of step with the ancestral spirits and had been for a long, long time. It was now more than she could bear. Bleak as it was, a future without Amidu would be better than one with him with things as they were. She had tried on previous visits to broach the subject more forcefully, but always her courage had deserted her, and she had allowed herself to wallow in the lukewarm comfort of acquiescence. How did she get herself into this mess? For the thousandth time, she allowed her mind to wander back to the very beginning.

***

They were sitting in the large communal hut with its high arched roof; they sat on woven grass mats, drawn up in a semi-circle around a low fire, watching the shadows play about their feet. As was the custom, the subject was not immediately broached – the scene had to be set. And so, with circumlocutory artfulness, her dear brother, Madondo, now smiling with laughing eyes and gesticulating hands, had kept them spellbound with his stories about life on the sugar farm; slowly but surely, he led them to the inevitable conclusion that life outside the valley was not something to be frowned upon but was in fact what any sane person would want, for it offered so many benefits. Then he came to the point.

"Nchebe, the owner of the farm where I work, has asked the indunas to spread the word that he is looking for more women to weed his cane. He wants at least another twenty-five for the new fields that he is going to plant down by the Enseleni River. Yes, that's the very river that flows through our valley. Father, I think Busisiwe should come back with me to Nchebe's farm – she is fit and strong and can easily weed in the fields. She will earn good money there and there'll be one less mouth to feed here. Please, Father, say yes and let her come back with me."

From the way he spoke, Busisiwe surmised that Madondo had already solicited and gained their mother's support. It was crucial – he could not have confronted his father without it.

"I am on good terms with the Induna, and he has promised to keep a place for her."

Madondo had been looking at Busisiwe, but his words had really been directed to his father. How her heart had ached then for her father! She could still see him sitting there, pathetic in his alienation, somehow shrivelled and still, with his *bheshu* tucked under him. For a while he said nothing. They all waited in respectful silence. It was well known that he hated talk about change, hated to see the slow and insidious erosion of values that he believed had stood his people in good stead and for so long. How many times had she heard him say that new ways came like a thief in the night, stealing a bit here and a bit there until suddenly, one morning, one realized that half the crop had been pilfered?

"Makoti, what do you think about all this?"

His wife had glanced across at him but when she saw the deep-lined anguish etched on his face she had looked away quickly, unable to hold his fiercely imploring gaze. It was as though he were struggling with his own thought processes, like a swimmer treading water, trying desperately to hug the comforting shore of his own convictions. He seemed to have slipped from her grasp and was drifting out of reach. Vividly, Busisiwe recalled the grieved look on her mother's face and remembered being flooded with overwhelming compassion, knowing at once that her mother, feeling inept and useless, was powerless to plunge into the deep waters of this controversy and rescue him. Thinking about it now made her nauseous, but back then, filled with the impetuous exuberance of youth, she had softly egged her mother on.

"Yes, Mama, tell us what you think."

Though Busisiwe had kept her voice respectful and barely above a murmur, she had been unable to mask the excitement that quivered through it when she spoke. She remembered the anguish that assailed her as she watched her mother struggle to find words that would not offend – words that seemed beyond her reach. It was her mother's wildly imploring eyes that she remembered most that night – eyes that swept the darkness like a flaying torch, as though the missing words were hiding from her, tucked into the shadows.

"Baba," her words were soothing, *"I know how you feel, but as you yourself have said so many times, the world has changed –"*

"You want to throw our daughter away, do you? You want to see her lose her honour, become a plaything for worthless young men ... do you want to see our girl lose everything and become ... you know, an isifebe before our very eyes?"

"No, no, no, I don't! You know I don't. But there is nothing for her here, nothing at all. It is not the same as when we were young. She is

just about the last one in the valley to go. We cannot make them all come back and also, we cannot stop the way things are going. I do not like it any more than you do, but for how long will corn stand against the wind? Who knows, perhaps she will bring us back some money, I don't know. There is no money here – that much I know."

Busisiwe looked at her father, *"I am your daughter, Father. I respect and love you. You know that I shall always try to be true to the ways of our ancestors. But I want to go with Madondo. I want to see the world. I want to get away from here for a while and earn my own money. Why would I want to lose my honour? Do you not trust me?"*

And then her father had smiled that thin, knowing smile of his, a smile that would haunt her for years to come. *"Ah, my child,"* he had said ever so gently, *"I know that. But it is not you that I am frightened of. It is the others out there who do not share our ways. All those men on the farms out there are herded together like animals. They get drunk all the time and they fight like dogs whenever a woman appears. It's not right,"* he said, shaking his head emphatically, *"not right at all. Those izikelemu pose a real problem for nice girls like you. They are very skilful at talking their way into a woman's heart and getting what they want. Heed my words, my girl, I know what I am talking about."*

A long uncomfortable silence had followed this pronouncement – she remembered that no one had dared to speak. After what seemed like an eternity, her father had raised himself slowly to his feet and, taking a deep breath, had drawn himself to his full height – on tiptoes, it seemed – so that he had loomed over them, dwarfing them with the full force of his presence. Busisiwe remembered his eyes and how they had flared briefly with bright intensity, like the raked coals of a dying fire. Yet when at last he spoke, his voice was vibrant and strong.

"I do not understand any of this and my sadness makes me tired. You can go, my girl, but mark you this and mark it well: I am a proud man who has always done his duty – did I not stand with Zipephu at Tshaneni? Did we not fight to preserve our own ways? Yes, you can go, my girl, but do not ever try to tell me that your place is anywhere but here with your mother. I hear all this chatter about working for the white man and making money, but nowhere do I see people who are better off because of it. I may be old, but I am not stupid. All I see with these tired eyes is that our fences are being broken one by one and the cows are now in the field, trampling our customs into the ground. Those customs took a long time to grow, and they fed our people for a long, long time. Now, there is nothing and we scrap like dogs for any bone that the white people toss over their shoulders.

"You go – I cannot hold onto you any longer. May the spirits watch over you and keep you safe. Please remember your calling, my child. You are a Dlamini. Don't ever dirty our good name. And you, Madondo, take care of Busisiwe. Anyone who harms her, harms me. And anyone who brings her into disrepute, brings me also into

disrepute. So, beware, my son, discharge your duty as our forefathers would have."

Then he turned around and latched his eyes onto her face. Oh, those eyes, how they had tormented her – they saw everything.

"While you are in my house you still have customs to observe. Before you leave here, you will tell your qhikiza what you are doing – that she can wash her hands of you, can let you go. It saddens me that you want to turn your back on our ways, but then the young always know best. So, go, my child, go and clear things with your qhikiza – at least you can do that for me."

With that, without so much as a backward glance, he had bid them goodnight and was gone.

***

Busisiwe never forgot that night. Even now, all these years later, she could see her father's face and hear his words, like iron on stone, it still rang in her ears.

The wooden door scraped open and brought Busisiwe out of her reverie with a start. Gordon held the door open for Thandi and she trotted into the room ahead of him.

"You all right, Ma?" Gordon, ever attentive to even the slightest shift in his mother's mood, looked at her anxiously. "Is everything all right?"

"Yes, my son, I am fine. I've been dreaming, that's all. When the door opened like that, I got a fright. But why aren't you playing with Nkosana Lichad?"

"Mpango came for him. He's gone now."

"What's the matter?"

"Nothing."

"Nothing? What happened? You look upset."

"No. It's nothing. I'm just tired. We can play again tomorrow."

"Maybe not. We may leave tomorrow. They will not let us stay here long. Depends on your father." Busisiwe handed Gordon a threadbare towel and a bar of carbolic soap, "He will be here soon. Go now and wash. Get all that dust off you. And take Thandi. There is hot water on the stove in the kitchen. Be careful."

She looked around for the kettle, found it low down on a shelf, and was about to go and fill it with water from the outside tap when there was a sharp rap on the door. Startled, she glanced at her watch. Too early for Amidu – he would still be at work. She swung the door open and stepped back. There, smiling like an owl through his thick, black-rimmed glasses, stood Reverend Mkhize.

"Oh, my goodness! What a nice surprise to see you again, Umfundisi!" She took his proffered hand with light, quick fingers and stepped back, straightening her shoulder straps, and smoothing her dress down over her hips. *"How come you are here?"*

"Sawubona, Busisiwe. It is indeed a pleasure to find you here. Now, how many times must I tell you not to call me Umfundisi? I much prefer Titus, my Christian name. But may I come in?"

"Oh gosh, so sorry. Yes of course, please do come in. But only for a minute. The children are bathing, and I am waiting for Amidu – he'll be here soon. It is pay day, you know. If I do not get here on pay day, then there will be no money for us – you know, same old story."

Reverend Titus Mkhize came inside but did not sit down. *"I have just arrived and thought you'd be here, so I came to see you."* He opened the door and prepared to leave. *"I won't keep you now, I can see you are busy. I'll be free at lunch time. If you are still here, I shall come over –"*

He saw a tear roll down her cheek. The sight of it, unheeded and unchecked, made him squeeze tight his own eyes. Something in his chest, long quiescent, stirred like a bird on a perch, preparing for flight. He shut the door. *"Come now, my child, don't cry. Here, take my handkerchief. Is it about Amidu?"* She nodded.

"So, you are going to force the issue?"

"I cannot face him, Titus. I cannot say what I have to say – what should have been said long ago. Help me. Help me – I do not have the strength for this."

"No, Busisiwe, this you must do on your own. You will never have peace of mind if I do it for you. Now, be strong. My advice is this: tell him. Make it short and plain but tell him."

She handed back his handkerchief. She was aware of his hand, lingering on her shoulder.

"Tell him, you say? That's not easy. Do you know how many times I have tried? Do you know how hard this is for me? Have I not told you how clever he is with his words?"

"I know. But today is different. In the past your courage failed you. But not today. You have made your decision. Stick by it. This is not the time for an argument. It is an ultimatum – he must decide. Only when he decides will you be able to hold your head up high. Be brave, Busisiwe. If you need me, I shall be here. I promise you. Now, prepare yourself and do your duty as God in his wisdom sees fit to guide you. God bless, Busisiwe."

7

Molly liked the time after dinner, especially after Richard and Mary had gone to bed. She liked it because she could put her feet up, have a drink, and let herself go. She could free her mind up and get things off her chest. Tonight, with the lounge lights dimmed and the curtains wide open, she was keen to discuss Richard with her husband.

"You know, Bill, Richard had a bad experience at school today. Apparently, the bigger kids have drawn a line across the playground – English on one side, *Afrikaans* on the other. The teachers must be aware of it. Anyway, at break this morning a boy went across the line to pick up his top. And you know what? The boys on that side of the line beat the daylights out of him. Rich was quite upset about it. You know, Bill, this is not the school for our son. I'm not going to put up with behaviour like –"

"Moll, don't you think you're over-reacting? I mean, kids will be kids and –"

"For God's sake, Bill, the *Boer War* is over. This is unacceptable. What sort of message do you think this conveys? Those kids think that rough stuff like that is perfectly acceptable. Well, it's not. I won't stand for it. Do you really want Rich to grow up with these sorts of ideas in his head?"

"Well," he said slowly, carefully choosing his words, "I agree with you – he's certainly picking up some funny habits, but then don't all kids do that? I mean, didn't we also do it when we went to school? Our parents would probably say the same –"

"Speak for yourself, but I'm sure my parents would have been appalled by such behaviour and would have whisked me away from such a school in a flash. Here's something else. Richard swore at an old Zulu gentleman the other day. I had to spank him then and there –"

"You did what? Spanked him? In front of a native? Whatever for?"

"He can't be allowed to use language like that to someone old enough to be his grandfather."

"But smack him in front of –?"

"Does it matter who it was in front of? Bill, he's not using language like that. I made him apologise. Hope to God he'll think twice before using language like that again. Anyway, what are we going to do?"

"Do?"

"With Richard, I mean. He's learning bad habits. Not just unacceptable language, attitudes as well. We don't talk like that, do we? We don't draw lines in our playroom – Richard on one side and Mary on the other. Of course not. He's getting all this from school and I'm not going to put up with it. Sorry, Bill, but we must make a stand. So, what do you think?"

Bill sighed before responding.

"Tell you what," he lay back and crossed his legs, propping his feet on the nearby pouf, "what about a cup of coffee first? Ring for Mildred, that's a good idea."

Molly nodded. She leaned over and rang a small silver bell that sat on a low table beside her. The fingers of her other hand, as if obeying some innate preoccupation with neatness and order, straightened the crocheted tablecloth that lay beneath it.

"While we're waiting, any gossip from the club?" She looked at him sideways and smiled, "You only told me that you beat Kobie on the last hole. Nothing else? No juicy titbits?"

"No, not really. You know that I steer away from all that stuff. Can't think of anything. Oh yes, Kobie told us something – not sure it's gossip, though. Anyway, he said that the police were getting tough on the curfew and that they've started doing night raids to lock up any Blacks caught without a *dompas*. Now that the Nationalists are in power, we're going to see a lot more of this, I'm afraid."

Molly pouted. She stood up and began to pace around the room with her hands clasped behind her back. For the moment, she forgot about Richard and what he'd gotten up to. Politics, she believed, was something to be taken seriously and whenever it crept into conversation, it aroused deep-seated passions that, in her mind anyway, needed articulation. Whenever she heard something she did not agree with, she felt that she had to challenge it and test it against the template of her own convictions. For this reason, many people, tired of her moral rectitude, and finding her far too intense, tended to give her a wide berth, or, if her presence was unavoidable, then to make sure that they talked only of homespun, trivial things and did what they could to keep her away from her hobby horses.

Bill liked her intensity and her passion, but even he, in moments of introspection, wished that she would back off occasionally, and simply let things be. She was like a dog with a bone. He knew the tell-tale signs – saw the narrowing of her eyes, the clench of her jaw, even the upward tilt of her head – he knew that she was about to unburden herself, so he watched and waited as she walked round and round, marshalling her thoughts.

"I detest talk like that," she began, as though commencing a lecture that nearly caught Bill off-guard, "it is so dehumanising and so unfair. It sets people apart. And now this government … This new government …"

Before she could get into her stride, there was a knock on the door and Mildred entered. She looked nun-like, swathed in white, and stood with her head bowed as though she was entering the chancel of a church. When she saw Molly freeze, as though in mid-step, she hesitated, fearing that she was interrupting something important.

"Yes, Mildred?"

"You rang, Madam," Mildred dropped her eyes in respectful observance of native custom and her words barely rose above a whisper.

"Ah yes, so I did. Please bring the coffee now. Then you may go – don't wait up. I'll put everything away later."

"Yes, Madam."

Mildred had just reached the door when Bill's voice stopped her, mid-stride.

"Mildred, I hear that Busisiwe's here. What does she want? Doesn't she know that she cannot stay here without a permit?"

"She is here, *Inkosi*. It is pay day. She knows the law. I think she came to see Amidu."

"Not about *lobola* again? Haven't they sorted that out yet? All right, tell Amidu that I want to see him after breakfast –"

"Thank you, Mildred," Molly's voice, keen as a sharp knife slicing into a pound of butter, severed their conversation, "that will be all. Please get the coffee. And bring a plate of biscuits as well."

She turned to her husband, blue eyes twinkling, and reached for his hand.

"I don't think we should discuss Busisiwe's situation – or Amidu's for that matter – with Mildred, do you? Why involve her? I know you were thinking of what Kobie had said, but why not speak to her on her own? What would Mildred know about their affairs? She can hardly speak for them, can she?"

She placed her hand on his chest and straightened his collar. Up close, the blueness of her eyes dazzled him. He kissed her. And ran his hand down her back, allowing it to linger briefly where the soft contours of her bottom flared from her waist.

"Talking of Busisiwe," she said, stepping back, "I do miss her terribly. I'd love to have her back here – she was such a quick learner and is so incredibly good at everything she does. When can we bring her back, Bill? Surely she's better off working here than wasting away in the reserve?"

"It's not quite so simple. Firstly, she cannot stay here with her children – work or no work. Secondly, as I've told you a thousand times, our good friend Amidu has blotted his copybook with her father. From what I gather, he still hasn't paid for her yet. You remember I lent him £15? Yes, that was specifically for his *lobola* when her second child was due. Silly bugger didn't do the right thing – he lost it gambling, I think. From what I hear, her father is a bit of a tiger – you know, very much of the old school. He wants his pound of flesh. She has tremendous respect for him, and she wants to do the right thing. You know, her father is highly respected in the district – even the chief listens to him."

"Bill, we're talking about Busisiwe."

"Well, as I said – if she is not employed, she cannot stay here, certainly not with children. Those days are over – *umhlaba ujikile,* as the natives would say, the world has changed. Now that the Nats are in power, magistrates are enforcing the Dutchman's law very firmly. I told you what Kobie said. Molly, my dear, whether we like it or not, formal separation of Whites and Blacks was an election promise that got these guys into power and –"

"It's wrong, and you know it. I don't care about the law – especially if it causes hurt and upsets people's lives. I mean, how would we like it if we were in their shoes?"

With his mind in turmoil and now feeling quite weary, he turned back to her, brandishing a broad grin that he hoped would mask his irritation. He shrugged his shoulders up and down, then presented his hands to her, palms forward, in a pose of mock surrender. He smiled again, an exaggerated smile this time, showing more teeth, and playfully arching one eyebrow above the other.

"My dear, you are the last person I want to argue with. All I am saying is that the law is the law. This one happens to be one of ours – Smuts put it on the statute book when our side was in power. The difference is that when we were in power, we paid lip service to it. Now that the Nats are in, they are going to enforce it as hard as they can. That's the way the cookie crumbles, I'm afraid.

"But, getting back to Busisiwe, she has to be bloody careful, or they'll lock her up. Quite simply, if you are black, you must have a *dompas* and you have to be employed in order to stay legitimately in a so-called white area. The days of her coming in from the reserve and shacking up with Amidu for a couple of days, are over. Blacks cannot stay in white areas – that includes our place – without a permit. No, I know you think it's unjust and immoral and what have you – but, Molly, please! Please listen. I'm happy to agree with you, I really am, but the law is the law. Apart from that, it is not fair to the other staff, her being here with her kids – they'll think that she is getting preferential treatment."

The resentment began to rise in the back of Molly's throat. She was about to respond when there was a knock on the door and Mildred reappeared. She watched Mildred set the coffee tray down, then leave. She poured coffee into two cups and added milk.

"Now, where were we?" She handed Bill his coffee and offered him a biscuit. "Oh yes, Richard. How did we end up talking about Busisiwe? You know, I feel quite exhausted. I wanted to talk about Richard and see what you think about sending him to a boarding school. But I'm feeling quite tired now. Why don't we call it quits and talk about it in the morning, when we're nice and fresh?"

Bill sighed happily. There is a God, he thought to himself. They drank their coffee in silence and went upstairs to bed, turning out lights as they went.

8

Busisiwe was furious. She could not sleep – her anger, roiling like an upset stomach, kept her awake. How dare Amidu come home and pretend that nothing was amiss. How dare he invite his friends over to play cards! To add insult to injury, they were gambling with money that

Amidu could ill afford; money that should be set aside for more important things, like her *lobola*. It was well past midnight, and she could still hear the murmur of their voices in the outhouse kitchen; she had seen it so many times and could visualise them, squatting around in a tight circle, peeping red-eyed at their closely held cards, and hoping against hope that they had made the right call.

She sighed and tried once again to make herself comfortable on the narrow bed. She had just rolled over and was drifting off when she heard a door bang, loud voices, and scuffling feet. The door burst open, and a torch was thrust into her face, momentarily blinding her. A pencil of bright light drew arcs around the room, looking everywhere – it even stole a glance under the bed.

"Who are you?" She knew. Panic welled up and gripped her throat; she gagged.

"Hey, you, get out of that bed."

This voice belonged to a white policeman – she knew that because he spoke poor Zulu and with an awful accent.

"Why are you here? Where is your dompas? Come on, hurry up." He gripped the doorframe with his free hand and leaned out. *"Zondi,"* he said to the African constable outside the door, *"watch this woman. I want to see her papers. Bring her to me when she's dressed."*

Busisiwe lit the paraffin lamp with shaking fingers and dressed as hurriedly as she could. Thandi began to wail, and she crawled over the tussled bedclothes to her mother. Busisiwe picked her up and carried her over to Gordon who stood cowering in the corner, hugging himself. He looked at her, eyes wide and pleading for answers. She wrapped him in her arms. She could feel his heart beating wildly in his chest and she nearly fell over as powerlessness engulfed her. She wanted to cry.

"It's all right, it's all right," she said, her words clotted with dry sobs. *"They don't want us. I won't be long. Look after Thandi and keep her quiet, please. I shall be back soon."*

She stepped around Constable Zondi and stopped in front of him. His face was bathed in sweat. *"Why this, brother? What have we done?"*

He flicked his eyes at her, then took hold of her upper arm. His face was impassive, as blank as the wall beside him. She tossed her head. He escorted her outside into the torch light where the white policeman and two other black constables had Amidu and his friends lined up. They were handcuffed and stood with heads bowed, like cattle in a slaughter yard. The white man had his back to her and was trying to read their pass books in his torch light but gave up in disgust.

"We'll take this lot back to the station for questioning. Get them into the wagon."

"What about the woman? She has children with her."

Sergeant van der Merwe turned around and undressed her with his torch. Good looking, he thought appreciatively, but cheeky – he could see it in her eyes.

"Where is your pass?"

"I have one, but it has expired. I am visiting my husband."

"My girl, you can't do that. You need a permit to be here. *Which one is your husband? Him?* Well, Zondi, get her details and we'll leave her here with her children. The rest of you get into the van."

The door banged shut, making a sharp, high-pitched bang. The sound, ricocheting into the night, died quickly. It was then that the dogs started to bark.

9

Molly Barclay was a light sleeper and so when the dogs started to bark, she was instantly awake and within seconds her heart was sounding like a trip hammer in her ears. What had disturbed the dogs? In England, her childhood fears had been benign – small flames, held at bay behind a grate – but once she stepped foot on South African soil, ghastly stories of women being molested – white women, they were always white women – had fuelled her imagination and set her fears ablaze. She groped for the switch on the base of the bedside lamp and was at once relieved to find that all the familiar objects in the room stood unmoved, washed clean in the yellow light, like rocks on a beach at low tide. Mollified, but with her heart beating wildly, she listened carefully, filtering the outside sounds, desperate for meaning.

"Moll, what the hell's got into you? Turn that bloody light out."

"Can't you hear the dogs? There is something out there – up at the back, do you think?"

"Probably those damn cats again –"

"Bill, hear that? The dogs are going mad. Out back I think, at the native quarters."

"Okay, okay! I'll have a look."

He swung out of bed, wrapped his *kikoi* around his lean waist, and stomped off down the passage, turning on lights as he went. He unlocked the top half of the kitchen door and peered out. All he could see was his shadow, spread-eagled in a pool of pale light. He whistled for the dogs twice, and they emerged from the darkness, trotting on silent paws with their pink tongues slopping over their bared teeth.

Then, just as he was closing the door, he thought he heard voices up at the native quarters and he stiffened.

"Inside! Rusty, Bruno, come here! Inside! Settle down now! Settle down!"

"Everything all right?" Molly appeared behind him and stood well back from the door. She hugged her dressing gown tight, pulling the collar up around her ears. "Can you hear anything? See anything? Any idea what set the dogs off?"

"Bugger all to worry about. Might have been a cat or something up at the quarters –"

"What, with the staff? What could possibly be going on up there?"

"Nothing. Thought I heard something but must have been mistaken." He held the dogs back from the door with his foot and closed it. Then he bolted it, top and bottom.

"That's it, the dogs are in and the door's locked. Let's get back into bed. I have a big day in theatre tomorrow and I need all the shuteye I can get."

***

A harsh, jangling sound, incessant and jarring, brought Bill's hand out from under the sheets. He groped back and forth for the light switch, found it, then, with clumsy fingers, picked up the bedside phone and brought it back to his shoulder where he cradled it against his pillow. It was a ritual he had performed many times – the hospital often called him during the night.

"Dr Barclay?" A strange voice. Bill pulled himself up into a sitting position.

"Yes, who's that?"

"Dr Barclay? Yes? Sorry. Sergeant van der Merwe here. South African Police. I'm afraid I have bad news for you. There was a raid in your street last night and we picked up some *Bantu* men in your native *khaya* –"

"At my place? What for?"

"They were gambling. Gambling for money – it's illegal. Also, their permits –"

"Come now, Sergeant. They weren't causing a disturbance – we all gamble. Surely you have better things to do than chase after house servants who are only having a bit of fun?"

"Doc, orders are orders. I was ordered to conduct a series of raids in the village. That's what I have been doing. Last night, we were in your street. These men were gambling on your premises. Also, their permits are not in order. But I am calling to inform you that a *Bantu* male by the name of Amidu Kabishi is deceased."

"What? What did you say? What the hell are you talking about? Deceased? He's dead?"

"Yes. He died last night in the cells. There must have been a fight. The holding cell was full, so we put them in with the other prisoners. That's what we do when –"

"This is bloody awful. How does someone die in detention, for God's sake? Aren't you supposed to keep an eye on them?"

"We do not keep an eye on them as you put it – we lock them up and then process them in the morning. His body was discovered when we went in for roll call and latrine change. Doc, what these animals do to each other after lights out is beyond our control."

Bill shuddered. He had an inkling of what went on. He had been there many times as the overseeing medical officer when lashes with a cane were being meted out – a magistrate could impose corporal punishment of not more than ten lashes with the cane. That sort of brutality he could live with – after all, it was done by the state to uphold and safeguard the citizens of the state. But this was different. This was savagery, pure and simple. Here, it dawned on him, was a paradox that he had difficulty grappling with, one that left him unnerved. For behind the very walls that were meant to represent the bastions of applied justice – inside a place that he thought would have been teeming with police and where, he would have said, personal safety ought to be guaranteed – the rule of law was in fact utterly impotent and quite useless. It was replaced by that of the jungle. Here, survival went to the fittest – the weak succumbed, and if they had to, traded sexual favours for protection from the strong.

"Bill, for God's sake speak to me. Who's dead?"

"Amidu. Last night. There was a raid here – remember the dogs barking?"

"How? What happened?"

"Don't know. That was the police. They've just found his body in the cells." He kicked off the bedclothes and leaped out of bed. Molly stared at him, stricken. She found her voice.

"Dead. Amidu, dead. Oh, my God." Tears welled up; they didn't spill but wobbled on her eyelids. "What are you doing?"

"Getting dressed. I'm going up to the native quarters to see Busisiwe. Have to tell her. It might be better if you came too."

But Busisiwe was not there. Nor were the children. Amidu's room was empty; the door hung open like the mouth of a dead bird. His clothes and what few worldly possessions he owned were stacked neatly on the bed.

"Bill, it's still dark – they can't be far –"

"No, Molly, it's not up to us to –"

He heard footsteps and went outside. The pre-dawn sky was beginning to mould the shadows; what could be seen, was bathed in a cold, leaden light. Mpango, standing there before him with a dark blanket wrapped around him, reminded Bill of a pewter figurine that stood with crossed hands on his mother's mantelpiece.

"Yes, Mpango?"

"Nkosi, the police came in the night. They took Amidu."

"Yes, I know. Now Amidu is dead."

"Yes, Nkosi, we have heard."

"Where is Busisiwe?"

49

"With the Umfundisi." He extracted his arm from beneath his blanket and pointed next door. *"She went there after the police left."*

Bill called out over his shoulder to Molly who was still in Amidu's room. "Molly, she's next door. I think we can leave now –"

"I must see her. Come, let's go and see what we can do."

"No, Molly, come away. Let her be. If she wants our help, she'll come for it."

They walked back down the path to the big house, hand-in-hand with the dogs trotting behind them, and they did not look back, not once.

The children were still asleep in their rooms upstairs, so they sat on the veranda drinking tea, with the dogs coiled around their feet. They watched the sun inch its way into a cloudless blue sky. Beams of sunlight slanted in, reaching under the eaves and illuminating some filigree spider webs which had appeared overnight and now, suspended high up in the interstices of the wrought-iron latticework, reminded Molly of the intricate doilies that her grandmother used to crochet.

"Somebody said – can't remember who, probably Gandhi – evil begins when you treat people as things," Molly said in what was almost a whisper.

"What's that?"

"Evil. I was thinking about evil. What happened to Amidu is evil. He was treated like an animal. Should never have happened, should it? What are we going to do?"

"Do? There's nothing we can do, Moll – nothing will bring him back."

"Bill, I'm thinking of Busisiwe and the children. What should we do about them?"

The phone rang. Bill rose quickly and went inside to answer it. He was glad to escape another interminable discussion with Molly, especially one about what he should or should not do for Busisiwe. It was the Reverend Jim Dingley, calling from next door. The conversation was brief. Bill hung up and went to rejoin Molly on the veranda.

"That was Jim. Said he'd heard about Amidu and offered his condolences. He says that one of his African priests, Titus Mkhize – you know him, the one that has the hots for Busisiwe – anyway, Jim says he's taken Busisiwe and her children under his wing and right now they are all on their way back to Somkhele. He says not to worry and that everything will be all right."

He smiled at her, and his smile told her that he considered this to be a perfectly satisfactory outcome – that this should be the end of the matter. She gathered up the teacups.

"Still feel we should have done more, Bill. Busisiwe was my friend and Amidu has been working for your family for a long, long time.

There will be an inquest, won't there? Will you go? And what about the children, what will we say to them?"

"Moll, of course there'll be an inquest. This isn't Stalinist Russia, you know. People don't just get bumped off; the rule of law does apply here, even if you don't think much of it. He was murdered. The police will investigate. There will be a trial. But I'm not going to get involved. I'll speak to Kobie about it – that's a promise. Now, as far as the kids are concerned, it's probably better coming from you. I'd just stick to the facts if I were you – there's no way to gild this lily, is there?"

Molly told Richard and Mary what had happened. She also told them that people were not things. A month later Richard went to boarding school. One door closed and another opened – a new world with new friends.

10

Three men walked in from the car park entrance to the Royal Hotel in Durban and sat down at an unoccupied corner table in the open-air restaurant. It was lunch time and the tables, with their red and white checked tablecloths, clung to the dappled shade of the verandas that ran down each side of a spacious courtyard. The two-toned, tiled floor resembled a large chess board. Turbaned Indian waiters, dressed in white and flitting soft as shadows between the tables, served drinks or off-loaded plates of curry and platters of cheese. This was the Royal Hotel's famed *Ulundi* Square, popular with lunch-goers for its central location in the city's business centre – popular also for its ambiance and for its quick but obsequious table service which suited both the local business community and out-of-town visitors alike.

One of the men on that day was black and his presence caused the volume of chatter from people sitting at the other tables to momentarily wax and wane, as though a draught of cold air had blown across a candle in an ill-lit room. Directly opposite them, on the other side of the courtyard, two men had just ordered their lunch and were reaching for their beers.

"What's he doing in here?"

"Who?"

"That black fellow over there – just walked in. Didn't you see him? No, no. Other end, three people at a table in the corner, see? There's an elderly priest with him – he's facing us. And somebody else who looks vaguely familiar –"

"Oh, got it. I see what you mean. That chap is Arthur Barclay – I know him quite well. As it happens, he's from Empangeni – one of those wealthy sugar daddies who thinks his bum doesn't smell. Hold on a minute, I'm sure I know that priest too. That's what's-his-name, yes, it's Reverend Donald McIntyre, if I'm not mistaken – from England. Many years ago, before the Great War in fact, he was the Anglican

51

priest in Empangeni. I'm sure it's him. He and Arthur were as thick as thieves back then. Have no idea who the black chap is – cheeky looking bugger if you ask me, look at the way he sits, legs crossed over, leaning back like that – thinks he owns the place."

"Well, your friend Barclay should know better. Natives are not allowed in here."

"I'm afraid you're right – give them your finger and before you know it, they've taken your hand. If we let them into places like this, then they'll start chatting up our women – can't have that, old chap, not here. And they can't hold their liquor – get pissed as parrots then fall off the perch. Hopeless, just hopeless. See what happened in India? The minute Britain got weak at the knees and pulled out – you know, gave those curry-munchers their independence – then all hell broke loose, and they were at each other like dogs after a bitch in heat. Truth is, they simply aren't up to it, not without a whitey keeping a firm grip on things. Bloody good country gone to shit. Glad I left before the rot set in. And you know what? Your friend, Smuts, was getting soft – horribly so, I reckon. Such a pity because he's quite clever. But he spent too much time trying to out the English. He and his UP think that racial integration in this country is inevitable, and they talk about 'gradualism' – have you ever heard such poppycock? It's nonsense, absolute bloody nonsense. I'll tell you this much, in last year's general election, I voted for Malan and his Nats." He leaned forward, warming to his theme, "I did, I don't mind telling anyone that, and I'm glad that they got in. Smuts has had his time, you know – did a good job in the war, I give him that much, but his time was up – as they say, every dog has his day and he's well and truly had his. I tell you, the Nats won't allow that lily-livered liberal thinking that has stuffed England up to come here and stuff up a damn good country. They'll keep the wogs in their place – well away from us – and, what's more, they won't sell us down the river or let that den of vipers at the UN and their Communist mates push us around. You know –"

"Hey, see that, Brig? They've bought the black bugger a beer. He's drinking it! I'll be damned! That's not on. Someone should say something."

The older of the two men shook his head vigorously, as though he couldn't quite believe what he was seeing. He put his glass down on the table in front of him and then stood up, straightened his khaki jacket, and looked around. The impression he wished to convey was that he was expecting someone to join his table. From his elevated position, he was able to see that many of the other diners, especially those close by, shared his outrage. They too, apparently, had noticed the presence of an intruder in their midst and shrank back, in a manner of speaking, much as hens do when a snake is spotted in the henhouse. They huddled together around their tables and twisted their heads around in twos and threes, trying to see without being seen. While others, less inhibited perhaps, peered over their menus at this affront or, as many of the women present did, whispered to each other behind their soft white hands.

"I'm going to say something to Art. This is too much. Everyone is incensed."

Despite his age, he still maintained a no-nonsense, straight-backed walk that years in the military had allowed him to assume was right and proper for an officer of his standing in His Majesty's imperial service. He marched across the square with his thoughts lined up behind him – a commander leading his troops into battle. When he reached Arthur Barclay, he bent forward, coughed discretely to prelude his interruption, and tapped him on the shoulder with his long, bony fingers.

"Hello, Art, sorry to interrupt – didn't know you were also in town? Got a minute?"

"Ah, Brigadier, hello." Arthur Barclay got up and stretched out his hand. "Do you remember our old friend Don? He was our parish priest if you remember, long, long ago."

"Why of course! How are you, Don?" the Brigadier effected genuine interest. "It's been a long time, hasn't it – you out here on holiday? Did Dot come with you?" He shook hands, glad that he had remembered the name of the vicar's wife. Don has aged a lot, he thought, he seemed tired and washed out. He half turned around and glanced at the man who had remained sitting in his seat, watching them with a bemused smile playing with his dark lips.

"Ah yes," said Don, following the Brigadier's eyes, "allow me to introduce my son, Jack. Jack, this is Brigadier Willkie-Scott. He's from Empangeni – or he was when I was there."

Jack rose from his chair and extended his hand. He gripped the Brigadier's hand with strong fingers and held it, then clamped it with his other hand, pumping it up and down.

"A pleasure to meet you, Brigadier. How do you do? I don't often get the pleasure of shaking a brigadier by the hand."

The Brigadier retrieved his hand and put it into his pocket where he rubbed his fingertips in the loose folds of his pocket handkerchief. His thoughts, like troops under fire, were beginning to waver. *A black man speaking the King's English like that! And with such a cultured voice! And looking me in the eye like that! And that handshake! Who does he think he is?* Then a thought came to him out of the blue – like a carrier pigeon it came, flying fast and furiously across enemy lines. He turned to Arthur.

"Is he the person I think he is – the one who –?"

"That's right, Brig. This is Jack. Don and Dot adopted him and his sister, remember? Took them back to England with them. Jack was in the British army, weren't you Jack?"

"Yes, sure was. Fourth Royal Tank Regiment." Jack placed himself between Arthur and his father and reached back possessively, drawing them to him with a loose arm around their waists. He spoke to the Brigadier, looking him straight in the eye. "Yes, I served in France – was wounded there. I was lucky to get out. After a stint in hospital back home, I was seconded to the Eleventh Hussars in North Africa. Was captured at Tobruk in 1942 and spent the rest of the war in a POW camp. That's my history in a nutshell. I've just resigned – had enough of square-bashing and the old spit and polish, you know – time to get out and spread my wings."

"Jack's being modest. He was awarded the Distinguished Conduct Medal for gallantry – won it in a tank battle at Arras. Where they gave the *Krauts* a bit of stick. Pity they had to fall back. This was just before Dunkirk, you know. He won't tell you about it, but –"

"Come now, Dad, the Brigadier doesn't want to hear about all that. In case you're wondering, I am returning to South Africa – have just arrived. This is the first time I've been back since I left. I want to discover my roots and learn something of where I came from."

"That's right. Jack is my godson. I came down and met them at the docks when the mail ship berthed. I'm going to drive them to Polela Mission – you know it? The one near Impendle. Thought we'd pop in here for a bite of lunch before we headed off. Oh, here I am rambling, did you want to ask me something?"

The Brigadier shook his head. "Just thought I'd come by and say hello. I'll be on my way."

Without further ado, he excused himself and went back to his table, not quite as straight-backed as when he left it, and not quite as firm of foot. His companion leaned over towards him, chin in one hand and his bread roll poised in the other; he waited.

"Well?"

"He's from here. The black fellow, I mean. Jack's his name. Was adopted, by a Limey priest. Brought up in England – now he thinks he's a bloody Englishman. Speaks with a hot potato in his mouth. Served in the war. Decorated, I'm told – almost felt I had to salute him. Can you imagine that? Bloody hell, what's the world coming to? Too much education is not good for these buggers, not by any stretch of the imagination – makes them uppity you know, and far too big for their boots."

11

Three weeks later, Richard came home from boarding school for the Easter holidays. He and Mary were spending the day with their grandparents Arthur and Jess on the farm. On this occasion, Aunty Trish was with them because she had taken Jess with her to a garden club meeting in Richards Bay that morning, and upon their return, Jess had asked her to stay for lunch.

"Hear the news lately, Mum? The troubles in Durban and on the Rand are still going on."

"What's that dear? Mind passing the *maas* down to Richard, please?"

"The Zulus are still at it. Still thumping the Indians – can't say I blame them. Silly buggers, those Indians, they rob the *coons* blind – then muck around with their women. Mind you, shouldn't bother us – not many *coolies* in Zululand –"

"Language please, children present."

"Sorry," Aunty Trish changed direction. "Did you hear that The Prohibition of Mixed Marriages Act has been passed."

"What's that, Aunty Trish? What's it mean?"

"It's to stop *coons* –" Arthur's raised eyebrow stopped Aunty Trish in her tracks. He took over.

"It means," his words, slow and deliberate, were for Richard, but his eyes were fixed on Aunty Trish, "that it is now against the law for a white person to marry a black person, or the other way round." Arthur unfurled his table napkin from its silver ring, shook it out, and then laid it across his lap. "Nothing you need to worry about – just putting into law what obviously should have been done a long time ago. Each to their own, I say."

"Well, not everyone would agree with that," Aunty Trish went on without looking up. "I mean, the Mercury quoted this Trevor Huddleston chap the other day, saying something like kind-hearted Whites are wrong-headed – they want to believe that separating the races is good when in fact it is evil and un-Christian."

"He's a priest. A do-gooder. A troublemaker. He's only been here five minutes but thinks he knows everything and can tell us what to do. Priests should stay out of politics and stick to 'hatches, matches, and dispatches.'"

Trish frowned. It didn't really matter to her, one way or another. She picked up her spoon, twirled it around in her fingers a couple of times as if thinking of something to say, then shrugged and began to eat.

"Politics bores me to tears," said Jess, looking for neutral ground. She turned to Richard and smiled encouragingly, "Why don't you tell us about what you've been up to at your new school? Here, have some sugar."

CHAPTER FOUR:

1954

1

It was the first week of the July school holidays and Richard was in his last year at preparatory school. His parents allowed him and his sister to visit their grandparents knowing how much they loved being on the farm. There was always something for them to do there. A special treat was horse riding which, for Richard, allowed him to enact the feats of horsemanship that he saw so gallantly portrayed in comics and American cowboy films. There was nothing overt in this – it all played out in his head, especially when they would canter along the cane breaks, riding abreast, with the dogs barking and running out wide. They would be woken early by their grandfather, well before the house servants entered the house; they would follow him, tucking their shirts into their jodhpurs as they went, stumbling into the crisp morning air that was still heavy with dew. The stable hands had been up even earlier and had their mounts waiting for them. Arthur would swing up into his saddle and off they would go at the trot, down the drive, and onto the farm to inspect the labour in the fields. They always visited the cane cutters first, which suited Richard as he liked to get them behind him as soon as he could. This was because the cane cutters, wiry as *biltong*, yet supple and incredibly strong, frightened him – they reminded him, in a vague sort of way, of wild animals that were alright to watch but not to get too close to. Arthur Barclay would dismount and confer with his *indunas* while they sat on their horses and watched the cutters cut and stack bundles of cane. Richard had difficulty in digesting the notion that grown men, covered in scraps of clothing and toiling in the glare of a harsh and relentless sun, should have to do such arduous work – nobody he knew worked like that. These things were never said; he just felt them. He would sit there, pinched and withdrawn, and would watch them as their cane knives sliced through stalk after stalk; would watch them with narrowed eyes as they gathered up and shouldered the fallen sticks, stacking them into piles that grew up from the ground to ultimately assume the shape of large, rounded beehives which, by noon or a little thereafter, would dot the open field in hap-hazard profusion. Each man was tasked to cut and load a stack a day. Every time, as he sat there playing with the reins while his horse stamped its feet or shook its head to ward off worrisome flies, Richard would feel uneasy, and his chest would tighten. It did not seem right that he, a youngster astride a horse, in his pressed jodhpurs and boots polished by someone else, should be in such an elevated position as to look down on grown men while they went about their inglorious work. Relief would come as soon as his grandfather had finished his business and had remounted his horse.

"Richard, I am going to the compound later on this afternoon, and I was wondering if you'd like to come? The boys have arranged for a witchdoctor to come and sort something out for them."

Richard could hardly suppress the surge of excitement that welled up and all but throttled him. He wondered if it would be a good idea to find out more from the house staff, but in the end decided not to – if his grandmother found out that he was talking to them about *thakathi*, that would be the end of it. Gathering up his reins, Richard cantered after the old man, happy to be rocking back and forth again, like a metronome, in tune to the rhythm of hooves pounding with iambic monotony beneath him and, at the same time, enervated by an untrammeled wind that, free as blank verse, played through his hair and narrowed his eyes.

***

Richard felt good. They were driving to the compound and as far as he could see, basking in the warm glow of that sunset, were familiar things that gave him an immense sense of belonging. His grandfather, armed with a theodolite and an ox-drawn plough, had tamed this land, dividing it with long straight lines into neat, rectangular fields that lay spread out before them like a quilted blanket. There was something very reassuring about those straight lines and the order they imposed. He sighed and turned to the old man who sat beside him, loose-limbed and draped over the steering wheel.

"Pops, do you think the witchdoctor will be on time?"

"Don't know, Rich. Mdletshe said that we should be there at 5:00 pm – what's the time now?"

"We're early. Five minutes to go. Do you reckon there is anything in this stuff?"

Arthur took his eyes off the road for a moment and peered at his grandson with a lopsided grin.

"Stuff, Richard? What do you mean, stuff?"

Richard ducked his head. He was pleased to be there with his Pop and wanted to show it by asking what he thought would be a grown-up question. But stuff was the wrong word.

"I mean, do you think that the witchdoctor really can tell if there is any *thakathi* here in the compound? It's all a lot of –" here he paused, trying to find the right word, "codswallop, isn't it?"

"Well, Rich, you might think it is codswallop, but to these people it's real alright. Just as real to them as your mother's religion is to her."

"Religion? This isn't really religion, is it?"

"Absolutely."

"But it's all superstition and fear, isn't it? That's what they told us at school."

"That's how religions work, Rich. All of them."

"Ours too?"

"Yup. Your religion depends on geography, you know – where you were born."

"But superstition. We're not superstitious, are we?"

"Of course. People say the number thirteen is unlucky. People go to fortune tellers. People buy newspapers just to read their stars. People everywhere are superstitious."

"But that's not really religion, is it?"

"Look, is there a Heaven and a Hell?"

"Isn't there?"

"Nobody knows, but people go to church just in case. Are there good spirits and bad ones? Nobody knows, but these people go to the *Sangoma*, just in case. What's the difference? Isn't that superstition, not being sure and taking a punt, just in case?"

Richard thought about that for a moment. He wished he had an answer. Mum would know, he thought, she believes in God and goes to church. But I've never thought that she was superstitious. He felt the ground shifting beneath him, like quicksand.

"But, Pops," he shook his head, "we don't cast spells on people, do we? I mean, well, Granny calls this stuff pagan mumbo-jumbo."

"Mumbo-jumbo, hey? Don't you listen when you're in church?"

"Yes, but do you think that –?"

Richard broke off and grabbed at the door and held on as Arthur double-declutched and swung the Land Rover sharply to the left. The gum trees, now directly in front, leaned over them, tracing their fingers in slow, parabolic curves across the red sky. There were lots of swallows, Richard noted, all flying low – a sure sign, according to the natives, that it was going to rain.

A large crowd of Africans had gathered on the wide-open space that lay spread out below the single quarters like a wide, threadbare apron. Arthur nosed the vehicle around the edge of the crowd, waited for a few stragglers to pass, then drove slowly up the slope away from them. He stopped beside the white-walled kitchen block. This didn't give them a clear enough view, so he started the engine again and turned the car into a better position. Now they could see everything.

Richard knew that this was going to take a long time, so he settled back and made himself comfortable. Arthur lit a cigar and puffed on it. Richard hated the smell. He sat up again and stuck his head out the window. There, leaning his chin on the sill, he mulled over what his grandfather had said earlier. He felt that the conversation had posed more questions than it had answered but, not sure how to resume it, he looked around instead.

He heard a noise. He turned his attention to it and saw the crowd had grown bigger. Including womenfolk, he reckoned that there were nearly two hundred people milling around in front of where they sat in the parked car. People stood in closely-knit groups, talking among themselves, and laughing. It took Richard a while to pick out Mdletshe, the head *induna*. He was of average height and so was partly obscured by the other *indunas* and police boys that crowded around him. He saw Mdletshe turn around, see the vehicle, wave, then needle a path through the crowd, and angle his way up the slope towards them.

"Greetings, Nkosi. Greetings, Nkosana," he said in that deep, onomatopoeic voice that Richard liked so much, *"the Sangoma will be here soon. Do you want to meet him?"*

"No, no," said Arthur, waving his cigar, *"you carry on. We will sit here and watch. Please give him our regards."*

Mdletshe bowed his head and smiled. Richard saw him bend down so that they could see each other more clearly. *"What about you, Nkosana? Would you like to come with me?"*

"No, thank you, I'll stay here."

Richard glanced sideways at his grandfather. He watched him take a cigar from his pocket and pass it through the window to Mdletshe who took it with both hands. "Here you are, old man. Have a smoke on me."

Mdletshe walked back down the slope. Funny, thought Richard, Pops is always handing out cigars – I wonder if they really want them or even like them.

Just then they heard a motorbike. It came into view on the road that ran past the married quarters. It hushed the crowd. Sitting astride it, dressed in a smart, fawn-coloured safari suit, and wearing polished black shoes and dark sunglasses, was a man whom Richard supposed to be in his mid-thirties. Richard glanced at his grandfather – this was not what he had expected. This man, so European in his appearance, took Richard by surprise – he had expected someone old and wizened, with a crabby face and piercing eyes, someone whose appearance would strike dread and fear into the hearts of all who beheld it. Why wasn't he barefoot and dressed in traditional skins? Where were the customary gall bladders and other accruements that in his mind were so typical of a witchdoctor's apparel? This couldn't be right – this man must be having them on, must be a sham.

"What do you reckon, Pops? Is this guy for real?"

"He's real, alright. The boys reckon he's the best – they have put together a lot of money for him to come here – they've got what they wanted." He tapped Richard's knee. "Why, don't you think he's genuine?"

"Well, he's not what I was expecting – too young, I think. Too classy looking. Not in traditional gear, is he? I mean, he almost looks like a clerk or someone from an office, a businessperson. Shouldn't he be wearing skins and stuff? Riding a motorcycle! Isn't that crazy?"

"And why shouldn't he ride a motorbike? He's a successful *Sangoma*, very well known around here. You mustn't judge a sausage by its skin. You watch, he'll deliver."

"Deliver? What's he going to deliver?"

"Well, they say that someone is practicing *thakathi* here, invoking the evil spirits and –"

"Yeah, but how do they know that?"

"Oh, Rich, I don't know. They say there are signs. Don't ask me."

"Sounds like rubbish to me."

"Rich, don't curl your lip like that. Listen, they'd most likely say that the virgin birth is rubbish. But what's the point of you or me foisting our views of *thakathi* on them, telling them it's all rubbish and that they should go home and forget about it?"

"I'm not saying we should tell them it's rubbish. But –"

"No buts, Rich. Respect their customs, that's all. It's not about proving who is right or wrong, it's about what makes them tick. You want to know something, my boy? If you want happy workers, then sometimes you have to play along with things you don't believe in."

By now the crowd had spread out so everyone could see. There was a wide-open space of flattened earth between where they and the *Sangoma* stood. All eyes were riveted onto the *Sangoma* – they watched his every move. Richard scanned the faces lined up along the front of the crowd. They seemed solemn to him, apprehensive even, yet at the same time, expectant. They could have been waiting for a bus.

Mdletshe approached, crouching forward with his hat in his hand. He spoke to the *Sangoma* who took off his sunglasses. Money changed hands. The *Sangoma* must have explained what he wanted done because Mdletshe nodded, then straightened up and jogged back to where the *indunas* stood. Next minute they were forming all the men into a long line. The women, some in faded print dresses and others still in their brown work smocks, were directed to stand to one side, with the children. They stood bunched up, waiting. Richard watched the *indunas* with a wry smile. They, ever eager to demonstrate their importance, waved their *knobkerries* back and forth as they moved up and down the line, straightening it and pushing the men into place.

The *Sangoma* had his back turned on all this. He opened a small imitation leather suitcase which was tied to a carrier on the back of his motorbike and took out a long red robe which he knotted around his neck. It hung over his shoulders and fell to his knees. Richard couldn't help feeling that the smart safari trousers protruding below it were somehow out of place. Next, the *Sangoma* removed a short stick which had the tail of an animal hanging from it.

Richard turned towards his grandfather and fanned aside the cigar smoke that hung like mist between them. He jabbed his finger at the front window.

"See that, Pops! That's the tail of an *nkonkoni*, isn't it?"

"I suspect it is." Arthur flicked the stump of his cigar out the window. "You know, in Shaka's day, if the *Sangoma* at the royal *kraal* struck you with that, you were a goner – royal slayers would drag you off for execution."

"Yuck, that's gruesome. And barbaric," said Richard, pulling an ugly face. "What if you were innocent? Imagine getting bumped off for nothing. Thank God we live in civilized times."

"Oh, I don't know about that."

"You don't think so?"

"Well, civilisation is a bit like makeup, you know. It just hides the bad spots. Being barbaric is part of human nature – lurks beneath the surface then boils up, like *chorbs*."

"But not everyone. I mean, you and Granny aren't barbaric. I'm not barbaric, am I?"

"No, not everyone. But our so-called civilization is founded on skullduggery, treachery, thievery – in short, on things we call barbaric when others do them."

Richard searched Arthur's face. He felt himself slipping again. He tried to regain his footing. "Maybe long ago, not now. I don't think we are barbaric."

"Well, we have just fought two world wars – they were barbaric, I can tell you. Civilised people, Richard – the cream of Europe, people who should have known better – did things to each other that would make your hair stand on end."

"But that was in war. We don't have witchdoctors or things like that."

"No, we don't. But we have priests, and they aren't much better."

"But they don't have people killed."

"No, but many wars have been fought because of religion. What about the Crusades, the Thirty Years' War? The Conquistadors in South America? The Inquisition? You heard about any of that? All done for God. Come to think of it, history is one barbaric episode after

61

another. That's the way it is, I'm afraid. Good or bad depends on who writes the story."

Just then a drum began to beat. It was a loud reverberating sound, primitive and wild. For the two of them sitting in the car, the throb of that drum was unsettling. They turned towards it and saw the brewing woman, bent over at the waist, thumping a large cowhide drum with a wooden stick in each hand. There was no change in pitch or tone, just an ominous, measured beat that mesmerised them and filled their heads. Richard wound up his window.

"Look," said Arthur, nudging Richard with his elbow. "See, the *Sangoma* is beginning to do his thing. See how all his movements are in time to the drum? Watch."

The *Sangoma* was moving in a sort of dance. He kept moving in a clockwise direction, making long shallow circles in front of where the men stood. He took big steps, raising his knees high and stretching his feet forward. As he went, he swished the *wildebeest* tail from side to side. Then he would stop, mid-stride, and stand dead still while the drum kept beating. He would sniff the air like a hunting dog, at times turning in a full circle. Not satisfied, he would shake his head as if to say he couldn't pick up a scent. Then he would begin all over again, starting with his strange, prancing gait. Richard lost count of the number of times he did this, but he noticed that each time the *Sangoma* completed a circle, he got closer and closer to the line of men who stood before him, so still that they could have been carved from petrified rock.

"Rich, see the cutters standing at this end? Look at their faces. They are scared stiff. Each time the *Sangoma* gets near them, they just about die of fright."

After ten minutes or so, the *Sangoma* stopped his strange dance and walked to the end of the line. Then, bending low, he ran down the line, so close to the men that he could have touched them. Their eyes were on the *wildebeest* tail which passed in front of their noses. He held it straight out in front of him with both hands as though it was a direction finder. When he reached the end of the line he turned, pivoting on the ball of his foot, and stood quite still. He sniffed the air, making deliberate but exaggerated movements with his head. Then he moved slowly back down the line. This time, he stopped before each man and sniffed him, up and down, like a dog sniffing a tree. It was a slow process. The tension was palpable, even the trees stood still. The drum, pulsing like a vein, was the only sound that could be heard. Richard noticed that the men sucked in their breath as the *Sangoma* approached them; he watched them stare straight ahead and saw the fear that pinched their faces. He imagined that they were praying – praying that the tell-tale scent would not be on them.

At last, he reached the end of the line. Then he walked out to the centre of the line with his left hand cupped to his ear. He stood like that, listening. Then he did the same with his right hand.

"Great theatre, isn't it?" Arthur fished in his pocket for another cigar.

"Theatre?" Richard stared at him. "What do you mean?"

"Well, all priests do it. The more drama they can inject into what they do, the better it is."

"So, it's all nonsense after all. Is that what you're saying?"

"You're missing the point, Rich. It doesn't matter what you and I think. It's what they think that counts. As you can see, they are all believers. He just plays to their expectations – and he does it well, I reckon."

"Then it is just a show?"

"That's right. It's theatre."

"Really?"

"Of course. Same for our priests, with their robes and incense, their crucifixes and what have you. They too stand in front of their congregations as if they are on stage. Theatre, pure and simple. And good theatre, you know, keeps the faithful coming back."

"So why do we go to church then, if it's all a show?"

"Because your grandma likes to go, that's why – so does your mother, come to think of it."

Richard stared out the window. Where was the sanctity of certainty? Conflicting thoughts made his ears ring – each one led him off on a wild goose chase with no end in sight – it was as though he was on a bicycle that had no brakes. He was in this state of mental agitation, trying to think of something sensible to say, when the *Sangoma* pounced. In a flash he ran up to a man who stood in line, close to them. He struck the man across the face with the *wildebeest* tail. The drum stopped. He struck twice, in quick succession. The tail whisked across the man's fear-stricken face so fast Richard could hardly follow it. A great wail went up. The women, holding their ground, began to ululate and stamp their feet. It was a raw, eerie sound that set his nerves on edge.

But there was no holding the men; the line stretched then snapped like a necklace, scattering bits and pieces everywhere. It was bedlam. Men that Richard knew well and liked, now howled with such contorted faces that he could hardly recognise them. They were animals, baying for blood. He watched them surround the condemned man, taunt him, and push him back and forth like a sack of meal. It was merciless. Richard shrank back in his seat, horrified. His worst nightmares were confirmed – Blacks really were savages. The blokes at school were right after all, these people could cut your throat for sixpence without blinking an eyelid.

Mdletshe and the *indunas* forced their way into the crowd that swirled around the stricken man. They reached him and formed a protective ring around him. He was ashen-faced and motionless, like a man in a trance.

Well clear of this heaving throng, and seemingly satisfied with his work, the *Sangoma* stepped back and held up his hand. The police boys spread out in front of him, and they too held up their hands, calming the crowd. The *Sangoma* began to speak.

"This man has been casting spells here. The amadlozi tell me there is a woman here, married to a tractor driver, who just last week gave birth to a dead child. Is that not so?"

A great cry went up. *"Yes, it is so."*

"This man caused it. He placed muthi in the roof of her house, right above where she slept. He is a sorcerer, this man. He comes here to cast spells and cause trouble. He rides a hyena at night."

With that, an anguished howl erupted from the crowd. Some people stamped their feet, others shook their fists. The *Sangoma* raised his hands again and waited for silence.

"Who here has heard the hyena call at night?" Many voices called out. *"You see, I have never been here, but I know that the hyena calls here. Have not some of your chickens disappeared at night? That is the hyena, I tell you – it feeds at night. Now, I have never seen this man before, but I know he is new here. And he works as a roof thatcher, in the building gang, does he not? How else could he get to the tractor driver's roof?"*

He raised his hands, fanning them up and down. *"Quiet please, quiet. Let me prove myself to you. Let me ask your mlungu some questions."*

He turned towards the car and called out in a loud voice.

"Tell me, Nkosi, have you ever seen me before?"

Richard watched his grandfather get out of the car and push the door shut with his hip. He took a cigar from his pocket. Richard slid across into the vacated seat. He watched the old man take his time to light the cigar. *"No,"* he heard him say, exhaling a stream of smoke, *"I have never seen you before."*

"Never on this farm?"

"No, never." The crowd roared.

"This man is new here, is that not so?"

"That's right."

"He is married with two children, a boy and a girl. Is that not so?"

"That is right." Again, the crowd roared.

"He lives in that house over there?" He pointed to a thatch hut near the married quarters.

"That is right."

"Did he not ask you last pay day for a loan? Did he not say he wanted money to pay lobola?"

"That is also correct."

"You did well to refuse him. Tell me, Nkosi, did your daughter from Empangeni not take your wife with her this morning to Richard's Bay to see flowers? Is that not so?"

Richard couldn't see Arthur smile, but he heard his amusement. *"It is as you say."* This time, the crowd went wild.

How the hell did he know that, Richard wondered, that's smart. Maybe he does have supernatural powers. The thought released a flood of images gleaned from books – paramount among them was King Arthur, drawing the sword from the stone, and Merlin – they were good people, he was on their side. But this, this was disturbing, and he could feel himself shrinking. The *Sangoma* turned back to the crowd with his hands above his head. The *wildebeest* tail dangled from his wrist.

"Now, how do I know all these things?" he asked, addressing the crowd. *"If I have never seen the Nkosi before, have never even spoken to him, how would I know?"*

As if on cue, voices in the crowd shouted back, *"Amadlozi! They tell you! Amadlozi!"*

Then, Richard heard his grandfather shouting, bellowing like a bull. *"Mdletshe, get that man out of there!"* Richard leaned out of the car and watched the old man walk a little way down the hill, then stop. *"Stand back!"* he shouted, *"Stand back. Leave him alone!"*

Richard jumped out, hesitated, then ran to his side. He clung to him, like a baby baboon to its mother, with no intention of being prised away.

"No, Rich, you go back to the car. Stay there. This could get ugly."

"But what about you?" He gripped Pops, fiercely.

"I'll be okay. Now, get back in the car."

Richard's mouth was dry, he could feel panic welling in the back of his throat. But he nodded and let go slowly. Then he ran back to the car, fast. He jumped in and locked the doors. It was getting dark; all the straight lines were melting. He was scared. But he could still make out the farm police boys. They emerged from the crowd, dragging the man with them. He offered no resistance, just allowed them to pull him along like a tethered goat. They took him to where the *Sangoma* stood, now beside his motorbike. Richard, alone in the gloom, listened to the screams and wild cries coming from the crowd. They gave him goosebumps. He noticed that some people had armed themselves with sticks, and several cane cutters were brandishing cane knives above their heads. The blades glinted in the fading light and Richard, seeing them, shivered involuntarily. Tears stung his eyes.

Then he saw his grandfather's tall figure push through the crowd and make his way to the *Sangoma's* side. The *Indunas* and police boys, hemmed in, were struggling to keep the crowd back. Arthur joined Mdletshe and they began shouting at the crowd and waving their arms. Richard couldn't hear what was said, but whatever it was, it created a lull, a moment of respite when the surging tide ebbed back a little and everyone paused, held their breath, and stood still.

In that moment, as though at the flick of a switch, the condemned man leaped into action. He broke free from the police boys, darted behind the *Sangoma*, skirted the motorbike, and then sprinted as fast as he could for the safety of the nearby cane field. In seconds he was swallowed up by the tall cane which closed behind him with barely a ripple. It all happened so fast – he was well into the field before the crowd realised what had happened. There was pandemonium. Three or four men with sticks in their hands broke from the crowd and gave chase. They fanned out and ran into the cane after him, each one in a different row, and they called to each other as they went.

In the chaos that followed, the *Sangoma* mounted his motorbike, kick-started it, and rode away. People swarmed all over the clearing. Arthur ran back to the car. He was breathing heavily and banged on the door. Richard leaned over and unlocked it.

"Sorry, Pops, I locked it, just in case. What's going to happen?"

His grandfather started the engine. He paused, turned on the headlights, and then gave Richard a long, pensive look. "I don't know, my boy, I don't know. I don't think they'll find that chap, he got a good start and he's running for his life."

"Hey, Pops! There, behind you! Look! People are carrying fire."

Arthur twisted round to see out the rear window. He cursed and spun the car around.

"Bloody hell! They are going to torch the man's house. Let's go."

Richard watched the headlights slice through the darkness, picking out figures that ran like fireflies towards the married quarters. The lights swept past them, onto the brick buildings, found the thatched huts at the end, steadied, then settled on one at the bottom of the slope. It was surrounded by the *indunas* and police boys. They had their backs to it and held their sticks high, warning the mob not to come closer. The car stopped. Mdletshe's face loomed up, filling the window, eyes as big as saucers. He was in a state of high agitation; beads of sweat ran down his face, soaking the stubble on his cheeks. Richard wound down the window and then shrank back, a chick running to its hen.

"*Nkosi,*" said Mdletshe, looking past Richard, "*there is danger here. They want to burn down that man's house.*"

As he spoke, the crowd surged forward. The police boys braced themselves and raised their sticks even higher. By now there was a mass of flaming torches, borne high overhead; they cast macabre shadows that danced on the walls of the surrounding huts. Mdletshe scuttled around to the other side of the car. Arthur opened his window.

"*Nkosi, can I have a driver and a vehicle?*"

"*What for, Mdletshe?*"

"*Nkosi, we must get his family out of here. They'll kill them. Please, Nkosi, a car.*"

Without waiting for a reply, he shouted into the dark. *"Someone call a driver – find Josiah. Tell him to come here quickly."* He turned back to the car. *"Nkosi, Josiah is from the wife's area, he will drive them there for us."*

The crowd pressed forward into the headlights and bunched up like swimmers crowding on a riverbank, waiting to see who would take the plunge first. Sweat glistened on their faces and their eyes, large and round, shone like pieces of wet coal. Mdletshe turned to them, this time with soft words. He went around that tight-knit circle again and again, pleading with each person for restraint. Richard could feel his heart pounding in his chest; he knew that if one person broke, they would all break. Nobody moved, the line held. Then they began to chant and stamp their feet. He could smell them; they were that close; fear widened his nostrils.

At last, Josiah stepped into the headlights. He elbowed his way to the front and approached the car. Arthur opened the door and got out.

"Josiah," he said, reaching out with his arm to draw him closer, *"I want you to help me. I want you to take the woman and her children back to her home. Will you do that for me?"*

Josiah looked around. *"Yes, Nkosi. Right now?"*

"Yes. If she stays here tonight, there will be trouble. Hurry to the workshops and ask Dunn to give you the big pickup – he must fill it with petrol for you. Tell him I said so. Come back here and load all her things onto it. Mdletshe, get the police boys to help load it!"

All this happened not a moment too soon. The woman and her two terrified children were climbing into the vehicle when the torch bearers, urged on by the shrill cries of those behind them, ran forward and hurled their torches at the hut. Within seconds it was a roaring inferno. Richard could feel the heat from where he sat in the car, spellbound. Hungry flames licked their way up the reed walls, swallowing them whole. Thatch that for so long had withstood wind and rain, disappeared in a puff of smoke. The roof collapsed, showering sparks everywhere. Wild cheers rent the night air. The *indunas*, wet sacks in their hands, dashed around, swatting, and dousing sparks wherever they could. People cavorted about, shouting and gesticulating, ghoulish figures in the red light. There was no wind. The flames seemed to be sucked straight up into the sky, a twisting, roaring column that cast lurid shadows far and wide. Smoke stung Richard's eyes. He wound up his window and hid his face, appalled.

At that moment another vehicle drove up and Frankie jumped out. With him was his seventeen-year-old grandson, Isaac. They approached Arthur's side of the car. "Is everything okay, Sir? We saw the flames – thought you might need a hand. I asked Isaac here to come along. We've brought some backpack weed-sprayers from the shed with us – filled with water. I thought they might be useful."

"Thank you, Frankie, well done. I'd forgotten the sprayers. I'm afraid it's all over. Happened so very fast. These damn savages have just burned this house down – can you believe it? Give the sprayers to the *indunas* – tell them to hose everything down. Would you mind staying on for a little while? To keep an eye on things for me till they've done it? Good man. I've got to get young Richard here back for his dinner. See you in the morning."

***

At breakfast the next morning Richard approached his grandfather who had his newspaper propped up against the toast rack in front of him. He was buttering slices of toast.

"Pops, have you spoken to Josiah? Did he manage to get them home safely?"

"Yes, Richard, he did."

"Shouldn't we have taken them?"

"No."

"Would it have been better if we had called the police?"

"No. The police are no good in situations like that."

"What happened to the man? Did those men catch him?"

"No. He got away. He'll be alright."

"And Mdletshe, did he say anything about last night?"

"Not much. He thinks that the *Sangoma* did a good job."

Richard thought about that. He walked around the table to the sideboard and helped himself to a bowl of cereal. He carried it back to his place and sat down.

"Pops?"

"Yes?"

"Why did they burn the man's house down?"

"Oh, I wouldn't worry about that if I were you. They have gotten rid of someone they didn't like, that's all. You wait and see; life will return to normal now."

"Didn't like him? Why not?"

"Well, for starters he is a *Shangaan*. Apparently, he has done something bad – the word is that he does not have a good relationship with the ancestral spirits. They don't like that, you know."

"Do you think he had something to do with that stillborn birth?"

"Of course not. But everyone in the compound thinks he did. That's all that matters."

Richard frowned. He poured milk over his cereal and then sprinkled a little sugar over it. He picked up his spoon but did not eat. Something bothered him.

"Pops, how did the *Sangoma* know that Aunty Trish took Granny to Richard's Bay with her yesterday morning?"

Art took off his glasses and put them down. He leaned across the table and took Richard's hand. He squeezed it.

"It's quite easy. The *Sangoma* has eyes and ears everywhere. We have garden boys and house servants, don't we? They are his eyes and ears. A vast network of informers. There's your answer. Now, be a good chap and pass the marmalade."

2

Reece Thornicroft was a senior partner of Shepparton Lawyers, a well-known law firm in Durban, and he had just returned to his office with his good friend Arthur Barclay – they had lunched together at the Royal Hotel and both men were feeling replete after an excellent curry. They were now awaiting the arrival of Jack McIntyre.

"While we are waiting, what do you think of this?"

Reece picked up a folded copy of the Natal Mercury and jabbed a long bony finger at an article on the front page. "Have you seen it?"

Arthur reached over for the paper, ran his eyes over it and then pushed it away. "Yeah, I've read it. So what? American politics, isn't it? Doesn't interest me that much."

"Well, Art. It's tremendously significant, I feel. In the case of Brown versus Board of Education, the United States Supreme Court has voted unanimously that the racial segregation of children in public schools is unconstitutional. That kills the 'separate-but-equal' argument stone dead."

"Well, Reece, I don't know that much about it, I'm just a simple farmer. You know me – you know that I'm not interested in politics at all. Who gives a shit about what happens over there? You're a UP man – you've had a bee in your bonnet ever since Smuts got kicked out. You do know I voted for the Nats last time, don't you? But hang it all, man, let's not allow politics to rear its ugly head and ruin what till now has been a good day."

Reece laughed. He picked up the paper, folded it, and placed it on the shelf behind him. Then he swung back in his swivel chair and faced Art with a disarming grin.

"Hell no. The last thing I want right now is a political argument. All I was saying is that this civil rights thing is gaining momentum in the States –"

"Yeah, but what's the fuss? Why get your wee in a froth about something that's happening far away? If you ask me, the Yanks have allowed – what do they call it now? A fifth column, I think it is, to infiltrate their government and turn it against them. That guy McCarthy had it right, I reckon – the commies don't have to win a war, do they? All they have to do is keep out of view and white-ant the government. Now, can you believe it, the powers that be over there want to shut the poor bugger up – seems like nobody there can bear to hear the truth."

"Well, Art, I'm not sure I agree with you about Senator McCarthy – or about the truth. I think he's dangerous and a threat to the democratic process –"

"Reece! Reece! Why do you lawyers go on about democracy so much? Too much idealism. Get real for a change. It's about governing with a firm hand. All that soft stuff might be okay in theory, but in the real world, the strong rule the weak and –"

"Art, this US Supreme Court ruling will affect us, that's why. When America sneezes, the rest of the world catches a cold. Seems to me that the world is going one way and that we, against the flow, are going another. Worrying times, Art, worrying times. But, changing the subject, what do you think of this guy from the Cape, Sir De Villiers Graaf? Was the only pick-up seat the UP had in 1948. I see people are now touting him for party leadership. Zululand is UP country, isn't it – what are people up there saying about him?"

"I wouldn't have a clue. I don't discuss politics if I can help it. Listen, Reece, before Jack gets here, I just want to say a couple of things."

Arthur stood up, fidgeted with his beard, then walked around his chair and leaned against it with his arms braced on the backrest. He wasn't sure how to begin or indeed, exactly what he wanted to say.

"I told you Jack's history on the phone the other day – he's unique, you know. Not many Blacks have been raised as Whites overseas and then come back. Give him his due – he came back, determined to learn to speak in his native tongue, as he put it. He went to Polela Mission to learn Zulu and now he's fluent – bloody fluent – you'd think he was a local. Though he's my godson, after a fashion, I haven't had much to do with him at all. Used to send him and his sister a fiver each at Christmas – before the war, that is – but that's about as much as I did. The sister? I lost touch with Jill, that's her name – the last I heard she was giving piano lessons in Edinburgh – I gather she's a very talented musician. But back to Jack. I did meet him when he came back but have only seen him once since then and that was to give him some money that he'd asked for – a loan, he insisted on calling it. We met in Mtubatuba. He didn't tell me what it was for, and I didn't ask. What's that? No, Jess has not seen him – not once since he's been back.

"Reece, he's a square peg in a round hole. Must be tough to be brought up as an English gent only to discover that you aren't one after all. I gathered from the last meeting I had with him that he's a bit at sea, floundering, I reckon. He's neither one thing nor another, if you know what I mean. Made it quite clear that he doesn't want any help from me, or anyone else for that matter. He's had a few jobs and lost them because ... How shall I put it? He'd say because of personality clashes but reading between the lines I'd say it's insubordination on his part – he doesn't mind airing his views and telling people where to get off. Because of his army background, he got this job with the Durban City

Police, with the Blackjacks, right here in the city. Right now, he's assistant to the Chief Constable. You know him? Withers, Ray Withers? Plays golf – I've met him a few times at the Country Club. He told me not long ago that Jack's doing a pretty good job – good enough for them to overlook his outbursts. But there are problems – grog mostly, and anger. Ray says he's very touchy and short-tempered. He can't stand what goes on here and gets quite hot under the collar when he talks about what he calls the 'iniquities'. You know, when I had that meeting with him in Mtuba, he asked me – quite out of the blue – about job reservation. Asked me if I approved of government policies that decree – his words – that certain jobs are to be reserved for Whites only? He nearly bit my head off when I said something about it being reasonable for the government to look after its own people first. You should have seen the fire in his eyes – thought he was going to explode. So, it's delicate. You just need to be aware of all this and treat him with kid gloves. What's that? No, he won't go back to England – nothing there for him, I suppose – especially now that his parents are dead."

"Thanks, Art. I'm keen to meet him. Don't worry, I won't –"

The phone rang. Reece picked it up, mumbled a few words and then set it down on its cradle again. He got up and went to the door and straightened his tie.

"Jack has just arrived. I told my secretary to bring him in."

Jack walked in. He shook hands with Reece and then, with exaggerated bonhomie, threw his arms around Arthur. They hugged, patting each other's back. They came apart, but held onto each other's arms, and laughed together.

"Uncle Arthur! Great to see you! I must say I wasn't expecting to see you."

"Hello, Jack – good to see you again. It's been a long time, hasn't it? Let me introduce you. This is Reece Thornicroft. The lawyer in England who's handling your father's estate contacted Reece and asked him to get in touch with you. Reece and I are old friends."

Reece shook Jack's hand and steered him towards a leather-bound chair. Then, with a sweep of his hands, he indicated that they all should be seated.

"Jack, pleased to meet you and thanks for coming in. Thomas Watson of Watson, Williams, and Wycliffe – all W's, I note – is the lawyer in England who is handling your parent's estate. Sorry to hear of your parent's death. Train crash, the one at Harrow and Wealdstone, was it? So many dead and so many injured. Absolutely awful – big news, even out here. I've known Tommy for a long time – his firm has used us, every so often, on other matters and so he contacted me and asked if I could help him find you. He said that he'd been in contact with your sister Jill, but she too hadn't heard from you in ages and didn't have a forwarding address. The only lead he had was the Polela Mission – found a note in your father's papers. So, he wrote to them, twice actually. Eventually he received a letter back saying that you had left there about three years ago and that they had no idea where you went or how to contact you. So, the trail went cold, so to speak. Then Tommy contacted me and asked me if I could help. I made a few enquiries, but nobody seemed to know of a Jack McIntyre or had heard of him –"

"That's because I always use my Zulu surname. Mkwanaze. Whites don't take kindly to a Black who they think is masquerading as one of them, especially when he's looking for a job. Sorry, I didn't mean to interrupt you. Go on."

"Well, quite frankly I sat on it for a while, wasn't sure where to go after that. Then I remembered a conversation I'd had some years ago with Arthur – don't know what reminded me of it, but I recalled that he came to see me after he'd met someone from England on the mail ship who was, how shall I put it, non-white. So, I gave Art a call on the off chance and here we are."

"When Reece called me, I was quite surprised. I'd have thought that there would have been some reference to me in Don's papers, but apparently not. Would have saved a lot of mucking around. Come-on, Reece, out with it. Tell him why your friend Tommy wants to contact Jack."

"Well, Jack, your parents were not well off and did not have much money. But they owned their house – still had a small mortgage on it, but for all intents and purposes, they owned it. Anyway, in your father's will, Tommy was instructed to sell it and to settle any outstanding debts. Whatever was left was to be divided equally between you and Jill. The house sold better than expected. I am here to tell you that you are the beneficiary of £500, and so is Jill. Tommy saw to it that she received her portion of the inheritance. He is waiting for instructions as to what he should do with yours. Also, your father left you his watch, his writing case, and his signet ring. There is also a letter for you – from him to you. Oh, I nearly forgot, your mother left you something as well – her engagement ring and a broach."

Jack got up and walked over to the window. Their eyes followed him and stayed on his back. His shoulders appeared to sag a little, as though the sinews that kept them taut and ramrod stiff had been nicked by a knife but the movement, if it was there, was lost with the downward motion of Jack's hand as he reached into his trouser pocket for his handkerchief. He kept his back to them and blew his nose. There were rickshaws on the other side of the street, lined up in front of the Dick King memorial, and though his eyes scanned each one and unconsciously compared the feathered headdresses of the drivers, he saw nothing.

"Thank you. Thank you. Thank you." The words bounced back off the windowpane, startling him and jolting him from his reverie. He turned around. His eyes were like puddles and his cheeks were awash with tears. He heaved and strained to contain the emotions that he could not swallow. They stood staring at him, searching his face with inquisitive eyes.

His gaze shifted between the men. "You know how sick and tired I am of being told how lucky I am, that I should count my blessings and be grateful. Of course, I'm grateful, very grateful. But I'm sick and tired of being pointed at, as though I'm something of an oddity, you know, like something in a zoo. Dad simply did his Christian thing, did what he felt had to be done. That's more than can be said for ninety-nine point nine per cent of the Whites in this country. But what's so special about it, I ask myself, is it because I have black skin? Is that what makes his Christian charity so unique? You tell me! Yes, I am touchy about who I am … "

He paused for breath, knowing that this was not really the right audience for his outburst, but the impetus of his words pushed him into the tangled undergrowth of his resentment and he blundered on, heedless of thorns and scratches, like a bushwalker obsessed with ever-distant blue hills.

"I don't like so-called Christian people – especially holier-than-thou white ones – telling me to count my blessings when, in fact, their white skins have given them a hell of a lot more blessings than I could ever dream of. I came back here because I wanted to. Sure, Mum and Dad didn't think it was a good idea, but they understood, understood that Africa with all its enigmatic charm was pulsing through my veins and calling out to me. I had to come back, had to see for myself. Bloody daft, you might say, who in their right mind would want to come back to this? This … this cesspool of moral degradation! You know, I can come and go as I please, just about anywhere in the world, but not here. Not in the country of my birth. I can fight for freedom in the white man's war, but not here – there's freedom here only if you are born white. You can speak better English, have a better education, behave with better manners – you can have all that, but God help you if you have black skin, because nobody else will. Here, we are the 'hewers of wood and the drawers of water'. We Blacks are the sons of Ham, aren't we? Says so in the bible. You know what sticks in my throat? That I should be grateful for the very things you take for granted – things you take in your stride, but which I must fall on my knees for. You know, had they been there – the righteous, god-fearing Whites of this country, I mean – had they been there, they would have snored through the Sermon on the Mount, and then said afterwards that they still knew better. Have you any idea, even a scintilla of an idea, what it means to be black? Have you even the foggiest idea what it's like to be born black and raised white?"

They heard it, heard the silence. It rang like a bell marking the end of a round in a ring. Like punch-drunk boxers they went back to their corners on leaden feet. Arthur shuffled to the window. Reece went to his chair behind the desk, sat down heavily, and then got up again. He went to Jack, approaching him as he might an accident victim – wanting to help, but not sure how.

"I'm sorry," Jack said, in a squashed-flat voice, "it's not your fault. There is a Zulu saying, which you've probably never heard – a proverb I suppose you'd call it, *Unayaw' alunampumulo* – the foot has no nose. With no nose, the feet cannot smell their way. That's me. My feet have no nose – nothing to lead them or to show them the way. You are lucky, your feet follow your noses like bees to a honeypot – but the scent they follow is for white nostrils only. Now, where were we? Mum and Dad. My inheritance." He turned to Arthur. "I see little point in bringing all that money here, do you? How much do I owe you? £50, was it? Well, let's fix that up right away. Reece, would you mind asking your friend Tommy to send me £250 and to put the remaining £250 in an interest-bearing bank account for me? Ask him to send you the other things from Mum and Dad as well, please. When all that gets here, would you then mind forwarding £50 to Uncle Arthur and £200 to me?"

Arthur cleared his throat and opened his mouth to speak, but Jack's raised hands stopped him.

"No, Uncle Art, I insist. I always said it was a loan, didn't I? Money isn't everything, not by a long chalk – that's one thing Dad taught me. But the £200 will come in handy. I have a lady that I want to marry. Mavis is her name. We have three children, but we never got married. It's time I did the right thing. The money will give us a good start, I reckon, a very good start. You know," he paused as though what he was about to say was akin to letting a genie out of a bottle, "I've had white girls – back in England, before the war – had quite a few in fact. I even had one I could have married, but she disappeared from my life. Just like that." And he snapped his fingers. "Never said a word – just vanished without trace. That was a long time ago. I have Mavis now – she's been good to me, very good. She's teaching my nose new tricks."

He looked around, nodded at them, and then went on. "Good, seems like we are done. I must get back to work. If you'd excuse me."

Jack shook them by the hand and was just about to leave when Reece's voice stopped him at the door. He kept his hand on the doorknob.

"What about the letter?"

"Letter?"

"The one from your father. Shall I wire Tommy and ask him to mail it out straight away? Been a while since it was written, and I just thought you might like it sooner rather than later. What's the best way to contact you?"

Jack went back to the desk and scribbled down his work address and phone number.

"That should do it. Thank you, Reece. And thank you, Uncle Art."

He tugged the back of his coat down with both hands, squared his shoulders with military correctness, doffed his head at each of them in turn, and marched out of the room.

"Well, well," said Arthur, turning to his friend, "what did I tell you? He's a troubled soul, isn't he? And touchy, very touchy. Look, Reece, I won't keep you any longer. Told Jess I'd meet her back at the Royal at 4:00 pm. I've got ten minutes. We're driving back this afternoon – I don't like driving after dark these days – too many bloody fools on the road. I'll give you a ring next time I'm in town – perhaps we can fit in some golf. Say hello to Laura. Goodbye, old chap."

3

There were no schools for coloured people in Empangeni, so Isaac went to school in Mandini, the heartland of the Dunn clan. Weekdays he stayed with his aunt Phyllis and her three boys. Her dissolute husband had left her a long time ago – good riddance, her friends would say, because he was far more devoted to the bottle than he was to Phyllis and, worse still, he beat her when he was drunk. Then, on Friday afternoons, and every Friday it was the same, *Oupa* Frankie would borrow one of Arthur Barclay's vehicles and would come to fetch him and would take him home to the farm for the weekends. Rosie never came; she stayed at home, waiting for her son and father while she prepared one of Isaac's favourite meals for him. The journey home was always a delight for Isaac – just him and the old man, two peas in a pod. Frankie reached behind him and retrieved an old biscuit tin from the space behind the passenger seat.

"Here, your mother never forgets. *Padkos* for you. She's made *koeksisters*. Don't eat them all at once. Now tell me, how was school this week? You going to pass, hey? You'd bloody better."

He took a *koeksister* from the tin and chewed on it slowly, revelling in its honeyed sweetness. "Have you decided what you want to do next year? You'd better pass your matric. How are your studies going, anyway? If you want to go to university, I can manage that. Or trade school – we can do that as well. Just tell me which way you want to jump, and I'll help you – but I'm not going to let you sit on your arse."

Isaac stared out the window. This was not a conversation he expected nor one that he wanted. He hated books; he'd had enough of them. He was thinking of a girl he had met – she had big breasts and long, shapely legs. The *koeksister* thickened in his mouth.

"Well, couldn't I just work with you on the farm? At least for a while?"

It was on the tip of his tongue to point out to his grandfather that he himself had had no formal training – that he'd gone off to work and had made his own way. He'd done well, hadn't he? But he knew that argument would be like pushing water uphill – he'd tried it before. So, he modified it.

"What about we ask *Baas* Barclay if I can be your assistant for say six months? That'll let me know if that's what I really want to do. You know, if I want to spend the rest of my life in a workshop fixing things. *Oupa*, if I do like it, then I'll go to trade school and get my ticket as a welder, or a mechanic, or whatever – promise."

Frankie sighed. He didn't like being fobbed off. Nobody had offered him a choice like that when he was a boy. Things were too easy for Isaac's generation.

"I'm not sure what *Baas* Barclay will say to that. Sure, he doesn't mind you hanging around the workshops and giving me a hand. But not sure if he wants to pay you for that. He's tight, you know – wouldn't give you a block of ice in the middle of winter. But I could ask him."

Cigarette smoke was beginning to hurt Isaac's eyes, so he leaned forward and opened the triangular vent window as far as it would go – it caught the crisp evening air outside like a stiff sail and funnelled it into the cab.

"My boy," Frankie's voice droned on, catching Isaac off guard, "I'm worried that if you stop studying now then you'll never go back to the books again. You'll become a bum, chasing skirt, and going from job to job. That's not good. I know what I'm talking about, seen it all too often. I had just started my time as a builder when the war broke out and off I went, young and silly – for king and country – can you believe that! I never did finish. I've told you before, I got interested in mechanical things in the war – you just had to know how to fix things if you wanted to survive. When I came home, I joined a firm in Umbilo Road that was making trailers – that's where I learned to weld. And that's where I met *Baas* Barclay. Built him a cane trailer, I did, best one he ever saw. And he was so impressed he offered me a job back on his farm. He said he had a house for me, and Gracie and I didn't think twice – we were there within a month. Been there ever since. She died there. Your mother was born there – we Dunns are part of the furniture now. But you might not be so lucky – there are not many Arthur Barclays hanging around, waiting for an Isaac Dunn to show up. Many of the blokes I grew up with didn't get lucky – they took to the bottle and drank their lives away. Happens all the time. Here's another thing, Isaac. Your mother and I went to a lot of trouble to ensure that you were born in England – that gives you the right to a British passport. I couldn't do it for your mother – didn't have the money – but I was able to do it for you. A British passport! That's big, bloody big. Opens up the world for you, my boy, it really does. Like the war did for me, only a lot better. But you'll need a qualification, something to prove that you can work wherever you go – they won't want you if you cannot get a job. This is your last year of school; come December, I want you to tell me what you've decided. If you want to –"

They were approaching the bridge over the Msunduze River, just past Nyoni. It had massive concrete arches that straddled a single lane for cars. A large white police van blocked their entrance to the bridge. Frankie stopped the car as quickly as he had stopped the conversation, and they climbed out. There had been an accident on the far side of the bridge – two vehicles, head-on. One, he could just make out, looked like a white Mercedes and the other, a lorry carrying a load of cut timber. Arthur Barclay had a white Mercedes he thought. Frankie shaded his eyes as he walked, trying to see if he could recognise the vehicle. It was too far away. He could see that there was an ambulance drawn up behind the lorry. Its roof lights were flashing. A white policeman walked up to intercept them.

"Go back. Go back. There's been an accident. Do not pass this point."

Frankie peered round the policeman. "What happened?" He pointed at the far end of the bridge. "Is it bad? Can we help?"

"Pretty bad. There's nothing you can do. Luckily, I arrived shortly after it happened. I've radioed for an ambulance from Empangeni. Once it's here, we'll clear the bridge. Go back to your vehicle and wait."

"Do you know who it is?"

"Yes, but I'm not revealing that now. If there's a fatality, then the next of kin need to know first. Standard procedure."

"That ambulance. What's it doing there? Surely it can help?"

"No. That's an ambulance for Blacks. A white male is unconscious – has head injuries. A white female is conscious. Shaken, crying a lot, but seems okay. The male needs an ambulance – a white ambulance. That one's waiting to cross the bridge – it's going to Stanger."

"What about the lorry – anyone hurt?"

"Single occupant. *Bantu* male. Pissed. We're taking him into custody. He didn't stop, drove straight onto the bridge and into the other vehicle. Says that his brakes failed. *Coons*, they're bloody hopeless."

Frankie stared at the policeman. Such a careless remark from a face that did not look unkind. "Maybe I can help when you clear the bridge. I have a winch in my pickup and tow ropes –"

"No, thank you. I've ordered a tow truck. It's on its way. Just go back and see no cars try to get onto the bridge for me. I'm going to assist Sergeant Breytenbach back there. The ambulance will be here soon. If we need help clearing the bridge, we'll call you. In the meantime, stay put. Thank you."

Frankie and Isaac tramped back to their car in silence.

"*Oupa*, why can't that ambulance take the injured man to hospital? Would save a hell of a lot of time, wouldn't it?"

Frankie looked away.

"It's not about what makes sense, my boy. It's about the law. This country wants Blacks and Whites to be kept apart – everything separated, squeaky clean, even when it doesn't seem to make sense. A white man cannot be taken to hospital in a black ambulance – he might catch something and die, heaven forbid. That's crazy, fucking crazy. Only in South Africa. It's another reason why I wanted you to have a British passport – so that you can escape all this shit."

He turned to Isaac and drew him close. Isaac's heart surged and he laughed. He put his free arm around his grandfather and hugged him.

"Listen hard, Isaac – listen to your *Oupa*."

Frankie wanted to think, so he fished out another cigarette for himself, lit it carefully, and looked around. Several cars were lined up behind them, engines off and doors closed. Nobody came to enquire what the problem was. Far away, across the river, he heard a bird calling and knew from the rising distinctive "*kok, koks*" that it was a *gwalagwala*. He turned towards it and saw that the shadows had reached across the river and were climbing towards the egrets, branch over branch. He nudged Isaac and pointed his nicotine-stained fingers at the bridge.

"What's happening over there is only going to get worse. Get yourself a ticket. Go to university. Or trade school. You can always give me a hand during the holidays – I'll teach you all I know. But for God's sake, don't piss it against the wall now, just because you want to 'do your own thing'. For fuck's sake, man, there's plenty of time for that afterwards, do you hear? Don't give me crap about being tired of school. Just because your mates who have shit for brains and hot nuts want to rush off and sow their wild oats, doesn't mean you have to copy them. Hey, you listening to me, fella? Get smart. Get qualified. Get ahead of the pack. Give yourself a red-hot chance to get out and explore the world. Please, Isaac, not for my sake, or your mother's, but for your own sake."

Fortunately for Isaac, at that precise moment providence made a timely intervention. Far across the river, just visible to the naked eye, a flashing light caught their eyes. It inched its way along and then, gathering speed as the road curved downwards, it dropped from view into a sea of green – a sunlit drop of water, Frankie thought, running down a leaf. It was the ambulance. When it was closer, they heard it more than they saw it; the road, twisting and turning through the cane fields, was unable to dampen much less shut out the siren's shrill wail which, even from where they stood on the opposite end of the bridge, annoyed their ears. Then, about ten minutes later, the tow truck arrived. They strained their eyes in the gathering gloom and were just able to make out white-clad figures, moving like ants between the vehicles. Then the ambulance left, siren screaming and its lights searing the evening sky. About twenty minutes later, they were waved onto the bridge.

They drove across slowly. The other cars waddled after them, like ducklings following a gander, and they reached the accident site. As they passed, their tyres crunched on broken glass. A native policeman waved them on. Frankie kept his hands on the steering wheel but raised the fingers of his right hand in acknowledgement. When they emerged, they saw the tow truck operators right in front of them – men in overalls, busily securing the badly smashed Mercedes Benz onto the back of their lorry. There was something familiar about it. Frankie felt a knot form in his stomach. He slowed down so that he could get a good look. The number plate. He knew it. Arthur Barclay's. His boss. Not wanting to believe his eyes, he stole another look. Understanding rose slowly, like sludge from the bottom of a disturbed pool, soiling his senses. Tears flowed from his eyes. The devil's work, this. To think that the *Ou Baas* may have died while he was sitting in his car just across the bridge was too much for him to bear. He instantly regretted not telling the *Ou Baas* things he wanted to say to him ages ago. He was angry with himself and angrier still that God hadn't even given him a chance to say goodbye.

4

When Busisiwe heard the news of Arthur Barclay's death, she was sure that the sun had fallen out of the sky.

Her heart ached. *Nchebe* was dead. *Nchebe* had given Madondo a job and Madondo had gotten her a job; it was *Nchebe* who got her into the Barclay household, and it was *Nchebe* who arranged for her and Amidu to work for Bill and Molly in the village. If she had not been in the village, she would not have met Titus. How strange the ways of the world – happy one minute, sad the next.

Death, it seemed, cast a long shadow. What was it that Titus had said at a funeral recently? Something about us being as water spilt on the ground, which cannot be gathered up again. Small consolation that, but fitting, nonetheless.

Busisiwe made up her mind. She would go to visit Molly as soon as she could. She had not been back to the Barclay residence since Amidu's death, nor had she tried to see Molly on any of the rare occasions when she had been back to Empangeni in the ensuing five years. Rather, it had been the other way around – Molly had visited her at the Mission and always brought a gift with her. Much had happened. She had married Titus and had given birth to their son, Peter, who was now nearly four years old. Gordon, a late-starting scholar, was at the Mission School and with patient help from Titus who sat down with him each evening after dinner, had not only caught up to his peers, but was now top of his class. Thandi too, was doing well at school. Despite his firmly held convictions to the contrary, Titus had done the right thing and had honoured tradition by meeting Busisiwe's father and agreeing to pay *lobola*. But instead of cattle – of which he had none at all – he offered cash, and, in the end, an undisclosed amount of money changed hands. They were married in church, and she wore a white dress. It was the happiest day of her life. Busisiwe was just about to walk across to his office when the kitchen door opened, and Titus stepped in. He removed his hat and sat down at the kitchen table.

"Ah, I was just coming over to see you, but you've saved me the trouble."

"I felt like a cup of tea. What did you want to see me about?"

"Titus, I would like to attend the funeral. *Nchebe's* funeral, I mean."

She scanned her husband's face with anxious eyes. All she saw coming back at her, in an unchecked torrent, was his pity which, she had come to understand and not to resent, was at the core of his adoration. His eyes, magnified by his glasses, were moist with concern. Stung by his love, and not wanting to burst into tears herself, she hurried on.

"You said it was going to be on Friday afternoon. I owe it to Madam Molly. She was so good to me. I really would like to go. What do you think?"

***

Titus and Busisiwe had arrived early for the funeral, but they did not go into the church. They knew their place and stood aside, in the uncontested strip of bright sunlight on the further side of the hearse; there they waited for the house servants and farm workers who arrived shortly afterwards on a tractor and trailer. Thandi, who was now eight years old, clutched her mother's skirt as she watched them pour in through the churchyard gate and make their way to where they stood. Titus had his hand on her shoulder and when she felt his grip tighten, she twisted around to look up at him. *"Strange, isn't it,"* she saw Titus leaning over and whisper to Busisiwe, *"even in death, when grief should bring people together, the old divisions hold fast – see, Blacks are on one side, Whites on the other."* Thandi squinted up at him. She didn't understand – wasn't it always like that?

Busisiwe felt a tap on her shoulder and turned around. "Hello, Busisiwe. Nice to see you again after all these years. You remember me? Frankie? The farm mechanic, on *Nchebe's* farm, remember? You remember Rosie? She's my daughter and this here is Isaac, my grandson. Such a sad day, isn't it."

"Of course, I remember you." Busisiwe shook their hands. Frankie looked older and greyer, but his eyes were as friendly as ever. She was pleased that he not only had recognised her but had actually bothered to come and greet her. "This is Titus, my husband," she said proudly, standing aside so they could shake hands, "we live at Somkhele Mission now." She was about to say more when a convoy of four cars drew up on either side of the large wooden gates and parked in the spaces that had been reserved for them. The Barclay family had arrived, all dressed in black except the chauffeur who drove the lead car – his freshly starched white coat and peaked cap set him apart.

Busisiwe watched Molly wipe her eyes with a handkerchief and then help Jess from the car. "Oh shame," Busisiwe felt the words wobble then fall from her lips, "the old lady is hurt." She must have been injured in the accident because Molly had to hold onto her mother-in-law and keep her propped up and steady until the chauffeur brought a wheelchair from the boot of the car. The family gathered around. Richard was there, in his school uniform, wearing long pants. Molly had fetched him from his boarding school so that he and Mary could attend the funeral of their grandfather. She turned her attention to the wheelchair. Bill took over from the chauffeur and settled his mother in it. Though the white hair was thinner, and the face more deeply etched, Busisiwe could see even from where she stood that the old lady had lost none of her feistiness. She smiled, recalling that her Zulu name *Qhotho* referred less to her skinny appearance and more to the fact that like the thin, dried piece of leather on the end of a long whip that made the cracking sound, she made things happen. So many memories came back to her just then as she watched the old lady, watched the familiar toss of her head and the quick, imperious flick of her hand as she exhorted Bill to move her forward. He bent down, straightened the crocheted blanket on her lap, and then, with both hands on the wheelchair, he trundled her inside. As though in slow motion, the rest of the family shuffled in behind, like cattle at milking time, following their matriarch. During all this, no words were spoken, no looks acknowledged and indeed, nobody from the assembled onlookers ventured forward to help. They hung back, like theatregoers arrayed behind the lights, and watched the drama unfold.

Standing outside in the heat was almost unbearable; Peter began to fidget; glancing down, Busisiwe noticed that his hands were scissored between his legs. She patted Thandi's back. *"Peter needs to wee. Take him round to the back. Over there, behind that building. Or find a tree where no one can see. Hurry now."*

No sooner were they behind the building and out of sight, then Peter looked up at Thandi with big apprehensive eyes and uttered just one word. *"Bhosha."* Thandi panicked. She looked around desperately. He couldn't *bhosha* here – urinating might have been alright, behind a tree, but not *bhosha* – not in an *abelungu* place. She took Peter's hand and dragged him round to the other side of the building and realized that this was the ablution block that adjoined the church hall. Relief swept over her, even though she knew these facilities were for white people only.

"Quick, Peter. There are toilets here. They are for the abelungu, so be quick." She hustled him into the nearest cubicle and helped him

remove his trousers. When they were finished, Thandi opened the door and peered out. She was at the wash basin, when two white girls burst in, their light-hearted chatter interspersed with giggles and face-pulling. They stopped dead.

"What are you doing in here?" The older, dark-haired girl asked, "This is for Whites only."

Thandi's English was unpractised. Titus tutored the children most nights around the dinner table and made them read English books aloud. She understood but was shy to speak.

"There was nowhere to go. Sorry. Velly sorry. We are going now."

The two girls stood aside and watched them go. "Honestly," said the dark-haired girl, raising her eyebrows with exaggerated artlessness, "these *munts* think they can go where they like. Which one were they in, do you think? I don't want to sit where a black bum has been."

The service had already started when an old pickup drew up alongside the Barclay cars and continued to wheeze and splutter after it had come to a stop. They saw a man jump out. He was tall and angular, and he wore dark pants and a sports coat. He paid the driver and hurried towards the church door where, oblivious of the stares that greeted him, he proceeded to work his way through the crowd that stood in front of it. Who was this latecomer, Busisiwe wondered, where did he get the cheek to push his way through all those people, as if he had more right to be inside than they did.

"Can I help you?" Someone asked him.

"Sorry, old chap," the newcomer said to a wide-girthed, grey-haired man who blocked his way at the door, "but if you don't mind, I have to get in."

"The church is full. Standing room only. That's why we're outside."

"That's all right. I'm happy to stand. Now, if you'll excuse me, I'd like to go in. I know Arthur. He's my godfather." And with that, he pushed past and made his way inside.

***

The wake was held in the church hall. Jess Barclay sat in her wheelchair at the front door and greeted the mourners who lined up to offer their condolences. Her family was gathered around her. Inside, the neon ceiling lights washed the room with a bright white light that seemed to rinse those who assembled beneath them of their sorrow for, as they entered as though from quarantine, their tongues were loosened, and they began at once to chatter without restraint. They moved in and out of ever-changing groups, drinking tea and coffee, and helping themselves to plates of sandwiches that were borne aloft by waiters in white tunics. Only when the line of mourners outside had dwindled to a few, did Frankie and his family join it. They paid their respects and moved inside, making their way discreetly to the back of the hall where they stood by themselves. Jess looked around and was about to ask Bill to wheel her inside when she saw Busisiwe.

"Bill. Molly. Look. There's Busisiwe. Over there. Bill, be a dear and wheel me over." Molly spun around, saw Busisiwe, and ran ahead with her arms outstretched.

"Oh, my God, Busisiwe! How nice to see you again. Thank you so much for coming." They hugged each other.

"Oh, Madam, I am so sorry. He was a good man."

"He was indeed," Titus shook Molly's hand, "my condolences, Madam. We never know why we should suffer like this, but God knows. It is in His hands."

Jess and Bill joined them. Busisiwe turned to Jess. Their eyes ran over each other's face, like fingers in the dark, seeking intimacy from half-forgotten features. "*Khosikazi*, we are so sorry to hear about the *Inkosi* passing, very sad. He was a very good man." Then she saw Richard and Mary standing partly behind their father. She pushed Thandi forward. "*Hawu, Lichad! You are grown up! Thandi, have you lost your tongue? Say hello to Inkhosana Lichad and Inkhosazana Meli.*"

The three children stood there, momentarily self-conscious, and uncertain, shyly appraising each other. Tremulous smiles, in mirror image, broadened into grins that split their faces wide open and then they hugged each other. Snatches of conversation and the occasional guffaw of muffled laughter drifted towards them from the hall. Bill gestured towards the hall behind him.

"Come, let's go inside and have some tea."

"Thank you, but we thought we would visit you tomorrow –"

"No, no, please come. I insist," Bill placed his hand on Titus's shoulder, "Molly, tell them to join us."

In that moment of indecision, while Busisiwe and Titus looked each other up and down, a tall figure approached from the direction of the church. He walked right up to the wheelchair.

"Aunty Jess?" He was about to put out his hand but then thought better of it. Instead, he dropped to his knee beside the wheelchair and put his arm around her shoulder. "It's me. Jack. Jack McIntyre. The last time you saw me was, I think, on the Union Castle mail ship when I was a baby."

"Oh my God," Jess reached for him with both hands and grabbed the lapels of his jacket. She pulled him to her and buried her face in his shoulder. "Is it really you, Jack?"

"Yes. I'm so sorry about Uncle Art. He was a good man."

"Oh, Jack, that we should meet like this. Why, in the car on our way back from Durban, Art was telling me about his meeting with you and Reece. Oh, my God, Jack, it's awful. Thank you for coming. It means a lot and Art would be so proud." She heard him sob, a loud shuddering sound that stirred her deeply. She gripped him even tighter, listening to his muffled words.

"Reece contacted me. I only heard yesterday. I am so sorry." He leaned back and stared at her. "I feel so guilty. If it wasn't for me, he wouldn't have had to go to Durban for that meeting. He would be still alive."

***

Most of the mourners had left. Molly was in earnest conversation with Busisiwe who had Peter playing with her skirt. Titus was with Frankie. Thandi, Mary, and Richard were out on the veranda, sitting in a line on the wall and swinging their feet together. Bill and Jack had moved away from the tea tables and were deep in conversation.

"So, you say you manage people? The Blackjacks – you're in charge of them, aren't you?"

"That's right. I have a couple of hundred policemen under my command. Can't say I love doing it, but you know, the pay isn't too bad for a black fellow like me."

"Have you ever thought of doing anything else?"

"Like what?"

"Well, farming for instance."

"Farming? Me?"

"Yes, you. Come farming with me."

It was more than an invitation; it was flattery, pure and simple. Jack could feel his nerve ends tingling. Just for the perverse satisfaction of hearing it again, he asked, "Sorry, what's that?"

"I'm asking you to come and work for me. Now that Dad has died, I have inherited the farm. It looks very much as though Molly and I will move back onto it and live there with my mother. Someone must take over from him and my mother is hoping that it will be me. I guess I knew that I'd have to face this one day, but you know, I have always shrugged it off. And now he's gone. Happened sooner than I had expected. I'm quite happy to move back onto the farm – in fact, that tickles my fancy, and it would be great for the kids. So, I'm happy to keep an eye on things, the business side of things I mean, but I'm a doctor, you know, not a farmer. While working for the Provincial Administration sticks in my throat, I'm happy enough doing what I am doing."

Bill paused for a moment. It was an outlandish idea, but its appeal was growing by the minute. He could keep doing what he was doing, and Jack could help Molly with the day-to-day running of the farm. Molly's lack of Zulu would be more than compensated for by Jack – not only that, but he'd been raised in England and knew how to conduct himself properly – she'd be comfortable working alongside him. And

84

there would be savings – a European manager would cost a lot more money and he couldn't have that.

"Jack, I'm serious. I'm going to need someone who can handle the labour for me. Molly can't do that. But, with your Blackjack knowhow and Molly doing the books, we'd manage well. And, we'd have Frankie, our coloured mechanic, looking after things in the workshop. What do you reckon?"

Jack walked over to the low veranda wall and lit himself a cigarette. He puffed on it, giving himself time to think. He wasn't sure what to think. He was still suffused with the warm glow of flattery – he couldn't remember when he'd last been appraised as an equal. Was this the break he had been looking for – the unknown, unrequited thing that had been tugging at his soul for so long? He flicked the ash off his cigarette.

"What the hell, I'm interested. Let's talk."

5

The year 1954 was, in many respects, like a fulcrum that balanced the old with the new. Arthur Barclay's death marked the end of an era – Bill and Molly moved out onto the farm and Jess, now comfortably ensconced in a suite of downstairs rooms that had been added onto the house specially for her, began a new life that took a while for her to get used to – though she was the titular head of the family, she was no longer the mistress of her own home and found it irksome that she had to defer to Molly in all matters relating to the day-to-day running of the house.

Richard was in his final year at preparatory school and basking in the warm glow that he and his mates contended was their due, having reached what in their eyes was the top of the pecking order. While he stood out academically, he was, as his father sometimes said – often in pique and always with a clenched jaw – a watcher rather than a doer. Little did Richard know about the high school that his parents had chosen for him, the one with the mores of faraway England embedded in its core, with its erstwhile liberal traditions and lofty aspirations clutched to its bosom and its grand, red-bricked buildings setting it apart in the verdant rolling hills of the Natal Midlands. Still, less was he aware that his happy and carefree life would, in the next year, be thrown into turmoil and disarray by the release of savage forces he had never encountered before: inflexible rules upheld by a primitive fear of a freely wielded cane, a deeply entrenched hierarchical system that awarded status and privilege according to age, and a pervasive culture of athletic chauvinism that championed sporting prowess above all else.

For Thandi, the year was significant as she became aware of difference   not mere difference as revealed by sight and sound, but a difference of understanding, one that was nurtured within the body politic of her emotions. Arthur Barclay's funeral was an eye opener – she knew that she would never forget the words that Titus had whispered to her mother beside the hearse or the curiosity that they aroused in her, nor would she ever forget the way Molly had greeted them on the lawn of the church hall. The warmth and spontaneity with which she had flung her arms around her mother had made her eyes sting and would remain with her forever. Only Molly had done that – a few other *abelungu* had nodded a greeting, but most of them just walked on by. And she had seen Richard again. She had not seen him for a long time and had been shy, reluctant to greet him, as though the boy in the long pants was a stranger. But the shyness was, she discovered, reciprocated and made his face look funny. Then it evaporated and the old intimacy returned; the warmth of his smile marked her mind as surely as if it were a knife in his hands and he was carving his initials into the bark of a living tree. And he had sat next to her on the wall. She liked that – liked the feel of his thigh against hers as they swung their legs back and forth – liked also that he had fetched cake for her and Mary from the table in the hall. He was so nice. She couldn't wait to see Gordon again and tell him how grown up Lichard was.

For Jack McIntyre's part, whenever he looked back, he would say that 1954 was in many respects a tipping point. It was the year that he resigned from the Durban Municipality. He took up Bill's offer and moved onto the Barclay farm where Bill had a three bedroomed house built for him. It was built from cement blocks made on the farm, was comfortable and set aside from the compound so that he was able to enjoy his own peace and quiet. He was now, as he saw it – in all but in name – manager of the Barclay farm. He liked his new life and felt that at last he had arrived – felt that he was valued and appreciated for who he was, not what he was. He got on well with the entire family – especially with Molly. He forged a special bond with her and found her liberal outlook both uplifting and enervating. They talked politics with a refreshing lack of candour, and it was obvious that she was genuinely interested in his point of view.

That year was also significant for Jack in another, equally important respect – it marked the time when his past, whirling like a randomly thrown stone, struck him on the back of his head and all but knocked him to the ground, senseless. About a month after the funeral but while he was still working with the Blackjacks, he received a package from Reece Thornicroft. He had been expecting it and he carried it home in two minds – keen to open it, but apprehensive as to its contents. At home, he brushed past Mavis and the children and went into his bedroom. In the dank, sparsely furnished room that was his lair, he took a bottle of Castle beer from a box under his bed and opened it. Jack tipped back his head and poured the warm beer down his throat. He wiped his mouth with the back of his hand and removed his tie. The package stared at him, daring him. He opened it. There, lying on the crinkled brown paper, unadorned and crushing in its simplicity, was all that remained of his father. It made him sad and lonely. He opened the writing case and ran his fingers over the worn leather binding, as though doing so would bring his father back to life. The signet ring caught his eye. He picked it up and stared for a long time at the engraved initials.

He opened the letter and time stood still.

The door opened and Mavis came in, closing it behind her.

"Jack, what's happening? You've been in here more than an hour. Not a word from you. Why are you lying there like that? You look awful. Come on, tell me, what's the matter?" She went to the bed and sat down beside him, facing him sideways. She could smell beer on his breath and saw the empty bottle on the table.

"Aah, Mavis, I'm buggered, I really am. Honest to God, I don't know where to begin."

He took her hand and held it there, imprisoning it across his chest with one arm while the fingers of his other hand, obeying their own impulse, stroked it back and forth. He loved her hands, loved the voluptuous silkiness of her skin and the softness of her touch. Mavis looked into his eyes and blanched. She had never seen them so empty, so hollowed out, as though what used to reside there – warm, palpable, and secure as a squirrel in its hole – had taken leave of its inner sanctum and had fled. Such abject emptiness frightened her, and she could feel unease welling in her throat. She reached over with her free hand and stroked his cheek.

"You don't know where to begin what?"

"This letter. It's blown my mind."

"What letter? Who from? What's it about? Tell me, Jack, are we in trouble?"

"No. No we aren't in trouble, nothing like that." His mind was far away. "It's about something that happened a long time ago … something I thought was dead and buried … "

"You done something bad? Is that it?"

"No, Mavis, nothing bad – well, not intentionally. The letter, written by my father, was to be sent to me after he died. It is very long. There are a lot of nice things he said about me and how much he loved me. But it also had something else in it – something from my past that he wanted to share with me. You can read it if you like but let me tell you first. Long ago, before the war even, I was a brash young man in the army. One night, I went to this dance hall in Bristol, where I met this white girl – a real corker, could dance like crazy. We clicked. No effort, no beating about the bush – we just clicked. We became lovers. It was short and sharp – just a couple of months or so, that's all. But I fell for her – hook, line, and sinker. For a little while I was even silly enough to think that I could marry her. Then she disappeared. Vanished. Just like that – into thin air. Never saw her again. It just about killed me. Couldn't understand what had happened. Had I said something, done something, you know, to piss her off? Couldn't think of anything that half made sense. She was gone – gone for good. Not a word – no goodbye, nothing. She had a friend that used to come dancing with her, but I never saw her again either. I didn't know who to call or where to look. Believe it or not, I hadn't a clue where she lived. Whenever we could, we'd duck off to a room behind a pub that belonged to a friend of mine – we'd shack up there –"

"What's her name?"

"Her name was Elsa."

"You loved her? This Elsa, you would have married her?"

Jack began to feel like a fly in a spider's web; the more he struggled, the more entangled he became and the harder it was to find the right answers for Mavis.

"Hell, Mavis, it was a long time ago. I was young and silly, full of passion. So was she – we couldn't keep our hands off each other. Marry her? No, we never talked about it, though it crossed my mind. But the point is that she disappeared. For a long time, I was like, you know, a wounded animal. I kept to myself, laid low, and licked my wounds. It occurred to me that somehow me being black and she being white had something to do with it – not that anyone had said anything. For a while I was very bitter and twisted. I began to see everything in black and white. Nearly drove me mad. It was during this dark time that I made up my mind to go back one day to Africa and discover my roots – it had never bothered me much before, but now, after Elsa left, it was a thought that took me by the throat and wouldn't let go."

"Oh shame, Jack. Poor you. But the letter, can we get back to the letter?"

"Of course," he released her arm and reached up to stroke her cheek. "You're very special, you know, very special. The letter. Well, it transpires that Elsa was pregnant. She had a baby. And yes, I am the father, apparently. Let me explain. My mother was ill and had to spend a couple of weeks in hospital. I never knew about it – I was already here in South Africa. Anyway, there was a nurse in the hospital called Dora Murphy. It seems she and Mum got on well, because late one night after a ward round, she sat down and had a long chat with Mum, sort of poured her heart out. Told her this incredible tale. Turns out that she was one of the midwives when Elsa came in to have her baby. She said she got the impression that Elsa didn't want to be there – showed no interest in the baby. Imagine that, not wanting her baby! Here's the interesting part. There was another mother in the same hospital, at the same time – also there to have her baby. Now she was very excited and was looking forward to it. But she was worried. She thought there was something wrong because when she got there, she could not feel the baby moving. As it happened, Elsa and this other woman had their babies at the same time. Elsa's baby was a healthy boy. The other lady's baby was also a boy, but it was stillborn. They swapped them around –"

"Swapped them? What do you mean? How can you swap babies?"

"Don't know. Dora said that the senior nurse made the decision. She was the midwife for the other woman. Dora was merely the assistant. She said that the babies were swapped. Elsa came to her senses, thinking that she'd lost her baby. The other lady was delighted to discover that her fears had proved to be groundless – she went home happy as could be."

"So how does this get back to you? I mean, who found out –"

"Dora told Mum that her conscience wouldn't give her any peace. Being a devout Catholic and knowing what she knew was like witnessing a crime being committed and doing nothing about it. She felt strongly that Elsa should know that she had given birth to a healthy child. I presume that's why she took it upon herself to start digging. You see, Mavis, after Elsa left the hospital, Dora went and checked the paperwork. She found the father's name on Elsa's admission form. It was Jack McIntyre, occupation was army, address unknown. But Elsa's address was on it. So, one day Dora went to that address and asked to speak to Elsa Duncan. The man who answered the door – must have been her father – said there was no Elsa Duncan there. Dora told him about the admission form. He said that Elsa no longer lived there – that if she had the right Elsa, then that Elsa was in South Africa and wouldn't be coming back."

"Did your mother know? Did she know it was you?"

"Not for certain, but she and Dad put two and two together. The name, army, white girl with black baby – it all added up. In the letter, Dad says that he advised Mum to see it as a sort of adoption – that everything ought to be done to protect the child. He said as far as the parents were concerned, he felt that bygones ought to be bygones – he could see little point in opening a can of worms after all those years and besides, he says right here, looking for Elsa would be like looking for a needle in a haystack."

Mavis took in all that information and watched Jack in silence, sensing that there was more he needed to get off his chest.

"Oh, Mavis, it seems that I am the father to someone I never knew about. You could have knocked me over with a feather when I read this. Came as a hell of a shock, like a kick in the guts. I've just been lying here thinking about it, trying to digest it all. I feel as though I've been turned inside out – I never knew, never had the faintest idea that she was pregnant – why didn't she tell me? That's what I can't figure out. Poor girl must have gone through hell. Reckon her father found out and put the fear of God into her – why else wouldn't she tell me? It's got me flummoxed. All this time I thought that she had just walked out on me, you know, had abandoned me. Now this. Mavis, it's quite scary.

I mean, think about it – there is someone out there, my flesh and blood, who doesn't even know me. What if he's looking for me? What if I bump into her? The letter says she went to South Africa – we could have passed each other in the street without knowing it … "

"What are you going to do?"

Jack stared at her.

"Do? What am I going to do? Why nothing, nothing at all. I have you and that's all that matters as far as I am concerned."

He straightened up and drew her to him, right into the maw of his arms, and hugged her. He was back in control. Reading the letter was like being ambushed on patrol – the first instinct was to run for cover and then, when panic had been brought to heel, to escape. Now, hunkered in his foxhole, he was able to return fire.

"The lad," he said, speaking over her shoulder from the nape of her neck, "if he's alive, is about eighteen now – would have left school, I reckon. He has no idea he's my son, so I'm going to leave it like that. And who knows where Elsa is – South Africa is a big country and she could be anywhere, if she's still here, that is. Would I like to meet him? Of course. Would I like to wind back the clock? No. What's done is done. All this was a long time ago, before the war. A hell of a lot of water has flowed under all our bridges since then. Who knows, the Elsa that I knew back then might be quite a different Elsa today. And I'm sure she'd find me different as well. So, my love, you are my wife, my rock, my all. What more could a man possibly want? We have our own family. That's all we need, isn't it. Come now, let's go to the children. They'll be wondering what's going on."

Jack went with her to the door and stopped. "Mavis, let's keep this between ourselves, okay? We don't need to tell anyone, and the kids are too young to understand."

<h1 style="text-align:center">6</h1>

Frankie was lying on his back, looking up at the underside of Bill's Mercedes. His feet stuck out at right angles. Someone nudged his foot. He lifted his head enough to squint down his belly and looked out. Through the vee of his own two feet, he could see a pair of clean, well-polished boots. Jack's – his boots were always like that; old army habits die hard.

"Frankie, sorry to bother, but you got a minute?"

"Yup, hold on a sec, nearly done. Am just checking the tyre rod ends." Using his feet, he pulled the trolley that he was lying on from under the car and stood up. He took a piece of towelling from the back pocket of his overalls and began to wipe his hands with it. His assistant approached him. *"Shall I let the car down now?"* Frankie did not look up but continued to methodically clean his fingers. *"Yebo, Zebulon, you can let her down now, everything's alright under there."* He put the cloth back in his pocket and faced Jack.

"What's up? You went to the meeting with Madam?"

"Yah, just got back. We've been asked to help out with the cane fire at the Charters' place. The owner is an arrogant prick. And stingy – wasn't keen to pay fire money for our cutters. Anyway, we're going to give them ten men tomorrow and fifteen two days later, when we've finished cutting here. I'm going to speak to Mdletshe about it now. We've also promised two tractors – must be licenced as they will be hauling straight to the mill. Yes, that's right, on the main road – with our trailers. What do you reckon? Which ones? Can you have a think about it and get two ready for me, first thing in the morning? Must be licenced and road worthy. Say Frankie, which drivers would you recommend?"

They were still talking when Isaac walked up. He waited for them, changing his weight from foot to foot. Frankie stretched out his arm, urging him closer.

"Jack, this is Isaac, my grandson – don't think you've met him. He's at farm school in Mandini. Boards there with Phyllis, my niece. Only comes home on weekends. Isaac, this is Jack. I told you about him. He's an ex-cop and our manager."

Jack smiled broadly and stuck out his hand.

"Not sure about being a copper. Or a manager, come to think of it – still have lots to learn before I qualify as one, I think. Glad to meet you, Isaac. At school hey, what are you going to do when you leave?"

They shook hands. Isaac shrugged. "Haven't made up my mind. Would like to do something like what Pops here is doing – I mean, working on a farm." He could feel Frankie's eyes boring into him, so he added, "Need to get a certificate first, don't I?" The last thing he wanted to discuss right then was life after school, not with a stranger. But he was intrigued by the man standing before him, by the tilt of his head and the way be braced his legs, by the shape of his clipped goatee, his smart khaki clothes – indeed, everything about him breathed difference. He had never heard an African speak English so fluently, with such easy familiarity.

"You speak posh."

"I do?"

"Hey, Isaac, that's rude. Apologise."

"No, Frankie, it isn't. He means well, I'm sure. Fact is, Isaac, I was brought up in England. Can't help speaking like I do."

"England? I was born in England, wasn't I, Pops?"

"Sure, you were. But we're not here to talk about that. Your mother's sent you, hasn't she? What's she wanting this time?"

Isaac laughed. He kept looking at Jack.

"Mum asked me to tell you that your tea is getting cold. Wants to know if you are going into the village? If you are, she wants to go as well. Better let her tell you. Nice to meet you, Mister Jack. I'd better get back. Bye."

Jack watched him go. "Hey, Isaac," he shouted after him, "you want to be a farmer? I'm going to have a drive around later on; would you like to come?"

So began a friendship between two people who knew each other without knowing who they were. Whenever he came back from Mandeni on weekends, Isaac made sure he caught up with Jack; he loved nothing more than driving around the farm with him, with his feet up on the shelf below the dashboard, listening to stories about the war. Jack taught him to drive, and it wasn't long before he was doing the driving and Jack was his passenger.

7

By the time Richard came home for the holidays, life on the farm had returned to normal. The neighbour's fire was a thing of the past. Molly was absorbed in the school that she had started, and Jack ran the farm on his own. Every morning, after breakfast, Molly would meet with him to discuss the day's activities – she kept a scrupulous eye on the finances and attended to most of the administrative paperwork.

The only concession to change that Richard could see – apart from the fact that nearly every day Grandma Jess would plonk herself down with her knitting needles and balls of wool in the only chair in the house that gave her a proprietorial view of both the internal goings-on in the house and, at the same time, a wide sweep of the garden – was that on most afternoons his mother would seat the house staff round the dining room table and would teach them to read and write – in English. She had a chalk board on which she'd write large letters for them to copy. She also had a whole series of little cards with words on them, broken into syllables to help them sound the words phonetically.

Richard loved farm life. He would spend hours and hours each day with Fanakanye, who was Mdletshe's son, and was about his own age. Fanakanye was Mamuhle's barefoot assistant – he herded the cattle and assisted the old man with the milking. The two boys were inseparable and in a carefree world of no tomorrows, they pursued their pleasures with innocent self-indulgence. They were often seen down at the river exploring, looking for hippos in the backwater or for monkeys that had the temerity to venture forth from the trees and raid the adjacent cane fields.

On the last day of the holidays, Richard and Mary went horse riding. It was mid-morning when they returned to the stables. Richard undid the girth of his mount and folded it across the pommel. Then he lifted the saddle from his horse and placed it astride the top rung of the wooden fence. Charua, the dark-skinned horse boy from Mozambique, removed the bridle and replaced it with the halter that was hanging over his shoulder. For a few moments Richard stood lost in thought, watching Charua rub the horse down with a curry comb. Absent-mindedly, he lifted each leg in turn to adjust his jodhpurs. Mary's horse had already been done and was now rolling in the sand, trying to remove the sweaty imprint that the numnah had left on its back. Richard loved that horsey, sweaty smell – especially after a nice long ride.

"Hey, come and sit up here," said Mary. He turned, squinting at her, and climbed up onto the top rail of the fence, and sat beside his sister. It was nice and warm, and he felt at peace with the world, though thoughts of going to school the next day were already impinging on his happiness.

"Horses went well, didn't they? Funny how they quicken their pace when we turn for home. They just seem to know and can't get back here fast enough."

They sat there, hunched up with the sun on their backs, and gazed out over the paddock which dipped down to a narrow ditch where the grass grew tall and green, and then rose up on the other side, gently, to a wire fence. Beyond the fence, beyond the orchard and surrounded by immaculate swathes of green lawn, sat their two-storied family home, basking comfortably in the morning light. Beyond the house to the south, were fields of sugar cane that rose and fell in green undulations, like slow waves on a languid sea.

"I wonder why Pops left those trees in that field over there. A bit scruffy, isn't it?"

"Where?" Mary shaded her eyes, "What trees?"

"That clump of bush, over there. See? Past the house, on the ridge. There's a tall *marula* standing right in the middle."

"Yah, I see it. Maybe there are rocks there and they couldn't plough it out."

"No. There are no rocks on this farm. Seems odd – you know, leaving a small clump of bush right in the middle of a field. Pops was an engineer and Dad says he loved things to be neat and tidy, loved straight lines. I mean, just look at the pine trees – whichever way you look at them, they are in straight lines. And the cane fields, all on the square. You must admit that that clump of bush is messy – looks like it was somehow left behind."

Mary wasn't really interested. She was about to climb down when she saw Mamuhle come around the corner of the stables. He was a fine old Zulu man, wedded to the past; he wore a *bheshu* which hung skirt-like beneath his short-sleeved khaki shirt – this, and his ubiquitous black felt hat were his only acknowledgements to modernity. In one hand he carried a *knobkerrie* and in the other, swinging in time to the step of his finely sculptured legs, he held an empty milk can.

"Hey, Rich, there's Mamuhle. Let's ask him."

Mamuhle had been on the farm since he was a boy, had always worked with the cattle and for a long time had had his own span of oxen that hauled wagon after wagon of cane up to the halt, where the train took it to the mill. Now, in the autumn of his life, he kept his hand in by overseeing the milking. He named the calves, said which cow would be covered by which bull and generally made all the decisions about animal husbandry on the farm. If Mamuhle said the vet needed to be called, then the vet was called – nobody, not even Arthur when he was alive, dared to question him, much less countermand his decisions.

"Rich, are you listening? If you're so worried about those trees over there, ask him – he's been here forever. If anyone knows, he will."

"*Sawubona, Mkhulu,*" Richard turned deferentially to the old man, "*how goes it?*"

"*Yebo, sawubona.*" The old man put the milk can down and waited.

"*Mau, you see that bush over there in the field? Over there, way past the house. Why did Nchebe leave it standing there?*"

Mamuhle took a small tin from his breast pocket and tapped a little snuff onto the back of his hand. Then he sniffed it up, and slapped his hands together, ridding them of the residue.

"*That's where my family is buried.*"

"*Your family?*"

"*Yes. We used to live there.*"

"*You used to live here?*"

"*Yes.*"

"*On this farm? Are you sure?*"

"*Yes. This is where my family lived. Those trees mark the place.*"

"*But why did you leave?*"

Mamuhle took another pinch of snuff and sneezed.

"*We lived on this side of the river. One day people from Indabazabantu came and told us we had to move. What could we say? Then some more white men came on horses, and they camped nearby. They looked through a popola and lined up sticks which they stuck in the ground. They put their sticks right through this area, even on the other side of the river. Then one day Nchebe came, also on a horse. We were told that he now owned the land inside the sticks. So, we moved. Nchebe removed our houses and ploughed right up to the trees. He left them there out of respect. When my father died, Nchebe allowed us to bury him there, near his father. That was in the Kaiser's war.*"

Richard's hands tightened their grip on the wooded rail. He could feel his ears burning. There was that knot in his tummy – his surroundings shimmered, just for a moment, making him feel unsteady. It was as though some bigger truth had been revealed to him – something enlightening, something that ought to have been immediately obvious – but he just couldn't see it. He felt like a blind man struggling to find the door in an unfamiliar room. It bothered him

– what made it worse was the fact that he couldn't even put his finger on why it bothered him, but it did.

Mary grabbed his arm. "Wakey-wakey, Richard. What's got into you? I was asking you what he said. Hey, why are you looking like that?"

"Looking like what? Sorry. Mau says that's where his family used to live."

"So?"

"I never thought about it. I had no idea."

"Never thought about what?" Mary jumped down. "Come on, breakfast time. I'm starving."

Richard climbed down. Mamuhle, straight-backed and lithe as a man half his age, strode off on his broad bare feet towards the milking shed. Charua was herding the horses out to pasture. Richard jogged up to Mary and fell into step beside her. Whatever had triggered his discomfort, had done nothing to her – her face was as clear as the sky and her voice, bubbly as a brook.

"Yah, breakfast. I'm going to ask Dad." He watched her face intently.

"Ask him about what?"

"You know … I mean … the trees in that field … how Pops got this farm."

"Who cares, Rich? Pops bought it, didn't he? Race you to the kitchen door."

8

Titus and Busisiwe sat in their kitchen. He sat with his elbows on the table, she with her chair drawn back so she could cross her legs and fold her hands in her lap. They waited for Gordon. He was at soccer practice, and they expected him at any moment. Titus took off his glasses and cleaned them for the umpteenth time.

"What's bothering you, my love?"

"Bothering me?" Titus, submerged in his own thoughts, surfaced slowly, and blinked at his wife. There was a flurry of brown and white at the window behind her that caught his attention – an Indian Myna. No sooner had it landed on the open window frame than it flew off, calling loudly. "Why, nothing, really. I was just thinking of my Fort Hare days. Those were happy times. I felt like a sponge, soaking everything up – I couldn't get enough. Did I tell you that I was there with Professor Matthews – in fact, he encouraged me to go on to seminary school and take the cloth. Did I tell you that?"

"Yes, you did, many times. He's the fellow you wrote to, isn't he? You know, Titus, you are so much more educated than me … you know people, know so much about everything! You make me feel quite stupid. I'm just a simple country girl who never went to school … I know nothing."

"You are better educated than most in the things that matter – the things that *really* matter." He found her hand and squeezed it. "You are a very good mother, a wonderful wife, and you have a heart the size of a house. I don't think you have a bad bone in your body. Tell me, what's the point of having an educated mind if the heart is a lump of stone? No, my dear, you are not uneducated at all – you are self-taught in the things that matter and –"

"Really? Like what?"

"Well, for example," he knew that she was playing with him but, undeterred, he began to count on his fingers, one by one, "you have wonderful instincts that seldom let you down; you know the difference between right and wrong; you have compassion – much more than most; you are kind and selfless; you are loyal and brave; you are big-hearted; you are a loving daughter, wife and mother; you are the most honest person I know –"

"Oh, Titus! Stop! In your eyes I can do no wrong! I'm not that perfect, am I?"

"You, my dear, are gold – pure gold. No amount of education can buy that. No, sir, it cannot. You know, the Lord was smiling when you were born, he really was."

He got up and went to the window and looked out. The evening light was blurring the shadows and the distant hills, always so blue and cleanly cut, were now melting into a cloudless sky. He returned his gaze to Busisiwe, his eyes gleaming with pride. "You know, this is very exciting – a great moment for Gordon. You must be very proud."

Busisiwe smiled, but her mind was in turmoil. Her thoughts were usually nice and tidy, like piles of paper laid out neatly on a desk for easy access but, whenever she opened the window to the past, they would fly all over the place and became quite unruly. Now, images of her father, Madondo, Molly, Nchebe, and mostly of Amidu, all swirled around and landed, in no particular order, on the floor of her mind. She persevered, trying hard to straighten them out.

"Yes, he would have been proud –"

"Not him. I'm sure he would have been. I was asking you –"

"Sorry, Titus, I was just thinking back to the beginning, to Gordon's father. Yes, I am proud of my son. But he couldn't be where he is today without you. Had Amidu lived, then Gordon would most probably have turned out … very differently."

"Don't torture yourself with the past and do try to stop imagining what it could have been – we shall never know, so let it pass. I always say that when you look back too much, all you get is a stiff neck. *Qonda phambili*, Busisiwe, look to the future. How we live today will shape it much more than gazing over our shoulders will. Why? Because we can change what we are doing today, we can make choices. The past is the past and no matter how hard we try; we cannot pull it back and alter it."

The door burst open. Gordon, with his soccer boots hanging around his neck, had Peter in one arm and held Thandi by the other. They were laughing. Gordon saw Titus glance at his watch. He put Peter down and pulled out a chair.

"Sorry we are late. It was my turn to pull the goal nets down and put them away. Took time because this young man here wanted to sit on my shoulders and undo them, didn't you?" He made a playful lunge at Peter who ran around the table and climbed up onto Busisiwe's lap.

"That's all right. Thandi, please take Peter and bath him. We just want to have a quick talk with Gordon. Thank you, we won't be long."

"You want to talk to me? What for? Anything wrong?"

"No, nothing wrong. Only good news. Shall I go on or will you, my dear?"

"No, Titus, this is your making. Please go on."

Titus left the window and pulled a chair out and sat down between Busisiwe and Gordon.

"You have been accepted at Fort Hare! Next year! Isn't that wonderful? Professor Matthews phoned me this afternoon, just after you left for soccer. Of course, it depends on you passing your matric. But that's a foregone conclusion. So, my boy, you are off to Alice in the *Ciskei*! Congratulations, Gordon! Your mother and I are so proud of you."

For a moment Gordon sat there, waxen and nonplussed as he slowly digested what he had just heard. He had always tried to do exactly what was expected of him – especially to satisfy the eyes of those whose adulation he so desperately sought. He was deeply conscious that his father was seldom referred to in conversation and that whenever he was, it was more often than not in a desultory, offhand manner. It was as though Amidu had not done enough to earn either esteem or respect – as though he had failed himself as much as his family. Gordon, ever fearful of a similar opprobrium, did all he could to attract notice as a 'good boy' and to remain, therefore, firmly ensconced in the warm glow of his parent's approval. But now, with the advent of adulthood, a dichotomy had appeared in his thinking and was beginning to irk him – on the one hand he wanted desperately to please them and, on the other, with growing impatience, he wanted to please himself, and establish a path to his own, inviolable independence. University, he had told himself so many times, was a door – an entrance to a bigger, wider world.

"That is wonderful news," he gushed, finally, "the best news ever! All the hard work has paid off!" He jumped up and punched the air above his head, his arms pumping like pistons, "Oh, what a relief! I'm so, so glad!" Then a dawning realisation struck him, like a thrown *ukhandi* strikes a bird in mid-flight, instantly collapsing his euphoria. It brought him, suddenly contrite and subdued, to his mother's side. He bent down and nuzzled her, kissing her cheek. Then he turned to Titus, saw the moist glistening behind his glasses, and he hugged him, tightly.

"All this is because of you," he said in a voice as thick as treacle, "both of you. Thank you, thank you from the bottom of my heart."

"Ah, my son. I am so proud. Now you can become educated like Titus here – you can get a good job, maybe even become someone important. You still want to become a teacher? Do you know any teachers who are important, Titus?"

"All teachers are important, my dear – perhaps the most important people of us all. But if you want names, well you need go no further than Professor Matthews or, better still, Albert Luthuli. They taught at Adams College together."

"I do want to become a teacher, Ma. I want to help young people. Like *baba omusha* taught me."

"To see you on your way now, well, *jabulisa inhliziyo yami*. But I was not alone. Who looked after us, cooked for us, fed us, washed our clothes, kept us happy? I couldn't have done it without your mother."

"Ma, I have told you how grateful –"

"Many times. And you have repaid me in so many ways. Oh, Gordon! This is so exciting!"

"Together in excellence," said Titus, head down and playing with his fingers.

"What's that?"

"That's the motto of Fort Hare. Actually, the real motto is '*in lumine tuo videbimus lumen.*' That's Latin, which you'll learn if you decide to study law, and it means, 'In your light we shall see the light.' Reflects the Christian origins of the university – it was started by missionaries. The college has produced some excellent people – in fact, lots of our finest people came from there. They shone their light so others could find their way in this dark, dark world of ours. Teaching is a great calling, Gordon. Be a good teacher. Shine your light and help others to see. You are extremely lucky to be going to Fort Hare before ... " He paused, drawing a question mark in the air with his forefinger, "before the government gets its hands onto it and messes it up –"

"Messes it up? What do you mean?"

"Well, last year the government introduced its *Bantu Education Act* ... How can I describe this for you? Think of South Africa as a big field in which our *Nguni* cows are grazing, fat and content. Mixed up with them is a much smaller herd of white cows, also fat and content. One day the farmer decides that his white cows need their own space. So, he separates the herds – he fences off our cows into about ten percent of the field and his white cows have the rest. That was the Native Land Act of 1913. Our bulls bellowed, but that was all – they went with our cows to this much smaller place and tried to make the most of it. All too soon, it was overgrazed, and our cattle lost condition. Then in 1948 a new farmer takes over. He reckons that the *Nguni* cows still have too much land and also, they need to be fenced off according to their colours – you know, the *bomvu* here, the *nsundu* there, the *inkone* over on this side – and so on. That was the Group Areas Act of 1950. The farmer is still not satisfied. Someone has not closed the gate properly and some *Nguni* cows have had the cheek to wander out and are now fattening themselves on his corn. What does he do? He rushes back and closes the gate so no more cows can get out and eat where they are not supposed to eat – that's the *Bantu Education Act* which was passed by parliament last year … "

A wistful, faraway look glazed his eyes.

"*We are not worthy so much as to gather up the crumbs under your table, O merciful Lord* … " He smiled at the cruel irony of these borrowed words from the *Prayer of Humble Access*. "Sorry, was just thinking aloud. So, Gordon, since the Nationalists came to power in 1948, they have introduced new laws and changed plenty of old ones with the sole purpose of cutting us out – they have been busy fencing us out and slamming shut all the gates. They want to keep us black people or us non-Whites, as they like to say, separate and apart from them. Notice, as we do not vote, we have had no say in any of this and, in fact, we have never been consulted. The white man knows best, he thinks … there I go again – I shouldn't allow my personal feelings to side-track me. What I wanted to say right at the beginning was this: this *Bantu Education Act* is all about enforcing racially separate education facilities and ensuring that ours are inferior to theirs. It's a gate shutter. Here, just listen to the words of this *hlyana*, Verwoerd, the Minister of Native Affairs, when he introduced the Act, 'I just want to remind the Honourable Members of Parliament that if the native in South Africa is being taught to expect that he will lead his adult life under the policy of equal rights, he is making a big mistake. The native must not be subject to a school system that draws him away from his own community and misleads him by showing him the green pastures of European society in which he is not allowed to graze.' See what I mean? But why am I telling you this – why in so much detail?"

Gordon blinked at Titus owlishly. It was a rhetorical question, yet it pinged in a corner of his mind, so he sat up, self-chastised. Titus's words had been leading his attention into a maze of unexplored pathways, distracting him. Titus droned on.

"Because I want you to understand what this government is up to; because I want you to understand how important it is for you to get qualified before our institutions are run down or, as I said earlier, messed up; because you must move fast – before the gate is slammed in your face. Professor Matthews says this Act will make big changes – changes that will dictate who will teach what and to whom. He believes it spells disaster for our people because it is designed to keep us in the bush – it proves, and these are his words, 'that we are to provide the white economy with manual labour and little else.' Anyway, Gordon, Fort Hare is your chance to slip through the gate before Verwoerd closes it. Yes, you have earned it, but please, Gordon, please do not waste it. Believe me, there are many temptations there and you will have to make choices – hard decisions that will test your *isibindi*. Remember, Gordon, we are the sum of all our choices – our choices say who we are."

Titus paused. He picked up his half-empty cup and drained it. "Anything you want to add?" He asked Busisiwe. She raised her hands, palms out, and raised her shoulders. "No. Carry on, just as you are." Gordon cleared his throat and was about to speak but Titus raised his forefinger to his lips and arched his eyebrows, silencing him.

"Sorry, Gordon, just hear me out. I have spoken to you about the events that are shaking this country to its core. We have read the newspapers together, have listened to the wireless – no topic was ever too sacred that it could not be discussed around our dinner table. When you asked about the Defiance Campaign, we told you what we thought about it, didn't we? How many times have we discussed what is happening to our people – I'm talking about those who were arrested for civil disobedience, especially since the *amaBhunu* have come to power? Thousands arrested – what for? Not for rebellion or for taking up arms – no, simply for their defiance. They did it peacefully, and they went to jail. You know my feelings about all this, know my ANC sympathies and my admiration for people like Luthuli; you also know that I am a man of peace. I do not like violence of any kind, nor do I think resorting to it is a good way to resolve disputes. I think I've told you that I am also an admirer of Mahatma Gandhi – he spent a lot of his formative years in this country, you know. His non-violence worked in India, the British left without firing a shot. But the Whites here are not going to leave – that's for certain. This is not India. A new language is emerging – I am sad that it is not based upon the Good Book, but there you are. The talk now is swinging away from peaceful non-violence. You will hear a lot about this. You must make up your own mind; I will not tell you what to think. Professor Matthews says that at Fort Hare many people are saying, even the intellectuals, that violence begets violence. The argument is, I think, that talk and peaceful protests – I mean boycotts, rallies, marches, things like that – have got us nowhere and the only thing that will make Whites sit up and take notice is to respond in kind: with violence. Now, I don't agree with that, I am a man of God and I dislike war. So does your mother. But you make up your own mind, see? You will be confronted by ideas that will challenge everything you believe in or have ever stood for. It happened to me. It was a glorious time of self-discovery. Many of the people that I met there found their calling in politics. Others, like me, didn't; we found ours in religion or, quite simply, in service to our communities. They all have their place – one is not better than the next. The point is this, you have to choose and all I want to say is think long and hard before you get drawn into something that you might later regret. Gordon, just be true to yourself. And remember, whatever happens, wherever you go, we will be here for you, your mother and I; we will not forsake you. Ever."

Gordon was stunned. Only then, staring at Titus, trying to hard see behind the glasses which held his own reflection, did he begin to comprehend the magnitude of what he was about to take on. Apprehension tingled up his spine; for a moment he felt cornered, that he was being saddled by responsibilities that did not belong to him. Whenever he had thought of university, it had always been from the perspective of the first person, singular – that is, university was to be *his* experience, exacted on *his* terms. He longed to find himself, to make his own way. Never, in all his imagining about this new world had politics featured – not once. As he listened to Titus, he realised that university was not a right or simply another step up the education ladder – it was, he now realised with percipient clarity, a privilege burdened by the enormous sacrifice and self-denial that his parents had expended on his behalf. More than that, there was the expectation that he would one day rank amongst the illustrious alumni that had preceded him – that he would make his mark and, in so doing, would validate their sacrifice. The hairs rose on the back of his neck.

"Ma, Baba, I do not know where to begin. First, I want to say thank you – no, hear me out. The goal that we set many years ago, was for me to get to university. I have thought about it a lot – I have dreamed of life with a degree, what it could do for me, and how it could raise me up in the world. But I have never really thought about getting there. I knew I had to work hard, and I think I have, but until now I never really understood how much I owe you both for making it possible. It is the *isihlilingi* that sends the stone on its way, is it not? You have been my *isihlilingi* and sent me on my way. How far you have sent me! All this time I have been thinking that my journey was because of me. How ungrateful was that! So, I say thank you. I will not let you down. I will study hard at university and one day I will make you proud, very proud. But now, all I can think of is how much you have done for me and how happy I am to be going to Fort Hare. Thank you. Secondly, I want to thank you, Baba, for your wisdom. You have taught me more than the books – more than all of them put together. You have made me aware of the plight of our people, of the injustice that we bear because of our brown skins – you have taught me that in the end, good triumphs over evil – you have given me hope. Your 'cows in the field' story opens my eyes – I assure you, I shall get through the gate before it closes. When the

101

time comes, I shall choose wisely – before that though, I shall consult you and seek your advice. I cannot thank you enough for all this – you are a wise and kind man. *Ngiyanibingelela*."

"Oh, Gordon! You are a mother's dream! Titus, shouldn't we celebrate? I think we should. Shall I get the bottle? Here, give me your keys."

Titus smiled and held out his keys to her. Busisiwe went over to his filing cabinet and unlocked it. From the bottom drawer, she withdrew a bottle of port. "It was a farewell gift from Father Jim when he left," she said, as though an explanation was warranted, "it's been with us ever since and is hardly ever touched." She did not have port glasses or, for that matter, any small ones so took down three water glasses from the cupboard above the sink and poured a splash of the luscious liquid into each one.

"Titus, will you?"

"Of course," he raised his glass and faced Gordon, "I'd like to propose a toast. To Gordon and to Fort Hare – may each enrich the other."

They raised their glasses together and drank. Gordon gagged as the dark red liquid slipped down his throat, warming its way into his belly. His only exposure to alcohol thus far had been the discreet sips of communion wine, taken on Sundays. This was a mouthful. He ran his tongue around the inside of his mouth, savouring the taste.

CHAPTER FIVE:

1960

1

" I'm so looking forward to this – it's going to be so much fun. Are you?"

Richard was barely listening. The thrill of driving the family car was still novel to him – not because it was new to him, but because he had only recently passed his driver's licence and now could drive it on the public roads and could go just about anywhere he pleased. Bill had allowed him to use his new Mercedes Benz, custom-ordered, all the way from Germany. It was very grand, the first one in the district, and turned heads wherever it went. He hadn't been able to work up much enthusiasm for this outing and had only agreed because he knew that Mary was keen to go and had been asked by Molly to chaperone her.

"Am I what, Mary?"

"Looking forward to the party! Think about it, Rich – the Club Ball! And all on our own!" She pulled down the sun visor to look at herself in the mirror on its back. All she could see were the whites of her eyes. She reached up for the roof light and switched it on.

"Won't be a mo. Just want to check my lipstick. Don't want any on my teeth."

Satisfied, she switched off the light and snapped back the sun visor. She settled back in her seat. He was suddenly aware of her perfume, as though in moving her body, she had carelessly allowed this fragrant aroma to escape and tease his nostrils. The scent of a woman. Though she was at school – in her final year – he realized that his little sister was now grown up. It made him conscious of his own masculinity.

"Funny thing, isn't it? We have lived here all our lives and yet we hardly know anyone. That's boarding school for you. It took us away, didn't it? We know lots of people but have few friends. And now I'm at varsity – makes it even worse. Don't you feel a bit like an *uitlander*?"

"Not really – probably not as much as you. Quite a few girls from Zululand are at school with me – some live here. I'm lucky – in the holidays I play tennis at the club and so know a few more people than you do. But you're right – we're not really bosom buddies with the locals, are we? But what about Shelly? She's from here – Heatonville really, but close enough. You took her to your school dance last year – thought you took a shine to her? She'll be here tonight, for sure. She's pretty. And nice. Did you know that she was a Rag Princess at varsity in Durban this year?"

"No, I didn't know that. Isn't she going out with that rugger bugger – what's his name?"

"Who?"

"That guy from Ging. Also plays polo –"

"Oh, you mean Mike? Mike de Lyle? He's a dish, I reckon. Don't know if she's going out with him. Lucky her if she is. He's very good-looking."

Richard nosed the car into the carpark and began to look for a vacant parking bay as close to the front doors as he could. A stab of jealousy narrowed his eyes. Bloody hell! So, all you need is to be good-looking! Despite himself, he began to dredge his memory for any defects of character that he could use to level the playing field. Nothing came to mind.

He switched off the motor and got out. No clouds, just millions of stars, mere pinpricks of light, stared down at him. The cathedral of the great outdoors, he could hear his mother saying. Just for a moment, as he stared up at them in their icy fastness, he felt infinitesimally small and utterly insignificant, like a mote of dust. He dropped his eyes quickly to the ground and went round to open Mary's door for her, comforted by the crunch of gravel underfoot.

"Come on, let's go in and have a good night. You've got the tickets? Which table did you say we're at? The Sangsters? Excellent! They're always great fun. Let's go and party!"

Inside, the room was ablaze with colour. Strings of coloured lights hung low, giving the room a cavernous ambience that encouraged an intimate cosiness. Round, candle-lit tables, arranged in a semi-circle around the dance floor, bore testimony to refinement and genteel living. Each was bedecked with ten identical place settings that dazzled with gleaming silver, chinaware, and sparkling glass. Symmetry caught the eye; everything was immaculately positioned and just as it should be. Even the flowers, set precisely in the middle, matched the colour of the cleverly folded napkins. In the corner, the bar was busy serving drinks; here and there white-jacketed waiters stood hunched over their trays like patient Marabou storks, watching and waiting for darting hands to pick them clean of *hors d'oeuvres*. A five-piece band, dressed in matching gold jackets, played soft music, and stared about them with faces that registered little more than bored indifference.

Richard and Mary stepped into the ballroom and paused.

"Can you see the Sangsters? I feel like a fish out of water. Are they here yet?"

"There they are," cried Mary and rushed off, threading her way through the crowd. Richard watched her go. He was about to follow when he felt a tug on his sleeve.

"Well, hello! If it isn't Richard Barclay! How are you?"

Richard whirled around. His heart stopped mid-beat. Then began again. Thumping wildly. His ears were on fire. He swallowed. Smiled. Looked away. Eased his collar. Touched his hair. Felt idiotic. There, standing before him, was the most beautiful girl he had ever seen. He knew in that instant that this was a picture that would forever be riveted to the wall in his mind. He stared, utterly undone. Lustrous shoulder-length hair framed a high-cheeked face of extraordinary loveliness; full red lips, parted in a radiant smile; white, evenly-spaced teeth; a wet, deliciously pink tongue; large dark eyes that twinkled and danced – such beguiling beauty! He ran his eyes over her features again and again as though they were the fingers of a blind man, reading Braille.

"Sorry … hello … "

"It's me, Magda. Magda Celliers. Andre's sister. Remember?"

"Of course, of course! How silly of me! Gosh, what a change! It's been a long time."

"Andre's here as well." She turned and searched the crowd. "We came over from Eshowe especially for the ball," she said without looking back. "Sorry, I haven't introduced you. Jaco, this is Richard Barclay. Richard, meet Jaco Barnard – from Durban."

Only then did Richard realise that she was not alone. He peeled his eyes off her and turned them to the tall man standing beside her. He was very good-looking. Richard felt his stomach beginning to tighten.

"How do you do," he said, shaking hands, "glad to meet you."

"Jaco, can you go and fetch Andre for me? He's over there, at the bar. Thank you." Magda took Richard's arm.

"So, tell me, what have you been up to? I hear that you're studying medicine. Going to make lots of money, huh?"

"Money? Well, that would be nice, but it's not exactly –"

"Just teasing."

They chatted, interspersing their inanities with laughter and, every now and then, with comical facial contortions that were meant to express delight. Richard was mesmerised; she was so vivacious, so intoxicatingly sexy that he couldn't take his eyes off her. Whenever she glanced away, he would drop his eyes and allow them to run up and down her body, greedy, feasting them on her cleavage, her breasts, and the flair of her hips.

"Hello, Rich! Long-time no see." Richard recognised the *Afrikaans*-accented voice at once and turned to greet Andre. They shook hands, paused as each surveyed the other, then embraced, laughing, and patting each other heartily on the back. Richard stepped back. Andre was just the same; he exuded the charisma of old, carried himself with the same self-assurance and was in every respect still the heroic figure that Richard would have given his back teeth to be. His hair was short – a crew-cut made his head look fuzzy like a tennis ball. He saw Richard looking at it and laughed.

"I'm in the army, *boet* – was in the ballot and got called up. Doing national service. I've nearly finished my three months of basic. Got a leave pass – a long weekend. One of the guys with me lives in Melmoth of all places – he also had one and was coming home, so I hitched a lift with him. We only have to be back by midnight on Monday. Magda wanted to come to the ball, so I said okay, get me a ticket as well. Here I am, being the good brother!"

"Wonderful to see you again after all these years. After the army, then what?"

"Man, I'm joining the force – have been accepted into the police – going to the academy straight after army. I'm going to catch the bad guys and lock them up." He laughed. Richard just stared.

"I'm so proud of my brother – you should see how dashing he looks in uniform. Were you balloted, Rich? You going to do national service?"

Richard blanched. Military service was anathema to him, and he balked at the very idea. His father had been in the war, and he thought military service was the right and proper thing for every young white man to do. Richard's objection had been shaped over a period of time by the chisel of his mother's implacable pacifism – she chipped away at his schoolboy façade and slowly smoothed the rough edges to reveal a palpable and sensitive underlay. Molly had inculcated into his thinking many new notions that were yet to be tested; one of them was that war was morally repugnant. She abhorred violence of any kind and vigorously asserted that war was a horrible and barbaric way of resolving differences and was not the way that civilised people ought to behave. She also said that it was a case of old men sending young men to fight and die for ideas they had absolutely no understanding of. He took great comfort in her logic and wrapped her thinking around him like a blanket. In his final year at school there had been much talk in the dormitories and common rooms about being called up – most of his contemporaries were for it and vied with each other as to which branch of service was best – army, navy, or air-force. Fortunately for him, he had not been balloted. He did not have to burden his conscience, nor did he have to defend his thoughts on this matter in public.

"No, I wasn't called up – didn't get balloted."

"Yah, but you can volunteer. You know that?" Andre watched him closely.

"Yes, I suppose I could. But I want to get my studies behind me – I want to qualify in medicine first. Then I'll see what happens."

"I was in the Army Gym," Jaco chipped in. "It was a lot of fun. I played a lot of rugby there."

"Oh, Jaco, you didn't go there just to play sport, did you? You went out of *plig – plig teenoor koning en land.*"

Jaco wrapped his arm around Magda's shoulders and gave her a hug. "You're right, Angel, for my country yes, but not for king. We all have to defend the fatherland, I reckon – otherwise the *coons* will drive us into the sea."

Angel. The word knifed into Richard, and he turned away, his thoughts wounded and in disarray. "Oh, I don't think anyone is going to drive us into the sea –"

"You don't think so? There's Macmillan, the English Prime Minister sprouting his 'winds of change' nonsense in our parliament – in Cape Town, this very year – and what happens? The very next month the PAC organises thousands of *coons* to burn their passbooks in a so-called peaceful protest. Peaceful my arse. What a joke! You saw what happened at Sharpeville? The police there were badly outnumbered by a viscous mob baying for blood – they had to shoot in self-defence and the bloody world went mad, saying that it was the government's fault. Poppycock! That Sobukwe fellow should be locked up for good – him, the PAC, the ANC and all the rest of them *betogers* who want to kick us out. No man, I might have played a lot of rugby in the army, but I also learned how to shoot straight and how to defend my country – I'm proud of that, that's for sure."

"Well," Richard's mind was in a scramble. His view of the 'winds of change' speech were diametrically opposed to what he had just heard – he didn't agree with the Sharpeville comments, either. "I think Macmillan was merely stating the obvious – that everything is, you know, in a state of flux. Africa is in the throes of massive change – you know, empires are disintegrating, colonialism is beginning to unravel. Change is the one constant in all our lives and just about the only thing that we can be certain of. Politically speaking –"

"Hold on, Richard. We're talking about the real world here, not some arty-farty debating point. I tell you; the *coons* are being stirred up and they want blood – our blood. And you forgot to mention God – He's constant. And we can be certain of His word."

Richard looked at Magda, desperate for a reprieve or, better still, a sign that she was with him. She gave nothing away and only smiled her gorgeous, red-lipped smile, so he plunged on. His sole objective was to sound erudite, to say something that would make a favourable impression on her, something that would offset the athletic magnetism that he so envied and which was so apparent in the bloke standing beside her – the man who had had the temerity to call her 'angel'.

"Jaco, I hear you. But there are valid reasons for what the PAC is saying. The Freedom Charter sets out a South Africa shared equally by all her people, not just the Whites – there's nothing in it about driving Whites into the sea or, for that matter, shedding our blood. Surely, if our government was more consultative and not so prescriptive –"

"Ah, there you go with your fancy words. That Charter was written by communists, so please don't quote it to me. You can talk with the *coons* until the cows come home. All they want is to take over. That's it. Well, over my dead body. If you don't understand that, then I am sorry for you, I really am. Maybe if you spent less time in your ivory tower and –"

"Ivory tower?" Richard was incensed. "Nonsense! It's all about change, Jaco –"

"Enough, enough!" Magda pretended to cover her ears, "Let's not let politics spoil the evening before it starts. Why do men have to talk about politics all the time? Rich, you and I were having a nice little chat about the good old days, weren't we? Come boys, let's go and find our table. I'm dying for a drink. See you, Rich. Bye."

Magda sandwiched herself between Jaco and Andre. She took each by the arm and swung them around, revealing as she did so a glimpse of pale leg that got Richard's heart galloping. He watched as they marched off across the dance floor. Then, over her naked shoulder, she looked back and called, "Do you like dancing, Rich? We're on table fourteen."

Richard's heart surged. He was smitten. Never before had his passions been so enflamed – never before had he been so drawn to a woman, so captivated by lustful thoughts that he could think of nothing else. He saw himself dancing with her and couldn't wait to hold her in his arms – the anticipation was excruciating, almost more than he could bear. Richard swept back his hair with both hands and took a deep breath to steady himself. Then he set off through the tables, looking for Mary and the Sangsters. Out of the blue, an ugly thought reared up and nearly tripped him up – he would have surely fallen had he not been able to grip the back of a nearby chair and hang onto it: How in God's name was he going to get past Jaco.

Later, after dinner had been served and couples were once again drifting back onto the dance floor, Richard went up to the bar and ordered a port from Chetty, the Indian barman.

"Hello, Rich, all on your lonesome? Thought you were going to ask me to dance?" Magda asked.

Richard spun around, his heart in his mouth. "Just getting myself a port – would you like one?"

"Come along, you can get that afterwards. Come and dance with me."

"You sure? What will Jaco say? Shouldn't –"

"Say? He doesn't own me, does he? Why should he worry? Come on, let's dance."

She took Richard by the hand and led him, blushing and bumbling, onto the dance floor. He had hoped for a slow number and got exactly that. Now was his chance! At last, he could show off his ballroom skills. He took her into his arms, led with his left foot and immediately spun her into a chasse reverse turn. She followed effortlessly, light on her feet, and looked up at him, unperturbed. Richard's spirits soared. Holding her close, with his left hand held out wide, keeping her outstretched fingers high in a delicate clasp, and, with his right hand pressed into the small of her back, he wove this way and that, gliding her, silk on glass, back and forth across the dance floor. A little later, during a slow foxtrot, she seemed to nestle closer, unleashing a cascade of erotic thoughts. Had he imagined it? No, he couldn't have – wasn't her head now pillowed on his shoulder? There by design, not by accident. Feeling licenced by this discovery, but scared to break the spell, he brought her right hand up to his chest and gently, ever so gently, he tucked it beneath his chin, holding it snug and close. At the same time, ever so slowly, he lowered his nose into her hair, inhaling her fragrance deep into his lungs. She neither protested nor encouraged him – as if this were the most natural thing in the world. Exultant and dizzy with excitement, he tightened his arms around her and surrendered himself to the voluptuous contours of her body. Her breasts were firm against his chest; her thighs moulded his; her warm breath caressed his cheek – all this made him want to throw back his head and burst into song. He knew then, knew without a flicker of doubt, that he could have died right then and there – died complete, his worldly mission done. Nothing else mattered; not the other party goers inside or even the stars outside; not medicine or university; not even, closer to home, the farm, or his parents; nothing mattered right then, nothing except the lady in his arms.

The band stopped. They unwrapped themselves and came apart. The singer announced the coffee break, and couples began to leave the floor. Magda smiled at him again – drawing him to the edge. "Give me a call some time – we're in the telephone book. The Eshowe book, I mean."

With that, she walked off – this time, much to Richard's chagrin, she did not look back. But she knew he was watching. With each step, and he was sure about this, there was an added lilt to the swing of her hips; no doubt about it, her bottom was waving at him.

When Richard returned to his table, Mary looked up and straight away noticed a glazed, far-away look on his face. She turned in her chair and examined him closely.

"You're looking quite odd, Richy. What's up?"

"Nothing. I've just been dancing –"

"Yes, we watched you. With the Celliers girl. She's a bit of a tease, I hear –"

"Tease? Says who?"

"Well, I don't know her at all. But Shelly does. She was saying that Magda has a bit of a reputation, you know. A reputation for being, well, how should I put it, a bit loose with her favours?"

"That's baloney. You can't believe rumours. I thought she was rather nice."

"Ask Shelly then," she turned around and tapped Shelly on the shoulder. Shelly was seated at the table behind them. "Hey, Shell, sorry to interrupt. But didn't you say that Magda, the girl Richard was dancing with just now, has a reputation for being fast and easy?"

Shelly twisted around and looked at Richard; she gave him a long, hard look. Then she smiled, a knowing smile, as if she had divined some unassailable truth from his face. "She does. Has men eating out of her hand – they trip over themselves to get near her. They say that she picks them up, chews them for as long as it suits her, and then spits them out. So many stories like that. Apparently, she had an affair with the pharmacist in Eshowe – he's a married man. Can't say for sure, but hey, where there's smoke, there's usually a fire."

Richard said nothing. He was furious. Rumours, just unkind rumours – where was the evidence? He didn't believe a word of it. These lesser luminaires were all jealous of her, they envied her beauty. Of course, men would be drawn to her, what red-blooded man wouldn't? In the same way that people said there was no such thing as an ugly rich man, so, he reasoned, plain women would say that anyone more beautiful than they were, had to be flawed.

2

Throughout his time at Fort Hare, Gordon's mind had been, in so far as his political thinking was concerned, a swirling mist of contending ideas, one minute clearing and affording him tantalising glimpses of a way ahead; the next, so thick and impenetrable that he could barely see his hand in front of his face, let alone find where to put his feet. Notwithstanding his stepfather's injunction to remain focused on his studies and not allow himself to become too distracted, he found himself drawn willy-nilly to a brand of political activism that was being advocated by ANC disciples on campus with near religious fervour. He attended their meetings whenever he could, but always sat at the back – inert, like a lump of formless wet clay – so keen was he to uphold his parent's trust. He listened. And sympathised. Outwardly, especially in his early years, he appeared to float, allowing the ebb and flow of ideas that were being bandied about the campus to rise and fall beneath him.

His focus never wavered; he pursued his studies with single-minded devotion. But the outside world would not keep still and went on spinning, heedless of the machinations of mere mortals; external events wrapped themselves around him, fingers in that wet clay; slowly but surely, they shaped and moulded him.

By the time the *Azikwelwa* campaign kicked off in Alexandria two years later, he was a senior and his degree was all but in his back pocket. By now the clay was taking shape; with little persuasion, he found himself on a committee that was charged with the coordination of student support. Those who framed the Freedom Charter, along with members of other organisations who had been instrumental in setting up the Action Committee in Alexandria, invited this Fort Hare group up to the Rand to see for themselves. Gordon was desperate to go. After quibbling with his conscience for some time, he, at last, plucked up the courage and called Titus in Somkhele, asking for help. He and Busisiwe dug deep; without demurring, they sent him ten well-worn pound notes by express mail which arrived just in time. He joined the group, and they went by bus, travelling all through the night.

Alexandria blew his mind. They stayed with local activists and helped wherever they could. The bussing protest was the kiln in which activists and sympathisers from far and wide came to be fired – they came to be joined together, welded to the ideal of justice. It was an exhilarating experience and brought Gordon for the first time to the front line of political activism. He watched thousands of defiant workers streaming off to work each morning, long before the sun was up, and saw them trudge back, well after sunset – tired and spent, but with their heads held high. At night, he attended meetings that flowed one into the other – people hurried in, had their say, and hurried out. It was madly exciting, and Gordon couldn't get enough of it. In this annealing heat, a new Gordon was forged.

***

Three years later, now in his second year as a form teacher at a co-educational junior school just outside Pietermaritzburg, Gordon and his fellow-teacher friend, Lucas Thusi, found themselves spending a night in jail. They were in a car with two white girls, driving back from Durban, after attending a multiracial meeting billed as one about moral rearmament that had been addressed by George Daneel, a Dutch Reformed Church minister, when the police pulled them over and accused them of being members of the ANC. They had tried their best to explain that they were only offering their assistance to the girls by giving them a ride, and that the meeting had nothing to do with the ANC. The girls were let off with a warning, and they found themselves in a police cell.

Gordon was galled by this experience; hunger for justice gnawed at his innards and he ached for release from this onerous burden which chafed him like an ill-fitting harness. He knew that inequities of this sort, commonplace for so many non-Whites, went unheeded by the majority of the white community and that thought needled his resentment even more. But he also knew that in black communities all over the country, hurts like these were stacked up, like straws on the back of the proverbial camel, light and seemingly of no significance in their own right, but heavy enough to one day break the animal's back. The memory of his father's death, long festering and unresolved in his mind, now helped to crystalize his thinking and when he juxtaposed that tragic event against what he perceived to be his own lesser slight, it magnified his outrage, intensified his anguish, and amplified the cry for retribution that reverberated in his brain, giving him no peace of mind. The arbitrariness of it, the sheer audacity of the assumptions that underpinned it, became his *hluzo* through which, hereafter, he passed his thoughts, straining them of sentiment and humbug. For Gordon, this experience was all that he needed to galvanise him into political activism. The impenetrable fog which, for so long had been heavy one day and then swirling ever so lightly the next, now rose to reveal blue skies and unimpeded vistas for as far as he could see. The way ahead was clear and unambiguous. With a feeling of almost rapturous joy – of transcendental kinship even – he understood now more perfectly the dilemma that Titus had faced when he came to his own crossroads. This was his burning bush moment and set him off in the opposite direction to that which Titus had taken. He joined the ANC. A year later, he surreptitiously joined *Mkhonto we Sizwe* and settled down to a bifurcate life – by day, he taught and by night, he plotted. No one who knew him then – not even his parents on the infrequent times that he visited them in Somkhele – would have suspected that this friendly, avuncular teacher who inspired and impressed students at work or at play, was the alter ego of a single-minded and very focused political operative.

3

It was the end of the first semester and all the students went home for the mid-year break. Richard liked being back, back in step with the unhurried rhythm of the farm and luxuriating in the warm glow of belonging. And though he would never have said it, he missed his role as the heir apparent, one whose presence commanded deference if not obedience and whose word, for those who lived and worked on the farm, carried more clout than all the *indunas* put together.

Molly was making one of her interminable goodwill trips to Somkhele mission and Richard, having nothing better to do, decided to accompany her. When they arrived, Busisiwe rushed out and ran up to the car, waving her arms and hollering with joy. She embraced Molly and they stood together, holding hands, and laughing. Then she saw Richard. She drew back, her hand at her mouth. He knew. Knew that she knew he was a man now, no longer the tussle-haired boy she was used to.

"Hello, Busisiwe," he said, with a smile he hoped was wide enough to bridge the divide, *"it has been a long time. How are you?"* She laughed. They hugged.

"Hauw, Lichard, I nearly didn't recognise you. You are so grown up!"

Richard laughed and went round to the boot of the car. He offloaded the boxes of books his mother had packed and closed the boot. Busisiwe and his mother were still paddling questions back and forth to each other as though they were in a game of ping-pong. He turned to them and was about to ask where the boxes should go when, to his surprise, he saw there was a young woman standing next to Busisiwe. He sucked in his breath and stared. It was Thandi. Breasts. She had breasts. And rounded curves. A surge of excitement caught him by surprise. He struggled to keep his eyes on her face as he walked round the car to greet her.

"Hello, Thandi." Unconsciously he ran his fingers through his hair. *"How are you?"*

"I am fine, thank you." Her eyes were lowered respectfully, but he could see them, big and round and shining. *"We didn't know that you were coming."*

"Thandi, go and make us some tea," Busisiwe pointed to the house. *"And go and tell Titus that it is teatime. And tell him that Khosazana Molly is here. Hurry now."*

"Wait, Thandi," said Richard, picking up a box and offering it to her, *"if you help me with these boxes, I'll help you make tea."*

The kitchen was small, and they moved around each other like a pair of wary cats, eager for more, yet fearful of touching each other. Once, they reached for the kettle at the same time and their fingers touched. Instantly, they whipped their hands back and clutched them to their chests, as though the kettle was boiling hot. They giggled, and the nervous awkwardness that had kept them pussyfooting around each other evaporated. Richard grinned sheepishly; he liked the way she looked at him now, her eyes laughing and full of adoration. Another upwelling of feeling. This is crazy, he thought, she's only a girl. But there was a fluttering within him, and he could feel the blood rising to his ears. He turned away and went to the window. The kettle began to hiss. Thandi removed it from the stove and turned to see what he was doing. He had a cigarette in his mouth and was about to light it when laughing voices approached the kitchen door, staying the match in his fingers. The door burst open. Silence. For what seemed like an eternity, they gawked at one another. Gordon and Peter had soccer boots hanging around their necks and Titus, behind them, had his hat in his hand.

"Mister Richard," Titus recovered first, "what a nice surprise. We did not know that you were coming today." His voice was warm, and he shook Richard's hand vigorously, "I mean, Busisiwe told me your mother was coming this morning, but she forgot to say that you were also coming."

"That's not her fault. I only decided to come at the last minute." He turned to Gordon, genuinely pleased to see him again. "Hello, Gordi. I did not expect to see you either – I heard you are a teacher now. So glad to see you after all this time. And hello, Peter, you've been playing soccer, have you?"

Something about Gordon bothered him and at first, he couldn't put his finger on it. But after exchanging a few words with him and laughing with him in the self-effacing way he always used to show friendliness, he realised that for the first time, they were speaking to each other in English and, more pertinently, that he found both Gordon's tone of voice and his level gaze unsettling.

After tea, Busisiwe and Molly began to assemble the knitting machine that Molly was so excited to bring to Somkhele. There was not enough room in the lounge for all of them, so Titus suggested that they each take a chair from the kitchen table and sit outside under the trees where it would be cooler. For a while, the lulling sound of their voices floated into the lounge and Molly heard it as if it were an outside radio – that is, she heard the music but not the words. When the knitting machine was finally assembled, she stood up and wiped back her hair. She looked around, perplexed. Voices. There weren't any. Just then, Thandi and Peter walked in and sat down.

"You don't want to sit and talk to the men?" Busisiwe rocked back on her heels, *"Or are they talking men's business?"*

"They are talking politics, Ma. And I don't know anything about it."

"What's that?"

"Sorry, Madam. I shouldn't be speaking Zulu. Thandi is bored. She says they are talking politics out there and she doesn't know anything about it."

Molly went to the window. The men were sitting close together under the trees. They were leaning towards each other, elbows on knees, the backs of the wooden kitchen chairs sticking out behind them like squirrel tails, stiff and upright.

"Men's business, is it? Never mind. Here, Thandi, come with me. I'll show you how to knit."

She opened some plastic bags and took out balls of wool. "Which colour do you like? This one? Good, let's start." She turned to Busisiwe. "Let me know what colours your sewing group likes, and I'll send them up to you. There's plenty more where this came from."

Later, when they were driving home, Molly noticed that Richard was quieter than usual and had a faraway look on his face. She turned to him and patted him on his knee, "You're quiet, young man, what are you thinking? Didn't you enjoy yourself?"

"Me? Yes. Of course, very much. It was nice, thank you."

Richard's mind was preoccupied. Thandi. That look. Try as he might, he couldn't get rid of those big dark eyes and the way they had looked at him. They haunted him. He couldn't stop thinking about her. Private thoughts they were, ones that quickened his pulse – he wasn't going to divulge them to a living soul, not even to his mother.

"Busisiwe seems to have got the hang of the knitting machine, hasn't she?"

"Yes. I'm so pleased for her sake." Richard saw his mother's happy smile and his heart lurched towards her. An appreciation of her goodness overtook his thinking right then that he barely heard her as she carried on speaking, her eyes now riveted to the road. "She'll teach the others, I reckon, and in no time at all, they'll be knitting jerseys and things – you know, enough to sell. What about the books, Rich? Where did they end up?"

"Titus has them. In his office – we put them there, Thandi and I. He was very pleased to receive them – didn't he say anything to you?"

"Yes, he did. Very effusive he was. But I didn't go to the hall and so I didn't see where they went." She glanced at Richard. "Tell me, how did you find Gordon? He's very self-assured now, isn't he? Must say I wasn't expecting to see him. You guys were in a huddle for a long time, out there on the lawn, what were you chatting about?"

"I was surprised to see Gordon as well. Was just trying to work out when I saw him last." He paused to look out the window and gather his thoughts. It took a conscious effort, but he managed to push Thandi and her big eyes out of the way and concentrate on Gordon. "He's not the same –"

"Not the same? How so?"

"Well, he's different. Pretty intense now. Argues all the time – it's very tiring, you know. Everything's political as far as he's concerned." He lit a cigarette and flicked the match out the window. "I found him quite aggressive. Don't get me wrong, he was friendly enough and I think he was pleased to see me. But it was the way he asked questions – like he wanted to debate everything, you know, to score points."

"So, what did you talk about?"

"Oh, I don't know. About everything. He asked me what I thought about Sharpeville. I was a bit taken aback – I mean, I wasn't expecting to be put on the spot like that."

"So, what did you say?"

"Not much. Said it was awful."

"What did he say?"

Richard could feel his irritation rising – he really didn't want to talk about it and was annoyed with himself for bringing up a subject that he should have realised his mother would latch onto. "He said, 'Awful, is it? Only awful – nothing more than that?' I wasn't sure that I liked his tone. So, I said something along the lines that it was a tragedy and should never have happened. Then he said, 'What are you going to do about it?' By now I was beginning to see red. I looked at him and said, 'What can I do? I'm not the government, I don't make the rules. What do you expect me to do?' At that point, Titus intervened and changed the subject."

"Did it work?"

"Not really. Everything came back to politics. He asked me about the Congo and what I thought about the Katanga secession. To be honest, I didn't know much about the Congo – other than the fact that the Belgians had walked out, leaving the place to chaos and savagery – but I wasn't going to tell him that. So, I returned serve and asked him what he thought about it. Off he went, rabbiting on about nationalism, about colonialism, about how Europeans like to draw straight lines on maps – lines, he said, that often cut nations in half or joined others together who had never been together. Mum, I tell you, he was full on. I couldn't get away fast enough."

Molly sat quiet for a while, digesting what she had heard.

"You know, Rich, it's inevitable. I mean his interest in politics. He's intelligent and he's been to Fort Hare – a breeding ground for political activism. The students there thrive on politics, it's their daily diet – their bread and butter, if you like. He's aware of what's going on. The Gordons of this world represent a new breed of thinkers, ones that will not accept the status quo – they have the weight of history on their side, and they want change." Molly's voice trailed off.

"The weight of history?" Richard did not like what he was hearing.

"Yes. In any conflict numbers are ultimately decisive. I do so worry about the future, Rich. The new intelligentsia is watching and biding its time. They see what's going on around them … they have their antennae up; they know there's change in the air –"

"Don't tell me. He went on about Macmillan's speech as well."

"There you are – that's my point. He's savvy and he knows what's going on."

"Well, if you don't mind, I've had enough of politics for one day. Can we change the subject?"

Molly laughed, more to herself than to him. She mulled over what Gordon had been talking about and every now and then, she shook her head. But Richard did not see this; he had settled back with his eyes half-closed, allowing his mind to slip back and contemplate more pleasurable things, like girls with nicely rounded bodies and luminous eyes.

4

It was the first day of the month. Pay day. Molly hated it. She could never stomach what for her was an odious, indigestible fact – that in money terms, she could eat in one meal at a restaurant what most of these people earned in a month. She grimaced and stared out the window.

The workers sat on the ground outside, staring at the office door and waiting patiently for their small brown paper packets that, for a few days at least, would afford them some small pleasures and would, for the time being, release them from the drudge of serfdom. For Molly there was something craven about this monthly ritual; she hated to see grown men sitting around on their haunches like animals, waiting to be fed. She could hear the low hum of their voices, punctuated every now and then by a raised voice or a guffaw of strangled laughter; the melodic cadence of African voices, like church music, always stirred her.

"You ready, Jack? Shall we get the show on the road?" She looked at Jack sitting beside her and watched him line up all the little paper packets in the order of the names that appeared in his time book. He checked the petty cash float and nodded.

"Ready when you are, Madam." He went to the door and paused with his hand on the latch, turning back to look at her. "Shall I call Mdletshe and the *indunas*?"

Molly took a deep breath. "Let's get this over with."

Jack opened the door and called in Mdletshe. After him, lined up one after another like a row of ants, came the others. Unlike the six-legged variety, who seem not to bow to rank or favour, these two-legged ones entered singly, and in order of seniority, starting with the *indunas*, police boys, and licenced drivers. These select souls, Molly couldn't help noticing, were fatter than all the others, wore lace-up shoes, and smoked filter-tip cigarettes – they constituted the intelligentsia of the workforce, if there was such a thing, for they formed an *ad hoc* council and when called upon, would help to resolve disputes, or make representations. Then, on bare shuffling feet, came the farm muscle – the cutters, planters, and weeders who were the brawn that kept the whole enterprise going, for without them, there would be no crop, and with no crop, there would be no harvest. After this phalanx had filed its way into and out of the office, the workshop staff followed close behind and with them, in their overalls, the building gang. Then came the compound staff – that is, the cooks, sweepers, brewers, and other hangers-on that were entitled to a shilling or two. Last in line, like runts fidgeting for a turn on a teat, were the *umfaans* who tended the livestock.

Each person would hand over his *dompas* to Molly who, with grinding teeth, would initial it and pass it back. While she was doing that, Jack would hand over the brown paper packet that contained the recipient's monthly wage.

When everyone had been paid, then those who wished to borrow money put on their most submissive faces and came forward to plead their case. For Molly, this was the worst part of pay day – she could barely look the applicants in the face, so distasteful was it to see people squirming for a loan, hope rimmed red around their pleading eyes. Jack did all the talking – he interpreted for her and added his own comments as to whether or not he thought the loan ought to be considered. She would have liked to say yes to them all, but she knew she couldn't. Compassion for her was a doing word, not a noun. Consequently, sitting still in the face of such abject pleading was more than merely heart-rending, it was akin to a mortal sin. This was the great tension in her life: giving in to her passions, headlong and without reserve, or reining them in, grudgingly, and gripping them with a tight fist.

"Remember, Madam," said Jack, raising his fingers, one after the other, "loans are dependent upon three things: length of stay, the amount, and the loan history of the borrower. Of course, we could add gutfeel to that. Some people may be more deserving than others." He saw the pinched look on her face. "If you'd like, I'll give you a thumbs up or thumbs down – like this, okay?" And he winked as he wiggled his thumb. "That way, you're not on your own – I mean, you can breathe easy, saying it was my decision and I can tell myself it was yours."

There were not many requests and Molly was thankful for that – the monthly task she so dreaded was over for now. She began loading papers into her bag when Frankie approached and stood in front of her. She sensed he wanted her attention and smiled up at him.

"Yes, Frank? Something bothering you?"

"Not sure if this is the right time, Madam, but I might as well say it now." He looked at her reproachfully, "I've been talking to Jack about it for a quite a while now, but the truth is I'm sixty-five this year and I've been working here for nearly forty years. The *Ou Baas* was very good to me – gave me a break, a real *lekker* break, and it helped me. I'll never forget that. But I'm thinking of retiring. Just thought I'd let you know – maybe you could have a talk to the Doctor about it? See what he thinks?"

"Thank you, Frankie. It's not really a surprise – none of us is getting any younger, are we – it had to come, sooner or later. My father-in-law always spoke highly of you, and I know Bill thinks the world of you as well. Can't imagine the farm without you – what an awful thought! But let's not rush things. Let me speak to Bill about it and we'll get back to you."

"Thank you, Madam. There's something else. I've been turning this over in my head for a long time, trying to see if it would be good for the farm. I always put the farm first – you know that. But I don't want you to think I am being, you know, selfish or anything like that. Oh, it would be good for me, no doubt about that, but whether or not it would –"

"Out with it, Frankie." Jack nudged Frankie with his elbow, "Don't beat about the bush. Or shall I tell Madam for you?"

Frankie raised his hands and stepped back a couple of paces. "Thank you, Jack, but this is my *indaba* – I can manage on my own." He returned his gaze to Molly and took a deep breath – he would have given just about anything for a cigarette but thought it inappropriate just then. "About Isaac, Madam. He's been working in the village, at Dingley's garage, for a few years now – he's good, you know, a good mechanic. He loves the farm. I had always thought that he should get qualified and then go overseas. To England. He can get an English passport – he was born over there. The *Ou Baas* –"

"He was born in England? I never knew that."

"Yes, Madam, the *Ou Baas*, Mr Barclay senior, he helped me take Rosie over there. Isaac was born in Bristol –"

"In Bristol! Well, I never!" She suddenly realised how little she knew about the lives of her staff. How long had she known Frankie Dunn, and yet she didn't know that.

"Yes, in Bristol, Madam. But I don't think Isaac will ever get there. He's a farm boy, he loves it here. Besides, he's not much interested in books or studying. I've come to the conclusion that you can't push water uphill. Face facts, I keep telling myself. So, after a lot of sleepless nights, I realised his place might be here – he could settle down, right here. Then I just thought, well, you know, why couldn't he take over from me? That didn't seem such a silly idea to me – in fact, the more I thought about it, the more I liked it. Of course, only if you want him to. But I could stay on for a while – if you agreed, that is – I could watch over him, help him take over – I could make sure he's up to speed before I pull the pin. But only if you and the Doctor want me to. I mean, it's your decision."

"Bless you, Frankie. You're a treasure. Have you discussed this with Isaac?"

"No. Didn't want to get him excited – in case it all fell flat."

"Well, I think it's a wonderful idea. But I don't want you get your hopes up either. Let me have a chat with Doctor, and we'll get back to you. Jack, what do you think?"

"Me? I think it makes a lot of sense. I have spent a lot of time with Isaac – as Frankie says, he loves the farm, is good with his hands and now that he's been at Dingley's working on engines for as long as he has, he is, I'm sure, a useful mechanic. I'd like to have him here. Also, the shop boys know him, and they all like him. Good fit, I reckon."

"Well, there you are, Frankie – seems like we are all in agreement. I'll get back to you."

After Frankie left, Jack picked up Molly's briefcase for her and accompanied her to her car.

"You know, it'll be good to have Isaac here. He'll have a place. He'll be somebody. Not easy for coloured folk here – not many of them in this part of the world and those that are, tend to hit the bottle. Frankie's world would come undone if Isaac went down that path."

Molly paused. She tried to imagine being coloured and how that would impinge on her outlook on life. Once again, the irony of 'coloured', emanating from the mixing of 'white' and 'black', struck her as cruel and hypocritical. After all, nobody applied any defining epithet – certainly not one with derogatory connotations – to someone whose one parent, fair-skinned and blue-eyed, came from Scandinavia say, and whose other parent, olive-skinned and dark-eyed, came from south Mediterranean stock. Ah, she reminded herself, it's the hair that's the problem – white South Africans didn't mind the dominance of black hair over white hair, so long as it didn't have any of the give-away curliness and springiness that was so uniquely African. People are funny, she mused, fancy being so caught up in such tiny details – not being able to see the wood for the trees.

"It's a funny world, isn't it? I was just thinking of the word 'coloured'. For all intents and purposes, it is an adjective, but in this country, it is used as a noun – a pejorative one at that. Why do you suppose we focus on difference? Why do we like to put people in boxes? I mean, what's so sacred about "us" that makes "them" so fearful? Aren't we all just people? Come to think of it, why does the lowest common multiple invariably determine the highest common factor?"

"Sorry, you lost me there. Do you mean why are –"

"Sorry, Jack. I'm rambling again, talking to myself. I was thinking about Isaac. Tell me, how are you and Mavis enjoying the farm?"

"Couldn't be happier, Madam – we really couldn't. Nobody bothers me here," he said, looking at the ground in front of him and drawing in the dust with the toe of his boot. "I can be myself. You know, it's not easy. Frankie and his family are different – they stand out because they are neither one thing nor the other. But they have their own communities – they stick together. Like them, I stand out because I am different – like them, I'm neither this nor that. But where's my community? I'm not white enough for you folk and I'm too "white" for the chaps in the compound, so who the hell am I? Even my own people – my blood family – do not accept me. Oh, they're nice enough if you know what I mean – they will talk to me, listen to me, and will be civil enough not to upset me, but they will not trust me. They think that I think I'm above them. That's ridiculous. I don't ... Sorry for the outburst ... it's not easy, not easy at all. But thanks to you and the Doctor, I am happy now and don't have much to worry about."

"But, Jack, you have friends, don't you?"

"Yes. We do have a small circle of friends. There are, you know, a few people in the village like us – nurses, teachers, one or two lawyers … you know what I mean – people who … how should I put it, have been made different by … education. We tend to find each other, spend time together – we're able to escape, to hide from the world … to console one another when the going gets tough. These other folk also feel estranged, they feel that in a way they have left their communities behind and can no longer return. Of course, they can return, in body – and they do – but not in spirit, if you know what I mean. They know that they are different and that this 'difference' sets them apart. That's what education does … it liberates and enslaves at the same time. The burden of loneliness – the loneliness of spirit, I mean – can be too much for some to bear. Many seek salvation in the bottle … I've been there, I've drunk myself stupid … But then I found Mavis – or she found me. Thank God for Mavis. She saved me. Mavis and the kids keep me on the straight and narrow – and sane. You know what? I've mellowed, I no longer get hot under the collar at being treated as sub-human – it still irks me, but now I let it ride. So, am I happy here? Yes, a thousand times yes. You and the Doctor have been very good to us – I really can't thank you enough."

It was getting dark. Molly shivered. She opened the car door.

"Well, Jack, you really don't have to thank us – besides, we're indebted to you. I could not possibly manage the farm without you. If you weren't here, then Doctor would have to leave the hospital and that would break his heart. Or he would have to find someone else to manage the farm for us. So, thank you, Jack. And, if it's any consolation – no, it couldn't possibly be – but I too feel like a fish out of water at times. I'm not used to this apartheid stuff – drives me up the wall. And it wins me few friends in the village. You're right about difference, about thinking differently – it does set one apart, doesn't it? People around here are nice enough and I guess they mean well, but you know what? Nice people are middle-of-the-road people – they bore me to tears. There I go again, rambling on and on. Sorry, Jack. Gosh, look at the time! I'll see you tomorrow. Bye."

5

Richard had been invited to a New Year's party in Kloof, just outside Durban. He had thought twice about attending before he replied in writing to the gold-embossed invitation card, but as the invitation came from his old school chum, Brydon Hamilton, whom he had not seen for ages, he decided to make the three-hour drive and attend. His parents gave him a key to their flat on Durban's Esplanade and said he could spend the night there. Brydon was an articled clerk at Shepparton Lawyers and studying law part-time at the Durban campus of Natal University. Kloof parties were always grand affairs and a lot of fun. He knew that many of his school friends would be there, and this made the decision for him even easier.

The party was held at the Hamilton residence. Space had been sacrificed for views – the house clung to the side of a hill and from this lofty vantage point, it cast its imperious gaze downwards, all the way to Durban's jutting skyscrapers which by day lay against a hazy shoreline like an incomplete jigsaw puzzle, and by night, twinkled beguilingly like a candle-lit Christmas tree. Whether by day or by night, the eye was drawn to the distance and marvelled at what it beheld.

Richard was in awe as soon as he entered the large, spacious foyer. Colour, light, sound, and movement all caught his senses and drew him into the heart of the party. The downstairs rooms were full of people. As he made his way to greet his hosts, he noticed thick Persian carpets, polished mahogany furniture, large bay windows, and numerous paintings on the walls. He paid his respects to Brydon's parents and moved out onto the front veranda where a bunch of men, all in dinner suits, thronged around the bar. Brydon was there, so he joined them and was soon laughing and joking with the rest of them.

It was a fun time. Many old school friends were there and seeing them again, after a year in Cape Town where he had felt like an *uitlander*, made Richard realize how much he had missed them – missed their familiarity, their inter-connectedness, and their good-natured ribbing. He also knew many of the girls and so was able to dance without having to go through the ordeal of rejection. It was bad enough having to dredge up the courage to ask a stranger who caught his eye to dance, but then to suffer the humiliation of rejection was almost more than he could endure. Unlike most of his friends who, it seemed, couldn't wait to get onto the dance floor, Richard was a bit of a wall flower – he tended to hang back and watch. The truth was that he lacked confidence – he felt inadequate, that he was not handsome enough nor sufficiently interesting enough to attract the eyes of glamourous girls. Of course, he always hankered after the pretty ones, the ones that everyone found irresistible, but despite being surrounded by an ocean of beauty, the vision of Magda never left him. It didn't matter that she never returned any of his calls after that night; he held her high up on a pedestal, pining for the day when he could hold her again.

There were only so many table seats, so dinner was served from a series of copper-domed *bains-marie* that allowed people to help themselves and to sit or stand wherever they wanted to. After he had finished his curry and rice, Richard took his plate into the kitchen as an excuse to have a chat with the African staff. Some people, walking into somebody's house for the first time, are able to form indelible impressions of the occupants, just by observing the things that they possess: their furniture, nick-knacks, and artwork – even how they are positioned – say much about the importance that they attribute to inanimate objects. Books, on the other hand, drawn up shoulder to shoulder, speak more about thoughts – they whisper about the animus, that compendium of driving interests that flows through the household like a subterranean river. Richard used these cues almost without being aware that he was doing so and, without conscious effort, liked to test his hunches against what he could find out from the native staff. Just a few minutes in their company was all it took for him to crystallize his thoughts and to confirm what he perceived to be the personality of the home.

He was still in the kitchen, joking with the cook while keeping out of his way, when a breathless Mrs Hamilton entered, her long crimson dress bustling around her pointed feet. She was beside herself.

"Quick, Joseph," she said to the young man at the sink, "one of the dogs has vomited on the veranda. Please go and clean it up." Then she saw Richard. "Damn dogs," she said, moving from the doorway so Joseph could get past, "I thought I asked Brydon to lock them in the garage while we were having the party. You looking for something?"

"Oh no. Just brought my plate in. Was having a chat with your cook. He was just telling me his surname is Mkhize. So, I asked if he was from the Mkhizes in the Kranskop area –"

"Charlie's been with us for years, haven't you, Charlie? Don't know what we would do without you. Did you say Kranskop, what made you ask him that?"

"*Khosikazi*, he speaks Zulu very well. He is one of us." Richard laughed and turned back to Mrs Hamilton. She was smiling at him, waiting for his answer.

"Well, I don't know about that. But I do know that there's a big Mkhize clan in the Kranskop area – many of them worked at school, that's how I know. He owns land there –"

"I know all about his land claim. He now has the title deeds – acquired by prescriptive right. Fred, my husband, did the legal work for him – took ages, but eventually it got done."

"That's amazing. Not many Africans can say they have title to a piece of land."

"No, don't suppose they can. Have you had any pudding yet? Charlie makes a mean trifle and everyone's getting stuck into it. Stay here as long as you like – Charlie seems to be enjoying your company. Would you like me to fetch some trifle for you? Or ice cream? What would you like?"

"No thanks, I was on the point of leaving when you came in." Richard nodded at Charlie and said to him, *"Sizobonana."* He opened the door for Mrs Hamilton but jumped aside hastily as Joseph came back into the kitchen.

"Deduka," he said with his nostrils scrunched up and his eyes pinched tight. He carried his mop and bucket well out in front of him, *"Nukela. Nukela kabi."*

They looked at each other; Mrs Hamilton's finely plucked eyebrows were arched into question marks while Richard's, matching his deadpan face, were flat and impassive. Without a word, they walked off down the passage and joined the party.

A number of parents, friends of the Hamiltons, had been invited to the party and they kept more or less to themselves. After dinner however, a group of fathers were gathered around Fred Hamilton near the bar – he had a box of Cuban cigars in one hand and a decanter of port in the other. Richard and a girl named Felicity squeezed past them to approach the bar. He had known her for a long time and enjoyed her company. She offered to help him carry a round of drinks back to where they had been sitting. While they stood in line waiting to be served, they couldn't help overhearing the conversation just behind them.

"Hear that?" Felicity whispered in Richard's ear, "They're talking politics – at a party! Such a bore, isn't it." Richard held up his hand – he was listening to what was being said.

"Those buggers who left us to form the PP should be shot. They were elected as UP members, not Progs. It's disgraceful, walking out on us like that."

"I agree," someone chipped in, "all it does is split the opposition."

"Well, they're all pink, aren't they? Aren't we better off without them? Let the bleeding hearts go if they want to – who needs them? I'm with Div. I reckon he's our man –"

Richard heard another voice cut in. "What's all this nonsense about a qualified franchise? If we don't keep the *wogs* in their place, we'll be done for. Once you give them your finger, next it's your hand, then your arm, and before you know it, you're a goner. Just look at what's happening in the rest of Africa. France and Belgium have upped stumps and bailed out. Britain has gone weak at the knees and is ditching her colonies as fast as she can – remember Macmillan's bullshit 'Winds of Change' speech? And what about them letting Dr bloody Banda back into Nyasaland? Been out for forty-odd years and could hardly speak the local lingo. And he'd been carrying on with a white woman in England, hadn't he? He's a shit stirrer, that's what he is."

"I actually think the Progs may be onto something." Fred Hamilton, speaking for the first time, and sounding very much like the lawyer that he was, continued in his carefully modulated voice, "You know Maurice, a qualified franchise makes sense. It's a halfway position between the Nats and the Liberals. It'll put the brakes on if you know what I mean – will give us time to get the Blacks up to speed. I don't want to throw away all that we have any more than the next person, but we cannot keep on this track and become the pariah of the world. The UP has nothing to offer except a watered-down version of separate development which the Nats are busily ramming down our throats. And we cannot afford another Sharpeville disaster, can we? Leave the Nats in charge and that's all but a certainty. No, as far as I'm concerned, the UP has run out of ideas and is clinging to the wreckage of the past. So, as I see it, the choice is simple. You can stick to the course and vote Nat and face the consequences, you can vote Liberal and know that you haven't even a snowball's chance in hell of ever being able to change things because the electorate won't buy it, or you can vote Prog. I rule out voting UP as in my book that'll get us nowhere."

"Hold on, Fred, you're being a bit savage on the UP. I'm not sure I agree with you. Surely, if we want to oust the Nats, then we ought to get behind the UP, they are the opposition and numbers-wise, are the only option. Personally, I like what they say, I really do. Mark my words, the Progs are all fart, no shit – they will bow and scrape to black demands and will end up selling us down the river."

"But we cannot continue as we are. The world is changing. Colonialism is being dismantled. We may not like it, but that's the reality. Integration in some shape or form is inevitable. The question is how it will be achieved. The UP has no more of an answer to that question than the Nats. Stick with the Nats, and we'll be forced into a *laager* that is getting smaller and smaller. At the UN –"

"Pardon my French but fuck the UN. That mob of bastards couldn't organise a piss-up in a brewery. They sit in their ivory towers like bare-bummed baboons on a cliff and hurl abuse at everybody and everything. And look at the Congo – five minutes after independence and the *coons* are at each other's throats, aren't they? In comes the UN, silly blue berets bobbing around everywhere, supposedly for law and order, but what do we get? More murder and mayhem! Even nuns are being raped and killed. What a bloody mess. Don't get me started on the UN. I didn't go to fight in the bloody war just so these idiots could tell us what to do."

Richard heard all this with the incredulity of a child listening to a fairy-tale; in a trance-like state, he stepped aside to let someone through and inadvertently bumped into one of the speakers who then spilled his drink.

"Oh gosh, I'm sorry, Sir. I didn't mean to. Here, let me get a mop."

"Ah, Richard, don't worry about that," said Fred Hamilton. He called out to his wife who at that moment was walking by, "Darling, get Joseph over here, please. With a mop."

He turned back to the group and moved aside, making space for Richard, "Come and join us." He ushered him into the circle. Richard felt awkward and out of place. He shuffled into line and put his handkerchief back into his pocket.

"Would you like a port? We're talking about the new political party – the Progressive Party, that is. Gentlemen, this is Richard Barclay, from Zululand, he's a good friend of Brydon – they went through school together. Let's all move over this way a bit, out of the way – we seem to be blocking the traffic. Thanks. Tell me, Rich, if you don't mind, what are young people thinking? You're at the University of Cape Town, what are they saying down there? Whom do students support more – the Progs or the UP?"

Richard squirmed. He hated being put on the spot. The music had started again – he'd have given anything right then to be dancing, even with the ugliest girl in the room. "Well, I'm not really into politics, but I think that the Progs are quite popular – on campus, I mean." Someone prodded his arm. "Sorry, what's that? You're a student? Which University did you say? Doing what?"

"I've just completed my first year at UCT, doing medicine."

"Wonderful. But tell me, what do you think about NUSAS? I'd like to hear from the horse's mouth as it were – I have two daughters, one's a nurse and the other is training to be a teacher. Neither of them has had any involvement with NUSAS – or none that I'm aware of. They're in the papers quite a lot though – mostly for political interference it seems. What are your thoughts? I mean, should students be dabbling in politics?"

Richard could feel the old familiar knot forming in his stomach – he looked around, desperate to escape. Felicity was already at the bar. "Just a minute, Sir. I think Felicity may need a hand with the drinks." He reached over and tapped her on the shoulder. "Sorry, Flick, you have the drinks? All of them? Let me give you a hand. Sorry, Sir, looks like I'm wanted."

"No, don't worry, Rich, I'm fine. Carry on – Micky here is giving me a hand."

Richard cursed under his breath. Instead of saving him, Felicity had cast him back into the lion's den. He was annoyed that he had allowed himself to become entangled in a discussion with people he did not know – with people swathed in cummerbunds and reeking of self-importance, people who looked down their noses at him and, he felt, expected him to show them due deference if not respect.

I know what Mum would do right now, Richard thought, she'd go in with all guns blazing. But I hate arguing, so much easier to keep one's thoughts to oneself. What do I even say? Should I agree with them, tell them what they want to hear, and then bail out, or should I tell them what I really think and become embroiled in an argument that might go on for ages?

Trying hard not to show his unease, he turned back to face his interrogator who, port in hand, was waiting for him with the slightly bemused look that a cat has when it plays with a mouse.

He took a deep breath.

"Well, NUSAS is a student union," he said, choosing his words carefully, "all students belong. I mean, there is a small annual levy which I understand is deducted by admin and paid to NUSAS on our behalf. So, in that sense, all students are members of the organisation. As to political –"

126

"Do you think that's fair? Shouldn't only those students who want to join be levied?"

"Well, I guess it's a bit like taxes. We all have to pay them, and we all benefit from them."

Someone interjected. "Well, talking about taxes – we pay them, not you chaps. And personally, I don't like my taxes going to universities who then pass them on to a ragtag bunch of students who have never done a day's work in their lives and who, bugger me, Jack, think they have a God-given right to bite the hand that feeds them."

"With all due respect, Sir," replied Richard, balking at being tarred by such a broad, ham-handed brush, "I have never bitten the hand that feeds me, nor do I think that God has given me anything he hasn't given to anyone else. But you know, NUSAS is open to everyone – it's a union. If the majority of students don't like what it says or disapproves of the political stance it is taking, then they can change it. But it is popular, people like it, and support it. And it's not all politics, it really isn't. NUSAS runs lots of activities on campus – well-supported ones that have nothing to do with politics – and it provides many other benefits. As far as I am –"

"Sorry to interrupt you," said a short, bald man wearing thick-rimmed glasses, "I agree with him, Ralph. When I was at varsity, before the war, NUSAS did quite a lot. I don't remember much about politics back then, but it certainly offered bursaries, helped students get jobs –"

"That might have been then, Ed, but now NUSAS is into politics, big time. We don't send our kids to university to become politicised, do we? We send them there to get educated, to get degrees, and then back into society where they can make useful contributions – not sponge off us. Tell me, Richard, is NUSAS political or is it not? Is it right for NUSAS to confront the government that feeds it?"

"Hold on, Ralph. Richard is studying medicine," said Fred Hamilton, pouring oil onto troubled waters, "he's probably too busy with his studies to be bothered with politics on campus. Anyway, I'm more interested in what young people are thinking about the Progs – NUSAS is another ball game."

"Fair enough, Fred. I'm also interested in his take on the Progs. But I'd still like to hear his thoughts on NUSAS and, you know, radical student politics. My view is that leftist lecturers and rabble rousers have infiltrated our universities and are trying to undermine the government. The same at Fort Hare and other black colleges – there are 'subversive elements' on all our campuses. Those are not my words; they are those of the Minister of Justice – he ought to know what he is talking about. Richard seems to be a reasonable, responsible young man – just wondered what his take on all this is."

Richard didn't like where the conversation was going. He felt as though his foot was being nailed to the floor. The last thing he wanted to do was to expose his political views to a scrutiny which he felt was jaundiced and which would, he felt quite sure, find him wanting, no matter what he said. He knew what he ought to say but decided against it. His mind was spinning at a thousand miles an hour. He wanted to construct a response that would be neutral and would allow him to retire gracefully and was rummaging for the right words when he felt a tap on his shoulder.

"It's alright, Richard," said a familiar voice from behind, "let me give you a hand."

Richard whirled around, his mouth working like a pair of bellows. There, standing right behind him and holding a whiskey glass in his hand, was Mr Carruthers, Bry's housemaster at school.

"Hello, Sir, didn't see you there. Everyone know Mr Carruthers? Brydon's housemaster … or was when Brydon and I were at school together."

"Thank you, Richard," Carruthers turned his attention to Ralph, "I overheard you quizzing young Richard here about NUSAS and student politics. Well, let me help him. Fred, you didn't send Brydon to our school for us to make him into a little 'yes' man, did you? I'm a history teacher and I always see my brief as teaching boys how to think, not what to think. I hope to God our universities do much more than that – I hope they fire young minds, make them so full of wonder and so curious that they doubt anything and everything. Universities have always been cauldrons in which conflicting ideas boil and bubble together – it's when we stew together that our true flavours come out. Seriously, do you want varsities to churn out cardboard cut-outs that won't rattle our cages?

"Now, with regard to NUSAS, I say thank G for it! NUSAS is the voice of liberalism on our campuses – the liberalism that you and I went to war for. Think about it, all the other voices that just about drown them out, are right wing – in fact, further right than Genghis Khan. So, thank God we have NUSAS, bleating bravely against the braying asses. And if the fees that you and I pay, when our sons and daughters go to university, happen to include a few bob to keep the voice of liberalism alive then so much the better, I say."

Richard could hardly believe his ears. He had been at school with Carruthers for four years and never had he suspected that this nondescript housemaster was so liberal in his thinking. How we conceal our true selves, he thought, what bland facades we hide behind!

After Carruthers delivered his little speech, there was a long pause. Some nodded, others stared glassily ahead but overall, it seemed, these craggy heads were numbed into silence. Old Carruthers had knocked the wind out of their sails. Fred Hamilton cleared his throat.

"Thanks for that, Patrick. Nicely said. We actually started off by asking Richard what young people thought of the Progs – you know, the breakaway party that's just been formed. The papers are full of it, and I just wondered what the leaders of tomorrow were thinking."

Richard was opening his mouth to speak but Carruthers held him back. "Here, Richard, get me another whiskey if you don't mind. I'd like to say a few words about the Progs." Richard took his glass, but hovered at the back to hear Carruthers who, like a bantam fluffing his feathers, was in full cry.

"Let me tell you what I think. If you want to find out what young people are thinking – the leaders of tomorrow as you put it – then you should really be asking young Blacks what they think. The future is in their hands, not ours. It's a case of simple arithmetic – they have the numbers and that's all there is to it. Remember what Napoleon said? A thousand cannons cannot supress an idea that strikes its time – or words to that effect. The Progs are a compromise, a halfway position – I doubt if black people will settle for what they are offering. Personally, I'm a Liberal. I believe in universal suffrage, a bill of rights and the dignity of man. And yes, in my book that means one man, one vote – irrespective of race, colour, or creed. Frankly, while their hearts are in the right place and their intentions are good, the Progs are too little too late. I won't comment on the UP – that's yesterday's news, done and dusted, and about as effective as farting in the wind."

Another long silence, one that swept through the ground floor rooms, snuffing out all sound as it went, even obliterating the dance music at the other end of the house. This time the group broke up. Richard watched two bald heads depart together – they reminded him of a pair of calabashes – one, not quite steady, tipped towards the other, "Bloody commie!" To which the other replied, "God help us – the world is going to pot!"

Fred Hamilton put his arm around the old man's shoulders. "Well, Patrick, you certainly put the cat among the pigeons."

"Not sure about that. Trouble is, there are too many bloody pigeons and not enough cats."

"Well, be that as it may. Go on, Rich, get this fellow a drink before he dies of thirst."

When midnight struck, everyone sang 'Auld Lang Syne'. Richard watched couples entwine and kiss. A pang of jealousy speared him, and he turned away wounded, squeezing his eyes shut. Magda loomed up. He wondered where she was right then and who was kissing her. He sighed and opened his eyes, making a concerted effort to rid himself of such a disturbing vision before re-joining the happy throng.

Brydon looked around for Richard and found him out on the balcony. He was standing all alone, smoking, and deep in thought.

"Hey, Rich! Is something wrong?" he asked.

"No, nothing at all." Richard smiled at Brydon and put his arm around his friend's shoulder. "Great party – a fitting end to 1960, I reckon."

"What were you looking at just then?"

"Oh, nothing really. Came out to enjoy the cool breeze. Then I saw the lights over there, the city lights – was just admiring them. I happened to glance down. Over there, see? I could just make out the shanty town down there on the flats. And that got me thinking."

"Really? What about?"

"Well," said Richard, not wanting to sound too serious on such an occasion, "here we are having a fabulous time. You know, music, good food, dancing, and all that. But what about the poor buggers living down there? They live cheek by jowl, don't they – like sardines in a tin. I was just wondering if they had cause to celebrate. What do you reckon?"

"That's pretty heavy stuff for this time of the night, Rich! But I get your drift."

He looked down in the direction of the shanty town that lay sprawled on the flat ground below. Though he could not see them clearly in the dark, he knew that there was a sprawl of grass huts and a motley collection of single-room dwellings, many of them covered with dried reeds, discarded plastic sheeting or lengths of rusted corrugated iron. Brydon sighed.

"Yup. Upsets me too whenever I look down there. In daylight you know, it's much more revealing. Especially if an easterly is blowing."

"Why's that?"

"Usually, you can't see much because there's a thin blanket of smoke hiding it. They're always burning something or other down there. The easterlies lift the blanket."

"Yeah, but that's Africa for you, isn't it? A bloody mess."

"Yes, but it's very much of our making. One learns to ignore it, I suppose. Dad says affluence is like wearing glasses that let you see only what you want to see."

He held up his hand, stifling the protest he saw forming in Richard's mouth.

"But you know what really gets me? It's the bare-bummed kids playing in the dirt. Should be in school, shouldn't they. And think about the women, Richard. Always bent over their fires – they know nothing but having kids and marital servitude. What a drudge that must be!"

Richard said nothing. He agreed but at the same time he didn't.

"You know what else, Rich? There are lots of young men down there – as there are in nearly every black township – all of them hanging around and waiting for breaks that will never come. They lounge about, smoke, play cards, chat up women or whatever – they all end up in trouble, don't they. Very distressing. Bothers me. It really does."

A girl's voice rose above the din inside the house, calling for Brydon. They both heard it and turned towards it. Brydon gathered himself and gave Richard a friendly punch. "Sounds like I'm wanted.

130

Let's not get all stewed up over things we do not like and cannot change – especially not on New Year's Day."

"What about your dad, Brydon? Does he feel the same way?"

"Absolutely."

"So why does he stay here? I mean, if all that down there gives him grief –"

"It's not grief. Sure, at times it's an eyesore, but it's also a reminder. A reminder of what underpins the 'good life' we all enjoy so much. 'There, but for the grace of God, goes I', he often says. Anyway, Dad likes it here. All his friends are here."

"Okay. But aren't you scared? Living so close to all this – to the *tsotsi* element down there?"

Brydon laughed. "Sure. That's why we lock everything up as much as we do. Dad says we hide behind lock and key – says it's the price we pay for living on these exalted clifftops."

A girl stepped onto the patio, saw Brydon, and hurried over to him.

"Here you are! Been looking for you everywhere. What's going on out here?"

Brydon drew the girl into his arms. "Nothing much. We're just having a chat."

"What about?"

"The lot of the dispossessed."

He was about to lead her away when a thought struck him, and he turned back to Richard and waggled his forefinger at him.

"You're from farming stock, aren't you, Rich? There are shit living conditions on farms as well. What's more, farms are private property, not so? All that land down there is municipal land – these guys are squatting. No squatters on farms, are there?"

"Yes, but on our farm –"

Brydon waved him aside. "Poverty and crappy living conditions on farms are at the behest of landowners. Instigated by good, God-fearing folk. By people who go to church on Sundays. People who should know better. Don't look at me like that! I've been to your farm. I've seen how your workers live – better off than many I grant you, but that's not saying much. Would you want to live in a farm compound? No, of course, you wouldn't. And nor would I."

He looked down at the girl in his arm and smiled at her. "Enough philosophising. Let's start 1961 on the right footing. Come along, Rich, let's go and get ourselves a drink."

131

CHAPTER SIX:

1966/7

1

After graduating from university, Richard returned to Durban where he joined the medical staff at Addington Hospital and was enrolled as a houseman. While he liked the Cape and had enjoyed his time there, he was pleased to be back where he felt he belonged. For some inexplicable reason, he felt like a migratory bird, returning to the place of its birth. He knew that birds did that instinctively, out of fidelity to the seasons – they were drawn back and forth blindly, yo-yos on a never-ending string. He, on the other hand, was coming home for good. Not so much to avoid the ravages of winter or to build a nest – though the material urge was undeniably strong – but more to appease an inner yearning, a desire to be at home with kith and kin, and with those other familiar things which, like water flowing over a stone, had imperceptibly shaped and smoothed him, giving him both identity and lustre.

He completed his first six months as a houseman concentrating on medicine and was now in the middle of his surgery rotation, something he enjoyed enormously. That said, he had neither the heart nor the singlemindedness of purpose to specialise and decided that he'd like nothing more than to be in general practice like his father, serving a rural community where he would know everybody and where his efforts would be noted and appreciated. He was happy. His old friends were waiting for him, and he picked up where he had left off. This, he told himself again and again, was the hallmark of all good friendships.

His social life blossomed – no longer in the thrall of exams, he partied with new-found zeal, enjoying for the first time as he saw it, the fruits of bachelorhood and the liberating independence that his salary now afforded him. He dated girls with increasing self-assurance, relishing visits with small groups of friends to the night spots and dinner-dance restaurants that he found hidden away in the hotels that, like sequins stitched to a hem, adorned the fabled Indian Ocean fringe.

He spent a lot of time with Brydon. Now a junior lawyer in a prestigious city law firm, Brydon was in a position to give clout to the political views that he had espoused as a student – he took on cases for social equity, representing black clients who had been charged with infringing one or other of the many statutes used by the government with such devastating effect to shore up and bolster the edifice of its own making, the draconian apartheid system. He championed the underdog and was becoming known as a lawyer with a social conscience, ready and willing to incur the wrath of the state in defence of what he regarded were inalienable rights that should be accorded to everyone, irrespective of race, colour, or creed. Richard was in awe of Brydon's political acumen and the incisive cut and thrust of his repartee. For Richard, there were two contending emotions that occupied his mind – fear and hope. He feared the forces of darkness; his heart quickened when he read of the savagery that independence had unleashed in the Belgian Congo; he applauded the Kennedys and empathised with the civil rights movement in the United States – the hairs on the back of his neck rose when he heard Martin Luther King's impassioned 'I have a Dream' speech – but he also shrank inwardly whenever the protests became violent; he squirmed whenever Africans rubbished colonialism or thumbed their noses at European values; he couldn't help feeling dismayed when he looked at the map and saw the red ink of English dominion slowly shrinking. Indeed, Richard had come to regard the English way as the right way – its magnanimity self-evident and its benevolence plainly manifest all around the world. In short, England brought light to shine where there was darkness. Thus, Richard feared change as much as he welcomed it – he needed safety just as a child needed a thumb to suck at night. Deep down, though he would never say it, he feared material loss; he feared that one day the accoutrements of the good life might be rudely taken away from him.

One Saturday night Richard had accompanied Brydon and some friends to a multiracial party on Salisbury Island and were just now returning home. It was a lovely starlit night and Richard paused to take in the view. His car was parked in the street, and he noticed dew drops glistening on its roof like tiny crystals of crushed ice. He followed Brydon and the others inside for a nightcap. Brydon and Angie were lying head to toe on the sofa. Jeremy was banging around in the kitchen, looking for glasses – he had a flagon of wine in his hand. The noise brought someone in pyjamas into the lounge. Richard knew him, his name was Patrick Duggan, a junior political science lecturer at the university and a brash, outspoken critic of apartheid who lambasted the government whenever he could. His letters to the Natal Mercury always attracted the ire and indignation of its more conservative readers.

"What's going on?" he asked, rubbing his eyes. "Shit, you buggers go to a party and then come back here to wake the dead. Jeremy, you've been here long enough now to know that the glasses are in the cupboard – not that one silly, the one above the sink. While you're at it, get me one as well. If you can't beat them, you might as well join them. Hello, Rich, didn't see you there. You staying for another late night session?"

Richard smiled. "Hi, Pat, sorry we woke you. Not sure about a session – it's already pretty late. I am happy to help Brydon flatten a bottle of port though."

A sleepy voice called from one of the inner rooms. "Patrick? Come back to bed."

"Who's that?" asked Brydon, "Do I know her?"

"No, I don't think so. Kathryn, her name's Kathryn – she's a teacher, from Maritzburg. Very sharp. She's one of us – not a comrade, but a card holder in the Liberal Party."

Patrick didn't go back to bed. He stayed up with them, drinking and chatting. Richard enjoyed their company, enjoyed sitting in on discussions that took him to places he had never been to before. They knew so much, were so well read, and could articulate their arguments with such rapier-like incisiveness that he felt like a babe in the woods by comparison. His career choice had led him into the sciences; but he wished at times like these that he had had more time for the arts, and more time to find himself philosophically.

***

In his befuddled state, Richard was unable to identify what had woken him. His head throbbed. An inky-black silence. The cushions were lumpy and uncomfortable. He pulled up the blanket and rolled over. Then he heard it again. A thumping sound, loud and insistent. He sat up on the couch and looked for his friends, thinking one of them was up and in the kitchen. He came to his senses and realised that someone was at the front door. He glanced at his watch and groaned. Nearly 4:00 am. He got up and groped for the wall light. He switched on the light and unlocked the door. Four men in long coats brushed past him and went inside.

"What's going on?" Brydon was now in the lounge. He had on a pair of underpants – nothing more. "Heard the commotion. What's going on? Who are you?"

"Police. I am Colonel Altman from the Security Police. We're looking for a Patrick Duggan. Where is he?"

Richard felt the blood draining from his face. His stomach balled up into a tight knot and he could feel his heart pounding in his chest.

The Colonel nodded at his men. They began to slink around the room like hyenas at a kill. Richard was appalled at their demeanour – so impassive, so cold and remote, not a flicker of emotion, nothing but a mechanical efficiency.

"Can I see the warrant?" he heard Brydon ask, "We have nothing to hide here."

Patrick walked in. A towel clung to his lean hips. "What's up?"

"Are you Patrick Duggan? Good. I am arresting you under Section Seventeen of the General Law Amendment Act Number Thirty-Seven of 1963. I am a commissioned officer and I do not need a warrant. Jensen, go with this man and stay with him while he gets dressed. Then bring him back to me."

"What the hell for?" Brydon's face was a picture of outrage. He knew – knew with bile rising in his throat that this was the infamous Ninety Day Detention Law, which meant that Patrick would simply disappear. Gone, just like that. For all intents and purposes, he wouldn't exist for up to ninety days. And without access to a lawyer or a priest. Even his parents would be denied access to him. "You can't just walk in here and arrest someone, just like that. What crime is he supposed to have committed?"

"His crime is politically motivated. He is an enemy of the State. I do not have to provide you with reasons."

"It's okay, Brydon. There's no point in kicking up a fuss. I'll go. Let me get dressed. Will you take care of Kath for me? And would you mind telling –"

"He'll do no such thing. Quoting a banned person is against the law."

Patrick left the room. They heard a female voice, loud and shrill, "Get out of here, you moron. I'm not getting dressed in front of you." Fainter, because of its lower tone, came Patrick's rejoinder, "He won't leave, love – just turn your back on him."

Altman turned his attention to Richard. He pulled out a notebook and stood with pencil poised. "Who are you? Another commie, hey?" Richard wilted. The stare from Altman's glassy eyes was too much for him and he crumbled; self-preservation was his only option.

"No, officer," the words flew from his mouth, "I'm Richard Barclay. I'm a doctor. This is my friend from school – I'm visiting him, that's all. Not really interested in politics. Don't belong to anything. I know nothing about –"

"Enough. Just answer the questions. I only asked for your name. Now, full name please. Date and place of birth? Address? Which university? Why that one? Employer? What were you doing at Salisbury Island? How do you know the detainee? For how long? Thank you. Sit down and shut up."

Richard felt he had run a marathon. He tottered across the room and collapsed into a chair beside Brydon at the dining table. His hands found each other; he began to pick his nails. Blood pounded his temples; he felt he was going to faint. He needed to concentrate on something, something to occupy his mind, so he watched the policemen searching through drawers and cupboards. They pulled books from shelves, flipped through them, and then tossed them on the floor behind them. Jeremy came into the room. Richard waved him over. "Sit down," he whispered, "Security Police. Shush! They've come for Pat! Yes, for Pat – not us. Don't say anything until you are asked to speak."

"What's this?" Altman held up a copy of *Lift the Ban* by Mary Turok, "This is banned – she's a communist. Is it yours? I'm confiscating it. And this one – what are you doing with Mao's *Little Red Book*? And this one by Lenin? Here's Lutuli's book. And this one, *Black Beauty* – what's it about? You black lovers are all the same, can't leave the black stuff alone. More filth – where did you get these Playboy magazines? They're *verboten*. And what do we have here? Karl Marx's *Das Kapital* – three volumes, what are they doing here? Man, you're sailing close to the wind – these are all banned. What? Don't give me that shit – I don't care if Duggan is a political science lecturer or not, this is subversive. And it's banned. You should know that – you're a lawyer. We're watching you. You'd better be careful my friend, very careful, or you'll be next for the chop."

Then he saw Jeremy. Without saying a word, he summoned him with curled forefinger, pointing at the ground in front of him. Jeremy got up and stood before him. He was subjected to the same questions. Then he was dismissed. "Sit," said Altman, "don't move unless I tell you to."

By the time Altman left, the sun was climbing up the trees outside, hand over hand. They took Patrick with them. And a pile of books and reams and reams of paper. The house was ransacked. The floor was littered with sheets of paper, cuttings, periodicals – all robbed from files that hung in desk drawers like frames in a beehive. And their treasured books, lying scattered on the floor in every room like gutted fish, stared at them with vacant eyes.

Richard drove home dangerously fast. He had no idea how to quell the demons that writhed and snarled in his tummy. To witness the iron fist of the state – to see it so supremely cock-sure and so omnipotent, so certain that its ends justified its means – was one thing, but to be accosted by it, to be ruffled by it so callously and then to be brushed aside with such contempt was for him, unnerving and filled him with dread. He made up his mind then and there that nothing on God's earth would ever induce him to run afoul of the law. He shivered. Terror spurred him to drive with reckless disregard – twice he drove through red traffic lights – he fled, with his tail tucked between his legs.

One day in May, Richard was sitting in the lounge of the Royal Hotel, waiting for his mother. A gentle breeze, wafting in through the open windows, ruffled the newspaper he was reading and chilled his ears. Winter was on its way – no wonder women had coats on and men were in jackets or cardigans. He got up and looked for a more sheltered seat. Then he saw Molly doubling up the stairs.

"Sorry I'm late, Rich," she kissed him and held onto his arm, "I know you have to get back to the hospital, but as I was in town for the day, I thought we could have lunch together. I booked a table downstairs – curry and rice, or cheese platters – quick and easy. Shall we go?"

The room was full. They were ushered to their table by an Indian waiter dressed in white. Richard ordered cheese platters for them both, a beer for himself and a rock shandy for his mother.

"How is Mary? Haven't seen or heard from her since her engagement party."

"Oh, she and Cam are busy getting everything ready for the wedding. I think that short engagements are the best – what's the point of waiting?"

"How long was yours?"

"I didn't have one. In fact, we didn't have a proper wedding either. We were naughty – we just moved in together and shacked up as they say. Happened a lot those days. During the war, there was no tomorrow – you just lived for the day and hoped like hell that you'd survive. Then one day we decided to make it official. So, we went to the local Magistrate's Office and got it done. Phoebe was the only member of my family there and your Uncle Ted was the only other Barclay. Which was nice because we never saw him again. Was killed the following year at El Alamein. Where was I? Mary. The sooner she can get herself up onto the game farm as Mrs Cameron Wilkes and give her husband a hand fulltime, the better it will be for everyone. Being a school teacher and only being able to help out during school holidays, hasn't been good. You know the wedding is now in December, don't you?"

"Yes. When Cam heard that I have September off, he asked if I wouldn't mind spending time at Mkuze for him – you know, keeping an eye on things – while he and Mary use the Michaelmas school holidays to get things done for the wedding. Of course, I agreed – I'm thinking of spending my whole leave up there. Wouldn't mind nipping off to Ndumu for a night or two while I'm there. Oh, by the way –"

"Richard! Hello! Haven't seen you for ages!"

Richard spun round in his chair. Magda. He closed his eyes and looked again, drinking her in. It was Magda alright, and her magnificent eyes shone right through him, warming his soul. He leapt to his feet dazzled, his mind racing, not sure if he should offer her his hand or kiss her cheek.

"Hello, Magda, nice to see you again," he could feel himself blushing and suspected that he was stumbling over his words, "yes, a long time. At the club, wasn't it? You were with Jaco then, what happened to him?"

"Jaco? Goodness, Richard! That was ages ago. Wasn't serious, you know – not my type. I haven't a clue what he's up to these days – but Andre still sees him."

"Gosh I'm sorry, you know my mother? Mum, this is Magda. Magda Celliers – you remember her, don't you? She's Andre's sister – they used to live near us in the village."

Molly had been appraising her. She remembered what Mary had told her. "Of course," she held out her hand, "but it was a long, long time ago."

"I'm here with some friends," she pointed behind her at a table where three girls were sitting, "we are going up to Shongweni this afternoon to watch the polo. How about you, Richard, what are you doing these days?"

"I'm at Addington. A couple more months and then I'll be going into private practice. How about you?"

"Oh, nothing as flash as you. I'm in public relations. Work for a property company. We do up-market estates all up the coast. Starting at Umhlanga. Come and have a look and I'll sell you a block overlooking the sea – you can have your own little piece of paradise."

Richard could imagine her getting people to sign on the dotted line. She would only have to flutter her eyelids or show a bit of leg and they would be tripping over themselves and reaching for their pens. He couldn't stop gawking – the memory of holding her in his arms came back, flushing his face crimson. Longing, like a released spring, sprang up and grabbed him by the throat, constricting his breathing. A little piece of paradise! His mind cavorted with a million wild ideas.

"I'm not in the market," he said, searching for something to say that would keep her standing beside him longer. "The property market, I mean. So, you live in Durban?"

"Yes. But I spent a while in England. Went to visit my mom's family."

"Magda, why don't you sit down? You two seem to have a lot of catching up to do."

"Thank you, Mrs Barclay, but I must go. Say, Rich, if you're not doing anything, why don't you come up to the polo this evening? There'll be something going on there for sure. Or we could go out for something to eat?"

There it was. A bold invitation from the prettiest girl in the world. It didn't matter that it jarred ever so slightly – simply because it seemed the wrong way round – but the aberration did tinkle a warning, as though from a tiny bell buried deep within. All the niggling little doubts which, since he had last seen her and which, in the intervening period, had accumulated in his mind like grass seed in the radiator of a car driving through long grass, were now flushed out and swept away by the torrent of regard he saw pouring from her big, luminous eyes. Richard hated himself, hated the way he succumbed to her charm, yet, at the same time, he loved being the focus of her attention. His mind was racing. Who could he get to do his evening ward round for him at the hospital?

"Why not? I don't have anything on – I knock off today at 4:00 pm. I could be there a couple of hours after that. Where shall I find you?"

"Wonderful. I'll be in the Nederburg tent. See you then. Bye, Mrs Barclay."

Richard watched her walk back to her table. The cheeks of her nicely rounded bottom, pressing full and firm against the sheath of her short blue skirt, took his breath away. He had an urge to rush after her, and grab them, one in each hand, knead them, and sink his fingers into them with voluptuous abandon. What he would have given right then to spin her around and crush her to him!

"Sit down, Rich," Molly tugged at his sleeve, "here, help yourself to some cheese – the waiter brought it while you were talking to Magda. She's quite something, isn't she? Are you sure you want to run off after her, all the way to Shongweni?"

"Not at all. I'm not running after her as you put it, I am simply accepting an invitation. That's all. You don't like her?"

"Me? I hardly know her. It's not a question of like or dislike. But she is madly attractive. Girls like that are used to snapping their fingers and having men at their beck and call. All I'm saying is, be careful. I don't want you to get hurt."

She studied her son's face and realised that there was little point in pursuing the subject any further – his mind was made up. She picked up the newspaper which Richard had brought from the lounge and flipped it over.

"Did you see this, Rich? Muhammed Ali has been found guilty of draft evasion in the US and has been stripped of his boxing titles. What do you make of that?"

Richard had a grudging respect for Ali as a fighter but couldn't help feeling that his antics were deliberately provocative, designed to rock the status quo. He knew it was ludicrous to be sensitive or to feel personally affronted, but he detested anything that ruffled his feathers. Guilt or complicity – for him they were one and the same – invariably brought out his goosebumps, just as surely as a cool draught always seemed to find his exposed skin. So, when people like Muhammed Ali wagged their fingers, his first reaction was to rug up, thinking that their icy blasts were aimed at him. He half hoped that a boxer would emerge with the wherewithal to put Muhammed Ali in his place and teach him some respect and manners – preferably a white boxer, for that would restore the order of things and would put the icing on the cake.

"Oh, I don't know." He couldn't get Magda out of his head. "Seems a bit of a loudmouth to me. Says it's because of his religion. And his opposition to the Vietnam War. Isn't he just thumbing his nose at everyone?"

"Well, you know the Americans now have nearly half a million troops in Vietnam. The mood in the country is changing – it's anti-war, isn't it, people are turning against it. They should never have gone in in the first place. Domino theory is a lot of –"

"Yah, but he broke the law, didn't he? You are always going on about the Rule of Law. He was drafted and he refused to go."

"Ah, but what if your conscience says the law is wrong? What if it likes the law, but finds the cause to be unjust or, quite simply, immoral? I think it was Gandhi who said, 'There is a higher court than the courts of justice and that is the court of conscience.' It supersedes all other courts. You cannot take issue with Ali for following his conscience, can you?"

"No, suppose not. But what's the world coming to? It's a bloody mess wherever you look. Communism is on the march, widespread protests in the States, Jews and Arabs at each other's throats, Africans demanding independence right across the continent and here we are, on the arse-end of Africa, pariahs of the world, trying to hold back the tide."

Molly watched Richard take a swig from his glass. He put it down and busied himself, buttering a bread roll. She reached over and helped herself to a piece of cheese.

"Rich, you look agitated. What's biting you?"

"Biting me?" He looked up. "Nothing really. It's just that the world seems to be falling apart. I mean, just look at the States – it's the most powerful country on earth and yet their own backyard is a mess. There is all this black power stuff – you heard Malcolm X, didn't you? The guy that got bumped off last year? He was a firebrand. Preached Islam, disobedience, violence – anything to upset the status quo." He held up his hand. "Let me finish. I know you're going to tell me about Martin Luther King and why he got the Nobel Peace Prize and stuff like that, but he too stirred up the mob – preached non-violence and all that but look what happened! Mayhem wasn't it. Cities on fire, looting all over the place, fights with the police – it was ugly, whichever way you want to dice it. And that's in America. Imagine what could happen here!"

"Well, I'm not as pessimistic as you are. I see the Blacks in America beginning to flex their muscle and demand the equality and justice that the Civil War promised them. They've been patient, for a hundred years. I think they are entitled to rock the white establishment and claim their just desserts. Wouldn't you? Wear their shoes, Richard. Yes, there has been violence. But who started it – is not white intransigence at least partially to blame? And what about the police – don't they have something to answer for as well? Tell me, how else do you get people to give you a place at the table and a fair share of the pie that your labour has helped to create? How do you get the sort of change you want when you have talked yourself blue in the face for a hundred years and have precious little to show for it? How else do you make Whites sit up and take notice of your predicament?"

Molly reached over and laid her hand on Richard's arm. She knew she should be trying harder to keep the teacher tone from her voice – should, at the same time, dismount from her political hobbyhorse, the one that gave Bill so much angst. She patted his arm and went on speaking.

"There is an argument, you know, one that says only revolution begets permanent change. Think of the French Revolution – or, talking about the US, the American Revolution. Evolution or revolution? They are a bit like the tortoise and the hare, aren't they – despite the lovely sentiment in *Aesop's Fables*, we all know that the tortoise is no match for the hare, don't we. You know what? Not long ago, Jack Kennedy said something like, 'those who make peaceful revolution impossible will make violent revolution inevitable.' Pretty perceptive, I reckon. You see, some people would rather die on their feet than go on living on their knees. Think about that too, Rich. Those who have power, cling to it – like shit to a blanket, as your father would say. Those who do not have it, find themselves in the end compelled to take matters into their own hands to get it – or to get enough of it to give them a say in how they want to live their lives. Simple as that.

"But, Richy, don't get your knickers in a knot over all this. We are living in exciting times – the tectonic plates are moving and there is nothing you or I can do about it. We have to remain alert and sure-footed; we have to move with the times and not fall through the cracks. The old world is dead, gone forever – what we are experiencing right now are the aftershocks. Colonialism and its complacent old-world thinking are in their death throes. A new world is emerging, creating new fault lines. We might be able to stop the clock, but we can never stop time. Everything is in a state of flux – nothing stands still forever. Embrace it! I actually feel thrilled to be part of it all, I really do."

"Well, I wish I could share your optimism. I would just like things to be more orderly, more settled. Wish I had a crystal ball. All that's going on now depresses the hell out of me – makes me want to escape to a deserted island."

Molly laughed. She passed the cheese platter back to Richard.

"Can't really see you on a deserted island – with no one else on it, not even Magda? Oh relax, Rich! I'm only teasing! I've said enough – Daddy would be pulling his hair out by now! If you want to sleep well at night, then, as I've told you many times, follow your conscience.

Someone said that conscience is a dog that can't bite, but never stops barking."

Richard grinned at her and took her hand in his. He was about to say something when he noticed the time on his watch. He had to go. He ate quickly, chewing on what had been said. Magda. The hospital. He had to make arrangements so that he could meet her. Molly's voice interrupted his train of thoughts and he looked up quickly.

"Sorry, Mum, you were saying?"

"I was just saying that Phoebe has written to say that she's thinking of coming out here for a holiday. Phoebe? Your godmother, remember? She's never been to Africa and would like to come and see us. She's been nursing in London now for twenty-five years and has long service leave coming up. That's exciting – you haven't seen her since your christening. Perhaps we can persuade her to come for the wedding. Daddy will have to help her – she doesn't have much money."

"Oh, that'll be nice. Coming here, I mean."

"Yes. You know that she introduced me to Daddy? She never quite made the boat – she never married. Blokes didn't take to her for some reason – can't think why as she's awfully nice –"

"There you are. When guys tell me a girl is nice, I know straightaway that she's unattractive."

"That's pretty crude. Beauty is only skin deep, you know – it doesn't last. There's more to a successful marriage than just good looks. Phoebe would have made a wonderful wife."

"I get that. But surely you need good looks to get you to first base? I'm not saying every girl has to be a corker, but she has to at least have enough to turn the eye, don't you think?"

Molly speared another piece of cheese and placed it on her plate. She was thinking of Magda. "Rich, looks do help, of course they do. All I'm saying is that there's more to it than that. Here's a thought for you. Think of a blind man – he cannot see at all. But he finds a woman, falls in love, and marries her. What help would good looks be in that situation? I say that the blind man sees beauty in a very different form. He finds it where his eyes cannot go – in happiness, kindness, companionship – things like that. Anyway, I think you've got it the wrong way round."

"What do you mean?"

"Well, I've just read Robert Ardrey's *African Genesis*. You should read it. He makes it quite clear that in the animal kingdom, it's all about territory. We are, says Ardrey, all animals – our instincts and behaviours, since we stepped out of the trees, have been shaped by our genes. So, the male of the species fights to establish a territory that females find attractive – big enough, I suppose, to guarantee the survival of her offspring. Or, where territory itself is not so important, then the male will rely on his physical attributes – his plumage, his strength, his horns, things like that. It's actually the female that makes the call – she decides who will suit her best, not the other way round."

"Well, I'm not sure about that. If that's so, then why didn't Aunty Phoebe find someone?"

Molly shrugged. "Good question. Don't know. Haven't finished the book yet."

Richard noticed that droplets of condensation on his beer glass were making the newspaper wet. He refolded it and moved it aside. Two words, 'Progressive Party' in bold type, caught his eye. They came into focus as a caption beneath the image of Magda in his mind and held his attention.

"Mum, we've just had an election and the Progs made no headway at all. One seat in 1961 and still only one seat this year. If it wasn't for Suzman, the Progs wouldn't exist, would they? Makes me so depressed. I mean, a qualified franchise makes so much sense. Why can't the voters see that? Even English-speaking voters – who you'd think would champion liberal causes – turned their back on it at the ballot box. Why is that?"

Molly took a sip of her drink. She glanced around the room, half expecting to find someone eavesdropping. "Well, that one seat represents the conscience of the country. Now, I know you like the Progs, but I suspect you do so because they make you feel safe."

Seeing Richard was about to protest, she raised her hand. "No, hear me out. You like them because their policies are reasonable and sit comfortably with your conscience. But you also like them because you fear the consequences of one-man, one-vote. You think that will be the end of civilisation as we know it. You think that moderate non-Whites, the ones that have a stake in the economy and therefore have something to lose, ought to embrace what the Progs are offering. Well, given the choice between what they have now and what the Progs offer, they'll go for the Progs every time. But that's not what they want. Only universal suffrage, irrespective of race, creed, or colour, will satisfy them, and rightly so, I reckon. That's why I'm with the Liberals – they have no parliamentary representation, by the way. That's why I come to town whenever I can and stand with the Black Sash girls. It's what my conscience tells me to do, Richy. My conscience.

"Now, getting back to the English voters. You know, so long as they can make money, enjoy their nice houses and their big cars – can have their gin and tonics, their compliant servants and what have you, then they couldn't care less. By and large, the English people here have been quite happy for the Nats to do the dirty work and keep the Blacks in check. What's that? Oh, not all, of course not. There are a lot of good people, from all walks of life, who every day try to make a difference. Yes, they hear the inner voice, yes, they respond to it and yes, they do what they can to make the lot of their fellow man easier to bear. And that's great – I'm not denigrating it at all. But collectively, us English have gone to sleep. We've been seduced by the good life – out with morality, in with prosperity, so to speak. It's as simple as that. You remember Titus? Busisiwe's husband? Well, he once told me something that I have never forgotten. He said that white liberals are not much better than the government. Why? Because at least with the Nationalists you know where you stand – in front of something hard and immoveable. But with well-intentioned liberals, you feel like you're in a bus that appears to be moving forward, but it's really an optical illusion – the engine is running, the wheels are turning merrily but in fact they are spinning in the sand and there is no progress. The do-gooders, he said, will always cluck sympathetically and promise to do everything they can for the black man – they will even mop his brow – they will do everything, except get off his back."

Richard reached out and patted his mother's arm. "Mum, I love talking to you. You are always so clear in your thinking and somehow you always see the bright side of things. I wish I could be more like you; I really do. I just worry that the world is coming undone." He looked at his watch. The ward that he was about to visit with a consultant surgeon flashed into his mind. Then Magda came back. Time, he thought, never enough time. "I have to go. I'll pay on the way out. No, no. It's my shout." He got up and kissed his mother. His hand lingered in her grasp.

"Before you go, how's Fanakanye handling city life? Is he looking after you properly? And cooking alright – not too many botch-ups, I hope?"

"He's settled in well. Took me forever to get him registered as a live-in domestic servant. But all good. I fixed his room for him, got him a decent bed and what have you. He's doing fine. Still a farm boy at heart – not used to city life yet."

"That's good. He's a good chap. Have fun tonight. With Magda, I mean. Bye."

"Thanks, Mum. Say hello to Dad. Bye for now, I must fly."

She watched him walk out. When he reached the door, he turned and waited for her eyes. He had that forsaken look, just as he had when she used to drop him off at boarding school. She waved. He smiled and waved back. Then he was gone. Her heart jumped and she reached for a tissue.

3

The sun, like the needle of the petrol gauge in front of him, was running on empty by the time Richard arrived at the grounds. The field of play was deserted – obviously, the tournament was over for the day. He parked his car and locked it. There was a lot of noise in the tents alongside the field and so he headed off in that direction. As he walked along the touchline, he could see the turf scuffed up and torn by

144

countless hoofmarks; they stood out, casting little shadows in the setting sun. Somehow, they reminded him of crabs on a moonlit beach that come out in their thousands to forage on the smooth wet sands when the tide is spent. He filled his nostrils with those familiar horsey smells which he loved so much, and he paused to take it all in. There in the distance were the horses, stamping their feet and swishing their tails. They were being rubbed down and readied for the night. He listened to the horse boys talking as they groomed, some to each other, others to the horses. Richard kept walking. The Nederburg tent was full of people and a haze of cigarette smoke made the inside lights look fuzzy. He stopped just inside and lit a cigarette, giving his eyes time to search the room.

Magda and two other women were seated on stools with their backs to the bar. In front of them, in a semi-circle, stood half a dozen men, still dressed in their polo regalia. They held glasses and laughed loudly at each other's jokes. With their dark jackets, white riding breeches and their dark, knee-high leather boots, they reminded Richard of bumblebees hovering around a flower, waiting for a turn at the nectar. The flower, in all her resplendent glory, was Magda. He hardly noticed her two companions who, by comparison, seemed like buds yet to open. There was another man standing by her side – close, but not actually touching her. He was tall and handsome and had a moustache. His face glowed – it was obvious that he believed that he was the chosen one. Magda looked up and saw him standing in the doorway. She waved.

"Rich! Over here. Come here and save me from these wretches!" She laughed and jumped off her seat and stretched out her hand to him. "Gentlemen, this is my old friend Richard Barclay."

She introduced him and he shook hands. The names meant nothing to him and were soon lost. He leaned on the bar with one elbow and beckoned the barman.

"Drink, Sir? What would you like?"

Magda perched herself on the barstool beside him and leaned close, allowing her perfume to envelop him. "I've just finished my drink. If you want one, go ahead. Or we could go. What do you think?"

Richard's heart began to hammer in his chest. "Go?" He searched her face. "I thought there was something happening here tonight. But if you'd like to go somewhere else, that's fine by me."

She leaned closer and whispered in his ear. "Let's go then. There's not much happening here. Besides," she reached up impulsively and cupped her hands around his ear. A muscle in his thigh began to twitch. "Besides," she said again, and this time he could almost feel her tongue, "I want you all to myself." She giggled; a hot, deep-throated gurgle that strung him as taut as a bowstring.

He replayed the words to himself. They were whispered, but what he imagined they suggested roared in his ears like an avalanche on a mountain – indeed, they induced in him a sense of floundering, as though the gimbals of his compass had been knocked out of kilter.

"Why don't we go into town and have dinner? Just the two of us?"

He wasn't dreaming. Her face was close, her eyes huge. "Sure," he said, "why not?"

He turned his head. The ring of pretenders were staring at him as though he had cuckolded them. Emboldened, and now feeling ten feet tall, he turned around and faced them, resting his elbows on the bar behind him.

"Sorry to break up the party, guys," he said with unfamiliar nonchalance that curdled the words in his mouth, "but we have to go. Got a table reserved in town." He couldn't help himself from adding, "Thanks for looking after her until I got here."

She clung to his arm as they walked in the dark to his car. He wasn't sure what he felt or how he thought he should feel. His life had suddenly concertinaed, one moment sandwiched into the next. Never had he felt so powerless, so like a puppet dangling on a string, moving only at the behest of some irresistible force. But, by the same token, never had he felt so reckless and so exhilarated as to throw caution to the wind.

They drove down into the city. From their conversation, one might have thought that they were a married couple returning from a day in the countryside – they responded to each other's questions with attentive civility, but for the most part they sat in agreeable silence and perused their own thoughts.

"Where would you like to go?"

Magda turned in her seat. "What about the Cuban Hat? We can sit in the car and have a toasted sandwich."

"Great. But you sure you don't want to go somewhere … well, more upmarket?"

"No." She laughed and prodded him with her finger, "You're a funny one – me, upmarket?"

"Ah, you know what I mean." Then added gallantly, "A classy place for a classy lady."

She laughed again, a deep throaty laugh. He glanced sideways and smiled at her. Streetlights lit up her face and danced on her eyes. They were shining. He gripped the steering wheel. "Here we are."

He turned off the motor and flicked on the indicator – the flashing light would be a signal to the waiters. One came and they ordered. He turned off the indicator and reached into his pocket for his cigarettes.

"Cigarette? You know, I don't even know if you smoke." She laughed and shook her head. "Mind if I have one – in the car, I mean?" Again, she shook her head. He used the dashboard lighter and lit it. Then he opened the window and exhaled. Anything to keep his hands occupied. There has to be a reason why she chose this place, he told himself – is it what I think? He knew that courting couples came here to

146

kiss and cuddle. He wanted to. Desperately. But he couldn't find the courage to make the first move for fear of rejection.

"Tell me, Rich, when's your birthday?" The unexpected question hit him like a bug in his eye and he blinked, repeatedly. What on earth did she want to know that for?

"What? My birthday, why?"

"I just want to know your star sign. You believe in it, don't you?"

"Well, not really." He thought astrology was rubbish, but he wasn't going to tell her that. He pulled on his cigarette. "Never given it much thought. But always willing to learn. So, my birthday is in March. Thirtieth of March, to be exact. Now, you tell me –"

"Why, Rich, that makes you an Aries. Amazing! I thought so. Mine is on the fifth of December – that makes me Sagittarius. That means we are meant for each other!"

His heart missed a beat and he gaped at her. She lifted her knee so she could turn and face him better. Her skirt slid back, exposing pale flesh above her knee. He swallowed. She saw his eyes fall downwards like a pair of gannets plunging into the sea and she toyed with her hem, watching him closely. He couldn't take his eyes away. Then, with languid fingers, she straightened her dress. He looked up, and when he realised that she had seen what he had been looking at, he blushed furiously and flicked his half-smoked cigarette out the window.

"Aries and Sagittarius have the same element – fire. That means they are compatible. Fire people are passionate and adventurous. Also, impulsive – they look after they leap. Do you?"

Before he could answer, there was a knock on the window. It was the waiter. Richard adjusted his window so the waiter could attach his tray to it. Richard checked the bill and paid him. He added a generous tip and then passed Magda her toasted sandwich.

"Do you always tip like that?"

"Like what?" He knew what she meant. "These poor buggers sink or swim on the tips they get."

"My Dad only tips if he gets really good service."

"Well, each to his own. Here's your coffee. I'll put it here."

"Can you put the radio on?"

He turned it on. Did that mean she was no longer interested in talking to him? Had he failed? They ate in silence for a while, and he stared out the window at the cars parked around them. He was desperate to regain the spell-like intimacy that he felt had been building up before the waiter's arrival.

"I don't think I'm the sort of person who leaps before he looks," he said with his mouth full, "but then again, we seldom know ourselves as others know us, do we?"

"Oh, I don't know, Rich. But I've read a lot about zodiac signs."

"Tell me what they say – the signs, I mean."

"Well, there's a lot to it, you know. People all over the world follow it closely – it can't all be wrong. I reckon it works; I check my stars every day in the paper. I know that Aries people, like everyone else, have lots of qualities in common – being passionate and adventurous is right up there. And they're also super competitive – won't stop until they've got what they want."

He stared at her. Something snapped inside his head. "Let me tell you what I want." The words were not his, yet their huskiness came from his own throat. "I want you. Only you."

His hand no longer belonged to him – it reached out on its own, following the words like a cat after a mouse, found the lock of hair on her cheek and held it between thumb and forefinger. He brushed it back. Gently. Slowly, and with infinite tenderness, he stroked her cheek, staring into her eyes, daring her to stop him. She reached up and drew his hand towards her lips. Her breath was hot and her lips, soft and moist. Then, wrapping both hands around it, she kissed it and clutched it tightly under her chin. Her heart fluttered against the back of his hand like a trapped bird. Richard leaned over and kissed her, more a brushing of lips than a proper kiss. He drew back, half expecting she would withdraw, but she didn't, only stared at him with hot, liquid eyes – so he kissed her again, more ardently this time. Her mouth quivered and then opened, salt-alive and deliciously succulent; almost without knowing what it was doing, his tongue found hers. There was the sound of crashing waves in his ears, a wild thumping in his chest as, with voluptuous disregard for restraint, they sought each other out.

His coffee cup rolled on the floor of the car, and outside, he could hear a car reversing. He came up for air. He hadn't imagined it; she was still there, panting, short shallow breaths through parted lips. She reached for him. "Kiss me again, Aries – kiss me." He dipped his head and kissed her. Never in his wildest dreams had he experienced anything like it. Her mouth seemed insatiable – it couldn't get enough of his lips, feasting on them greedily and sucking his tongue deep inside. An immense sense of pride, of being a conquering hero, overcame him – he felt he should throw back his head like a lion and roar to the world. His hand, with a mind of its own, began to work its way up her side. He kept his mouth glued to hers and closed his fingers around her breast. He felt her breath check in her throat, a tiny gasp that echoed through his ears, and then she relaxed, giving him licence. He squeezed it. The world stood still. Nothing was more important to him right then than the breast in his hand – he kept kneading it, and fondling it, and trying all the while to imagine it unclothed. She stirred and lifted his head.

"I'm feeling hot," she said, "what about we go somewhere more comfortable?"

He didn't reply. His fingers, scrabbling at the buttons of her blouse like a child opening a present, would not be denied. He tried to get it off her shoulders. She was wearing a black brassiere. In the dim light her thinly veiled breasts bulged and gleamed – she looked like a Greek goddess, carved from alabaster. He reached for her again.

"Wait," she said, stopping him, "let me."

She reached behind her and unsnapped her bra with practiced ease. For a moment, but only for a moment, he wondered how many men she had done this for, but then didn't care. Her breasts stared at him. There, in the carpark, cramped in the front seats and heedless of what passers-by might or might not see, he buried his face in her chest and nuzzled her breasts, from side to side, covering them with kisses. Above his head, wrapped in her arms, he heard faint crooning sounds that nearly drove him mad. He wanted more, and silently cursed the lack of space in the car. A bold thought struck him.

"Your place or mine?"

She sat back, surprised at his audacity. His eyes were shining bright and keen, like a hound with its quarry in a bolthole. Keeping her eyes on his face, she rearranged her clothing and covered herself up. A faint smile was playing with her lips. "Do you think we should?"

"God yes." And then, in an attempt to make his intentions less blatant and somehow more respectable, he added, "I just thought we could go somewhere a bit more comfortable; you know – somewhere where we could, well, sort of kick back, relax, have a drink – that sort of thing."

Magda arched her eyebrows in mock surprise and smiled. "A drink? Why, I'd love a drink. What about your place? Not sure we have much to drink at our place." She saw his eyes widen. "I share a flat with two other girls. On Ridge Road. Where's your place?"

"Along Chelmsford Road. I have a downstairs apartment. On my own. Just let me get rid of this tray and we'll hit the road."

They drove up Berea Road and turned into Chelmsford Road, which was lined with tall, leafy trees. All the way, Magda kept her hand on Richard's knee. It gave him a profound sense of possession that made his chest swell and filled his mind with indescribable wellbeing. She spent the night. It was the first time he had made love to a woman. He was grateful that she did not find him wanting – or, if she did, she said nothing to hurt his feelings. He awoke early in the morning. The night shadows were turning grey. He sat up, memories coursing through his mind and thrilling him. He felt incredibly pleased with himself and what he had achieved. She was awake; her dark eyes watching him. The beauty of her naked body stirred him to the quick and aroused him. She reached for him.

"Come," she said, "come."

He went into her arms. This time she slowed him. And taught him. They made excellent love.

Afterwards, she said that she had to get home and change for work. He looked at his watch. Fanakanye would be in the kitchen soon.

"Would you like something to eat before we go? I can get my boy to rustle up something for you if you like."

"You have a servant here?"

"Yes, Fanakanye and I grew up together on the farm. He's my man – we go everywhere together. He's pretty good in the kitchen – my mum taught him the basics. What would you like? Couple of eggs and bacon, toast – name it."

She was impressed. Sugar farmers had so much money. She didn't know anybody else in their age group who had their own personal servant. "No, thanks very much but I'd like to get back. I'll grab something to eat at my place. We really should go now."

He drove her home. In the early morning light, as the shadows retreated from the houses along the streets and the city began to slowly wake, doubt scurried back into his mind like a cat returning from its nightly prowl. Was this the beginning of a relationship? A one-night stand that he had heard so much about? When would she see him again? And the big one, the one that towered over him like a huge tree in a forest, where had she learned so much about making love – who had taught her? A thousand questions, all more or less around the same theme, crowded his mind and muddled his thinking. Oh, for just one sentence that would put his mind at rest! He told himself that what they had just shared was too fragile, still too young for him to press for answers – deep down though, he wasn't sure he could cope if they were not to his liking. Richard opened the car door for her and wrapped his arms around her, nuzzling and kissing her, and marvelling at the soft contours of her body, pressed up against him. He didn't want to let her go.

"Steady on, Rich. You'll get me started. Not here. Not on the street." She disentangled herself from him but held onto his hand. "I'm tied up for the next few days, but why don't you give me a call and we'll try to do something over the weekend?"

He was crestfallen. "That's three whole days away. I can't last that long."

She laughed. "Silly. I'm not going away forever." When she saw the doleful look on his face, she reached up with both hands and tweaked his cheeks playfully. She kissed him.

"I do have work to do. If it'll make you feel better, then here's a promise. I'll be here on Friday evening, ready to go out with you – for the whole weekend, if you like."

Mollified, but not entirely happy, he walked into the building with her, and they took the lift to the fifth floor. She unlocked her door, dropped the key back into her bag, and turned back into his arms. They stood in the doorway and kissed. Her eyes were shining, and she smiled happily at him.

"And now, my hot-blooded Aries, it's time to go."

Richard drove through the city centre and headed towards Addington Hospital. He had not showered; her scent, like suntan lotion worked into the skin and oozing from every pore, would, he hoped, linger in his nostrils, and keep her with him, all day long. He was in a state of unmitigated bliss, but he was going to be in theatre all day so reluctantly, and with great effort, he forced himself to concentrate on the operations he was about to perform.

4

Gordon came home to Somkhele on that weekend to surprise Thandi. He hadn't seen her for a long time. He knew that she was home between jobs and that on Monday she would start her new job, working as a nursing sister for the outpatients at the Mission Hospital up at Ubombo.

The purported reason for his visit was that he wanted to surprise Thandi and be the one to drive her to work, but in reality, he wanted to be alone with her to ask her a favour. He loaded her bags into the car, and they began their journey.

"Thandi, I have something to tell you."

"You are not getting married?" He laughed, and so did she.

"No. No time for that. Now listen. *Ungayigcina imfihlo?*"

"Can I keep a secret? Of course, but it depends. What is it?"

"I am telling you and no one else. *Hawu*, these cows." He slowed down and drove wide of two cows that were standing in the middle of road. He changed gear and Thandi noticed as they passed that one cow had a crooked horn and mournful eyes. "You must not tell anyone, not even our mother or Titus. You promise?"

Thandi turned back to him and gripped his arm with both hands. "A secret that we cannot even tell our mother? We have never done such a thing. It is unheard of. Has something happened? Are you in trouble?"

Gordon prised open her fingers and gently freed his arm. He kept smiling, while keeping his eyes on the road. The car rattled along and in the rear-view mirror, he could see clouds of dust billowing out behind them and hazing the view. "No, sis, no trouble. Before I tell you, I must know that you will not tell anyone. Promise?"

"I promise. But you are making me frightened. Tell me, what is it?"

"I am going away. *Ngizokweqa.* For some time, I have been working with my comrades in *uMkhonto we Sizwe.* They have asked me to go overseas. I cannot tell you where I am going or exactly when I am leaving – I do not know yet. Thandi, you and I are one. I am telling you just in case anything happens to me, and I do not come back. Please, be strong and take this key. It is to a box that a lawyer in Durban is looking after for me."

He handed her a sealed envelope. She pulled her hand back and would not take it. He looked at her and saw how scared she was. He slowed down a little and reached over to drop the envelope in her lap. Her fingers reached out tentatively and secured it; she could feel the key inside – it was large and felt quite heavy. This was not the Gordon she knew. And he was asking her to become involved in something she knew could land her in trouble.

"Gordon, please tell me. Why are you doing this? Making trouble – for me, I mean."

"The lawyer's name is Hamilton," he went on, "Brydon Hamilton. Remember his name. He works at a law firm called Shepparton, in Smith Street. The box is in a safe in his office. Only open it if I tell you to or if you hear that something has happened to me. In the box is a diary, my Will, and some other personal documents."

"But, Gordon, I am frightened. How –"

"Hush. One day, when the time is right, I shall resign from school and then, without anyone knowing why or how, I shall simply disappear. Nobody must know. Nobody."

She began to cry. Her big day was being ruined and she felt miserable and frightened. He pulled over onto the side of the road in the shade of some fever trees. She opened her window and a tepid stillness, so typical of the *bushveld*, poured in. He turned in his seat and took her hand. "Please, Thandi, if you cry, I shall cry. Listen, you have nothing to fear – you are not doing anything wrong. This is just an envelope with a key inside it. That's all. There is no law saying you cannot keep an envelope for someone you love."

"What's made you like this? Is there no other way?"

"You know, before I went to Fort Hare, Titus told me to be true to myself. I have thought long and hard about what I am doing, and I believe now that I am being true to myself. I do not want to trouble him or our mother with any of this – they are getting old, and this would worry them too much. After I am gone –"

"How will I know that you have gone?"

"I shall call you. After I have gone, you can tell them – Titus will understand. And I will write to you. Often. And you can share the letters with them, if you like – there will be nothing in them that they cannot see. I am asking you to do this because I trust you. Please don't worry. You may never have to visit the lawyer. I could be back without you ever having to open my box. So, *dadewethu,* please do not cry. I shall be alright. Trust me."

He leaned across and dried her tears with his handkerchief. "Now, let's forget about all this. Tell me about this new job you are going to at Ubombo." He settled back into his seat and steered the car back onto the road. He wanted to cheer her up. "I am so proud of my sister! Imagine, being a nursing sister at the age of twenty! Amazing!"

They drove on. She stared out the window with unseeing eyes. On their right, a prominent escarpment rose up and on the other side of it, across the flats, was the Indian Ocean. They drove past Hluhluwe and through sisal plantations, heading northwards to Mkuze. Two quite distinct mountains got bigger and bigger the closer they got.

"Do you know those mountains?"

"No," said Thandi and she ducked her head to see out Gordon's window, "should I?"

"That is Tshaneni and the other one is Gaza. It is where Dinizulu defeated Zibhebhu and our Mandlakazi forefathers with the help of the *Boers*. It was the last great battle our people fought. Thousands were killed. After that, the *Boers* came like jackals and picked the carcass clean. They took nearly all the land. It was the end of Zululand."

Suddenly Thandi remembered. She gripped Gordon's arm.

"Tshaneni? Our grandfather was there, wasn't he? I have heard –"

"Yes, he was an *imidibi*. I have heard him tell the story how our forces were betrayed. An English writer wrote a story about it."

"Really? How do you know that?"

"I'm a teacher, remember. The book is about the Zulu kings, seen through English eyes. Not very good. I saw it in the library one day when I was looking up something for a history lesson."

Gordon pointed out the window. "To think that *Mkhulu* was right there on those hills! He was lucky to escape. You know, our cattle and our women were hidden in the valley right below Ubombo where you are going. They had a terrible time."

They drove in silence. Thandi was thinking of her grandfather. He was very old now, but his mind was as keen as ever. Titus would take Busisiwe to see him as often as he could. She noticed a high, closely wired fence running for mile after mile alongside the road.

"What's that, Gordon? That fence is very high – cattle can't jump that high, can they?"

"No, they can't. That's a game fence. It's high so that the buck cannot jump out."

"Really? Are there buck there?"

"Yes," he sounded pensive, "fences like that are to keep the buck inside and us out."

"Us out? How so?"

"Yes. When our people see protein – the meat of wild animals, I mean – they see a way to feed their families. But well-fed Whites like to drive around and look at the animals. So, they build high fences and put wild animals inside. To them, we are poachers, but to us, we are hunters."

Thandi looked at her brother. His face was impassive, and he stared straight ahead. She wondered where his cynicism came from – he used to be so full of humour and such good company. Now he was serious and rather bitter, as though life had dealt him a bad hand. A car came roaring past and overtook them, spewing up stones that peppered the windscreen. They were enveloped in thick, churning dust that seeped in through all the little gaps in the old car. Gordon swore and covered his nose. He slowed down and waited for the dust to thin, then he changed gear and accelerated again.

"White people. Always in a hurry. If a black person had driven past that guy and covered him in dust, he'd have screamed blue murder."

"Gordon, are you always so bitter?"

"Bitter?"

"Well, you seem to think that all white people are bad. Are they? You know, I went home one time to surprise our parents and Peter – it was his birthday. The train was delayed, and I suddenly found myself at the station in Mtubatuba in the dark – there were no taxis. Then a white man, an *Afrikaans* man, gave me a lift. I was terrified – I had grown up scared of *Afrikaners*, thinking they were horrible people. But this man was very kind. He drove me all the way home to Somkhele and all the time I was thinking he wanted to, you know, *fundekela* me. But he was lonely, I think – he was just being nice. That was a big lesson for me – never judge a cow by its hide. Are all white people bad? No, I do not think so. That fellow who made all the dust may have been in a hurry to get to a doctor. We will never know. You really should be more charitable."

"Thandi, you are so kind. You only want to see goodness in people. Of course, there are good white people. Many of us have benefitted from the kindness of white people, no doubt about it. And, you and I have been lucky, we grew up in the Barclay shadow. Our mother worked for *Nchebe* and then in the village for Bill and Molly. They were good to us. Molly makes a difference – she stands on street corners for our cause. But how many others do? Being nice and kind to your servants is all well and good, but it is kind of meaningless when those same people go and vote in the Nationalist government –"

"*Awu*! You mention the government. That reminds me. I was going to ask you. What did you think of Verwoerd's assassination?"

"He was a madman. His ideas were like cows made of clay – they look nice, but they can't walk. Now we have his apprentice, doing all that he can to convince the world that they are alive and kicking."

"You think Vorster will be worse?"

"Definitely. Hard as *umsimbithi*. Mark my words, he'll rule with an iron hand. And he's also in the *Broederbond* – you don't know what that is? It's an exclusive white, secret society set up to further *Afrikaner* interests – their interests, not ours, or those of the country. You know, during the war he was active in what they call the *Ossewabrandwag* which made him a terrorist. Then he ends up being the Minister of Justice during the Rivonia Trial! So, yesterday's terrorist sits in judgement on today's terrorist! How strange is that? Now he's Prime Minister!"

"Why was Verwoerd killed?"

"Have no idea. A mad person did it, they say. But it makes no difference – cut the head off this snake and it doesn't die, it just grows a new one."

They were silent for a while. Thandi felt a twinge of guilt for not being better versed in political affairs, but it was a subject that really didn't interest her – not to the extent that it excited Gordon.

"Is this what being a history teacher does to you? I mean, make you political?"

Gordon laughed. "No, not really. But it teaches you to see things differently. Let me give you an example." He adjusted himself in his seat and took one hand off the steering wheel.

"You know the story of Dingaan? Okay. Well, the history books say that he was a treacherous person who deceived the *Boers* and then murdered them. That he was a criminal, a very bad man. But you remember what our grandfather told us? No? He couldn't read or write – he told us what he had been told. He told us that Dingaan was a great leader because he acted to defend his people and preserve their ways. Remember what he said? The *Boers* came to uMgungundlovu cocky as hell. They rode their horses across our sacred burial sites with impunity, they ogled the king's harem when they were bathing – something our own people were not allowed to do on pain of death – they even threatened to do to Dingaan what they had done to Sekonyela. So, people began to ask, who are these people who flaunt our laws? Who do they think they are? Do they have magic that protects them from our laws? Dingaan heard these whispers, so when he ordered their death, he said '*bulalani abathakathi*,' thereby letting his people know that nobody was above the laws of the land. What is more, the *Boers* were not given a warrior's death, nor even one meted out to common criminals – no, they were clubbed to death with the sticks that were used to soften the loincloths of women. That was the biggest insult he could give them. So, despite what else Dingaan might have been, *Mkhulu* grew up believing he was a national hero, a defender of our customs. But no history book will tell you that. Why? Because we don't write the history books.

"Now, just in case you think I'm being over-sensitive and upset at the way Whites have written our history, they do the same with their own. For example, our papers were full of stuff about how bad Hitler was and that he was the devil incarnate. I get that, but he was the symptom, not the cause of the war. At the end of the First World War, the Allies throttled the life out of Germany – Lloyd George famously said, 'we shall squeeze her until the pips squeak.' You see, Thandi, when they had the Germans down, the Allies put the boot in as hard as they could. They imposed impossible conditions on Germany which all but made it certain that one day a nationalist would rise from the ashes to redeem his people. But you never hear about that, do you – the victors never make mistakes. Never. They write history the way they

155

want it to be read and taught. Thandi, there are always two sides to every coin – history teaches us to see both. If that makes me political, then I am guilty."

Thandi sat in awe of her brother. She was a nurse and knew none of these things or if she did, she was unable to see their relevance in the way that he did. They had never had a conversation about abstract things like this, and she marvelled at his knowledge.

"Gordon, do you believe in God?"

"Why?"

"Well, Titus believes. And so does our mother. But I wondered if you do."

"Not in the way that Titus does. I certainly do not believe in the three -headed God that the Europeans want to ram down our throats – or, you know, that he is white and sits in the sky watching over us. If he exists, then he'd be as black as burnt wood – everyone in that part of the world was black in those days. I do believe in the power of love, in goodness, justice, honesty, those sorts of things. But whether they are from God or exist on their own, I don't really know – or care, for that matter. But I suspect that after what I just said about our grandfather, you are asking if I believe in our beliefs and customs – the *amadlozi*, right?"

When she didn't reply, but stared at him with large wondering eyes, he went on, "Those things have stood our people in good stead for a very long time. Do I believe them? No, I don't. But many do. Our customs are important – they are the *ingcino* that holds us together, makes us what we are. I only believe what can be supported by evidence. But I see no reason to root out what our forefathers believed in if all we are going to do is replace it with stuff from the Bible – that's one fiction replacing another. I am wary of all religion. Napoleon said that religion is what keeps the poor from murdering the rich. Thank God for Titus! He taught us to read – gave you and me an education. How many newspapers did he make us read out aloud around the kitchen table, just to improve our English? He made us different, set us upon a different path. Have you not heard *Shenge* say, 'do not feed me a fish, give me a fishing rod and I'll feed myself'? That's what education does for us – allows us to feed ourselves. Reading, you know, opened my eyes; it taught me to doubt, to challenge – to make up my own mind. Reading also gave me words which I can now use like bullets –"

"Bullets! No, Gordon, not bullets. Please, my brother, when you talk like that, you frighten me."

"Thandi, yes, bullets kill people, but words kill ideas. That's what I mean. Armed with the right words, you can kill someone repeatedly! No, no, I am joking. It's no wonder Whites don't want us to become educated – they only want our muscles, not our brains. They don't want us to have the words or the arguments that we can use to kill their crazy ideas. Getting back to beliefs. Someone once said something along the lines that men never do evil so thoroughly and as cheerfully as when they do it with religious conviction. More than anything, history has taught me to doubt. You know, Thandi, the more I read, the less I believe."

Thandi was lost in thought. Gordon was on a different planet to her – his mind was full of complicated things. She had never thought of education as a weapon or words as bullets.

The climb up to Ubombo was steep and the road was rough. There were a couple of sharp corners and as they crawled around them, Thandi looked over the edge and her heart lurched. The sides were sheer and way down below the bush was thick and foreboding. The engine strained in low gear and the needle in the temperature gauge began to climb towards the red. Eventually they reached the top. They paused for a moment, giving the motor time to catch its breath. Gordon wiped the sweat off his face and pointed.

"There you are, Thandi. We are here at last."

They turned into the driveway. The little car, covered in red dust and looking like a bushbuck tentatively nosing its way into a sunlit glade, made its way slowly up the concrete road towards a clump of white buildings which were huddled together and over-shadowed by large, leafy trees. Father Henley came out onto the veranda and waved. He had been expecting them.

5

Molly and Mary had had a good day. They had walked themselves to a standstill, visiting all the department stores on West Street at least a dozen times. They had come to Durban to buy things for Mary's *trousseau* or, as Mary quaintly liked to say, for her bottom drawer. This was a novel experience for Molly whose own mother had not been able to indulge her in a similar fashion – not for any other reason than that war was on and money in those days was tight. What they couldn't carry on these shopping forays, they had delivered to the Royal Hotel. They were exhausted. Molly wasn't keen to get dolled up as she put it and go down to the main dining room for dinner and so suggested that they have something sent up to the room. But Mary wanted to go out. She suggested a light dinner downstairs followed by a film. Molly readily agreed – if she didn't like the film, she could always nod off.

"What flicks are on, do you know?"

"Well, Mum, *Hawaii* is on at the moment. Everyone is raving about it. I wonder if we can get tickets. Shall I phone reception and see if they can get some for us?"

"Hold on a sec. Pass me the paper and let's see what else is on." Mary handed her The Daily News and she paged through it until she found the entertainment page.

"Mary," she said, without looking up, "there's one here called *A Man for All Seasons*. Good write-up. Paul Scofield is in it. He's a brilliant Shakespearean actor. I wouldn't mind seeing it. What do you think?" She glanced over the top of the paper, saw Mary's face, and immediately closed the paper.

"Alright, darling. If you'd prefer to see *Hawaii*, then that's fine by me. Phone downstairs and see if you can get tickets. Tell them to put them on my account."

"Thanks, Mum. It's a great film. I'm sure you'll enjoy it. We'll see your one next time. You know what? I think you should stay here and have a rest. I'll pop down to the Colosseum and get the tickets myself."

"Okay. But get seats as far back as you can. I'm too old for the peanut gallery."

***

Later, after a hot bath and a change of clothes, Molly felt much better. Mary had managed to get good seats and now she didn't mind what show she saw. They went to the downstairs restaurant and ordered an omelette each and a bottle of Simonsig Chenin Blanc.

"Not often that we can do this," said Mary, "I'm so pleased that Rich could go up to the ranch and keep an eye on things for us. Frees Cam and me up to sort out the wedding. Very nice of him."

"Very nice. Between you and me, I didn't think he'd be able to drag himself away from Durban – especially now that he's involved with the Celliers woman."

"I gather you don't like her?"

"It's not that. She's too worldly-wise for our Richie, I fear. I just don't want to see him get hurt. I've met her once. She is very attractive; I'll give you that. Attractive and extremely self-assured. What do you think, Mary?"

"Well, I don't know much more. I told you what others say – that she's a man-eater. Maybe they are jealous, I don't know. But Rich is smitten. Ah, here's our dinner."

Afterwards, cheeks aglow and in no hurry because they already had their tickets, they sauntered arm-in-arm along Smith Street and made their way to the Colosseum Theatre.

The foyer was teeming with people. They headed towards the ushers. Mary saw a girl in the corner selling ice-creams. She pointed.

"Look, Mum, ice-creams. Just what I feel like. We didn't have dessert just now, so shall we be naughty? Let me buy you one. Okay?"

"Oh alright. Twist my arm. I'd like an Eskimo Pie if she has one. Thanks, Mary."

Molly took two steps up the stairway and turned so she could better watch Mary's progress through the crowd. She watched her blond head bobbing in the crowd and make its way to the ice-cream girl. A surge of affection swept over her as she watched her daughter. She heard the bell ring – the film was about to start. People welled up around the downstairs doors while others passed her on the stairs and went on up. While she stared at Mary, she became aware of a face in the crowd across the foyer. She didn't know what it was that caught her attention, but it did. Molly gripped the balustrade and narrowed her eyes to get a better look. Her vision was blocked by heads drifting past, then it cleared. Good God, it was Magda! She was with a tall man who had a moustache. A handsome man. She was leaning on his arm. He must have said something for she bent in towards him with an upturned face and smiled. There was, in the way they looked at each other, a complicity that contravened mere friendship. Molly froze, her mind in turmoil and she had the worst possible feeling in her gut.

"Here's your ice-cream. Just what you wanted. We'd better take them in with us. The film is starting in a few minutes. You alright, Mum? You have a funny look on your face."

"Me, darling? I'm fine, thank you," Molly took the ice-cream. Her mind was struggling to make sense of what she had just seen. Mary's face was a picture of innocence. She was smiling and her eyes twinkled. Molly hooked her arm into Mary's arm. "Let's go in and learn all about *Hawaii*!"

6

Cameron ran the game ranch well – there was not much that Richard needed to do, other than to keep a watchful eye on the labour, hand out the rations, and attend to any emergencies. But this supervisory role did allow him to accompany the game guards on their mounted patrols. They would set out in the early morning mist, single-file and silent, and would follow game trails wherever they led. They never encountered poachers, though they did see and remove snares that had been cunningly laid overnight. On one occasion, they heard dogs barking and though they galloped headlong towards them, they did not see them or the hunters they belonged to.

There was, Richard told himself, no better way to view game and drink in the majesty of the *bushveld* than from the saddle. It was the solitude that appealed to him and the feeling of being utterly insignificant, like a flea crawling on the back of a rhino. It was a cliché, he knew, but its truth was inescapable – whenever he was in the bush, he felt renewed and marvellously rejuvenated. It was as if immersion into this empty but not-so-empty space somehow cleansed him, ridding him of humbug and make-believe. It allowed him to see the world with new eyes and to ask himself, without ever settling on a satisfactory answer, what exactly did it mean to be civilised? Out here, in these wide-open vaulted spaces, civilisation counted for precious little. The further he rode, the more he could feel the trappings of his urban existence falling away while, at the same time, reflective meditations on the imponderables of life rose, perplexing him and toying with his mind. He rode along, following the horse in front of him, feeling in tune with his senses and at peace with the world.

When he finally took a moment to relax on the veranda, his mind drifted off to Magda and how much he missed her. He had only spoken to her a few times on the phone since his arrival in Mkuze and was mildly irritated that he had not been able to reach her more often. But then, it was a trunk call to Durban, and often by the time the call came through, he wasn't there to take it, or Magda was not there. He wondered about her fidelity, but only fleetingly – that was a thorn-littered *donga* he had no intention of venturing into, fearful of where it might lead him.

He pushed all thoughts aside and picked up a two-day old copy of The Sunday Times. An article about Bobby Kennedy's visit to South Africa earlier in the year caught his eye. It was about his 'Day of Affirmation Address' in Cape Town. The Kennedys fascinated him; there was something magnetic about Bobby and his unruly forelock, something about youthfulness and keeping dreams alive that fired his imagination. He began to read.

"It is from numberless diverse acts of courage and belief that human history is shaped each time a man stands up for an ideal or acts to improve the lot of others or strikes out against injustice. He sends forth a tiny ripple of hope and crossing each other from a million different centres of energy and daring, those ripples build a current that can sweep down the mightiest wall of oppression and resistance."

Richard lowered the paper onto his lap. The 'ripple of hope' words stood out from the quote; he picked them up as he might the mellifluous notes of a flute, flying high above the trumpets in an orchestra. They struck a sympathetic chord in his ears. He read them again; aloud this time, as though they were foreign to his tongue. They were fine words, he knew that. But they pricked his bubble, deflating his self-satisfaction. It was all very well for the Kennedys of this world to come to South Africa and espouse liberal causes, to preach about freedom and individual liberty and things like that, but they lived in a country where the Whites were massively in the majority – they had nothing to lose. In South Africa, Richard couldn't help reminding himself, universal suffrage could unleash forces that could well topple his world into chaos – one from which there would be no return. How to transform society without losing all that one held dear was the problem – how to share without losing it all. Inexplicably, his mother's words came back to him, the ones about doing everything for a beast of burden except removing the load from its back. He grimaced. He loved the feelings that Kennedy's words aroused in his chest but now felt irritated – uneasy ambivalence hung around him like a bad smell.

"Nkosana, you are wanted. Someone is injured." Cameron's cook, Elias, was calling from the veranda.

"What's that? Injured?" Richard turned in his chair, *"Who is injured?"*

"Manuka. He has cut himself. There is much blood. He is at the kitchen door."

The man was standing on the back veranda. He had a bloody rag around his lower leg and was in considerable discomfort. Richard led him to a chair and sat him down. He uncovered the wound. It was cleanly cut, long and deep like a freshly gutted fish. There was a lot of blood.

"Okay," he said to Elias, *"bring me a basin of warm water. I must clean this. It needs stitches. I don't have anything here to do that, so I'll take him up to the hospital at Ubombo. It's alright, Manuka, we'll get this fixed for you. How did it happen?"*

Manuka said he was trimming fencing sticks with a cane knife and the blade slipped. It must have been very sharp for it had sliced into his calf deeply. Richard cleaned the wound and bandaged it. He turned to Elias.

"You'd better come with me. You can look after the dogs for me at the hospital."

They went out to the Land Rover. It was a shooting brake – it had no roof and the top half of the doors had been removed. There was a raised padded bench in the back behind the front seats where Cameron's hunting clients sat. The dogs leapt onto the back and started to bark excitedly. They loved hanging their heads over the side and having the wind in their faces. Richard shouted something to the garden boy about not being away too long. Between them, he and Elias eased Manuka into the front passenger seat. Elias climbed into the back and settled the dogs. Richard slammed his door shut and off they went.

They parked in the shade of some large gumtrees and looked around. A line of motely people stretched down a long path that was lined with white stones, all the way from the carpark to the Outpatients building. It twitched rather than moved, like a raised vein on a withered arm. Richard muttered under his breath. Babies clung to the backs of their mothers, children fidgeted around adult feet and, in twos and threes, men and women exchanged pleasantries while they waited patiently for their turn. Richard could see that this was going to take a long time.

"Wait here," he said to Manuka, leaving him sitting on a large log at the back of the queue, *"I'll see if we can get you to the front."*

He made his way up to the front of the queue and squeezed past the people standing under the awning which hung over the large open window that served as an admitting counter. A nurse was seated at a desk below the window. A fan on top of a filing cabinet stirred the air, ruffling the papers on a nearby desk. The nurse had her head down and was filling in a form. Richard leaned past the man at the counter and waited. He watched the pen move. He flicked his eyes back to her head and studied it. He noticed the hairpins that held her decorative white cap in place. They gleamed in the soft coils of her hair. She is mindful of her appearance, he thought.

"Excuse me," Richard said, leaning over the counter a little more and addressing the top of her head, "I have an injured man here. How long will it be before someone can look at him?"

"So," said the bowed head, "I suppose you think that allows you to jump the queue?"

Richard made a self-deprecating clucking noise and was about to respond when the nurse looked up. She had a cheeky smile on her face and her eyes, large and round, shone. He gaped at her. His mind shattered like a dropped mirror, scattering shards of glass everywhere. Then recognition, like some inexorable magnetic force, drew those pieces back together again and, piece by piece, a picture formed. He knew those eyes. Thandi. He shook his head. She stood up. Her hands were at her face, and she clasped it, as though without her cupping palms it would have fallen to the floor.

"Thandi! Is it really you?"

"*Awu*! Nkosana Lichard! I did not know it was you. Yes, it is me, Thandi. How are you, sir?"

For the next few minutes, they tripped and stumbled over each other's questions, trying hard to temper their curiosity with short, neutral answers. Richard could hardly believe that this woman, exuding a confidence and radiant wholesomeness that took his breath away, was the same shy Thandi of his youth.

The patient standing next to him at the counter heard this exchange. He did not know what they were saying but he knew that it had nothing to do with an appointment to see the doctor. He had been shifting his weight from one foot to the other. Now he coughed.

"Sir, I must keep going," said Thandi, sensing the man's agitation, "there are many patients here and they have waited a long time. Leave your man here – he is not an emergency, is he?"

"No. His leg needs stitches. I could have done it, but I do not have any instruments."

"Alright," she glanced down at her nurse's watch, pinned upside-down on her white-starched chest, "come back at 12:30 pm – doctor should have seen him by then."

"Thank you, I will. See you later."

Richard walked back to the vehicle feeling elated. He didn't know why, he just did.

***

At precisely 12:30 pm, Richard returned to the hospital carpark. Manuka was waiting for him. His leg was neatly bandaged and he seemed a lot more comfortable. Richard told him to get into the vehicle and said he wouldn't be long. He walked off down the path to

Outpatients, making a conscious effort to breathe deeply and calm his nerves. The patients who had not yet seen the doctor were now sitting in the shade, back from the path. They sat in a line, silent and listless. Richard scanned their faces as he passed. One or two raised a half-hearted hand but mostly they watched him pass, their faces etched with the resignation of those whose lot in life is to be perpetually at the beck and call of others. They knew that it was the doctor's lunchtime and there was little they could do other than to make themselves as comfortable as they could in the tepid shade and wait for the sun to slowly lower itself.

As Richard approached the open window, a woman got up, unstrapped the child from her back and took it to a garden tap protruding from the side wall. Thandi, with head bent and pencil poised, was speaking on the telephone, so Richard turned around to watch the woman. She splayed her legs wide and bent down, drinking from the tap with one hand while the other held the tap open. Then the child also drank, from tiny, cupped hands. Richard noticed the woman's feet. She had no socks, and her shoes had no laces. He wondered where she had gotten them from. They must have been hand-me-downs; they were too small for her, and the backs were folded over so her broad cracked heels could slide over them, allowing her to wear them like slippers.

Thandi put the phone down and came out to meet him. She stood with her hands at her waist and fidgeted with the buckle on her belt.

"Sir, I told doctor about you. That you are a doctor as well. He would like to meet you. His name is Doctor Schultz. He will be here just now."

"Ah, Thandi, please don't call me sir. Tell me, how is Busisiwe? And Titus? What of Gordon and Peter, where are they now?"

Before Thandi could reply, an inner door opened and a short stocky man in a white coat came striding out. He took his spectacles off and dropped them into his breast pocket.

"You must be Dr Barclay. How do you do?" He shook Richard's hand warmly. He had smiling hazel-coloured eyes and thick, bushy eyebrows. "I am Erwin Schultz. Pleased to meet you. Sister here has told me a lot about you."

Richard tried to place his accent. Was it German or Swiss? They walked down the path together and turned towards the main building. Schultz stopped and spun around.

"Look," he said, addressing Richard, "I am going to have something to eat. Why don't you join me? My wife can knock up a sandwich for us – she'll be delighted to see a new face."

"Thanks, but I have a couple of chaps in the car waiting for me. I have to get back. Perhaps another time."

"Ah, that's right. You brought the fellow with cut leg, didn't you? Nasty cut. A few stitches and a tetanus shot – he's right to go."

"Thanks for fixing him up. How do we pay? I'm not from here and this is the first time I've had to bring someone here."

"It's alright, *Nkosana*. I shall put it on account. That's what *Nkosana* Cameron does. He pays the account at the end of the month."

Richard couldn't contain his curiosity any longer. "If you don't mind me asking, where are you from? Is that a German accent?"

Schultz laughed. "Everyone asks me that. I'm Dutch but my mother is Swiss. I was fired by Kennedy's Peace Corp – you know, for doing something for those around the world who are less fortunate than ourselves. So, my wife and I went abroad to do our bit. We started in the Congo and just kept going south. Just love Africa – such lovely people. Worked in Ndola, Limbe, then we did a six-month locum in Vilankulos – you know it? In Mozambique. Then we came here. Been here a year now. Getting itchy feet – reckon it's time to move on. But we have two kids now, so it's not so easy. Schooling, you know. Next time you're up the hill, pop in for a chat. Bye now."

Richard watched him go, then turned to Thandi.

"Well, Thandi. This is a surprise. Tell me, how long have you been here?"

"Only six months. I was working in Durban. At McCord hospital. It's where I did my training. But I don't like city life that much. Titus knows Father Henley – he's the Superintendent here – and he asked me to apply. I like the work. But there is not much to do here – when we have time off, I mean."

"Look I have to go. There is so much I want to ask you. Why don't you come down to the house next time you are off and we can catch-up?"

Thandi looked at him and searched his face briefly. Then her eyes slid sideways and fell to the ground. She wanted to see him, but also she didn't – what would people say? After all, they were no longer children playing in the backyard. "Thank you. But it's difficult. I don't have transport –"

"Just call me. On the phone. Mkuze 1211. I'll come and fetch you."

She hesitated. "Maybe. I'll see."

"Tell you what. Let's fix the time now. When are you off next?"

She hesitated and looked away.

"I have tomorrow afternoon off. But I could ask Myeni if he is going down to Mkuze tomorrow. Maybe he can give me a lift."

"Myeni?"

"The ambulance driver. He drives down to the rail at Mkuze and other places. He goes every day. We often get a lift with him."

"Well, over to you. If you want me to fetch you, I will. Just call. Must go now, Thandi. Bye."

All the way back to the farmhouse, Richard was deep in thought. Thandi's eyes haunted him; they were as he remembered them – large, round, and innocent. But now they belonged to a woman, a very

164

attractive woman; an attractive lady who happened to speak perfect English.

***

From that first visit, when Thandi brought a friend with her as a safety card and sat stiff and upright on the edge of her chair right until her last visit, when she sat relaxed on the sofa with her feet coiled up beneath her - their friendship, born in childhood and long dormant, now quickly opened up, blossoming like a desert flower that unfurls itself at the first hint of rain. It became quite normal for the hospital staff to see Richard arrive in his Land Rover to pick Thandi up or to bring her back. For him it was companionship, someone to talk to and to share things with. He took her around the game ranch and showed her the animals. On one occasion, she told him what Gordon had told her, that her grandfather had been in the battle of Tshaneni which had taken place right there in front of them. She added that her grandfather was still alive. Richard was enthralled, and plied her with questions, many of which she was unable to answer.

One day they returned to the house and decided to stay indoors as the weather turned quite glum with a hot north wind blowing. Thandi wandered around looking at the bookshelves. She stopped beside the record player and ran her finger over its plastic cover.

"Do you like music?" he asked, "If you want, I'll turn the generator on, and we can play some records. Not sure what records Cameron has here. Go on, have a look. There's a big selection of long-playing records in the cabinet underneath. Here, let me show you." He joined her at the cabinet and squatted down to look inside. "What sort of music do you like?"

"Classical. Church music mostly. It is what I know. From Titus – he loves music. He often goes into the church at Somkhele and plays the piano for hours on end. He taught all of us to play."

"Really?" He looked up at her, wonderingly. He knew that it shouldn't have, but the notion that something so refined as classical music would be of intrinsic interest to a black person struck him as incongruous – as though someone was trespassing on someone else's turf. He'd never heard of black children learning to play the piano – that somehow seemed such a white preoccupation. But, why not? Weren't most of the great American jazz players black? Someone must have taught them. "Which composer do you like? If we find something you like, I'll start the engine and we can listen to it."

"Well, I grew up with Bach."

"Johann Sebastian Bach. Okay let's see –"

"No, not him so much. Titus prefers his sons."

"Ah, you mean Johann Christian?"

"Yes, him and Emanuel."

Richard had never heard of Emanuel Bach. "His brother?"

"Yes. Titus prefers the 'sensitive style' of Emanuel – he says it is more dynamic and more expressive than his father's style. I don't know, but that's what Titus says. He knows a lot about music. He says music is a place where you can go to when you want to shut out the world. I'm not sure about that, but I grew up with classical music in our home – I couldn't help liking it. There was a collection of records that someone gave to the church and Titus bought a wind-up player – this was before we had electricity – he played these records all the time."

Richard's mind was reeling. Here was a black person talking more intimately about an aspect of white culture than he ever could. He started rifling through the records, pulling them out at random and sliding them back into their slots.

"Wait! Is that the Messiah? 'Handel's Messiah'? Oh, that's beautiful. Could we play it? Just the Hallelujah Chorus would be enough. Whenever Titus played it, we would lie on the floor, hold hands, and close our eyes, and … and sort of give ourselves to the music."

"You'd all lie on the floor?"

"Yes, which is silly as traditionally, you should stand."

"Stand? For the Hallelujah Chorus?"

"Yes. Titus said that the King of England started the tradition a long time ago. Titus said he likes to lie down, close his eyes, and allow the music to take possession of his soul."

"Did it? Did it take your soul?"

Thandi's laugh was as timid as a faint breeze. "No. But I did enjoy lying on the floor – you know, with my family, and listening to the music. We did it a lot."

Richard extracted all the Messiah records. "Here you are. It's a recording by the Mormon Tabernacle Choir. Gosh, there are a lot of them."

"Can you find Part Eleven? The chorus is at the end of Part Eleven."

Richard paused and looked up at her. "You know a lot more about this than I do." Before she could reply, he straightened up and called out to Elias in the kitchen. "*Elias, run down to the workshop and ask Manana to start the lighting plant.*"

The engine throbbed into life and the lights came on. Richard found the right record and placed it on the turntable. He skipped the needle a couple of times until he found the beginning. She nodded and they stood listening to the opening bars. Richard had heard it before but had never given it much attention. Now, as the first chords sounded, he cocked his head and listened intently. Then the full-throated vocals crashed in with cathedral-filling volume – they flowed and ebbed like waves on a rising tide, lifting the hairs on the back of his neck. He glanced sideways at Thandi. She was rocking back and forth with her eyes closed. Her lips moved with the music.

Impulsively, he reached for her hand. "Come on. We'd better do it properly." She jerked her hand away and stepped back. "What? I thought you like to hear this lying down and holding hands?"

He sank to the floor and waited for her. The music surged around them, waves swirling on a beachhead. Thandi hesitated. She felt she was being enticed to trespass, to venture into a domain that was strictly out of bounds. She drew back, anxious, and full of mistrust. But then, when she saw nothing sinister in his clear blue eyes – no subterfuge or anything to confirm her suspicions – she quelled her trepidation and smiled as bravely as she could. The last thing she wanted to do was offend him.

"I will lie here," she said, hoping her smile would negate her reticence. She moved away from him and sat down on a zebra skin which was in the middle of the floor. Then she lay down, sweeping here arms back and forth from her sides, making the point that there was only enough room there for one person. She stretched out her arms and closed her eyes. Sitting at her feet and seeing her spread out in a crucified pose like that, reminded him of a drawing by Leonardo da Vinci that he knew, but couldn't remember its name. He shrugged and stretched out on the polished wooden floor, on his side, and watched the rise and fall of her chest. How different she was now from the little girl of his youth! For some unaccountable reason, he felt content and couldn't help smiling. He rolled onto his back and closed his eyes. He concentrated as hard as he could, listening to the nuances of the music and the repetitive words. It occurred to him that church music was similar to martial music; both had rhythm and an evenly measured beat, and both stirred the passions of the heart, invoking a noble sense of duty – one for war, the other for peace. Two sides of the same coin. He wasn't musical, but the emotional force that the chorus unleashed in him as he lay on the floor in the lounge, quickened his breath and filled him with awe. *'King - of - kings'* and *'lord - of - lords,'* one note per syllable, getting higher and higher all the time, and building to a climax – made him gasp and want to shout. He didn't, instead he flung out his arms. The fingers of his right hand brushed the fingers of her left hand. Their hands shied apart, but their eyes remained closed. Then slowly, almost of their own volition, those self-same fingers crept back together and became entwined, like the hands of two bathers steadying each other against the pull of a restless sea. They were still like that, long after the last strains of the tumultuous finale had drained away into silence.

Then the needle of the gramophone, hissing a short pause, broke the spell. Thandi stirred. A soloist's crystal-clear voice began to sing *'I know that my Redeemer liveth,'* presaging the start of Part Eleven. She knew the score. She opened her eyes and looked around. The music still strummed through her body and there were fingers still holding her hand. She fluttered her eyes and turned her head, expecting to see a family member at her side. Richard. She was holding Richard's hand. She sat up, horrified. Her hand. She yanked it away and clutched it tightly to her as though it had been a naughty child that had wandered without permission away from the sanctity of its mother's skirt. Richard was looking at her. She looked away. And took a deep breath. Her heart skipped. She was suddenly very scared. Like Eve in that primordial garden, aroused and newly aware, she thought only of covering herself.

"I am sorry," she said with pleading eyes, "I don't know what happened. I am very sorry. Forgive me." She got up and moved away with her arms crossed over her chest and a hand on each shoulder.

Richard was unsettled; he didn't know why, but he was. Something had happened. Was it the touch of her hand? The look in her large, frightened eyes? Something as revealing as a stolen glimpse at momentarily exposed underwear, set his mind galloping in a thousand different directions. An intimacy had been shared. He was sure of that. For some odd reason, and he couldn't quite see its relevance now, an old adage of his mother's wandered into his mind, 'once the genie is out of its bottle, you can never put it back.'

He got up and went to the record player, avoiding her eyes. He turned it off and removed the record. "No need to apologise, Thandi. Is there anything else you'd like to hear?" he asked, with his back to her, "There's a lot here to choose from."

It was no use. The genie had escaped. They talked, but in contrived careful sentences that were so devoid of warmth, they made him cringe. They seemed to have retreated into their own absorptions and stared sullenly at each other. Try as he might, he could not find common ground or anything to lift her spirits, let alone make her laugh. The smiles she tendered were fleeting, like shadows on a wintery day, and they seldom warmed her eyes. She stayed for a while, mooching, and distracted, but then said that she was not feeling well and asked if he wouldn't mind taking her home. He drove her back up the hill to the hospital, trying all the while to engage her in conversation. They parted uneasily. Then, with a single wave and not once looking back, she was gone. Richard drove home, bleak of mind and ill at ease. He knew, she would not visit again.

By the time he returned to the house, he was feeling better. He had tried his best with Thandi, had tried to be friendly and chatty, but to no avail. He opened the kitchen door, and the dogs came bounding out. Elias was sitting at the kitchen table, cleaning the silverware.

"*Nkosana*. The *Inkhosazana* called. On the telephone. After you had left."

"*Inkhosazana* Mary?"

"No. The *Inkhosazana* from Durban. Your *Inkhosazana*."

Richard glanced at his watch. 4:35 pm. Magda should still be at work. A sudden sense of unease overcame him, and he went to the phone in the hallway. He picked up the handpiece.

"Call on?" The line was clear. He rang a long ring and waited for the exchange in Mkuze to answer. While he waited, he dug out his wallet and found a piece of paper in it that had Magda's work number. The operator came online – he booked the call and was told that there would only be a five-minute delay. He stood by the phone and waited. Why on earth had she phoned him from work? She had never done it before. The seconds crept by, and he cursed aloud, anxious to hear her voice and put his mind at rest. The dogs sat around him, sensing his unease, and wondering what it was that kept him in the hallway. There was a low chair beneath the phone and a small table with notepaper on it and a sawn-off cow's horn holding a bunch of pens and pencils. Richard went back to it and sat down. He rested his elbows on his knees and allowed his head to hang down. What could be wrong?

The phone shrilled above him, jerking him from his reverie. Short-long, short-long, short-long. It was for him. He picked it up and heard his heart hammering in his chest. "Your Durban number is on the line," said the operator in a nasal voice, "speak up please."

Richard didn't recognise the voice. "Can I speak to Magda Celliers, please?"

He waited. Eventually, after a series of static clicks, he heard her voice.

"Hello?"

"Hello, Magda. It's me. Richard. Sorry to call you at work." The words tumbled from his mouth, tripping him up. "Elias – he's Cam's cook – said that you'd called. I was out. Sorry. Had to go up the hill. To Ubombo – to the hospital there. You alright? Is anything wrong?"

"Oh, Richard. Thanks for calling back. Yes, I called you. Spoke to the boy. I was going to wait. But then I couldn't. Still more than a week before –"

"Magda, I'm dying of suspense. Is anything wrong?"

"Richard. Promise you won't be cross –"

"Be cross? Why should I? Come on, tell me what this is all about."

"I'm pregnant."

It was as though he had been shot from afar – the word hit him like a bullet, smacking into his brain long before the sound reached his ears. Panic. His gut knotted, squeezing ice through his veins, and when he tried to speak, no sound came – his throat was constricted, as though gripped in a vice. In an instant his mind was swept clean. Thandi, the game ranch, and everything to do with Mkuze and Ubombo were obliterated by the awful contemplation of a new reality.

"You there, Richard? Please say something."

Fortunately, and he was to remember this afterwards, he did not trot out the first thing that came into his head – though for some time afterwards, it roiled around in his mind like an angry python and laboured to get out. "Well, that's a surprise! Are you … are you … pleased? I mean, what do you think? What do you want to do?" He waited for her reply, his heart leaping around in his chest like a frightened bird in a cage.

He was surprised how clear his thinking suddenly became and how quickly he was able to marshal his shocked emotions and bring them to heel. Yesterday was already cast in stone; how he handled tomorrow is what counted now, and his mind raced ahead like a threshing machine, sorting and discarding options at a furious pace.

"Do?" Her question sounded a long way behind him. "What do you mean 'do', Richard?"

"Well," he paused, not wanting to say something that might lie between them like a puff adder in the grass and one day rear up and strike. Then he took a deep breath and rolled the dice. "I want to marry you. That's what I want to do."

He heard the sharp intake of her breath before she replied. "So do I, Rich, so do I." Another long pause. He felt he ought to be more formal, so he cleared his throat.

"Magda, will you marry me and make me the happiest of men?"

"Of course! I would marry you tomorrow if you want to. Oh, Richard, we'll be so happy –"

"Magda, you are an angel, you really are. I love you – to the moon and back!" He went on, trying to introduce a note of levity by responding, "There are proposals and proposals, but this one, on a party line, takes the cake!" But she seemed not to have heard, for she went on, "Can I tell Mom?"

He stared outside, thinking hard. The sun was low in the afternoon sky. He had a ball of string by the end and now it was unravelling fast, rolling away from him and would end up who knew where. Mom. The word reverberated. Oh God, that's a bridge I still have to cross – Mum will be easy, but Dad will be a different kettle of fish. Brakes, put the brakes on – one thing at a time.

"Magda, let's not say anything to anyone just yet. I am leaving here in a few minutes, and I am coming down to see you. I'll be there before midnight. We can discuss everything and make plans."

"Will we have our own house?"

The question was like a mosquito bite – it stung, and he knew it would itch. It made him realise how little he knew of her. She had always lived in his head, an image without form. "Of course we will. But wait until I get there, and we'll talk about it all. With regard to telling your parents, I would rather you say nothing just yet. I'd like to ask them myself. For your hand, I mean. It's the right and proper thing to do. Yes, yes, I want to speak to your father. I think –"

"Hold on," the phone went quiet. Then she came back again. "Sorry, that was my boss. I have to go. It's 5:00 pm and we are locking up now. I won't tell anyone yet. I love you, too. Bye."

Richard put the phone down and went into the lounge. He sat down heavily. So, this was it. He never saw the storm coming and only now realised how ill-prepared he was for it. He had been quite content and self-absorbed – like a caterpillar laboriously spinning its cocoon – impervious to all considerations except those that shut out the outside world or added to his sense of wellbeing. How careless he had been, how short-sighted. For a while, he sat there, slumped over with his elbows on his knees. He could hear himself breathing through loosely parted lips; a slowly deflating balloon that left him devoid of emotion and not sure how to gather his scattered thoughts or even where to begin. Then, as his heartbeat slowed, his training began to assert itself; he started to examine cause and effect, slowly weighing possibility against probability, and assessing other such variables as might pave the way forward.

It was pitch black outside when Richard stood up suddenly and stretched. A plan materialised in his head. He would go with Magda to Eshowe and ask her father for her hand. There was no skirting that issue – he would front up and do the gentlemanly thing. Then they would get married. Quickly, before Mary and Cameron, and hopefully without upstaging them. He wasn't looking forward to it, but first, he had to break the news to his father. He would ask him if a house could be built for them on the farm – or, failing that, then in the village. His time at Addington was nearly up and the family knew that he was moving back to Empangeni to practice – they all knew that at Christmas he would be coming home for good.

Just an hour later, after he had packed his bags, Richard called Magda and told her what he was thinking. He fielded her questions as best he could, but when he heard the excitement growing in her voice, the tension began to drain out of him, and he could feel his own excitement beginning to grow. First up though, he had to see Magda – there was much to talk about. A warm feeling of voluptuous longing diverted his thinking – he couldn't wait to be back in her arms.

He smiled ruefully as he drove into the night, conscious that enveloping darkness always tended to condense his doubts and exacerbate his fears. Nonetheless, he took solace from the certain knowledge that love conquered all, or so he had been led to believe. Didn't love make the rough smooth, or as his mother so often said, make the world go round? Why wasn't he in the state of ecstasy he had heard so much about? He braced himself and lit a cigarette. He was determined to make this work.

And so, within two months, Richard and Magda were married. Richard would like to have had Brydon Hamilton as his best man, but in the end his preference gave way to prudence – he decided that it would be better to be seen as a bridge-builder and thereby cement himself into his new family. So, he asked Andre, a move which won him considerable kudos from his father-in-law – this, on top of nodding the approval he had already secured by agreeing not to invite any natives to the wedding, even those who he had grown up with. The service was in the Dutch Reformed Church in Eshowe and the reception was held at the Country Club. It was a splendid affair, nice speeches, good food, and the wine flowed freely. If anyone was surprised by the hastiness of this wedding, they did not show it, and if anyone wondered why the bride had the temerity to not only wear white, but to do it in such a vivacious manner, they kept it to themselves. Apart from the barman and the waiters, there were no black faces to be seen – in that respect at least, the wedding conformed to expectations and raised no eyebrows and took its place in local folklore as a happy and otherwise unremarkable event at which everyone had a thoroughly good time.

8

In the second week of December, Mary and Cameron were married in the Anglican Church in Empangeni. Richard and Magda came up from Durban for the weekend and used the occasion to see how their house was coming on. They were living in his Durban apartment and the intention was to stay there until the end of the month when Richard's tenure at Addington would be up. Then they would move back to the Barclay family home after Christmas and would stay with Bill and Molly until their house on the farm was completed and ready for them to move into.

Mary's wedding was one of those lavish Zululand affairs – no expense was spared and there were nearly three hundred guests, all smartly dressed and in a festive mood. The reception was held at the Barclay residence on the farm. Dozens of farm workers were seconded to the task of erecting the marquee – they rolled out the canvass panels, lifted them onto tent poles, hauled on ropes and held them all in place while teams armed with mallets, went around securing the whole edifice with hundreds of tent pegs. When it was finished, one of the workers stepped back and remarked that it was as big as Boswell's Circus tent which caused a ripple of laughter from his fellow onlookers. Then the ladies of the district, with their secateurs tucked into their aprons and working tirelessly over buckets of flowers, decorated the interior with skill and verve, transforming it into a place of elegance and beauty. And the menfolk, not to be outdone, brought in all the tables and chairs, arranged them according to plan, erected the bar exactly where Molly wanted it, and then laid down the dance floor with a similarly imposed preciseness. The lights were hung, tables set, and the acoustics tested again and again. Nothing at all was left to chance.

Not surprisingly, there were at this wedding, black faces in the church and in the crowd of well-wishers that gathered on the Barclay farm that sunny day, under the striped canvass of the marquee. They sat by themselves, at small tables at the back, and they kept themselves out of the way like family pets – there but not there – carefully avoiding entanglement and being trampled underfoot. Busisiwe and Titus had driven down from Somkhele, and they brought Thandi and Peter with them. Unfortunately, Jack had contracted a nasty bout of flu and at the last moment and was unable to attend. He spent the day in bed, but Mavis and the children were there, sitting at another fringe table – Frankie, Rosie and Isaac were with them.

At another table, purposefully positioned well away and, as it were, well above the salt, sat Kobie and Anna with Richard and Magda. Richard had been surprised to see Thandi at the church service and was dying to talk to her. Every now and then he sat upright and looked around quizzically, like a meerkat on its tail, as though searching for something. Try as he might, he could not catch her eye. Feeling disgruntled, he decided to bide his time and settled down beside his father-in-law, feigning interest in what was being said. Kobie, for his part, knew many people there and kept bobbing up and down, greeting old acquaintances as they walked past and shaking their hands. He was in good humour and smiled serenely throughout the proceedings – indeed, even when Cameron, in his rather long but witty speech, paid tribute to the African members of the farm community by name, his face never betrayed him, not so much as by the twitch of a single muscle.

Granny Jess sat at the top table with the bridal party – it was clear to everyone that she was the matriarch and what she said still carried weight, for all the guests paused whenever they passed her chair to say a few words or simply to doff their heads. She sat ramrod-straight and accepted these displays of deference like a bank teller at a counter, taking deposits. Phoebe was there, all the way from England. She sat at a table set aside for Barclay relatives and loved being in the thick of things; she fiddled and fussed with the cutlery absent-mindedly and watched everything that was going on around her with her head tipped to one side like a bird. When she spoke, her strong English accent turned heads and, for a few moments, she became the centre of attention in her own right when Cameron paid tribute to her in his speech and pointed her out. She had delayed her Africa visit to coincide with the wedding and was extremely grateful to Bill and Molly who had paid for her to fly on a BOAC Comet, from London to Johannesburg, on a flight that included a two-day stopover in Nairobi.

She marvelled at all she saw, shaking her head and smiling in disbelief at what she perceived to be opulence on a grand scale. There was, she noted, a careless exuberance to life in this part of the world, an insatiable desire to drink the cup of life to the lees – it was a lifestyle way beyond her ken, something she had never experienced before, something she thought was the prerogative of royalty only.

Phoebe listened to the sounds of merriment around her as she allowed her eyes to wander around the room. They settled on Richard and Magda – such a nice-looking couple, she thought. Her eyes moved fractionally to Magda's side. That must be Magda's parents. She hadn't met them yet and wanted to get a good look at them – in church, she had only seen the back of their heads. Phoebe sipped her champagne and watched them, her eyes darting back and forth. Something bothered her. She looked around for Molly, saw her at another table, and went to her.

"Moll, is that Magda's mother sitting over there?"

"Yes. You haven't met them yet? Sorry, I've been so busy. Come, I'll introduce you."

As they approached, Phoebe heard Kobie and Anna speaking to each other in *Afrikaans*. They switched to English as soon as they realised that Molly was bearing down on them.

"Great wedding, Molly," said Kobie, rising from his chair, "Mary looks absolutely radiant, doesn't she. And Cameron spoke so well." He turned his attention to Phoebe, "You must be the aunt who came all the way from England. Pleased to meet you. Kobie's the name. This is my wife, Anna."

They shook hands and exchanged pleasantries briefly, like kids swapping marbles. Richard had risen with Kobie as well; he excused himself and sauntered off. Phoebe tried to examine Anna's face without appearing to do so – she stole what she thought were discreet glances and kept smiling.

She was troubled. There was something vaguely familiar about the woman that she couldn't put her finger on. It irked her.

***

It was 2:30 am when Phoebe climbed into bed and turned off her bedside light. She lay in the dark, dead tired, and closed her eyes. What an incredible party! She went over it, scene by scene and couldn't help smiling. Suddenly, she sat bolt upright and scrabbled for the light switch. *Anna.* Something clicked. She climbed out of bed and reaching for her dressing gown, headed for the door. The lights in the hall were still on. She hurried towards them, belting up her gown as she went. Molly and Bill were sitting at the dining room table. They had their shoes off and their feet up.

"Phoebe! What's up?" Bill waved to a chair, "Can't get to sleep? Then sit down. We've run out of puff and are having a *regmaaker*, a pick-me-up. Care to have one?"

"No, no. Sorry to barge in on you, but it's just dawned on me."

"What's dawned on you?'

"Anna."

"Anna? What on earth are you talking about?"

"I was just about to drift off to sleep when it came to me. Molly, remember you introduced me to her – to Richard's mother-in-law, I mean? Yes? Well, I had a funny feeling that I had seen her before. It's been bothering me all afternoon. I'm pretty sure I know where, now. I could swear that I nursed her when she had a baby."

"Nursed her? I don't think so. She has two children, Andre and Magda – both born here in South Africa. No, Phoebs, I think you are mistaken."

"Well, it was thirty odd years ago. I could swear she's the person who had a baby in Bristol. It was the strangest thing. One day, I was asked to go to the maternity annex and help the midwife there. Jessie Wainwright she was, very experienced – taught me lots. Anyway, the reason why I remember this birth so well is that this woman – the one who I was attending to with Jessie – had absolutely no interest in her baby, none whatsoever. But that's only half of it. Sometime during the labour, the nurse in the other birthing room – her name was Libby, Libby Osborne, I think – came in and spoke to Jessie. Quite urgent, it was. There was a problem, she needed Jessie's help. So, because Jessie was the senior in charge, they decided to swap – Jessie went next door and took over the other patient while Libby stayed with me."

"Phoebe, what are you trying to tell us? Nurses swapping patients? So what?"

"Well, I'd say it's pretty unusual. They swapped. There must have been something very wrong for that to happen. I never saw the other mother. When I asked Dora – the maternity nurse assisting Libby – when I met up with her afterwards, she was tight-lipped and told me not to worry and to go back to my surgical ward –"

"Phoebe, it's late, can this wait until later?"

"Sorry, but it's all coming back. Here's the thing. She had a perfectly normal baby. Trouble is, the woman's name was Elsa, not Anna. Elsa Duncan, I think. She was dark haired, not blond."

"So? What are you getting at?"

"The baby was black."

The word was like a pistol shot; it cannoned against their eardrums, stupefying them. Silence. A long tenuous silence, broken only by the grandfather clock in the hall, ticking towards tomorrow with measured precision. Bill recovered first. He swung his feet off the table and sat up. "A black baby?" He leancd across the table and looked Phoebe in the eye. "Are you saying Anna had a black baby?"

Phoebe's gaze buckled. She turned her eyes to Molly. "I'm not saying that. All I'm saying is that I assisted a midwife called Jessie in delivering a baby in Bristol, many years ago. That pregnant woman's name was Elsa. She had a baby boy. I was out of the room when he popped out, but I saw him alright, Jess showed me – a bonny little chap. Molly, believe me when I tell you he was black." She paused, and took a deep breath, "This Anna looks like Elsa, she really does. I'm not saying it is her, but the resemblance is uncanny. I could be wrong. In fact, I probably am –"

Molly got up and put her hand on Phoebe's shoulder. "You know Bill, there may be something in this. While Phoebs was talking, my mind went back to the first time I met Anna."

Bill hung his head. He didn't need a long dissertation from his wife, not now. He looked up.

"Richard had been invited over to Anna's house one afternoon to play with Andre. Remember when Kobie was the magistrate in Empangeni?" Bill nodded and hurried her on with his hand. His bed was calling, and he really wasn't interested.

"Well, I'd never met her before. So, when I went to pick him up, I made a point of chatting to Anna – you know, to be nice and friendly. The more she talked, the more I thought I could detect a faint English accent. That made me curious. You know me, Bill – I had to find out. So, I asked her if she was English. I could tell straight away that she didn't like the question. She said rather stiffly that she was from Bristol. So, to make her feel better, I told her that's where I met you – at a Bristol hospital, just before the war. Told her my cousin was working there and that she introduced us. Anna suddenly pricked up her ears. She asked me when this was and which hospital it was, so I told her. That was the end of it. But two things struck me: one, she seemed quite interested in that Bristol hospital and I had no idea why, and two, it was clear to me that she had something against being English, which I thought was odd. She's very proud that she's fluent in *Afrikaans*. She and Kobie speak it at home – all the time, I gather. I wonder, could our Anna really be the Elsa that Phoebe's talking about?"

Bill got up and stretched. "I'm going to bed. It's none of our business. I reckon we park it."

"Bill," said Phoebe, "I'm not asking you or anyone to do anything. It was bothering me, that's all. I just wanted to talk to get it off my chest. I shouldn't have opened my big mouth. I'm sorry –"

"Phoebs, don't apologise," Molly squeezed Phoebe's shoulder, "I'm glad you've told us. We won't breathe a word to a soul, will we Bill? We can't really, can we – we don't know if Anna and this Elsa are the same person, do we? It's stretching a long bow. Let's all go to bed and sleep on it."

Bill and Molly kissed Phoebe goodnight and headed upstairs. Phoebe went to her room, ill at ease and feeling that she had stirred up a hornet's nest, and for no good reason. She closed the door and noticed as she did so that the click of the door latch sounded unusually loud. Anna was in her head and would not go away. If she could only resolve it, one way or the other, then she could relax and have peace of mind. She was about to get into her bed when a bright idea came into her head. If anybody could shed light on this, it would be Libby or Dora. Jessie Wainwright would have retired ages ago. She went to the cupboard and took out her old, worn leather handbag. She rummaged through it and found what she was looking for – her well-thumbed address book. She sat on the bed, kicked her slippers off and paged through it. No, she did not have a Dora Murphy or a Libby Osborne in her address book. But the telephone number of the Bristol hospital where she used to work was there. She got up, pulling her robe tight, and checked that the windows and curtains were properly closed and then, on second thoughts, went back to the door to make sure that it was indeed locked. Only then did she relax and climb into bed. She knew what she was going to do.

The next morning when nobody was around, she booked an overseas call. It took a while to get put through to the hospital in Bristol, but her spirits sank almost immediately; the trail had run cold. Dora Murphy still worked at the hospital but was not expected back at work till after Boxing Day. Phoebe sighed and closed her eyes, not entirely sure of what to do next.

9

The sun was going down as Molly and Phoebe pulled up at the workshops. The wedding had come and gone, and life was returning to normal. It seemed to Molly that the Barclay household had moved on and, like a boat that had slipped its moorings, was now lolling on a languid tide. "Chilly, isn't it? When the sun goes down, I mean."

"Yes. Want to go back? We can come another time."

"Gosh no. Not cold for a girl from Keswick. Do show me around, Moll – I'd love to know more about all that goes on here."

Molly talked fluently about farming and her life on the farm. Phoebe was intrigued and marvelled at the excitement in Molly's voice – clearly, she relished her life on the farm. It was while they were walking from one building to the next that Jack appeared from around the corner of the office block. He stood to one side and waited for Molly to stop talking. She turned to him and grinned.

"Ah, Jack, there you are! Hello. We missed you at the wedding. How are you feeling?"

"Good evening, madam," he said, "I am a lot better, thank you. This flu has been doing the rounds – I must have caught it from the kids. Really knocked me for a six. Felt like a piece of chewed string for a few days. But I'm as strong as an ox – I'll be back in harness tomorrow."

"Jack, let me introduce you. This is my cousin Phoebe. She's from England, came out for the wedding. And she's staying for Christmas. Phoebe, this is Jack, our farm manager."

Phoebe hesitated, but only for a second. Then, very deliberately, stuck out her hand. "Pleased to meet you," she said, locking her eyes onto his and then quickly looking away. She couldn't believe her ears. Here was a black man in the middle of Africa, dressed in crisply pressed khaki fatigues and sporting a dark-coloured, floral cravat. It seemed so incongruous. But even more incongruous than that was his perfectly modulated English voice which caught her totally by surprise. Had her eyes been closed, she would have sworn that the voice she was hearing belonged to an English country gentleman. This ran counter to all that she had come to expect, and she turned to Molly enquiringly.

"How do you do? Ah, I see that you are surprised, madam." Jack gave a self-deprecating laugh, "We are not all savages here, you know, nor do we swing from the trees," he stopped to cough and blow his nose. "Pardon me. This wretched cold has left me with an infuriating tickle in my throat." He coughed again. "Sorry about that. Yes, I am from the old country, from the 'Land of Hope and Glory' if you believe all that stuff. I was born here but was raised there. How does the poem go? *'If I should die, think only this of me: that there's some corner of a foreign field that is forever England.'* Not that I'm about to die, mind you. It's a funny world, isn't it?"

"Jack's been with us ever since Bill's father died, haven't you, Jack? What's that make it, about twelve years now? Gosh, time flies, doesn't it? Best thing that ever happened to us. I couldn't possibly manage without you, Jack. You are a godsend."

They entered the workshop and stood chatting for a while when the office phone rang. Molly excused herself to answer it, leaving Jack and Phoebe to continue chatting without her.

A short while after, Molly waved at Phoebe to indicate she was done with the call and ready to leave.

"Your Jack is an interesting fellow, isn't he?" Phoebe said, while getting into the car. "He was telling me his story. Fascinating. To think that Bill's father was instrumental in getting him to England all those years ago and now, by some quirk of fate, he ends up right here on the Barclay farm. Quite extraordinary! And can you believe this? He was also in Bristol during the war."

"You talked about that – the war, I mean?" Molly let out the clutch and reversed the car.

"Yes. He asked me where I came from. So, I told him that I was from Keswick in the Lake District, that I had nursed in Bristol during the war, and that since then I had become a Londoner. He told me he'd been in the army – the British army, mind you – said he'd been stationed in Bristol just before the war broke out. Then, out of the blue, he asked me a funny question. He asked me if, when I was nursing in Bristol, I had ever come across a nurse called Dora Murphy. I was gobsmacked."

"Really? What's so odd about that?"

Molly drove around the front of the workshops and saw Jack. Something about the way he was standing caught her attention. He seemed sort of slumped, as though the wind had been taken from his sails. She would down her window and waved, "Bye, Jack," she called out, "I'll see you in the morning." As she drove away, she watched him in her rear-view mirror. Jack was motionless, cast in stone; he neither called back nor waved an acknowledgement. That's odd, she thought, not like Jack.

"Who's this Dora Murphy?"

"She's the other nurse! Remember I was telling you about the time when I was assisting a birth and that I thought the mother was Anna? Well, Dora Murphy was the nurse assisting with the other birth – assisting Libby, remember me telling you that? Isn't that a strange coincidence – I mean, that Jack should ask me about her?"

Molly was only half listening. She switched on the headlights.

"Yes, it is a coincidence I suppose. So, what did you tell him?"

"I told him that I knew her but not well – because she was in maternity, and I was in surgery."

"And then what?"

"He kept saying that it was amazing – that I should know Dora. I asked him how he knew her, but he didn't answer my question. He just said that he wouldn't mind catching up with her one day. I think he wanted to say more but –"

Phoebe sat bolt upright, aghast, her hairs on end. A wild idea, hurtling like a meteor from outer space, pierced her composure and blasted all other thoughts to the distant corners of her mind.

"Oh my God," she grabbed Molly's arm with one hand and covered her mouth with the other, "too much of a coincidence to beggar belief? But could it be? Why didn't I think of it?"

"Phoebs, what's got into you? What are you gabbling about? Why didn't you think of what?"

"Well," said Phoebe, struggling hard to digest the enormity of what had just struck her, "I just wonder if – and it's a big if – but what if Jack knew Elsa? More than that, suppose … suppose he was the father of her child? It might sound preposterous, but –"

"Oh fiddlesticks! That's outrageous," said Molly, "he would have said something before –" Suddenly she jabbed her foot onto the brake. The car lurched to a stop, and stood trembling and on edge, as though holding its breath. "I was going to say – supposing you are right – that he would have recognised her long ago. But now that I think about it, he's probably never even clapped eyes on her. When he arrived here in

Empangeni, she and Kobie were already in Eshowe. My God, what a thought! Still, it's a hell of a long bow you're stretching, isn't it? Let me think about that."

They drove the rest of the way back to the house cocooned in silence. Molly parked the car and as she opened her door, she leaned over to Phoebe, detaining her with a hand on her arm. The internal roof light came on and Phoebe was at once struck by Molly's eyes – they were large and piercing. "I think we shouldn't say anything to anyone about this," she heard Molly say, fascinated by her eyes, "after all, what good could come from it if we spilled the beans? So what if Jack knew Anna before – or Elsa, if that was her name? And if she did have a baby and if it was his – so what? It's really none of our business. What do you think?"

Phoebe stared at Molly. She didn't know what to say. She was of half a mind to find out the truth – purely to satisfy her own curiosity – yet on the other hand, she felt she had no right to stick her nose in where it did not belong.

"That's fine, Moll. The last thing I want to do is upset the applecart."

***

But it wasn't as simple as that. The next morning, after breakfast, Phoebe decided to go for a walk. She took the dogs with her and went to see how Richard and Magda's house was coming on. It was a lovely day and the sun shone brightly. By the time she arrived there, she was sweating profusely and feeling rather tired. She heard a pickup arrive and turned to see who it was, squinting into the sun. Jack climbed out. Three men jumped off the back and began to offload what appeared to be large, outdoor terracotta tiles. He saw Phoebe and came over to her.

"Morning, Madam," he said. His English accent was rich and smooth, like icing on a cake, "Did you walk? I can give you a lift back if you like." He shouted something in Zulu to one of the men who was about to carry some tiles inside. The man stopped, nodded, and waved with his free hand. He retraced his footsteps and placed the tiles on the ground near the front door. Then he went back to the pickup for a second load. "These chaps do not listen," said Jack, shaking his head, "I told them very clearly that these tiles were for the outside and were not to be taken inside. You must watch them like a hawk, otherwise, God knows what will happen."

He looked down and, after a while, began to scuff the ground with the toe of his boot. The pause in conversation gave cause for Phoebe to study him closely and she peered at him, shading her eyes with her hand. He seemed to be wrestling with his emotions, as if he wanted to say something but did not know how or where to begin. She had a feeling that some unscripted play was about to be enacted – something outside the guidelines of the conversation she had had with Molly the previous evening.

"Yesterday, Madam, when you came up to the workshops with Madam Molly, I asked you if you knew Dora Murphy – you remember that?"

"Yes. Yes, I do," and then unable to stop herself she added, "but you never said why."

Jack looked up and locked his eyes onto hers. Without breaking their hold, she saw his goatee quiver, ever so slightly, and then his Adam's apple began to move. She stared back at him and waited, feeling fearful and horribly unprepared, yet greedy for more.

"I wouldn't know Dora if I tripped over her – don't even know what she looks like. But she assisted at the birth of a friend of mine – that doesn't sound right, let me say it better. When my friend was having a baby, in Bristol, this Dora assisted with the birth."

"So?"

"She could throw light on something that has been bothering me for ages. I understand that my friend's baby was swapped with another baby – one born at the same time."

Phoebe's throat constricted and her mouth worked for air like a goldfish. Swapped babies! She threaded together her recollections and found to her surprise that they could easily fit this narrative. She felt she was going to faint. The question had to be asked and she blurted it out, heedless of the consequences. "Swapped? Who told you that?"

"Yes, swapped. I learned about it in a letter from my father. Long story, but I'm pretty sure it's true. That's why I would like to meet Dora one day – she's the only person I know who can prove it."

"My God, that's incredible," Phoebe paused, groping for words, "the woman who had the baby ... Is she related to you? What's this got to do with you?"

"Not related. But I think the baby was mine."

"You! Your baby! Oh my God! What was her name?" Phoebe's voice was a thin whisper, but it singed the air between them like a charge of static electricity, "The baby's mother – what was her name? Do you know?"

"Why?"

"Because I ... Just tell me. Please."

"Elsa. Her name was Elsa Duncan. Why do you ask?"

Phoebe would have fallen, had Jack not reached out to steady her. "I don't believe it," she said, repeatedly.

"Madam, are you alright? What don't you believe? Have I said something to upset you?"

"Jack," she lifted her face and stared at him. "I was there, Jack. I was there when the baby was born."

This utterance was like a gust of fierce wind that comes without warning and is strong enough to collapse tents. Jack seemed to sag – as though his guy ropes had been uprooted.

"You were there?"

"Yes, Jack. I was there. And she had a baby boy."

"A boy! She had a boy!"

Phoebe turned away, unable to face his fierce eyes. She found herself looking at the shimmering waters of Nsezi Lake, way off in the distance, and thinking that getting in touch with Dora had just become a must. She contemplated telling Jack that she thought Elsa was now Anna, but she held her tongue and concentrated harder on the lake, trying to overpower her thoughts. The thin stretch of water, with bright green papyrus painted on its edges like lipstick, marked the end of the farm. And on the other side, barely discernible, were wattle and daub huts, pinned as it were in haphazard fashion among the trees that fringed the open grasslands of the native reserve, much like drawing pins stuck randomly around the edges of a noticeboard. Such a peaceful scene, she thought, so quiet and somehow so serene. Distance, she reminded herself, lends enchantment to the eye. The dogs lying at her feet stirred and got up, catching her attention. She watched them pad over to Jack's vehicle and flop down in the shade beside it. She sighed, wishing she could wander off and flop down somewhere – anywhere but here.

"Madam, are you sure? Are you absolutely sure? Her name was Elsa? And what about the baby? Who was the other mother? Do you know what happened to her or her child?"

"Yes, I was there – I remember it well. What a coincidence! Yes, the person's name was Elsa. She had a baby boy." Phoebe took a deep breath. "I distinctly remember it because the mother showed absolutely no interest in her baby – none at all. But I tell you Jack, I know nothing of any babies being swapped. And I can't help you with the other mother either – I never saw her or had anything to do with her. You see, straight after the birth, I went back to the surgical ward I'd come from. That was quite normal, you know, nothing out of the ordinary about that. I have no idea at all as to what happened to either of the babies – I certainly never suspected that they had been swapped or got mixed up. I can hardly believe such a thing could happen. Honestly, Jack, this is the first I've heard of it."

"Let me fill you in." Jack felt he owed Phoebe an explanation, "What I am about to tell you is strictly confidential – I have never discussed it with anyone. Like the war – I don't like talking about it at all. I'm only telling you this because you may be able to help me. So, here we go. I was in love with a girl in Bristol called Elsa. I had no idea she was pregnant. Our fleeting relationship ended so abruptly because she just disappeared from my life. I had no idea why, or where she went, though my father's letter suggested that she may have come to

South Africa. The lack of closure from our relationship had always bothered me, but I have moved on. It is the child I am concerned about. Knowing he's okay, and what he's like. I have a responsibility to him."

He got up and walked a few paces away. He felt like a cigarette, but his cold was still bothering him, and he knew that cigarette smoke would aggravate his lungs. Instead, he dug a cough lozenge from his breast pocket and popped it into his mouth.

"Do you know how to get hold of this Dora Murphy?"

The burden of truth. Phoebe was conflicted and her courage began to wilt. She felt she ought to say yes and tell him that she had already tried, but then she would have to tell why she had done so and that would lead to Anna – to another can of worms. Jack was more interested in finding out about his child so telling him about Anna could just confuse the situation even more. Her thoughts, like flowing water, found the line of least resistance and she followed them, glad to turn her back on the source of her disquiet.

"I'll tell you what I'll do," she said, her confidence gathered pace like a yacht tacking around a buoy, "when I get back to England – which won't be long, now – I'll try and track her down for you. Bear in mind though, it was a long time ago when I saw her, so I can't make any promises. I've been in London for more than twenty years – she could be anywhere by now. But leave it to me, I'll see what I can find out for you. I promise I'll let you know, one way or another. Is that okay? Good, let's leave it like that."

She got up and dusted herself off. "Now, Jack, if you don't mind, I'd like to take you up on your offer – would you mind giving me and the dogs a lift and driving us back to Molly's house?"

10

On Phoebe's last day on the farm, she asked Molly if she could telephone London on the pretext of making sure that her friend knew her flight details and would be there at the airport to meet her. Boxing Day had come and gone, and Phoebe struggled to shake off her uneasiness; she called the hospital in Bristol and was pleasantly surprised when the switchboard operator put her through to the maternity ward and, in just a breathless minute, she found herself talking to Dora Murphy. The call began cagily and did not last long, but afterwards Phoebe sat for a long time, staring out the window. Elsa Duncan had had a healthy baby boy. It was black. But the other baby, also black, had been stillborn. And they *were* swapped! By Jessie Wainwright – she did it. The other mother was a young, coloured woman from South Africa. Her name was Rosie.

Phoebe heard footsteps in the passage and thought someone might overhear her conversation. She said goodbye abruptly and put the phone down. It seemed as though Dora had wanted to get something off her chest. But she also seemed to be hanging back, as though waiting to be questioned further. A line of action appeared before Phoebe as clearly as a line on a map. She got up and went into the office to find a pen and paper. Then she hurried to her room and began to write. For the rest of the day, in between saying her goodbyes and getting her last-minute things done, she would nip back to her dressing table and write a bit more. After dinner, she retired to her room early on the pretext that she still had packing to do. She closed the door and sat down at her dressing table, reverently, as though she were in a confessional. And there, in the church-like quiet that pressed in around her and squeezed the words from her pen as though from a tube of toothpaste, she continued writing her letter. It was well after midnight when she finished; she folded the pages and placed them in an envelope, sealed it, and crawled into bed.

But sleep would not come. For a long while she lay on her back with the covers pulled up under her chin; she stared into the darkness and listened to the crickets outside, while her mind kept spinning at a hundred miles an hour. She found comfort in the letter she wrote, she had done her best to lay it all out and tell the truth – that was all that mattered to her. She knew that Molly would faithfully pass on the letter, and she knew that Jack could draw up whatever conclusions he needed to from it.

11

On the afternoon of New Year's Eve, Thandi was helping some of the nurses to get their common room ready for the party that night when she was called to the phone. She took the call in the hallway. It was her mother. Busisiwe was in an awful state and could hardly get her words out properly. Titus was in hospital. Empangeni hospital. Thandi gathered that Busisiwe had found Titus unconscious in the bathroom and had immediately phoned for an ambulance. While it was coming, he regained consciousness, but his speech was slurred, and he couldn't get up without assistance. Fortunately, Peter was there, and they managed to get him onto his bed. The ambulance arrived about half an hour later and took him away. Busisiwe was frightened. She didn't know what to do. "What's going to happen to us?" She kept asking. "Can you come and help me?" Thandi asked to speak to Peter. She told him to stay calm and not to leave Busisiwe's side. He said they had tried to get hold of Gordon, but it was school holidays, and he was in Johannesburg. Thandi said she would try to get there as soon as she could, but it was New Year's Eve, and everything would soon be closed. She would call him back. Thandi found herself in a quandary, unsure of her next step. She was on her way to the common room to tell her friends what had happened when an idea dropped into her head and quickly spread, like a drop of cochineal into a glass of water. She turned on her heel and walked over to the administration building and then went straight to the switchboard operator and booked a call to Empangeni.

With her heart pumping in her ears, she went into the cubicle and waited for her call.

***

Richard and Bill had just returned from the hospital. Bill wanted to show Richard a patient of his. They had just walked back into the house and were in the kitchen, asking the cook to make them some tea when the phone rang. Richard heard his mother answer it as he walked into the lounge. Magda was there, sitting on the settee, talking with Jess who watched her with a bemused smile while her fingers, with practiced ease, worked a pair of long silver knitting needles. Magda's large eyes lit up when she saw Richard approaching and she held out her hand. He bent down and kissed her, nuzzling her hair and inhaling her scent deep into his lungs. He had just sat down and was lighting a cigarette when Molly appeared at the door.

"Rich, can I have a moment?" The look on her face brought him out of his chair with a start.

"What's the matter, Mum?"

"I've got Thandi on the line. Titus is in hospital. Can you talk to her?"

"How does she know I'm here? What can I do?"

"She didn't. I told her you were here. Please talk to her. It's a trunk call, don't keep her waiting."

Richard left the room and Molly sat down. "The natives always want something," said Jess over her knitting, "what does she want, Molly? Why did she call us?"

Molly was about to react, but then thought better of it. "Not sure. She's worried about Titus. Thinks he may have had a stroke or something. She feels quite helpless – her being up at Ubombo you know, and him being down here."

"So, why's she phoning here? What does she expect us to do?" Magda turned back to Jess for support. "It is New Year's Eve and we're going to the Club tonight. I hope Richard tells her that."

"Magda," said Molly, trying hard to keep her voice neutral even as her hackles rose, "she's family." She went on, waving aside the objection she saw forming in Magda's mouth, "Not real family, not strictly speaking, but to all intents and purposes she and her family are part of our family. We do what we can for our friends. Now, we don't know what she wants yet, do we? So, let's wait for Rich."

"All I'm saying is we are going out tonight. Everything's arranged. I'm all for helping this girl, but only if it doesn't mess us around."

185

Jess put down her knitting. "I'm with you, Magda. Sometimes one has to be firm. My Arthur always used to say, give an inch and they'll take a foot –"

"That's enough, Mum. We are all jumping the gun. We have no idea what Thandi wants. Let's bite our tongues and wait for Rich to tell us what's going on."

Bill walked into the room. "What's up? You all look as though you're squaring off like bantam cocks. Just kidding, Moll, just kidding. Say, anyone mind if I turn on the radio? The Second Cricket Test is on at Newlands – the Aussies won the toss and chose to bat. They're going great guns."

He was fiddling with the radio when Richard walked in and paused in the doorway. "What's the matter, Rich?" He straightened up, "Something wrong?"

"No, nothing wrong. Was talking to Thandi. About Titus. He's been taken to hospital. Here in Empangeni. She is worried stiff. So is Busisiwe. I said I'd speak to you, Dad. Can we go back and check to see how he is? I said I'd call her back. Sounds like he's in bad shape – stroke or heart attack is my guess. I offered to go up to Ubombo and bring her back. So that she can be with Busisiwe. Everything is closed now. It's Saturday, and Monday will be a holiday so that means –"

"Richard, we are due at the Country Club tonight. Have you forgotten?"

"No, my darling, I haven't forgotten, but –"

"No buts. Going to fetch her is out of the question. What would she do if we weren't here?"

"But we are here, Mags. And she's a friend."

"Why can't someone else go? Why does it have to be you?"

"It doesn't. I suppose someone else could. But if I left now, I could be back by –"

"Well, suit yourself. I'm going to the Club." She got up and walked to the door. "I really don't think we have to go racing all over the country whenever someone gets sick. I mean, the man is in a hospital, isn't he? Isn't that enough? And why does she call here – does she think we are a soft touch? What does she expect? That we would drop everything and rush off to sort out her problems for her?" When she saw the stony faces arrayed before her and realised in that instant that she was on her own, her temper erupted and she swept on, regardless. "*My magtig*! I don't understand why you people fall over backwards to help Blacks so much. And you, Richard – you have the hots for her. I saw you looking for her at Mary's wedding –"

"The hots for her! Don't be silly. You're the only person I have –"

"Well, she has them for you. I can tell."

"Come on, Mags, be reasonable. She's just a friend – we grew up together. She called to ask if Dad could find out how serious Titus's condition is. She isn't expecting – wait, Mags, don't go. Mags, please."

But Magda swirled on the ball of her foot, flaring her skirt in a way that even then in that crowded moment, caught Richard's eye. She tossed back her head and stormed out, eyes blazing and her shoes drumming a retreating tattoo on the parquet floor.

Richard's head dropped. "Oh, God. What do you think, Dad?"

"I think you've upset your girl. In hindsight, perhaps you could have –"

"Rich." They all turned to Molly. She saw hope rising in her son's eyes. "Magda is overwrought – it's not uncommon for women to be overly emotional during pregnancy." She walked up to Richard and put her arm around him. "Call Thandi back, dear. Tell her Daddy will call the ward and find out how he is. Also, Rich, tell her to get ready. Tell her we are sending a vehicle to fetch her. Bill, I'm going to call Jack and ask him if he can get one of our drivers to go up there and –"

"What if he can't find one? What if they are all too full of hooch? It is Saturday, remember."

"I reckon they'll be as high as kites by now," said Jess, "especially today."

"Now, now, Mum," Molly raised a remonstrating finger, "let's cross that bridge when we get to it, okay? Bill and I will go if we have to, won't we, Bill? Or, if I have to, I'll go alone. I'm not going to the Ball. Go and call her, Rich. She's waiting, isn't she? And while you're at it, phone Busisiwe – the number is in my book. Then go and cheer Magda up – tell her what we've decided. Tell her you are not going to Ubombo. God forbid that she should be upset, especially on New Year's Eve. Now, off you go."

12

By the time the New Year dawned, Jack had read Phoebe's letter many times; he would lock himself away, night after night, and pore over it, like a monk scrutinising an ancient parchment for revelations that escaped the naked eye. Mavis watched him closely; she saw the agony etched on his face and she felt his misery. The house became as quiet as a tomb – the children tip-toed around him and even their dog, usually so playful, kept its distance, slinking around with its tail between its legs. Eventually, Mavis could bear it no longer.

"The past is the past," she said, holding his head between her hands and staring into his eyes, "it cannot be undone. Let it go, Jack. You did nothing wrong. How many times have I heard that quote of yours – you know, the one that goes something like this: *'learn from yesterday, live for today, hope for tomorrow'*. We have –"

"Einstein. I think it was Einstein who said that –"

"Whoever. We have so much to live for, don't we – living is what keeps our hopes alive."

"Yes, Mavis," he sat down heavily on the bed and stared up at her with wild, wet eyes. Tears ran down his cheeks, unheeded. "I might have done nothing wrong, but I have a son! The letter says so. It matches the letter I got from Dad. Elsa and me – a son. Oh hell! That takes some getting used to. I mean, what am I supposed to believe, hey? What am I supposed to do? No, listen. This letter says that the other mother was also from South Africa – is that simply a coincidence? That she was a coloured – more coincidence? And it says her Christian name was Rosie – yet another coincidence? Come on, Mavis, who else can it be but Frankie's daughter?" He stood up and gripped her shoulders. She took a step back; she had never seen him looking so wild before, nor had she ever heard such desperation in his voice. He went on. "Didn't he take Rosie to England to have her baby – how many times has he told us that, hey, Mavis? How many times? Dammit, the facts fit, don't they? And you know what all this means, what it adds up to? It means that as sure as God made little apples, Isaac is my son. Can you get your head around that? I can't. All these years we have known each other, yet without knowing –"

"Slow down, Jack, you're strangling yourself. You'll give yourself a heart attack. Your heart is breaking, and I feel for you. I understand, Jack, I really do. I can see the anguish on your face, the wild look in your eyes. I see that you feel something must be done but you don't know what to do or how. And, my love, I agree with everything you say. But what are you going to do about it? You can hardly go to Rosie and say, 'Isaac is my son, not yours. Your baby was stillborn.' For what purpose?" Mavis ran her hand around him and began to rub his back, as soothingly as she could. "Who are we, Jack – who are we to blow her world apart? We are not God; we have no right to kill her happiness as we might slaughter a chicken in the backyard. You are too full of love to do that. Rosie adores Isaac and he is her life. You know that and I know that, and it's lovely to see – but do we really want to destroy her happiness? She would die if she knew the contents of that letter, she really would. And, we have our own children, our pride and joy – are we going to upset them as well?" She curled around him and wiped the tears from his face with her other hand. "Did the letter say anything about Elsa – you know, how to contact her? No? Then let's keep all this to ourselves. You have always liked Isaac, haven't you? Now, you have reason to *love* him. You can father him without him knowing. Isn't that beautiful? Isn't that enough?"

Jack stared at her. It was as though he was seeing her for the first time. "Oh, Mavis, you amaze me! You are an angel, an absolute angel. Do you think we can? Won't it sort of leak out?"

"No. This will be our secret –"

"But can I keep it? I am bursting to tell him. You know –"

"Jack, you have told me so many times that God moves in strange ways … Well, so do the *amadlozi*. I think that they must be smiling now; they like to see good, harmonious relationships – ones that grow strong and get better and better … Isn't that something we can be proud of?"

Her words were like a sprinkling of rain on parched soil; new thoughts stirred and raised their heads. His gratitude was almost palpable. It was a moment of symbiosis, of profound togetherness, the like of which he had never experienced before. He hugged her and kissed her. Like an exhausted relay runner at the end of his race, Jack handed over the decision-making baton, happy to relinquish responsibility and defer to what on face value seemed to be her better judgement. He felt fatigued and, while he sucked in his breath, he luxuriated in an immense feeling of relief which seemed to reach right down to his toes. At her urging, he put the letter away and promised not to look at it again. Mavis said that no word about it should escape their lips, not to a living soul. He readily agreed – the bottle of unhappiness should be corked and put away. From then on, their silence was as absolute as it was inscrutable.

13

Richard picked up another magazine and glanced at his watch. He had been in the waiting room for more than two hours and still no word from the delivery ward. The magazine was old and didn't really interest him, so he tossed it aside and went back to his chair and closed his eyes. He stretched out his legs, content to entertain whatever thoughts wandered into his head. Since New Year, a lot of seemingly disparate things had happened. Funny, he thought, how they had piled up, one after another, banging into each other like rail trucks in a shunting yard. First there was Christmas with the Celliers family. Straight after that, Phoebe had left. Then there was The Ball. And there always had to be some unpleasantness – this came in the form of the debilitating stroke that Titus had suffered. Richard was in awe of his parents – their response, without hesitation, had been to build a house on the farm for Busisiwe so that she and Titus could be near to medical attention, if and when he should need it. His father went a step further and arranged for Thandi to work at the hospital with them. Richard approved – she was a damn good nurse, and he liked the idea of her being close. All these moments happened one after the other, and now here he was, ready for his very own big moment. He was going to be a father.

Richard had his reservations about the General Practitioner, Piet. He would have opted to go to Durban for this, but Magda had insisted that Piet was to deliver her baby.

The door swung open and Piet appeared, snapping Richard back to reality. He took off his mask and revealed a rakish grin and a lot of even, white teeth. In that instant Richard saw what he suspected Piet's female patients mistook for medical competence – a dashing virility that made Richard pull his tummy in.

"Congratulations, Rich." Piet stuck out his hand. "A boy. Easy birth, all went very well indeed. Mother and child in great shape. You can go in. They are cleaning up."

When Magda saw him approaching, she smiled and turned her dark eyes onto him and they, belying what she had just been through, smouldered with such intensity that his knees nearly gave way and his voice died in his throat. He was stung by the beauty of the scene before him – his wife, now a mother, holding her swaddled baby for the first time, exhaustion written all over her pallid face, yet radiant beyond belief. And the baby, dark haired, slightly yellowish and wrinkled like a prune – his son! A vague feeling of being instrumental in the creation of something unique – something profound and irrevocably connected to him – seeped into his consciousness, causing him to hover at the foot of the bed, unsure who he should go to first. Magda stretched out her free hand, so he went to her quickly, misty-eyed, and bent down to kiss her. He heard her whisper, "Are you happy, my love? A son. Born under Taurus, strong and dependable. And sensual, like his father ... The Barclay name lives on." He lifted his head and caressed his son's cheek with a curled forefinger and noticed again the slight yellow tinge to his complexion. But then his little mouth moved, and Richard felt a surge of love rising in him, and he smiled at his son – what grand thoughts flashed through his mind then! There was so much he wanted to say but the words swirling around in his head could not find his mouth. Instead, he reached for her hand and kissed it. Sitting down beside her and staring into her eyes, he grinned foolishly. For a while they whispered sweet nothings to each other, smiling uncontrollably, until the nurse arrived to take her to the ward to rest.

"Rich, we agreed on Ben, didn't we? Ben suits him nicely. Say goodbye to Ben."

Richard walked back to the bed and patted his son. He remembered them paging through books, looking for neutral names, ones that were pronounced the same in English and in *Afrikaans* – and the shorter the better. Ben for a boy, Fleur for a girl.

"Bye-bye, Ben," Richard stroked his son's tiny fingers, marvelling at how delicate and finely sculptured they were, "look after Mum for me, little man, while I'm gone. I'll be back soon." He kissed Magda again. "Might be mid-morning – I have a ward-round first up. Now, get some rest. Bye."

On the way home, he switched on the radio and listened to the news. The headline story was about the government's newly introduced Prohibition of Mixed Marriages (Amendment) Bill, which said that even marriages between people of different races that had been made abroad would not be recognised in South Africa. The announcer, apparently unaware of the irony of what he was saying, went on to add that in the case of Loving versus the State of Virginia, the US Supreme Court found by a majority of six to three that the Virginian law banning interracial marriage was unconstitutional. Richard wondered why the local government got so wound up about sex across the colour line. Weren't there already nearly one and a half million Coloureds in South Africa – a third of the white population. It made no sense at all – you couldn't stop people from falling in love. Then came some news about the Terrorism Act – it was going to be extended to restrict political activity. The announcer went on to say that the ANC and the Zimbabwe African People's Union had formed an alliance against South Africa and Rhodesia. Richard felt his chest tighten – white people were being hemmed in. In response to this, the announcer said, the government was going to pass legislation making military conscription compulsory for all white males over the age of sixteen.

Richard thought about the state the country was currently in; the ANC wanted to murder people like him … and people like Bram Fischer, an avowed communist, lined themselves up to defend these self-same terrorists! Then there was Steve Biko, a medical student in Durban who was carrying on about Black Consciousness – Richard made a mental note to ask Brydon what his thoughts were of him. It felt as though the world was standing on its head – and his wife had just had a baby! It worried him. Deeply. He agonised about the state of things, and what lay in store for his child when he grew up.

He switched the radio off and stared grimly at the strip of road that the narrow beam of his headlights revealed to him. Everything else was black, out of sight, and remote as interstellar space. He couldn't wait to get home and into bed.

***

Richard felt like a million dollars as he made his way into the hospital, he felt free of the thoughts that troubled him the night before. He glanced down at the bunch of flowers he was carrying – he had picked them himself, first blooms from their garden. They had been in the back of the car and although he had wrapped their stems in wet cottonwool, they now looked a bit droopy. To him, it was the thought that counted. The world, it seemed, was infinitely benevolent and had, he told himself as though patting himself on the back, smiled bountifully upon him – he was married to the most beautiful woman in the world and now, to cap it all, he was a father! He had phoned Magda's parents and Andre. But, not content with just them and feeling he ought to be shouting his good news to the world at large, he had phoned as many people as he could – indeed, he had gone without breakfast in order to do just that.

He entered Magda's room with the flowers held behind his back. Magda's mother was there. She was sitting in a chair beside the bed. He stopped dead in his tracks.

"Hello, Richard. Don't look so surprised. After you called this morning Kobus said to me, 'your place is at your daughter's side.' So, I hopped in the car and here I am – I arrived ten minutes ago."

"Hello Mum," he went to her, wearing a broad smile like a strip of Band-Aid, and kissed her cheek. "Glad you came." Then he bent down and kissed Magda, keeping the flowers hidden from her view.

"Has our Ben made an appearance yet?"

"Not yet. Mom had a peep through the window, but you can't really see much from there. You're a doctor. Can't you ask the nurse to bend the rules so Mom can see my baby?"

"I'm afraid not. There will be plenty of other times –"

"Look at the flowers, Rich. Mom brought those. And the roses are from Piet."

"From Piet?"

"Yes, he was here earlier. *So gaaf en bedagsaam.* Such a nice touch, don't you think? Hope you're nice like that to your patients."

Richard winced. The flowers were lovely. By comparison his looked as though they had been run over. "Well darling, I brought you some too," he smiled brightly and brought them from behind his back with a flourish, "fresh from our garden. Picked them myself."

"Oh, thank you, Richy. Very nice. Barberton daisies – they are from the front garden, aren't they? And the chrysanthemums, so pretty – see, they waited for Ben before they opened their pretty little faces! So sweet of you. But they need water, don't they. Get a vase – from the cupboard over there – give them a drink. That's it. They'll soon pick up –"

"Tell Rich about the blood. What the nurse said."

"Blood?" Richard stiffened. His eyes swung back and forth between mother and daughter. "What's this about blood?"

"Oh," Magda waved her hand dismissively, "the nurse said that they may have to take some blood from Ben. Don't ask me, I have no idea. She said not to –"

"Yah, but tell him what she said about the sickness."

"Sickness?"

"Oh, Rich, she said something about Ben being a bit too yellow. Said Piet just wants to be sure. They're going to wait and see for a day or two, then decide. She asked me about my blood type, was it A? I said yes, it was. I said she should know that already. Then she babbled on about jaundice – that they were going to keep an eye on it. What's jaundice, Rich – I know it's about being yellow and all that, but what is it?"

Without going into the details about liver function, red cells and bilirubin levels in the blood, Richard did his best to explain it as simply as he could – he told her that new-born jaundice was quite common and usually went away in a few weeks. But if it didn't, then it could be treated easily enough. But as he extrapolated what he had just heard, worry wormed its way up his spine. He didn't show it.

Ben did not shake off his jaundice right away. With the spectre of Richard's inquisitive face peering over his shoulder, Piet made sure that he was extra cautious in all that he did. He called a paediatrician friend in Durban who endorsed what Piet was doing and suggested that Piet might want to have a blood group test done, just in case this was an ABO incompatibility episode. On that advice, he had blood samples taken – including one for a blood group test – and had them sent off to the lab for analysis. While the bilirubin level hadn't risen, it nonetheless remained frustratingly high. So, he had Ben placed under bright lights for two days. To everyone's relief, the phototherapy seemed to work because the bilirubin levels began to drop. Consequently, fear of blood type incompatibility receded. Four days later, a very relieved Piet told Magda that she could take Ben home with her. However, because antibodies could linger in his circulation for some weeks after his discharge, he told her that she had to bring Ben back to the hospital for ongoing blood tests until he was completely satisfied that Ben's bilirubin levels were absolutely normal and that there was nothing left to worry about.

14

One sunny afternoon, three weeks later, Richard came home early. He was in a good mood and couldn't wait to see his son. Magda was in the nursery with Ben and had just finished feeding him when Richard walked into the room. Her dress was off one shoulder and when she turned towards him, his eyes dipped, locking onto her exposed breast. It was heavy and faintly marbled. She ladled it gently into her brassier with a cupped hand.

"Well, hello! Home early! What a nice surprise. Here," she said, buttoning up her dress and sweeping her hair back behind her ear, "I've just finished feeding the little man – can you take him for me please and burp him? He's feeding so well now – and so greedy, just can't get enough!"

"I saw Dad at the hospital, and he asked if he and Mum could come round this evening for a look-see. I said sure, come for a drink. They'll be here shortly. You okay with that?"

"Yes, but you should have warned me – I don't have anything prepared –"

"Mags, please," said Richard, taking Ben from her, "you don't have to slay the fatted calf every time someone visits us – especially not for family. They're just popping in for a quick hello and I'm pretty sure they won't stay long. Don't worry about snacks – they're not expecting anything."

Magda shrugged and sat down. Her mother would never have accepted that – she always liked plenty of notice. She watched Richard walk round and round the room on soft feet, holding Ben over his shoulder and gently patting his back. Father and son, such a good sight. For Richard, it was a moment of indescribable joy, just the three of them in the room like that, with the world for the moment shut out and far away – and no sound, except for a tremulous whisper as his breath passed through his nostrils, and from his son, nothing but mewling snuffles and little burps that made his heart swell in his chest.

"Shall I take him now?" Magda could see that Ben was drifting off to sleep. "I'll put him down for a nap and then I'll go to the kitchen. You know me – I'll find something quick and easy. Oh, by the way, I saw Piet today. He's so happy with Ben – no more talk of jaundice. And he gave me a sheaf of papers – my discharge summary, copies of the lab reports – stuff like that. Said he thought you'd like to see them. They are Greek to me. Over there, on the table, next to my bag."

Magda went into the kitchen and Richard took a bottle of Castle Lager from the fridge on the veranda and settled himself into one of the reclining cane chairs. He heard a coucal call and looked up, searching the sky for rain clouds. It was a silly habit he knew, something that jangled his science nerve, but, he supposed, the coucal wasn't called the rain bird for nothing. There wasn't a cloud to be seen and for a few moments he sat and watched the shadows leave the building and crawl across the lawn. He wasn't really interested but he thought he'd better look at Ben's medical reports. He was rifling through them when he heard Bill's Mercedes pull up. He got up. Then stopped. He read it again. It couldn't be. Ben's blood type was B. He clutched the pages with both hands and brought them up for a closer look. But there it was, in black and white. There must have been some mistake with Ben's blood group test. Then, as though being struck by a falling tree, the enormity of what he was reading, hit him with such force that he staggered backwards and collapsed back onto his chair.

A few moments later, Molly walked out onto the veranda and saw Richard slumped with his head in his hands. "Good God, Rich! What's wrong? You look awful." His mind was crammed full of so many wild thoughts that he could not find the words to reply. "Oh, Mum, I'm shattered. Come into the garden with me. I don't want anyone to hear." He got up and took her hand and led her down the steps and onto the lawn. They walked until they reached the flowerbeds at the bottom of the garden.

"Where's Dad?"

"In the kitchen, chatting to Magda. Why? What's up?"

"I've just had a look at Ben's medical reports – Piet gave them to Mags to give to me. Funny, I wasn't going to look at them, but then I did. I've just seen Ben's blood type. It's B."

"So what?"

"Well, Magda is type A and I'm type O negative."

"Rich, what's that mean?"

"If Ben is B, then it's impossible for me to be his father."

The sky fell in. They stared at each other, seeking solace in each other's face.

Molly felt a knife turning in her bowels. Her mind went immediately to the time she was at the pictures in Durban with Mary. She recalled the scene and saw, as though it had happened only yesterday, not just Magda on the arm of a tall, handsome man with a moustache – much as that had alarmed her – but more so, the telling way they gazed into each other's eyes. There was a familiarity there, a shared intimacy that for Molly now explained so much.

"Gosh, Richard. That's … I'm not sure what to say … You're sure there's no mistake?"

"Quite sure. For a child to be type B with a mother of type A, then the father has to be type B or AB. I am neither – I am type O. It's as simple as that."

"Does she know?"

Richard said nothing, his eyes were screwed into his corrugated face.

Molly pursed her lips and hurried on, "Well, you'd only just started going out with her, hadn't you – you don't honestly think you were the first one … the first one to sleep with her, do you?"

"Oh, Mum, I'm gutted. I feel dead inside, like I've been duped. What am I going to say to her?"

His anguish made her want to cry. "Tricked? Remember, Rich, doubt feeds the brain but starves the heart. Keep a tight rein on it. What's there to say? I'd say nothing at all – I wouldn't even raise the subject. What would be the point?" She reached for his hands. "You weren't engaged, were you? She may have been in a relationship with someone else and then dropped him like a hot cake the minute she started with you. Dropped him, just like that. It happens a lot, you know. I mean, when you walked into her life, out of the blue like that, she ditched him for you. For you, Rich, the love of her life. Who knows? Be charitable, give her the benefit of the doubt. But does it –"

"Why me, Mum? What have I done to deserve this? Why couldn't I have had the fairy-tale, you know – the princess, the castle, and live happily ever after? Why did I have to draw the short straw?"

"You haven't. Stop feeling sorry for yourself – look on the bright side –"

"How can I? Will I ever be able to trust her?"

"Why on earth not? It's not as though she's been unfaithful to you, has she? What trust has she betrayed? It's your pride that has been dented, not her fidelity. But does it really matter? Why torture yourself? I'm sure things like this happen a lot more than we would ever know. If it hadn't been for the jaundice scare, you probably would never have known either. She may not know. In fact, I'm pretty sure she doesn't. What I do know – and she has told me many times – is that she loves you."

She kissed Richard on his cheek and hugged him. "You love her, don't you? She loves you, doesn't she? You have a beautiful baby boy. Remember, she *chose* you. Isn't that what matters? The last thing I would do if I were you, Rich, is put it on the line and confront her. For what purpose? You'll lose all that you hold dear. And you'll become bitter and twisted in the process. You're bigger than that. Pull yourself together – let it go."

She heard Magda call from the veranda, telling them that Bill had prepared the drinks – they'd better hurry, there was a gin and tonic waiting for them on the *stoep*. "Coming," she shouted back over her shoulder, "won't be long. Just enjoying the garden."

"Come now, Rich. Let's join them. Not a word to a soul. It's not the end of the world."

It wasn't the end of the world, but from that moment on, ever so slowly, the colour seeped from it – like a photograph exposed to sunlight, it began to fray around the edges and fade, and before long, it assumed a washed-out, sepia hue.

15

June has been a hell of a month, thought Richard. Firstly, for six days he had watched in awe as the Israeli forces, with brutal efficiency, imposed their will on what had been Palestine and carved out for themselves what they thought was their due, thereby redrawing the boundaries of their infant state. The majority of white South Africans, he felt, cheered and clapped, marvelling at Israel's military prowess and, as they saw it, the cocky way in which that tiny, beleaguered state thumbed her nose at the world. Richard found himself being carried along by this widespread backslapping – for him, the unfolding drama of the Middle East was akin to watching two bare-knuckled boys having a fist fight behind the school gym. His head was with the bigger, slower moving boy who, in this case his conscience told him, was more likely to be in the right; but his heart, thumping wildly against his ribs, was with the cocky little guy who was so nimble on his feet. For someone who had never been in a fight – he abhorred violent confrontation – Richard found these David and Goliath scenarios enthralling. More often than not though, he tended to side with the underdog. If Israel could stand up for itself like that and thumb its nose at world opinion, then why couldn't South Africa? But even as he tried to soothe his agitation with this comforting thought, another one, buried way back, in an inner recess of his mind like an old photograph buried in an attic, kept bobbing into his consciousness, muddying or obfuscating what he felt ought to be clear and straight forward – it was the haunting picture of his wife, naked and in bed with a faceless man, the father of his son.

Secondly, and much closer to home, Thandi's grandfather died. When Busisiwe learned about it, she straight away told Thandi that as Gordon was not able to represent her at the funeral, then she would have to. She explained that with Titus as incapacitated as he was, there was no way she could leave him – her place was at his side.

Busisiwe had also told Molly, and she in turn told Richard. His heart lit up and an idea rose in his mind like a kite on a string. Not quite sure why he responded with the alacrity that he did, yet feeling drawn blindly by some invisible force, he drove to the clump of white-walled houses behind the compound and parked in front of Busisiwe's house. Thandi greeted him at the door and invited him in. Without sitting down, he commiserated with Busisiwe and paid his respects to Titus who sat in a chair by the window. Then, turning to Thandi, he offered to drive her to the funeral.

"Thank you, Sir, very kind. But I thought I'd ask Isaac. He –"

"Nonsense, don't bother him. Let me. Besides, I would like to see your ancestral home – the home, I mean, where you came from, Busisiwe. I have heard so much about your grandfather and am sorry now that I never put aside the time to go and see him while he was alive. I feel I must go. And Madondo, your uncle. He'll be there, won't he? I would like to see him again. What do you say, Thandi? Want to come with me? I'll take you and bring you back – once we get there, you can do as you please."

Thandi felt conflicted. She looked at her mother. Busisiwe shrugged and looked at Titus. Richard was adamant – who was she to intervene. "You decide, my child," she said at last, taking her daughter's hand, "if the *Nkosana* is offering, then you might as well go with him."

***

Early on Saturday morning, Richard picked her up in his Land Rover and they headed off to the funeral. Thandi sat frozen beside him and stared straight ahead. In an attempt to thaw the atmosphere which, he felt he could cut with a blunt knife, he lit a cigarette, rolled down his window and rested his elbow over the sill with studied nonchalance.

"So, Thandi," he said, leading off with a disarming question, "what do you do for pleasure?"

"For pleasure?"

"I mean, what do you do when you're not working? What do you do for entertainment? I remember you telling me that there was nothing to do in Ubombo and I just wondered if life is better here in Empangeni."

She wasn't sure how to answer; she didn't like questions that pried into her private life.

"It's better here, thank you."

"Do you get out much?"

"Yes. Sometimes." She looked at him sideways, and he found himself staring at her long, delicate eyelashes. "You know Moodley?" She looked away quickly. "The Moodley who works in the chemist? Well, he shows films in the hall for black people at the back of the mill. On a sheet – he hangs a sheet up on the wall. Once a month. He borrows a projector from Mr Christenson and gets the films from somewhere in Durban – in Grey Street, I think."

"Movies, hey? Are they any good?"

"Yes. We saw *Bonnie and Clyde*. Ish, too much shooting. We also saw *Z*."

"Really?" He could hardly believe that a somewhat obscure European film would be of much interest to Moodley's audiences. "I'm surprised Moodley could get a copy. It's political. I saw it. Did you like it?"

"Yes, I saw it with Isaac, and he said –"

"You go to movies with Isaac?"

There was a sharp edge to his voice, and she glanced back at him, quickly, with suspicious eyes. "Yes. We go when we can. Isaac likes films. Says he likes ones that make him think."

Thandi and Isaac together. He could feel his hackles rising. Very deliberately he returned his mind to their conversation. How do non-Whites get access to such current films, he wondered, especially to political ones?

"What did he say about *Z*?"

"He says governments can kill a person, but they can't kill what he stands for."

"Did he now! Is that what you think?"

"Well, I'm not into politics. I like films that make me laugh. But it's true, isn't it? Titus always talks about what he calls the 'indomitable human spirit.'"

Richard sat for a while digesting all that he had heard. He decided to change the subject.

"Where is Gordon?" he asked, exhaling a stream of smoke. "Isn't he going to the funeral?"

Thandi's eyes flicked at him and then as quickly they flicked back to the road. "He is away."

"Away? He's always away. Haven't seen him for years. I thought he was teaching, somewhere near Durban. When you say he's away, where do you mean?"

"I don't know. He just tells us he is away."

Richard stared at her. She refused to look at him. There was something quite desperate about the way her eyes clung to the road – a vein twitched in her neck and the tip of her tongue peered out, like the head of a tortoise, and oscillated across her lower lip. He felt his heart lurch and he knotted his fingers around the steering wheel. Such vulnerability stung him. Compassion rose up in his bowels, flushing his entire body and making him hot. Instinct told him to reach out and reassure her – perhaps even to give her a friendly hug; learning told him not to, that she was out of bounds, so he didn't. And he recalled the time their hands had touched up at Cam's game farm and the enmity that their entwined fingers had unleashed. Then he found himself thinking about her and Isaac. Together. The thought was unacceptable, adding to his discomfort. He took a deep breath and changed the subject.

"You know those clinics that my mother and her church friends have set up," he asked, keeping his voice as light as possible, "with farmers? The ones bordering the reserves? Yes, just like the one on our farm. And you know that I visit them with her, don't you – that most of the time I'm the doctor at these clinics and I examine all the patients that come to them?"

She said nothing, but her eye lashes fluttered, catching the sunlight. "They're pretty popular, you know. Now people in these outlying areas don't have to catch a bus into town, just to see a doctor. Well, the church has asked her to set up more of them, more clinics. So now she's looking for a fulltime nursing sister."

He took his eyes off the road and glanced at her, eager for her reaction. Interest flared briefly in her large round eyes and then subsided, a flickering flame about to go out. He wanted to kindle it and blow on it gently, desperate to keep it alive. "She's looking for someone to look after them," he said, adding tinder as gently as he could, "a qualified nurse. A matron actually. Someone with experience. Someone like you." The flame wavered but did not go out. "It'll be fulltime. With good pay – the same as the hospitals pay. She didn't ask me to ask you. I think she is going to ask Jack if he wouldn't mind spreading the word for her. But would you be interested? Your time would be your own, you know. And you would be working from home. You'd have a good job and still be able to keep an eye on Titus for your mother. Could suit you perfectly."

"Thank you. I will think about it."

That was all. But the kindling was alight; he saw the glow on her face. Satisfied, he returned his attention to the road.

They drove on and attended the funeral. Richard had never been to a native funeral before. There was a big crowd and the Zulu king had sent one of his *indunas* to represent him. This was a huge sign of respect for the old warrior who all his life had stood proud for tradition, custom and ritual – never once had he forsaken the ways of his ancestors. As he was not a member of the family, Richard did not attend the *ukubuyisa* ceremony, but he did partake of the slaughtered ox which had been cleansed and purified with traditional medicines. And he noted with interest that the corpse was lowered into the grave in a sitting position. A spectator nearby explained that this symbolised the journey to the spirit world that the dead man was about to undertake. Grains of different cereals were placed in his hand – these would be for his welfare in the world of the *izithunzi*, the place of the living dead. His *isicoco* was placed below his bent knees and his snuff box, with freshly -ground snuff, was placed within easy reach of his hand. Also close to hand, were his personal assegais – calamity would befall the family were these important personal possessions not to accompany him on his journey to the next world. A number of other possessions were also interred – the only one deliberately omitted, Richard learned, was the old man's private beer-pot. It had great significance for it would be used later in remembrance ceremonies. This was not an untimely death, not one associated with witchcraft, and it wasn't an occasion for mourning. Rather, it was a time to celebrate a natural occurrence for it signified the continuation of existence.

Richard pondered about this as he looked around for Thandi. She was some way off, surrounded by womenfolk and was hard to tell apart. They all sat in similar fashion, knees together and their feet tucked demurely beneath them. Some of them, in traditional dress, had long twisted strips of beads around their waists and this he knew signified their unmarried status. Richard knew he could not join them, but he edged closer, hoping to catch her attention. But to no avail – she either did not see him or chose to ignore him. Frustrated, he lit a cigarette and turned back to the ceremony. The sun was warm on his face, and he wished he had brought a hat. Then he heard the praise-songs being recited in that marvellous Zulu voice he knew so well, and he forgot about Thandi and the heat. The laments were so poetic, so rich in metaphor, and delivered with such artful cadence and so much expression. He couldn't help feeling – from the snatches he was able to follow – that they had a lot more meaning or relevance for the people around him than any prayer book litany had had for him or for the congregations he had frequented, either in his mother's church or in the chapels of the schools he had attended.

On the way back, Thandi said, "Please tell your mother that I am interested in the clinic job."

"You are? That's great! What made you decide so quickly?"

"I mentioned it to my *qhikiza* – she was there. She said that the shades would approve – they would be happy if I did that. I would be helping my people."

"Aren't you a Christian, Thandi?" Richard asked, intrigued. "You don't believe that do you?"

"I am a Christian. But I also believe in what our people say. To be a good person I have to maintain a good relationship with the *amadlozi* – what harm is there in that?"

The ice was broken. All they talked about on the way home was medicine, and how best to dispense it at the farm clinics that Molly had initiated. It was something external that they had in common, and the more they talked, the more like colleagues they became. Thandi asked lots of questions and, as the conversation progressed, so their voices became more animated and less restrained. One thing she had found missing in the hospital environment, she told him, jabbing her forefinger up and down, was a place for, or an understanding of, traditional medicine and an acknowledgement that in African society the *inyanga* had an important role to play, healing both body and mind. She was looking forward to working in a place where, for the sake of her patients, she could join hands with the practitioners of traditional medicine. This was a red flag to Richard and ordinarily he would have voiced his hitherto fiercely held objections. But this was a moment of shared intimacy, one that lifted him onto his toes – it was a moment too precious to squander on semantics – so he kept nodding and urging her on with his eyes.

Driving with the sun setting in his rear-view mirror, Richard felt once again the inexorable affinity he had for Thandi, the one that had so captivated him when he was with her in Mkuze. He was entranced and let her talk without interruption, hanging on every word, and, as she warmed to the subject, he found that there was a lot more to traditional medicine than he had ever supposed. Whenever she paused, he would feed her with questions as though she were a bird in a cage – he would do anything to keep her talking, anything to hear her voice stripped of formality or reservation, both of which he abhorred and drove him to distraction.

***

Two months later, Thandi resigned from the hospital and became Molly's fulltime nurse and helper with her clinics. If Bill had objections, he didn't voice them – after all, the church was picking up the tab and Molly was happy. And the participating farmers were unfazed – it didn't interfere with their golf or tennis fixtures and, more to the point, there was a cost benefit: the absentee rate of the labourers decreased and, correspondingly, they seemed happier. Only Busisiwe had misgivings. She saw the increasing amount of time that Richard and Thandi were spending together, and she fretted at the intimacy she saw growing between them. But she accepted it with a bland face, telling herself it was founded on mutual professional admiration – she respected that – but at the same time, she couldn't help fearing that it would grow tendrils of its own, tendrils that would snake out with a remorseless inevitably and ensnare them. She remained silent. In this matter, her feet had no nose.

The sun was slipping below the trees and long purple shadows were beginning to spread across the front lawn when the last of the patients left, taking with them their chatter and the muted cries of their children. Molly stopped doing what she was doing and looked around. The sudden absence of sound seemed to hollow out the high-vaulted rondavel in which they stood, reminding her of the stillness she associated with a church. She looked at her watch and turned to Richard.

"Well, well. That's it. I have to run. Thank you. There were more patients today than I thought there'd be. You don't mind me going now, do you? Dad and I are going out tonight and I still have a lot to do. Rich, can you give Thandi a lift home? I really must rush. Bye."

After she had gone, Richard and Thandi tidied up and put things away. It didn't take long; they drained the autoclave and turned it off, locked the medicine cabinets and then closed the windows. Soon they were on their way.

Richard enjoyed working in the clinics with Thandi. Not only was she a very good nurse, but she had a way with the patients and easily gained their confidence. Many of them, womenfolk of the farm labourers, came straight from the reserves and Richard, knowing how suspicious they were of the white man's medicines, was grateful for Thandi's intervention and ability to make them relax, especially the children. And she had a marvellous way of anticipating him, as if she could read his mind – she seemed to know what instrument he needed or what medicine he wanted, long before he asked for it. Usually, Thandi and Molly would get to a clinic before he did and they would have everything sorted out by the time he arrived, often straight from theatre. It worked well. They were a good team, the three of them, and in between patients there was always time for a quick joke and a bit of light-hearted tomfoolery. Molly, doing the paperwork, would smile at their banter and marvel that it never spilled over into the time spent with the patients.

"Mind if I smoke?"

"You always ask me that and I always say, go ahead."

Richard laughed and blew smoke out the window. They were cresting a steep hill and as they did so, the setting sun came into view. It looked like a burnt-out orange ball, falling towards the horizon. It had plunged behind a large cumulus cloud, highlighting it gloriously and splashing vivid colours high up into the sky. It was a magnificent sight, and instinctively he slowed down.

"Good heavens! Look at that!" He stuck his hand out the window and pointed.

Thandi leaned towards him to look through his window. "Yes, very pretty."

He stopped the car. "See the sun's rays? See how they make that cloud stand out?"

She put one hand on the dashboard and bent over, leaning right across him to get a better look. "Yes," she said, holding onto the windowsill with her other hand, "that's beautiful, isn't it."

Closeness. It aroused him. Her hair was almost in his face. Close up, finely spun, and soft; he inhaled it, drawing the scent of it deep into his lungs. She heard him and turned her head and saw his face flushed pink. For a few moments their eyes were mere inches apart and they stared at each other, as though they were seeing each other for the first time. Richard swallowed. She sucked in her breath. Neither of them moved. Her lips parted, and he could feel the warmth of her breath on his face. He could have kissed her then, could have done it easily and gotten away with it – he knew instinctively that she would have let him. But he didn't. With a great effort that tested his resolve, he managed to keep himself in check. Fear. It rode him. But he did touch her. He raised his hand to her cheek and there, very lightly, he brushed aside her hair in such a way as he might have done to a child. The moment passed. The roaring in his ears died as quickly as it had come; she straightened up and moved away.

"Thandi, I'm so sorry. I don't know what came over me."

"No, I'm sorry. I shouldn't have leaned over you like that."

Richard engaged the engine and they drove off. Not a word was said about what had happened; they talked of other things, even laughed, and joked, all the while trying to reassure themselves and pretend that nothing out of the ordinary had happened. But they both knew. And that knowledge fell like a stone into a deep well, lost to sight but there nonetheless, lying on the bottom, inviolable and silent, and biding its time.

CHAPTER SEVEN:

1972

1

During the 1960s Richard had been aware of change in much the same way that he regarded smoke over the horizon – he only had a passing interest in it. He took the view that it was far away, in someone else's backyard and so really had nothing to do with him. But in the 1970s, with increasing alarm and much to his chagrin, he found himself compelled to look closer.

Change, he now ruefully conceded, was like a bushfire, threatening to get out of control. The newspapers were full of it – so were the news bulletins on the radio – every day there was some new revelation that sent his alarm bells ringing. Colonies right around the world were locked in a deadly struggle for independence; everywhere he looked, the disenfranchised were clamouring for things he knew in his heart they were entitled to; order was giving way to chaos and the certainties of the old world were now seen as nothing more than fanciful illusions. Richard kept asking himself what it all meant. Unease addled his thinking. He wondered what would become of them if power became vested in illiterate, uneducated people. There would be chaos and upheaval on an unprecedented scale – nobody would be safe, not even those who sympathised with their cause.

He could feel the tectonic plates begin to stir, deep beneath his feet. For many though, these were minor tremors and of little consequence – life would carry on much as it had before. The decade began with the Nationalist Party being returned to power, albeit with a slightly reduced majority. Richard took no comfort from this – while he deplored the harsh inequities of his government and rued its draconian laws, he could not see what an alternative political system would look like. He noted with apprehension that gold production, long the backbone of the South African economy, had peaked; he saw what an increasingly militant non-white labour force, striking more and more often for wage equity and better working conditions, could do to a contracting economy; he was aware of these things as though by osmosis – they passed easily and simultaneously through the semipermeable membranes in his mind. Richard felt impotent and disillusioned. External pressures only compounded his frustration and exacerbated his fears – that South Africa could be expelled from the Olympic Movement, ostracised from just about every international sporting organisation and could be pilloried by an increasingly vociferous UN – one that was hell-bent on tightening the sanctions screws as hard as it could – all seemed horribly unfair to him and filled him with despondency.

He knew he spoke Zulu well and, every so often, would read *Ilanga* newspaper – he knew what was going on around him. There was a distinct change of mood sweeping through the non-white community. He could feel it. The ANC, despite being truncated, banned, and forced underground, was proliferating as a grassroots organisation, and was nourishing black minds with new-found hope. Steve Biko and others launched the Black Consciousness movement in 1970 and it quickly captured national attention. Richard had a sneaking admiration for Biko but didn't like his strident anti-white outbursts.

To cap it all, the Prime Minister announced that all Coloured people were going to be removed from the Common Voters' Roll and, to rub salt into the wound, his government passed legislation that withdrew South African citizenship from all non-Whites in the country. Richard wondered why anyone would antagonise so many people for such little gain. He shook his head when, in what he saw was an attempt to off-set the country's increasing alienation on the world stage, the government went off and proudly signed a treaty with Israel – a country, which he felt, was another pariah state that also glared at the world with bared teeth. That was not all. Richard was acutely aware that the government was determined to cut down all the tall poppies that it didn't like – the Dean of Johannesburg, for example, had just been remanded under the Terrorism Act and Father Cosmas Desmond has been placed under house arrest. They may have dabbled in politics, but were they really a threat to national security? Richard was unconvinced. He recalled reading a thin book by 1970 Nobel Prize Winner Aleksandr Solzhenitsyn called *We Never Make Mistakes* – the irony of the title always flashed into his mind whenever the government did or said something with overweening arrogance.

Largely through discussions with Brydon, he had become aware of the political activism undertaken by what he regarded were brave, conscientious students on both black and white campuses. They were, as far as he could tell, ordinary decent people – not terrorists with guns and bombs. All they did, Brydon told him, was to hand out pamphlets to non-white workers – pamphlets that simply explained the Poverty Datum Line and urged them to demand a minimum wage of R20 a week. The government's Wages Board ignored this petition – instead, with what Richard now reckoned was staggering conceit and blinded by self-interest, it went and set the minimum wage at a paltry R8,50 a week! He knew what would happen – strikes would break out right across the country. Had to happen. Jack told him that on the farms, far from the epicentres of civil unrest as he so quaintly liked to put it, a tuned ear could detect a change in mood. Cane cutters, he said, were whispering among themselves, were becoming more restless, and were beginning to ask for more.

While these things played with Richard's mind, causing him endless agitation – he felt them closing in and stifling him – none of them, at home or abroad, seemed to trouble Magda in the slightest. This saddened him; he so wanted her affirmation and would have loved to discuss these things with her and share his thoughts, but she was unmoved and made it quite clear she had no interest in airy-fairy things like politics. The only things in life that mattered to her, she told him breezily, were the ones related to music – things that made one's heart sing and made her want to get up and dance. You can spend your time thinking about politics if you have to, but you know deep down you cannot change anything, can you? Besides, it's all in our stars so why bother. 'Loosen up, Rich,' she would say, 'loosen up – you're too serious. Life is a dance, not a funeral march.' Having danced through six years of marriage on light, nimble feet and hardly missing a beat, she found herself in the lull between dances – the band was no longer playing and now, with two children in hand, she felt side-lined and for the first time in her life, somewhat nonplussed and unsure what to do next. She was staying with her parents in Eshowe while Richard and some friends were on a fishing trip, up the Mozambique coast. Anna noticed the change in her daughter's demeanour – she watched Magda moping around the house with a glum look on her face. So, to brighten her up, she announced one morning at breakfast that she had invited Andre and his wife up for the weekend. When she heard this, Magda's face lit up – the band had struck up and she could dance again. That evening she called Andre on the telephone and had a long conversation with him – it began loudly, with giggles and laughter, but soon became earnest and subsided into hushed whispers.

Mother and daughter were sitting on the *stoep*. It was drowsy sitting there in the morning sun, and for a while they stopped talking. Andre and Betsy had gone into town, leaving their son Aldo with them so that he could play with his cousins. Magda reached for a glass in front of her and stared out across the lawn. The children were at play. Anna, unconsciously following her daughter, also picked up her glass and began to sip from it. She studied her daughter. She was perplexed; it was as though Magda was waiting for something or someone – a person perhaps, whose arrival had not been confirmed. But who could it be? She watched Magda's eyes flick back and forth between the children on the lawn and the veranda door beside them.

Anna pointed at the children. Ben, now five years of age and already tall for his age, was chasing Aldo who, a year younger, was a lot shorter. His little legs pumped up and down like pistons as he tried to keep ahead of Ben's outstretched hands. The two boys ran round and round a dark-coloured blanket, which was spread out in the shade of a large mango tree. They shrieked as they ran, happy as could be. In the centre of the blanket, surrounded by toys, sat three-year-old Fleur. She sat with one hand on her nanny's lap and the thumb of the other in her mouth. Her head followed the boys as they romped around her. Magda turned suddenly and saw her mother looking at her. She took a deep breath to mask her irritation and held it, swelling out her chest. Then she exhaled with a loud hiss, and winked at her mother as if to say, 'Nothing's wrong, Mom – I promise'. She drained her glass and turned back to the children. She could hardly believe that she was already the mother of two children – how time had flown! And Andre! She never thought he'd settle down. Betsy, his petite wife from Pretoria, was expecting her second – she was hoping for a girl this time, a sister for Aldo.

"So, you were saying that you couldn't stand another fishing trip?" said Anna, reviving their conversation, "Why? Where'd they go this time?"

"No, Mom, I couldn't. I've had a gutful of fishing trips." Magda's eyebrows were knitted. "They've gone to a place they call Kofferkweni, in Mozambique."

"Where's that? Anywhere near Xai-Xai? Your Dad went fishing there a few years ago. On a men-only fishing trip, with some golfing buddies."

"No, this is south of Lorenco Marques, not north. Miles and miles from anywhere – nobody would dream of going there, it's very isolated. But that's what they like – *bundu-bashing* and all that. You have to go through an elephant reserve to get there. No roads, just animal tracks." She toned her voice down, "His father discovered it – they love it and have been going there for years. It's okay if you like fishing but I don't. Rich has tried to teach me but quite honestly, I couldn't be bothered – just don't have the patience. And I'm not that fussed about camping either."

"But isn't it fun? You used to go, didn't you – quite a lot?"

"Yes, I used to go. And I've been where they are now – but only once. But you know me, Mom – I hate dirt and like to be clean and tidy. That's impossible on the beach – the sand is a curse, especially when the wind is blowing. It gets into everything. I don't like it in my shoes, in my clothes, my hair or, worse still, in my bed. There's no hot water – we just bath in the sea. And no privacy – everyone sleeps in one big tent, lined up in camp beds. *Magtig!* You should hear the noises people make when they're asleep! And the snoring! Fortunately, Fleur is still too young for all that right now, so I can use her as an excuse."

Anna frowned, as though she were struggling to understand what had come over her daughter. She had everything that opened and shut, was married to a wealthy doctor and shared two beautiful children with him, now lived in a posh new house in Empangeni, and drove her own Mercedes – a coupé no less – had servants at her beck and call, and she still looked sensational – what more could anyone possibly want?

"You alright, Magda? You keep looking at the door. *Seker niks pla nie?*"

"Me? I'm fine. *Niks is verkeerd nie.* Nothing's bothering me –"

"You seem … how shall I say? Different. You're not your usual self. When you came, I said to Papa that you looked bored and sort of flat – not the usual bubbly girl I know so well. And today you seem edgy. I can't put my finger on it. You sure you're okay?"

Magda ran her eyes over her mother's face. She didn't want to talk about herself, not now. But at the same time, she had to find a way of fending her off. So, she finessed by changing the subject.

"When do you think Andre will be back?"

"Lunch time. Magda, look at me. You sure that everything's okay? I'm your mother, you can tell me. You know what's said between us, stays between us."

"Oh, I don't know, Mom," she felt cornered and began slowly, "just seems that Richard and I are arguing a lot more these days. We're very different, you know. I know that opposites attract and all that, but when I say one thing, he says another. I like shopping, he doesn't. I love to party, he'd rather stay at home."

She got up and called out to Ben, "Be careful, darling, Aldo's smaller than you." She waved at the nanny and caught her attention, *"Pas op vir die kleintjie, Esther. Dankie."* She turned back to Anna, words tumbling out of her mouth.

"We think so differently, Mom, it's scary … I follow my stars and am interested in astrology, but Richard says it's all bullshit. I'm too stupid to argue … He's into politics, I'm not … He loves the Blacks, I don't, but don't get me started on that … You know that his mother is a bit of a do-gooder? A big one, actually – she rushes around the district trying to help their kind. She set up some clinics on a few farms in the district – you know about them? Well, Rich does the doctor bit, and he takes it very seriously. Whenever I want to do anything – say, for example, I feel like going to Durban on such-and-such a day – he'll say 'Sorry, I have clinic that afternoon.' So, most times I end up going by myself. We never take holidays at nice places – we could go to Joburg, to the Cape, to Rhodesia, wherever – no, if we go, we end up fishing or going to game reserves. Drives me mad."

An apprehension, long tethered to the back of her mind, broke free and scattered her thoughts. "And you know what, Mom? There's this damn nurse! Rich takes her everywhere with him. She's with him in Mozambique right now. Anyway, Rich says he needs a nurse for the clinic he runs up there. Yah, he runs one wherever he goes – the family is mad, I reckon – just a bunch of do-gooders, always falling over themselves to help the wrong colour. Charity begins at home, I say. And you know what else? The bloody nurse lives on the farm. Her job is to look after his mother's clinics I was just telling you about. Something to do with the church. You know, Mom, Rich just about spends more time with her than he does with his own family. Can you believe that? More time with a *coon!*"

"Magda! Wash your mouth out! Surely you're not suggesting –"

"Maybe not. *Sy hou te veel van hom. Sy kan my nie flous nie.*"

Anna turned away. Memories long dormant were waking from their slumber. She tried to ignore them, but they rose up, catching her mind's eye. Her heart began to beat faster. With a great effort, she forced her concentration back to the conversation.

"Don't be so hard on your husband," she said, struggling to keep her voice matter of fact, "he's a good man. Suspicion without proof, my dear, is like … like worry without a cause – it just eats you up. I would not think that Richard is the sort of person to play around with other women – White or Black. Relationships have their ups and downs. You have to –"

She broke off, listening. Her son's deep voice was booming in the belly of the house. "Ah, Andre and Betsy are back. Just in time for lunch. Magda, be a dear and tell Esther to bring the children in and wash their hands."

She got up as Andre and Betsy stepped onto the veranda. There was a tall man with them; he was very good looking and had a thick, dark moustache.

"Hello!" Andre threw back his arms as though he were unveiling a painting, "Look who we bumped into in town! Eugene! I've invited him for lunch, Mom – hope you don't mind. Eugene, you know my sister Magda, but have you met my mother?"

"No, I haven't," he said suavely, taking Anna's hand in both of his, "*aangename kennis*. Nice to be here, Mrs Celliers." But his eyes swept past her and settled on Magda, standing behind her. They shone brightly and in them, Anna could see the reflection of her daughter's own eyes, now wide and alive and, to her consternation, sparkling with unfiltered brilliance.

Richard picked up a folding chair and took it out of the tent. He set it down beside Brydon.

"I'm bushed," he said, "must have seen at least fifty patients this morning. Mind you, it's a big help having Thandi here."

"Does she always come with you?"

"No. This is her first trip to Mozambique. Bloody government – took ages for me to get her a passport. But she's been plenty of times up the Zululand coast with me. Having a nurse along –"

"Rich, tell me something – she's more than a nurse, isn't she?"

"What? What are you trying to insinuate?"

"Not trying to insinuate anything. Just stating what seems to be obvious. I mean, Blind Freddie can see it's more than just a doctor-nurse relationship or, another way round, more than just an employer-employee thing. I mean, the way you look at each other, talk to each other … You know, things like that … I mean, well … Simon even asked me if I thought you were having a bit on the side and –"

"A bit on the side? Come off it – you really think so?"

"Of course not. But you are close, aren't you? Just be careful, that's all I'm saying." He realised that he had been misunderstood – it wasn't the black-white thing that he was warning Richard about, it was the politics. It was on the tip of his tongue to tell Richard that he knew Thandi's brother, knew his political affiliations, and knew that he was now a fugitive abroad and any association with such a person, however oblique, could be dangerous. But professional integrity held, and he bit his lip. "Do you always do this?" he asked, changing tack, "Run clinics for the locals, I mean?"

"Just for the record," Richard's mind was still spinning from what he had just heard, "I am not, repeat not, having a bit on the side with Thandi – you can tell Simon that from me."

Instinct told him to raise the drawbridge – to island himself from a discussion that was making him uncomfortable, so he closed the subject and took up Brydon's innocuous question.

"About the clinics. Actually, they started a long time ago with my dad. One day we were fishing up past Bhangazi – on the Zululand coast – there was a sick native woman in a *kraal* behind the sand dunes and this guy came and asked Dad if he would look at her. He did and gave her some antibiotics that sorted her out. Mum said that was rent paid. She said that it was the least we could do since we were camping on their beach for free. So, every time we went fishing after that, we took a bunch of medicines along, and soon Dad was running clinics, especially up here – this country is pretty well buggered, you know. I've just followed suit, I suppose – perhaps taken it to a higher level, don't know. But we bring a lot more medical equipment now – Ed Christenson, the pharmacist in Empangeni, does a great job stocking me up with all that I need. I now bring things like plaster of Paris – for broken bones – phials of local anaesthetic so I can do procedures like pulling teeth – you watched me pull some the other day – I now bring heaps of antibiotics and other medicines that allow me to treat all sorts of ailments I'm likely to find out here in the boondocks. It's a funny thing, but as soon as we hit the beach, the word spreads like wildfire and before you know it, there are people lining up to see the "*Doketela*." Trouble is, there are no doctors here – certainly none in the elephant reserve – in fact, I don't think there's one from the border at Ora Point, right up to the Santa Maria channel. That's a bloody big area. Some of these poor sods walk thirty or forty miles to see me – imagine if we had to do that, just to see a doctor."

"Well," Brydon was still thinking about Thandi, "it's impressive, it really is. Just sorry I can't help. I'm a simple lawyer, can't speak the lingo, and to be quite honest, I feel quite useless. But I do admire what you're doing. I'm quite envious – you practice what I preach."

Richard, now safe on his island, smiled benevolently but wasn't really listening to his friend. "You know what? I feel like a beer, Bry. Want one?" When he saw Brydon nod, he twisted around and looked back in the direction of the camp kitchen, "Fanakanye," he shouted, "*ngicela niphathele obhiya ababili. Shesha!*"

Fanakanye brought two bottles of Laurentina, a local Portuguese beer that he rather enjoyed. They stretched out their feet and wiggled their toes in the warm sand and sucked their beers. The liquid was lukewarm but satisfying – there was no fridge or icebox in their camp or anywhere within fifty miles or so. They stared at the sea. Beyond the breakers, the water was a deep blue and looked rather foreboding, but once it rolled in and crossed the sandbar, rising up into round-shouldered waves, line after line, it became a translucent green that somehow seemed less threatening. They sat as though hypnotised, watching the waves surge forward like lines of advancing cavalry, row after row – the white plumes of their helmets tossing in the wind – they watched them trot forward, gather into a canter, and then, as though with sabres drawn, saw them break into a headlong gallop and hurl themselves at the beach in a frothing fury. White water swished up the sloping sand with reckless intent, smothering all before it, even mounting the rampart of sand that lipped the bay. But the rampart held and the waves, now vanquished and spent, turned in mottled confusion and retreated back to the sea, leaving rivulets of seawater here and there to scar the beach with their passing.

"Look," said Brydon, "they are going for a swim."

"Who? Where?"

Richard turned to where Brydon was pointing. Thandi and Isaac were about a hundred yards away; they waded into the water and stopped for a wave that splashed up and washed around their legs. Her nicely sculptured body stood out against the whiteness of the water, catching Richard's eye, and making him look closely. For a second, jealousy blazed white-hot through him; just as quickly it died, leaving the acrid taste of envy in his mouth. Brydon's words flew back into his mind, tormenting him. He kept watching. Isaac was holding her hand; Richard saw him lead her into deeper water and then flop down beside her, their bodies almost touching. Their playful laughter carried easily over the sea and made his pulse quicken. He wrenched his eyes back to the horizon but saw nothing except what was in his head and heard nothing except Brydon's words which refused to leave him. He was cross with Isaac and cross with himself. The beer tasted bitter, so he poured the rest of the bottle into the sand beside him and covered it with his foot.

Brydon stood up and stretched. "Wonder if the others are catching any fish round the point – you feel like joining them?" Richard shook his head. Brydon turned around. "What's that?" he asked, pointing back towards the camp, "Looks like we got visitors. Hey, look, Rich, an oxcart. It's coming here. What do you reckon?"

Richard jumped up and spun around. "Not another patient. Not now." He squinted under his raised hand. "Something's up. Let's go and have a look." They hurried back up the beach.

It always amazed Richard how fast news travelled in the bush – there were no telephones or anything like that, yet by the time the oxcart came to a stop, many of the locals had materialised out of the bush and were waiting to meet it. They gathered around it, patient and silent, heads bared as though in supplication. When he got closer, Richard was at once struck by how old and decrepit the oxcart was; the wooden spokes and rims had been repaired countless times and were bound with bits of wire. It must have come a long way for both the oxen that drew it were standing in their yolks with splayed legs and lowered heads. Then he saw a figure lying on the flat wooden boards. A woman. A young woman. Richard was shocked – the agony he saw twisted on the face of that young woman took his breath away. She was in the advanced stages of labour, and it was patently obvious that her situation was desperate. Her face was beaded with sweat and the hand that lay on her belly outside the thin blanket covering her, opened and closed fitfully, like the mouth of a beached fish, gasping for air.

There were two men standing close beside the wagon and every few minutes one of them would bend over and try to comfort the woman. This, Richard concluded, must be the husband. His face was knotted with worry, and he kept the sun off the woman's face with an ancient, black umbrella which he held high above his head. The other man was Ben Sithole or, as the Barclay family liked to call him, Peg-Leg. Richard knew that many years ago, when he was working in a Johannesburg gold mine, he had lost his leg below his right knee in an accident. When he walked, he would swing his wooden leg around in a wide arc and it would sink into the sand, giving him a lop-sided gait. He used a well-worn stick to help him keep his balance. Everyone liked Peg-Leg; his grizzled old face was seldom without a smile. Because he had worked as an itinerant worker in South Africa, he spoke Zulu quite well, and so, whenever Bill or Richard examined patients at this particular campsite, they made sure that Peg-Leg was available to translate Tonga into Zulu for them.

Richard eased past the man with the umbrella and gently removed the blanket from the woman. An awful smell wafted up. It wrinkled his nostrils, causing him to flinch, momentarily. He ran his fingers up and down the woman's bulging stomach, pressing here, and probing there. Whenever he asked a question in Zulu, Peg-Leg would translate for him. Richard's fears were confirmed. He looked up and found Brydon standing well back, staring at him.

"Brydon, this woman is in serious trouble," he said, rubbing his hands up and down his pants, "she's been in labour for a long time. Go and fetch Thandi for me, please. Tell her to come quickly. I need her. Hurry, there's no time to lose." An obscure thought lit up a dark corner in his head, as though a single candle had been lit behind a windowpane, high up in an attic; he found himself focusing on it, relishing the idea that he was prying Thandi and Isaac apart.

He turned back to Peg-Leg. *Is this her husband? Good. Tell him his wife needs to get to a hospital fast. There's nothing I can do for her here. Ask him if he will allow me to drive her to the hospital in Lorenco Marques. And tell him that he can come and keep her company.*

Richard studied the man while Peg-Leg spoke to him. He looked fatigued and at his wits end, like someone who had survived one ordeal only to find that another now blocked his way. He listened with his head on one side, and then asked a question. As he did so, the umbrella in his hand dipped and swayed, as though caught in an unexpected gust of wind.

"He wants to know how much it will cost. He says he has no money. I told him no money. I said you do not charge. He said thank you. He will go with you."

"Good. Tell him not to go anywhere – we are leaving as soon as the vehicle is ready."

Thandi and Brydon appeared. She was in her swimming costume and had wrapped a towel around her waist. They pushed through the crowd towards him. "What's wrong?" she asked. Then she saw the woman lying in the cart and reached down for her hand, instinctively taking her pulse. "I see. She's in bad shape. What do you want me to do?"

"We are going to take her to LM. Yes, you too. In the Ford – it has more room in the back than the Land Rover. You'll have to come and keep an eye on her for me while I drive. Can you get her ready for the trip? We'll put a stretcher in the back – Fanakanye will tie it down for you. Tell him how you want it set up." He pointed to the woman. "Can you get a cannula into her arm, please? We're going to need pethidine … Also, you'd better get dressed and bring a change of clothes with you – we might have to stay overnight there."

Then he saw the look on Brydon's face. "Want to come along, Brydon? Fancy a trip to the big smoke? Could do with some company. And another pair of hands might be handy. Great. Ask Isaac to come here please and then take the beach buggy and nip around the corner and tell the others what's happening. And tell them not to wait up for us tonight – pretty sure we won't be back until tomorrow. Get your gear and get back here as quickly as you can."

Richard didn't wait for his reply; his mind was racing at a million miles an hour. He turned to Peg-Leg. *"Can you come with us? To LM? Thank you. I might need you to translate for me. You and the husband can hold the stretcher for Thandi and keep it from falling over. Yes, she will sit in the back with you. She will look after the woman. Fanakanye will sit up front with us."*

Within an hour they were ready to go. The sun had slipped off its noonday perch and was beginning its slide towards the green hills in the west. Richard kept his eye on the road but his mind, lulled by the monotonous *veld* that flashed past, began to wander and he soon found himself thinking about women and relationships he had had. Then, inexplicably, he found himself pondering about the meaning of love. He knew that time softens bumps in the road of life, just as surely as it conceals others yet to come – he understood that, but he could not forget. If only he could bury his bone and stop chewing on it. Magda. He still loved her, but not in the same way as he had at the beginning of their relationship when, he now grudgingly conceded, infatuation had got the better of him. Her magnetic eyes, firm breasts, and deliciously sculptured bottom no longer aroused his hunger with the same greedy thoughts as they used to – familiarity had slaked his craving. A bird swooped in front of the car, and he braked hard to avoid hitting it, then accelerated on. Here, on this mad dash, in the middle of nowhere, he felt wondrously alive and alert – his heart was pumping, and nerves tingled with a long-supressed sense of inner joy – for the first time in ages, he felt that he was doing something for a higher purpose. What would Magda think of all this? If she were here, would this mad dash to LM thrill her? He couldn't imagine her sitting in the back like Thandi, but then again Magda wasn't a nurse. Nor was she particularly fond of getting her hands dirty. Brydon's words floated back into focus, and he ground his teeth, chewing not so much on what had been said, but on what had been implied. His mind became stuck on thoughts that raised more questions than answers – clarity eluded him, and he felt as though he was chasing his tail. The old familiar knot was beginning to form in his stomach, so he lit a cigarette, opened the window, flicked out the match, and made a concerted effort to keep his mind on the road.

When they reached Catembe, Richard slowed down and motes of red dust overtook their car, settling on it like flies at a roadside kill. He wound up his window and fanned them away with one hand while with the other, he steered slowly down to the wharf. For the first time since they had left their camp on the beach, he felt he could relax. He exhaled a long sigh of relief and turned off the motor. He looked at Brydon and pointed. There, far across Delagoa Bay, pencilled against the evening sky, stood the high-rise buildings of Lourenco Marques; they stood shoulder to shoulder, promising with blinking eyes all the trappings of a bustling metropolis – including, Richard hoped, hospitals with emergency facilities able to save a patient like his. They climbed out and stretched their limbs. Their relief at getting this far with their patient and finding her still alive and conscious was palpable – they slapped one another on the back and began to chatter, brittle words riding on the back of nervous laughter. Thandi's face was haggard and drawn. The journey in the back of the Ford had sapped her energy for she could barely hold herself upright; she leaned against the car. Brydon went to her.

"Are you alright?" He asked, placing his arm around her shoulder, "You look as though you've been to hell and back."

She smiled, a tired stretch of the lips that quickly faded. She was wary of Brydon. She knew who he was – Gordon had mentioned his name – but she suspected he did not know that she knew. Keeping up this pretence made her feel awkward in his presence, so she stepped away. "I'm fine, thank you," she said, "the bumps and the dust. Nearly killed me." Then she turned her bloodshot eyes to Richard, and they lit up, warming him. "What now? Shall I get back in and stay with her?"

"No, no." If Brydon could touch her like that without fear of over-stepping the mark, then so could he. He moved to her side and placed a reassuring hand on the small of her back. "Should be a water taxi here," he said as though to a child, "one's always here – at least, whenever I've been here, there has been one." He dropped his hand but remained standing close beside her. "Ben," he said, pointing to some local Africans who were sitting on a low wall nearby, watching them. *"Go and ask them where the water taxi is. Hurry, we have to go."*

But before Ben reached them, a taxi boat appeared from behind the wharf and nosed its way along the jetty. It's like a calf, Richard thought, it knows where the udder is. *"Fanakanye,"* he called, taking out his wallet and opening it up, *"you and Sithole stay here and look after the truck. Park it where you can see it. Here's some money. Portuguese escudos, enough for both of you. There's a cafe back there where you can get food. And here are your travel papers and your dompas – just in case the police come. Don't let the vehicle out of your sight. One of you can sleep in the front and the other in the back. Stay well."*

They waved goodbye and carried the stretcher on board, laying it down carefully in the lee of the cockpit where it would be protected from spray. There was nowhere to attach the saline bag, so they took turns in holding it up, all the way across the bay. Thandi sat down beside the woman and held her hand. Her husband sat on the other side of the stretcher, his face hollowed and gaunt. A boatman fended the boat away from the jetty and soon they were on their way.

By the time they reached the docks at LM, the light was fading fast and the dockside cranes, silent and still and towering over them like roosting storks, peered down at them as they chugged slowly below, leaving sluggish patterns on the surface of the water behind them. They berthed and Richard paid; then he picked up the front of the stretcher and Brydon took hold of the bottom. Thandi walked alongside, one hand holding up the drip bag and with the other, she held onto the blood pressure monitor that lay alongside the woman's extended belly. Her husband picked up their bags. Once again, their luck held – there in the gloom at the end of the wharf, with a red cross emblazoned on its side, was an ambulance waiting for them.

"There is a God," muttered Richard, relief surging through him and rinsing tiredness from his body, "who said the Pork and Beans were hopeless? Look at that, bang on time!" The stretcher was loaded into the ambulance and Thandi crawled in behind it, still clutching her saline bag. A paramedic climbed in beside her – he quickly hooked the woman up to oxygen and then turned his attention to an array of life-support monitors beside him. The woman's husband hesitated, not sure what to do.

"You go with your wife," said Richard firmly, pointing to the open door, *"get in."* He lent in, talking to Thandi, "You go in this, and we'll follow in a taxi. See you at the hospital. There's a taxi rank just outside the gates – don't let them go until we are behind you. Got it? Wait for us."

They followed the ambulance to the hospital. As the stretcher passed through the emergency entrance, Richard heard someone shouting for plasma. Two white-clad figures wheeled the woman at the run towards the surgical unit. Richard turned to the others. "She's in safe hands now. These guys are on the money – they know what they are doing." He ushered them outside. The taxi was still there. The driver was leaning against the bonnet. His arms and legs were crossed, and a cigarette dangled from his mouth. How fortuitous, Richard thought, both for him and for us.

"Look, he's still there. Clever bugger. Let's go and get some grub."

"Well, shouldn't we find somewhere to doss down first?" Brydon spread his hands and lifted his shoulders, "I mean, we are spending the night here, aren't we?"

Richard looked at him. A thought, long tethered and kept out of sight, rose in his mind like a freed balloon. He swung his eyes to Thandi and watched for her reaction as he spoke.

"Yes, a hotel," he said, gazing at her steadily, "we need a hotel, don't we? Somewhere to kip. Somewhere to spend the night. I want to come back here in the morning – I'd like to find out if she made it. You okay with that Thandi?"

Thandi searched his face; she felt scared and took a while to answer. "In a hotel? We are going to sleep in a hotel? I can go back to the car."

Brydon saw doubt clouding her eyes and immediately set about allaying the fears he supposed underpinned it. "No ways, Thandi. You can't go back on your own," he said as disarmingly as he could, "Richard's right, let's stick together. We'll stay in a hotel. This is Mozambique you know, not South Africa. We'll be in separate rooms, of course." He turned to Richard. "What do you think, Rich – the Polana is probably a bit too flashy for the way we are dressed. What about the Cardosa or the Girassol?"

"No, bugger it." The words 'not South Africa' were swimming round and round in Richard's head like big fish in a small tank. "We're all bushed – we've had a hell of a trip. I say the Polana if we can get in. And then dinner at Costa do Sol. We're going to stuff ourselves to the gunnels with prawns at Gerry's – that's a restaurant on the beach – we'll have prawns *peri-peri*, and we'll wash them down with some nice, wickedly chilled *Vinho Verde*." He saw the look on Thandi's face and laughed. "Don't worry," he said, patting her back, "it'll be fun. And you'll be fine."

Then, as they walked towards the taxi, he suddenly remembered the woman's husband. He turned around. "Hold on a minute, we forgot to fix this chap up." Richard hurried back to the woman's husband who was standing in the foyer with a lost look on his face. *"You want to stay here?"* The man nodded but it was clear that once again he was not sure of what to do or where to go. *"Here's some money for food."* Richard peeled off some notes and stuffed them into the man's cupped hands. He folded his fingers around the notes, looked up, found Richard watching him and lost for words, smiled his thanks. His eyes were wet. Richard felt a lump growing in his throat – he coughed and took the man by the arm and walked him back into the hospital. *"Let's go and ask someone where you can wait."*

A short while later he joined Brydon and Thandi who by now were in the back seat of the taxi.

"He'll be okay. They've taken him and given him a place to wait until his wife comes out of surgery. All good. Let's go."

He tapped the driver on his shoulder. "Hotel Polana, *por favor*."

They booked into the Polana, freshened up, and then took a taxi out to Costa do Sol. This was a novel experience for Thandi – she had never sat in a restaurant before, not one that served alcohol, and never with white people. When she sat down, she was overcome by self-consciousness, convinced that people were looking at her out of the corner of their eyes; this tended to stilt her conversation and compound her uneasiness. Not sure if it was simply the wine – Richard kept her glass full – or because she was tired and no longer cared, but as the evening wore on, so her inhibitions began to evaporate, and she came to realise that her presence was nothing out of the ordinary at all. In fact, there were black and white people seated together at other tables; they were having a good time, laughing, and joking, and as far as she could tell, they all spoke Portuguese. This is what visiting another country does, she told herself as she sipped her wine, it shows you that what you've been brought to believe is normal, is not normal at all. She began to relax and enjoy herself. Their table was outside under the stars, where they could see the moonlit ocean and hear the surf, murmuring in the distance. There were some young boys playing with a soccer ball in a floodlit patch of beach not far away. She watched them. There was something about them, something about their back-and-forth play and their full-throated cries as they called out to one another that made her frown. Then she put her finger on it, the incongruous reality that stared her in the face: there were black children down there playing with white children – not against each other, but together, with each other. It dawned on her that children everywhere were born colour-blind – kids played with kids irrespective of their skin tone. It was adults who taught them to take note of difference; it was adults who taught them to apportion worth according to race and creed; it was adults who taught them that God had made some superior and others inferior; it was adults who, ultimately, taught them who to trust and who to fear – and fear she knew, was the bedrock of hatred. It's the wrong way round, she told herself – adults should learn from children. She recalled some words years ago from bible study, '*suffer the little children to come to me, for theirs is the kingdom of Heaven.*' She thought about it, pleased with herself – pleased as though she had discovered a theorem for a difficult maths problem. She did not hear Richard address her but jumped when she felt his hand squeeze her arm.

"Thandi, you were a million miles away. What were you thinking about?"

"Not much," she was embarrassed at having been caught unguarded and lost in thought, "I was just watching those kids playing on the beach over there, that's all. I'm sorry, what were you saying?"

"Would you like some more wine? Bry has ordered another bottle."

She couldn't help smiling. Here she was, enjoying a nice meal on a balmy evening – albeit in a foreign country – but being treated as an equal and, glory be, the sky hadn't fallen in. A delicious feeling of wine-mellow drowsiness set her heart humming and emboldened her reply.

"Why not?" She surprised them with a coquettishly raised eyebrow, "It's helping my poor body – the bumps on the road getting here nearly killed me. How that woman survived, I'll never know." Brydon topped up her glass. "Thank you. Not too much – you're not trying to get me drunk, are you?"

Richard laughed. "Heavens no, wouldn't dream of it."

He pushed his chair back and leaned back with one elbow on the table and crossed his legs. He lit a cigarette and flicked the match into the darkness. He watched her out of the corner of his eye, enjoying the profile of her breast. They sat there sipping their wine, replete and content, soaking up the ambiance and basking in the warm glow of accomplishment. Had the poor woman survived the ordeal of surgery? And what about the baby? These thoughts hovered in all their minds, in different ways, causing them to pause and reflect. The cries of the youngsters at play on the beach, high-pitched and tinkling in the cool night air like ice cubes in a glass, caught Richard's attention and he turned from his reverie to watch them over his shoulder.

After a while, Thandi excused herself and went to the toilet.

"She looks like she's beginning to enjoy herself."

"What's that? Thandi? Yes, I suppose she is."

"Pity we can't do this back home. Sit and drink like this, I mean. The bloody colour bar – it's so artificial and so fucking stupid. And it won't last you know – it'll go."

"I'm with you, Bry, I really am. But how do we get rid of it without pissing away all that we have? You tell me. You're the legal expert – you like to dabble in politics, what's the answer? The rest of the world hates our guts. Whatever they do to make us see the light or change our ways, only makes the bloody government dig in deeper. We're in a *laager*, aren't we – backs to the wall sort of stuff. Gives me the shits, it really does. Tell me, Bry, what's the solution?"

"Start with *liberté, égalité and fraternité*, Rich – you know, from the French Revolution –"

"You mean, one man one vote? Hell will freeze over before that happens – you know that."

"Well, anything short of that, then we'll have blood in the streets. Mark my words."

"Depresses the hell out of me. If only there was a peaceful way out. If only –"

Richard broke off – Thandi was approaching. When she reached their table, both men stood up.

"Thank you," she smiled at them and sat down, "it's funny, but I cannot remember white men ever standing up for me – not before this."

"Well, do Black men stand for you?" Richard felt slighted, "As for Whites, I don't suppose there have been many occasions for it to happen," then, trying to dig himself out of a hole, he carried on doggedly, "I mean, when was the last time you were with White blokes in a restaurant?"

"Never." She smiled coyly. The wine was loosening her tongue. "But it makes me feel nice. I was just thinking. There is no apartheid here and these things are done naturally here. But back home, across the border, we have rules that make us treat each other differently. It's strange, don't you think? Nobody stands for me back in South Africa. But it's nice – nice being treated like a lady. You know, Titus always says that everything comes down to geography and now I see what he means –"

"Thandi, I would stand up for you anywhere – in fact, I hope I always do. I pride myself on doing things like that and, by the way, as far as I'm concerned, colour has nothing to do with it."

"Yes, Rich, but Thandi's point is that here we sit together and she's the beneficiary of what we reckon are good manners. Back home we don't sit together, do we – we're not allowed to, by law – so we do not practice our good manners on those who have been set apart from us. Geography, hey? It's an astute observation." Brydon turned to Thandi, "I like it. Who is Titus?"

"My stepfather. A good man. He's not well now. Mr Richard knows him. Titus says that if you are born in India, you'll probably be Hindu, if you're born in Pakistan, you'll probably be Muslim. If you are born in Addington, you'll be white, if you're born at McCord, you'll be black. Simple as that. He says that geography determines everything – religion, customs, politics, education, even what we do and say to each other – all these sorts of things are determined by where we live, by geography."

"Funnily enough, my mother says much the same. Perhaps she got it from Titus." Richard saw Brydon get up and yawn. "Are we keeping you up? Long past your bedtime?"

"No, I was thinking what a wise man Titus is." He stretched. "I'm quite happy to kick on. But it's getting late. Looks like we're done here. Shouldn't we settle up and wander off for a cab?"

They walked down the restaurant steps and, three abreast, ambled slowly along the esplanade. Presently they approached what appeared to be a nightclub – coloured light spilled onto the pavement and as they got closer, they could hear soft music playing. They stopped and looked inside. There was a four-piece band playing a slow number and they could just see shadowy shapes gliding around a dimly lit dance floor. Thandi drew back. What she saw held her eyes fast – but it also made her heart beat in her ears.

"Come-on, let's go and have a look," said Richard, with a new-found spring in his step, "what about a nightcap – something for the road?" He hurried off and disappeared inside. Brydon and Thandi waited in the street. The cool night air eddied around them, raising goosebumps on their exposed skin. Thandi wished she had a coat. She hugged herself and rubbed her bare arms vigorously.

"He's hopeless," said Brydon, "next thing is he'll be wanting to show off his dancing skills. He's a Mr Twinkle-Toes, our Richard – especially when it comes to ballroom dancing."

"Do you want to stay?" Thandi's mind was on a knife-edge. "We can go back, if you like." Then, not wanting to show her apprehension, she added expansively, "Or we can stay. You decide."

Had he been looking at her, Brydon would have seen her anxiety written all over her face and the vein that stood out, throbbing at the base of her neck. But he was preoccupied, peering inside, trying to see what Richard was up to.

"Oh, I'm in no particular hurry," he said over his shoulder, "let's wait and see what he says."

Inexplicably, while she stood hugging herself to keep warm, Thandi's mind picked up on their earlier conversation – the one about manners and what Titus had said about geography. Perhaps it was because these things had a political connotation that she found her thoughts cascading towards Gordon – she wondered what he was doing and how he was.

"You know my brother." She raised her hand to her mouth, surprised and alarmed that the words had blurted from her mouth. She wanted to like Brydon, but he was a lawyer, and she was scared of lawyers.

"Do I?" He straightened up and turned to face her.

"Yes. His name is Gordon. He told me that he left a box with you."

"He did?"

"Yes. You know he did." She stepped closer. "He said that one day I may have to visit you. I know nothing about what he is doing. Just wanted you to know that I know you are his lawyer."

"I shall neither confirm nor deny that," Brydon smiled kindly and patted her arm, "but thank you anyway. Here's my business card. Let me write my home number on the back. You can call me any time you like – day or night. Now, let's leave it at that, shall we? Gosh, it is nippy standing around out here, isn't it? Wish Rich would hurry up."

Richard soon appeared at the door and waved them in. There was something boyish in the way that he beckoned to them that made Brydon smile – it was as though Richard was saying, come quickly before anyone sees us or before the grown-ups return. They followed him in and sat down. Thandi looked around her. Where they had dined earlier, the outdoor setting had been informal and, in a sense, neutral. Here, in a smoke-filled room with low, coloured lights, the atmosphere breathed of intimacy and even intrigue – she could feel her heart beginning to flutter loudly in her ears. The music had a nice beat to it – just right for the dancers to hold each other and, for those watching, just catchy enough to keep their feet tapping when they were not talking or, when they were, loud enough to make them lean forward towards each other's ears. Richard was in a jovial mood and ordered a bottle of champagne. Brydon and Thandi looked at each other and shrugged as if to say, 'Might as well, why not?' She sipped it slowly, thinking how bizarre it was for her to be in a nightclub like this. But at the same time, she couldn't escape a feeling of elation, an inescapable feeling that this was the way things were meant to be. She was glad she had had her conversation with Brydon about Gordon – at least now they were on the same page.

The bubbles tickled her nose, and she wondered if she was approaching the point of no return and ought to stop. She settled back and watched the dancers. Out of the corner of her eye, a movement on the tabletop caught her attention. It was Richard's right hand. He held the stem of his champagne glass between his thumb and forefinger and was sliding it back and forth, in a preoccupied manner. She glanced at him. A minute ago, he had been all smiles, but now he had the grave look of a man who was struggling with his emotions. Her pulse quickened and she looked away, alarmed.

The band picked up the tempo and the dancers, following suit, broke into a quick step. The clarinet player was bald and when he raised or lowered his eyebrows in time with the music, creases seemed to ripple over his forehead like waves.

"He's good, isn't he?" said Brydon into her ear, "The clarinet player, I mean."

Thandi smiled back, "Yes, very good. I like this music –"

"Would you like to dance?"

Her heart slammed into her ribcage. It had come. What she had both desired and feared was now upon her. "What? I'm sorry. What did you say?" She lifted her eyes, dreading what she might see. His eyes bored into her, undoing her completely. She tried but couldn't look away.

"I said, Thandi, would you like to dance?" Richard was standing in front of her like a man at a roulette wheel who, having made up his mind, has staked his all on a single number. He reached out his hand. "Please dance with me."

It was hopeless. His remorseless eyes. They pleaded with her. And said, 'Help me'. Whenever she was in his presence, ever since the time that they had touched hands, lying on the floor of Cam's house in Mkuze, and more recently, since their near kiss on that sunset evening after clinic, she had found herself on a tightrope, trying hard to keep her balance and not to fall. Even when they were working side by side in the clinics, when their professionalism kept them focused and emotionally unencumbered, she had made a conscious effort to distance herself and to keep her balance. Now, here she was, feeling giddy on a wire that swayed precariously. She tore her eyes away and swung them around to Brydon for support, hoping against hope that he would reach out with a steadying hand. But he just sat there smiling as if to say he knew this was going to happen. He lifted his shoulders. "Don't ask me. Go ahead and dance if you want to dance – I mean, it's a free world."

She turned back to Richard and dipped her eyes, staring instead at the wedding ring on his still outstretched hand. "I don't know how to dance like that." It was her last ploy. She knew it would be useless, but she felt compelled to use it anyway – as if, in so doing, she was convincing herself that she had done all that she could to avoid tipping over and cartwheeling into the void.

"Don't worry. I'll show you."

Thandi took a deep breath and stood up. She tipped back her head and looked Richard straight in the eye. Then, with blood roaring in her ears, she jumped. "Thank you, Richard, I'd love to dance." It was the first time she had ever addressed him by his first name. He heard it like a foghorn – his heart kicked in his chest and his smile, a triumphant slash of white in the dim smoke-laden light, split his face from ear to ear. She placed her fingers in his hand and followed him onto the dance floor.

For a while Brydon watched them dance. He knew. The tell-tale signs had been there right from the start. But he worried about where it would go. All he could see was a disaster in the making; someone was going to get hurt. He liked his friend immensely, and he liked Thandi, but how would the feisty Magda react to all this? Hell hath no fury to match that of a woman scorned, he reminded himself. He flinched – he had seen Magda once or twice on her high horse, with torrential fire and brimstone pouring from her magnificent eyes – he didn't fancy being on the receiving end of that. He felt a hand tap his shoulder and turned around to find a short, slightly built man with wire-rimmed glasses standing beside him.

"Sorry to interrupt you, but is that by any chance Richard Barclay?" He pointed across the dance floor, "I mean, the guy dancing over there?"

"Yes, why?"

"Thought I recognised him. Haven't seen him for ages."

"You know Richard?"

"Yes, Willie Simpson is my name. Richard and I were at primary school together. He spoke Zulu like one of them – I always remember that. He went to boarding school and about the same time my family moved to Johannesburg, so we lost touch." He sat down, crossed his legs, and nonchalantly lit a foul-smelling cigarillo. "Andre Celliers was our hero then. Funny world – now he's Richard's brother-in-law. You know Andre?" He nodded and took another puff. "Actually, I see quite a lot of Andre – we're good mates. He's in the police and I'm a reporter. Crime, that's my gig – I write for the Mercury and Andre often gives me, you know, good leads ... especially the juicy stuff."

There was hint of cockiness about Willie that Brydon didn't like, but it was the presumptive way that he plonked himself down and made himself at home without being asked that really made him see red. He decided then and there that he'd had enough. "Nice meeting you. I'll tell Rich you're here."

But Willie was unperturbed. He blew a smoke ring and watched it float upwards. "You guys here on holiday? Come over for a little bit of crumpet? Don't mind a bit myself." He winked and waved his cigarillo in Richard's direction. "I see he's into it."

Brydon got to his feet. "For your information, that girl is not a bit of crumpet, as you put it.' He struggled to control himself, "She's a nurse if you must know, and a bloody good one at that. She works for the Barclays and is a family friend. We, the three of us, have just brought a very sick woman to a hospital here in LM. He's just dancing, that's all. So, it's a bit rich of you to jump to conclusions –"

"Keep your hair on," Willie stood up and stepped back, "I just came to say hello. But if you think that he's just playing the family friend game, think again." He pointed at the dance floor behind Brydon, jabbing his finger like an arrow. Brydon turned around. Richard and Thandi were in the middle of the floor, barely moving, and dancing cheek to cheek. "They're more than close friends, if you ask me." Brydon heard the 'Gotcha' in Willie's voice and he seethed. "Don't worry, *boet*. I won't tell. This is LM – he can do as he likes." Willie stubbed out his cigarillo. "Tell him I said hello."

He walked away to the bar where his companions were waiting for him. They slid off their barstools and huddled around him. And then, as if on cue, they all turned round together and looked back at him. Even from where he stood, across the dimly lit room, Brydon sensed as much as saw their raised eyebrows. He watched them walk out. He was furious that he had been flat-footed by what he regarded was nothing more than a mealy-mouthed little twerp. There would be little point in telling Richard, so he decided to keep the Willie encounter to himself. He sat down and picked up his drink. An unpleasant smell caught his nostrils and he sniffed; Willie's crushed cigarillo, smouldering in the ashtray and giving off tired wisps of smoke, was spreading its obnoxious odour far and wide. After a while he got up and made his way onto the dance floor. Richard looked up.

"What's up?"

"I'm knackered. I'm going to get a cab and head back."

"Really? So soon? What's the time?"

"Nearly midnight. You two stay on. I'll see you in the morning, downstairs for *brekkie* – how does 8:00 am sound?"

"Don't go," said Richard, in a feeble attempt to detain his friend, "we won't be long, will we?" But Thandi just held his hand in both of hers and looked the other way. "Okay then, Bry, see you at breakfast. 8:00 am suits me fine."

When Brydon reached the door, he paused and turned around. Richard and Thandi were once again glued together – not so much in a dance, as in a slow, trance-like *pirouette* on feet that barely moved. They did not notice the band change its tempo, nor did they notice the couples follow suit and quickstep around them with their arms outstretched. Brydon smiled wryly and shook his head. Richard and Thandi seemed impervious to the swirl around them; it was now the world that moved, not them.

***

Long before daybreak – before the prawn boats had puttered back into the harbour and before the seagulls had even risen to hover around them with their plaintive, wheeling cries – long before then, the sky from Richard's open bedroom window seemed to him to be a blank page, awaiting his hesitant pencil. He stared at that opaque page, wondering. There was that tight knot in his stomach again. He wasn't looking forward to the morning – still less to what the new day might usher in. His anxious heart, simmering like a kettle, kept sleep at bay and Thandi's bare arm, lying across his chest with her hand clenched beneath his ear, kept him as still as a mouse. He wasn't sure how it had happened. He had always prided himself on caution, discretion, measured restraint – all the things which protected him from raised eyebrows – he, now in a bed of his own making, had given in to what, a foolish, vainglorious whim? No, not that – that was cheap and trite, had a hollow ring to it, and offended his ears. This was something more, he persuaded himself, much more – something wholesome and edifying, instigated by impulses beyond his control. He had crossed the Rubicon and there was no turning back. Before him yawned the abyss and behind him, lay the blackened carcasses of burned boats. Dread quickened his pulse and he tried to take stock. For the first time in his life, he had broken the law – not here of course, but in the country he called home. And he had wittingly contravened one of the strictest social mores of the day. The consequences of this single transgression could well be dire and could extract from him a toll he wasn't sure he could readily pay. Esteem, honour, standing in the community, all trampled underfoot – the family name would be dragged through the mud, forever soiled. Ruin. The word stared him in the face and followed his thoughts wherever they went. And he had violated his wedding vows, something he thought he would never do in a million years. Magda, and the children. How would he be able to look them in the eye and pretend nothing had happened? But … But then, why not? Did they have to know? Affairs happened all the time. Didn't people in similar situations manage to keep their philandering safely hidden without letting their lives come undone? He cringed at the thought of being found out. Into his swirling mind came a line form *Lady Macbeth* he'd learned at school, '*Things without all remedy should be without regard: what's done is done.*' Well, it was done. The question now was how to go forward?

When in trouble, he told himself, turn adversity into advantage – do whatever is necessary to deflect fault or avoid embarrassment. This survival strategy had served him well in the past and now he fell back onto it, quickly wrapping his mind around his predicament and moulding it into something he could live with. The rationale he fashioned was that going forward his actions should be interpreted as being done not for selfish reasons, but purely for the best interests of others – especially those near and dear to him. Surely it would be better to save them from hurt and humiliation. The more he worked this idea, modelling it with careful attention to detail, the more he liked it. If he could keep things under wraps and, at the same time, could maintain an innocent disposition, then nobody would get hurt and nobody would know. Nobody needed to know. And, with a bit of luck, he could keep seeing Thandi.

He wondered how Thandi would react, if she would trust him, if she would keep it a secret. Their friendship and professional regard for each other had ripened, he would tell her, as surely as had the apple on the tree in the Garden of Eden – they had eaten it, and now they had to cover their new-found nakedness. Would she accept his rationale – that from now on, their relationship would have to go underground – would she accept that this self-sacrifice was for a greater good that embodied her as well? Would she be willing to stay in the shadows and lead a double life? Is that what being a kept woman meant? He balked at that, finding the connotations associated with this reality to be both repugnant and distasteful, but there was no alternative. Nothing else he could offer, nothing that wouldn't rock the boat or pitch them into the turbulent waters of humiliation and disgrace. Richard pondered. They had simply succumbed to an irresistible force. A force that had been gathering momentum for a long time – one like the coiled spring in a grandfather clock, readying itself to strike the hour – and they had been powerless to stop it. His heart was squirming in his chest – if only he could freeze time, tomorrow would never come!

The first glimmers of dawn crept in through the window. His mind raced. It wasn't as though he had forced himself upon her or that she had been led unwilling to his bed – God no, she had been as eager and as willing as he had been. When he had asked her, hot of breath, "Should we?" she had stared at him with unblinking eyes and said, "If you want to, then so do I." The decision, like a finger on a trigger, had been his. She had given herself to him and this realisation kindled a fierce sense of pride, deep in his soul. With Magda, lovemaking was incredibly thrilling and intensely physical – an erotic journey mapped by his schoolboy fantasies. With Thandi, while it was equally as pleasurable, it brought with it a profound sense of accomplishment, and a pervasive peacefulness, the likes of which he had never before associated with sex. He tried to look at her without moving, but all he could see was the top of her head. It was still too dark to see properly, but he could not stop his eyes from wandering down the curve of her back and settling on where he knew the smooth skin of her bottom to be. A spasm of awareness flared hotly and just for a second, his hold on her body tightened. She stirred but did not wake; one hand pulled up the sheet and she nuzzled closer. Her breasts were warm against his ribs, her hair soft and fragrant in his face. An immense desire to protect her overcame him; he eased onto his side and brought his free hand over and there, with infinite tenderness, he stroked her back, up and down, up and down. He would not give her up, not this. His feet had always found the steppingstones of other people's expectations with unerring accuracy; now he was in uncharted territory, and they had to find their own way. Others had committed adultery and had managed to survive, keeping their reputations intact – he was determined to not be the exception.

His panic began to subside – in his mind's eye he took up his pencil and faced the blank page. He would write his own narrative – the idea of following somebody else's script filled him with dread – he alone would be the creator of tomorrow's story. Everything would work out just fine. He felt sure he could persuade Thandi to follow his footsteps and allow him to lead her, just as he had on the dance floor. Safety was the key and secrecy its *alma mater* – these would be his watchwords. His writer's block began to dissolve – words began to align themselves, slowly at first, but they soon gathered pace. One scene merged into the next, forming a coherent and plausible storyline with a fluency that made him smile. Unlike the proverbial rolling stone which gathers no moss, a rolling grain of truth on the other hand, often does – it can quickly become encased in layers of comforting half-truths, deflections and, at times, bare-faced denials. The writer's mantle settled on him like a blanket and Richard, now in fiction mode and feeling more content, closed his eyes, shuffling his thoughts like a sheaf of papers; soon, he was fast asleep.

4

Isaac felt a tug on his line. Was it a fish or a wave-bite? A rush of adrenaline made him jump to his feet – his fingertip reading the line and his body tense and poised, like a heron ready to strike. He wound in a few turns on his wooden Scarborough fishing reel to tighten the line. The tip of his rod was high above him and nodded knowingly at the sea. He stared at the waves and waited. Nothing happened. He relaxed, then decided to reel in and check his bait. It looked a little moth-eaten, so he added a bit more crab to his hook – just enough to hide the barb without choking it – and walked down to the water's edge. He bent down and washed his fingers and dried them on his shorts while he waited for a gap between the waves. Then, as a large one was sucked back into the sea, hissing, and gurgling as he ran after it, he quickly turned his back and swung his rod around in a long sweeping motion that hurled his trace over his shoulder high into the sky. He turned, keeping his eye on the bait and sinker, and when they began to arc gracefully downwards, to the mottled blue-green water well beyond the shore break, he used the palm of his hand to slow the reel and stop it from over-winding. Satisfied with his cast, he high stepped out of another receding wave and headed for the beach, carrying his rod high above his head and allowing the reel to let out line as he went.

Only then, while he was adjusting the slack on his line and wriggling his bottom to get comfortable on the sand, did he notice a figure walking towards him on the beach. At first, it was nothing more than a black dot, smudged by the haze, and so far away he could hardly see that it was moving. Isaac watched it curiously, wondering if it was someone coming to see the doctor. Slowly the figure got closer and closer. It metamorphosed into a woman; she was wearing pants – native women didn't do that; they only wore dresses. The woman was walking slowly along the beach, just above the high-water mark. Every so often she would bend down and fossick in front of her with a piece of driftwood. A few minutes later, he recognised her. It was Thandi. His heart began to flap like a bird in a cage. She was looking for shells. Isaac stared at her, spellbound. In her unguarded self-absorption, she seemed to him to be an ethereal spirit, something from a dream. Yet, at the same time, there was a poignant, flesh-and-blood vulnerability about her unguardedness that made his throat tighten.

"Hello, Thandi," he called out when he thought she was within earshot, "what are you doing? Looking for shells? Any nice ones?"

She looked up, smiled briefly, and carried on examining the tidal debris in front of her. Presently she reached him and sat down beside him, placing her bag of shells in front of her feet.

"Hello, Isaac. Caught anything?"

"No, nothing yet." He looked at her quizzically, "You okay? I mean, is everything alright?"

"Yes. Why?"

"You seem sort of quiet these last couple of days – ever since you got back from LM. Just wondered if anything happened there to upset you?"

She looked at him sharply – was she so transparent? "No. I'm fine," she said, as though reciting a familiar verse, "the woman died on the operating table. Made me so sad, you know, so sad. After all that we had done for her. And she so nearly made it. And the poor baby. Never had a chance. But I knew that – knew it before we got there." Thandi paused; sunlight, sparkling on the water each time the waves swelled up, caught her eye – such an enchanting sight. "So very sad," she said turning back to him, "her husband stayed in LM, you know – he's going to bury her. The Doctor and Mr Bryson gave him money for the funeral. The trip back was much better –"

"I know all that, Thandi – you already told me. About the woman. And her husband. Terrible business." He peered at her intently, "But you – what's happened to you, Thandi?"

"Me?" She searched his face. "Nothing's wrong. I'm just tired, that's all."

"Well, you're not the same. We've all noticed it." He piled up some sand with his foot, then kicked it away. "Fanakanye says you were quiet all the way back from LM. Something's changed. You slip around the camp like … like a ghost … or even like an *umgodoyi.*" He saw the look on her face and quickly recanted. "No, no, not like a dog. Sorry, I didn't mean that." She tried to hold his gaze but couldn't. "Thandi, it's none of my business, but you seem to be avoiding us. No more smiling face, no more laughing, no more the old Thandi we all like so much. Everyone's noticed it. You sure nothing's wrong? You seem to want to be alone. You go to bed early, go for long walks by yourself … Sure everything's okay? Nothing bothering you?"

Her lower lip quivered and her eyelashes, overburdened, fluttered briefly then capitulated. A tear spilled. She kept her mouth tightly shut, eyes looking straight ahead at the broad expanse of sea which heaved and swayed beneath a cloudless blue sky. A large flock of terns crossed her field of vision, distracting her. She watched them as she gathered her thoughts; watched the furious flap of dark wings, watched the angular shapes skim low and fast in a northerly direction, watched them arrow into the distance, tiny black specks that were soon swallowed up by the sea.

"Thandi, look at me."

Her mind was in turmoil and her emotions, bubbling as though in a kettle, were on the brink of boiling over. She hesitated, downcast, wanting to shut him out, but the concern in his voice undid her. She began to cry. Her shoulders shook. He watched and waited. At last, she wiped her nose with the back of her hand, and she turned her head to him. Her eyes found his and locked onto them.

"Oh, Isaac", she said, her voice wet and punctuated with sobs, "my heart. It's breaking. I don't know what to do."

"Why? What's happened?"

"I slept with him."

"Slept with who?"

"With Richard."

There was a long silence. Isaac stared at her wild-eyed and disorientated. He allowed the implications of what he had just heard to percolate his thinking and slowly dilute his disbelief.

"Why? Did he take advantage of you?"

"No. Not that. We … I spent the night in his room."

"You love him?"

"Oh, I don't know," she said, managing to control her tears, "I really don't know. We have always been fond of each other, right from when we were kids. And then one day, when I was nursing at Ubombo, we were listening to music together and I suddenly realised that there was more to it – the way he looked at me, the touch of his hand – my heart went boom-boom. Oh, how I ached! I was so afraid; I didn't know what to do."

"What did you do?"

"I ran away." She saw that he was about to speak, so she lifted her hand to silence him.

"All these years I have tried so hard to keep our friendship … well, just a friendship. You know, to stop it from growing into anything more. But I –"

"If you ran away, why did you go and work with his mother?"

"I don't know. Maybe I thought I could keep my distance. You see, I still liked him, liked him a lot. I enjoy being with him – always have. I knew he liked me. We have so much fun together. Isn't that enough for a girl? And he's a good doctor, you know – I like working with good doctors … I have had other boyfriends, but there was nothing for me in Ubombo, nothing except more peace and quiet than I knew what to do with … I soon got bored. I mean, it's a nice place and all that, but there were no educated men there … nobody interesting, nobody to really talk to … nobody that could make me feel special like Richard does … nobody there that would, you know, treat me like a lady. Then recently, coming home from clinic, it happened again. We nearly kissed. I got a fright – a big fright. I thought it had gone. The feeling. Thought it was gone. Is it love? I don't know. What is love? Do you know? Can you tell me? I am so confused." She lifted up her hand again. "Then, in LM, he asked me to dance. Maybe I was too tired to say no – or maybe it was the wine, or maybe I just wanted to – who knows. Why does anybody do anything – does there always have to be a reason?"

Thandi shook her head and rubbed her eyes with her knuckles. She took a deep breath.

"But you know what? I was having a wonderful time. I just let go and began to enjoy myself. After all this time, living … you know, in denial, holding myself back … Always such a struggle. So, I let go. Just like that. It was so good. So very good. I mean, we – the three of us – we were enjoying ourselves … just being ourselves … It was so … How shall I put it, so sort of natural. For the first time in my life, I was a woman in male company and colour didn't matter. It was an incredible feeling. I was on a high. All around me – at the restaurant and at the nightclub – there were black and white people sitting together and having fun. Then he asked me to dance. God knows I had been dreading it. I was going to refuse but then something in me snapped. I got up and we danced. I knew what was going to happen – I

230

am a woman, after all, I just knew. I was so excited. And very frightened. But right then I didn't care. At times like that, you … you just follow your nose … you just let go. The thinking comes afterwards. We danced a lot. And he kissed me. Then we went back to the hotel, and I spent the night in his room."

She waited for his reaction, but all he did was clench his jaw and stare at the sea while, without getting up, he slowly reeled in his line. He laid his rod down and faced her, cross-legged.

"And then? What now?"

"Then the sun came and woke us up. Had I been dreaming? I woke and straight away knew that this was a new me, if you know what I mean – I was now a stranger living in a new world. How should I, you know, conduct myself in this new place? I was suddenly frightened. There I was, in bed with a white married man. You can hardly believe it, can you? I am a Christian, not a heathen, but I wonder what the *amadlozi* would say. Isaac, please tell me, do you think that I have I sinned?"

He leaned forward and patted her knee. "No, of course not. It's not for me to –"

"Yes, but am I a bad woman? Was it my fault? I don't know what to think. I feel guilty, upset, frightened, happy, sad – all mixed up. I'm a mess, Isaac, a big mess."

"No, you're not. Not at all. Just a beautiful girl who dared to follow her heart. That's pretty special as far as I'm concerned. But tell me, what does Richard think?"

"I asked him what we were going to do. He said it would be best for all concerned if we played it safe and kept it quiet. I asked who the 'all concerned' were and he said everyone. That didn't make sense to me, but I didn't say anything. He went on and said that when we were with other people we should behave as we always had – like colleagues, like good friends – nothing more. But when we were alone and together, then we could be ourselves and love each other. That's living a lie, don't you think? He told me that it was going to be difficult for him, that he needed time to work it out – but it would work out okay, he promised me. You know, the more he spoke, the more upset I became – it was like he wanted to have two lives. A public one and a private one. That worried me. All the time he was telling me that he loved me … he said it a lot … Trust me, he kept saying, just trust me. But I soon found myself questioning what sort of love this is … I mean, how can you separate your heart from your head, hey? How can you live two lives? For what? And how would it end up?"

Thandi wrapped her arms around her legs and rested her chin on her knees. Talking to Isaac was turning out to be therapeutic, and much easier than she had thought. The more she confided in him, the more her sense of exoneration grew. Shame gave way to regret, and regret sat heavily on her, heavy as wet clothing. She regretted that she had let her guard down and had succumbed; regretted that she had enjoyed the night as much as she had; and she regretted that she had nothing to show for it – nothing but an aching feeling that a piece of her heart had been torn from her. Her misery was all-consuming; she told herself repeatedly that it was unfair – she wondered how the heart could be so cruel.

"Sorry to cry on your shoulder like this, Isaac – do you really want me to go on?"

"Yes. Yes, every last detail."

"Well, I could feel my doubts beginning to climb on top of his words," she said, avoiding his eyes now and staring back at the sea, "and I started to get scared. Then, as if he was talking to himself, he said something that was like a knife in my belly. He said that back home, back in South Africa that is, we will have to observe the law – even if it's stupid and unjust – but when we were out of the country, we could be ourselves and, you know, do as we like. He started talking about us travelling to Swaziland for weekends, or back here to Mozambique."

She burst into tears again, this time her sobs were loud and anguished. He did not move; just let her unburden herself, let her tears wash her conscience clean. He waited, and after a while she took out a tissue. "Sorry," she said, blowing her nose. "I can't help it." Then she went on.

"You know, I could feel my heart beginning to shrivel and get hard, like … like, like I don't know what. It occurred to me, right then, that everything he said was about what was best for him – not what was best for the two of us. Not once did he ask what I thought or what I wanted. He is so scared of being found out. I don't know what I was expecting … I just wanted … I don't know … I thought love would find a way, that's all. I didn't go looking for this, I really didn't. Our people say, 'Love does not choose the blade of grass it falls on.' These things happen on their own. Oh, Isaac, my heart is breaking. He did not say it, but the more I think about it, the more it seems he wants me to be a woman on the side. We'll be together but only when it suits him. Only when he's sure we will not be found out. I understand. He's married. We live in South Africa – he's white and I'm black. I know all that, but where does it leave me? Should I say, oh well that was LM and forget all about it? I can't. Am I being stupid?"

Isaac crawled over to her on knees that had their own mind. He knelt before her in the soft sand, and wrapped his arms around her and, in this unfamiliar pose, he tried to calm her as he might have a wounded animal. "There, there. Don't cry. It's not the end of the world." He looked down at her head, saw the haze of soft, fine curls and below them, the nape of her delicate neck, flowing like molten chocolate into her exposed shoulders. He looked away, aroused – looked for something out in the ocean, anything to distract him and cool the blood pounding in his ears. He knelt as though in homage and held her, soothing her with soft, inarticulate sounds.

"What am I going to do?" she asked with her face upturned. "What would you do, Isaac, if you were me? Help me. Please help me."

There was much that he would like to have said, but the words got all jumbled up in his mind and he knew they wouldn't come out right. So, he thought about his grandfather and what he would say.

"Benefit of the doubt. My *Oupa* – Frankie? He always says –"

"Give him the benefit of the doubt?" It wasn't a lifeline, but she clung to it. "Really?"

"Not him. Your heart."

"How? What are you getting at?"

"Try doing what he says. See how it goes. Give your heart a chance. Give both your hearts a chance. I reckon that's what you should do. I mean, you'll find out soon enough – your heart will tell you soon enough." Isaac sat back on his heels and took a deep breath. "Thandi, Richard is a nice man. A very nice man. But is he a *good* man?"

"Nice? Good? What do you mean?" She was surprised to hear him voice a distinction that she herself often used and she wondered if their thoughts were aligned. "Sorry, I don't understand."

"Well, anyone can be nice. Most of us are – most of the time. Nice people say the right things, but good people *do* the right things. There's a big difference, I reckon. You see, good folk aren't scared to stick their necks out if they think it's the right thing to do. Anyway, that's what my *Oupa* says. Question is, does our nice Richard have the balls to do the right thing?"

"The right thing?" Hope flared and widened her eyes. "What should he do?"

They were still on their knees, facing each other; he glanced down, surprised to see that her hands were in his – she seemed not to have noticed and kept her eyes on his face.

"Well," he said, bracing himself, "if I was him, I'd say fuck it to the world and fuck it to the consequences – pardon my French. I'd tell my wife it's all over, *klaar*. I'd say sorry, ma'am, but I'm moving out. I'd go the whole hog – I'd marry my new love. I really would. What's the point of living like a car with a flat battery – you know, looking good from the outside but inside nothing's working, everything's dead? Why would you do that? No, I'd go with my heart and if that meant getting into trouble with the law, well then, I'd get into trouble. But at least I'd be happy, wouldn't I? Like that English king – you know the one I mean? The one who gave up his crown for love? Remember that? Anyway, that's what I'd do."

"You would? Would that be doing the right thing?"

"Reckon so. Anyway, that's what I think. I'd let my heart tell me what to do, not my fear."

"You think Richard would? Is that what you think he should do?"

"I'm not Richard. I'm not saying what he should or shouldn't do. I'm just saying what I'd do."

"You're not married."

"No."

"I think you'd make a good husband."

"You reckon?"

"Of course."

He looked away. "Never found the right woman," he said with a thin smile, "at least not yet."

"What else does your *Oupa* say?"

Isaac laughed and squeezed her hands involuntarily, "He says lots of things. When things are not going right at home, he likes to remind my mom that every cloud has a silver lining."

They stood up together and for a while just stood staring at the sea, letting their minds pick and choose from the words that had been spoken and mulling over what they found.

***

A nice man or a brave man. The benefit of the doubt. Clouds with silver linings. These things that Isaac had talked about so filled her mind that she could think of little else. She mulled over them at length, and while they did little to ease her pain, they did, at last, lead her to a conclusion: trust. She would trust Richard. Trust him with everything. Titus had told her once that the essence of trust was not to expect anything. Well, she had no expectations – none that she could put into words – but when the time came, she would know. So, for the rest of their time there, Thandi conducted herself just as she thought he would want. She perked up, she fished with Isaac, joined Richard and his friends when invited, and when the last clinic came, she helped him without batting an eye. Nothing changed; what had happened on that sultry night in Lourenco Marques, lay hidden like a crab in a hole.

5

It was Magda's last night at her parents' home and they had just had dinner. Anna had invited a few family friends around to mark the occasion. She had excelled herself in the kitchen, cooking a magnificent three course meal and afterwards, they retired to the lounge where they sat curled up on the sofas and easy chairs, replete and satisfied. Andre had poured them all a thimbleful of dark red port and handed them around.

"So, you'll be leaving first thing in the morning?" He came back to where Magda was sitting and raised his glass. "*Gesondheid.*"

"Yes, I have a few things to sort out at home before Richard gets back. My ten days here with Mom are nearly up. Been nice to spend time with her – and she with the kids." She tipped back her head and smiled coyly at him. "So pleased, Andre, that you were able to come all this way, just for dinner. Must mean you're fond of your sis!"

"Of course," he laughed and sat down on the arm of her sofa, "if I didn't have a court case tomorrow morning, I'd have brought Betsy and we could have spent the night."

"What court case," asked Rita de Villiers, one of the guests who was sitting on the couch opposite them, "can you tell us?"

"It's an Immorality Act case," said Andre, and the way he glanced at her told Rita he really did not want to talk about it, "bad business, I'm afraid. You really don't want to know – such depravity is not good for delicate ears."

Magda pawed his arm. "But you can tell me, can't you – my ears aren't that delicate."

"Well," he turned back to her and paused, taking a sip of port, and swirling the fiery liquid around his mouth with his tongue, "we caught a black guy shagging a white woman. She's a teacher. Can't have that – what sort of example is that for our kids?"

"Awful." Magda pulled a face. "How did you catch them?"

"We received a tip-off. One of my men hid in a tree and watched through the window. When he gave the signal, Sergeant Mlondo and I went in. They were caught *in flagrante delicto.*"

"They were in bed together?"

"No, they must have got up when they heard us coming. But they were both naked. I felt under the covers. The area in the middle of the bed was warm. And both pillows were dented."

"My God! How humiliating – wasn't she upset when you barged in? Did she say anything?"

"Well, she did not have enough respect to be undressed in front of a non-White, or in front of me, a white policeman, so I didn't much care if she was upset or not. I watched her get dressed and then took her away. One doesn't have a lot of respect for such a person, you know – not for trash."

"That's sick. I couldn't imagine getting into bed with a black, not in a million years –"

"Happens more often than you think."

"What'll happen to her?"

"That's up to the court." He looked up. Kobie, on his way out of the room, overheard reference to the court and stopped in front of them. "Hey, Dad, Mags was asking what is likely to happen to a white woman caught contravening the Immorality Act. What do you reckon?"

Kobie wrinkled his nose. "Depends on the evidence. But it is in the nature of the native, you know, when he can have intercourse with a European, he prefers it. This has to be rooted out. *Met wortel en tak.* I haven't seen one of those cases for a while. The last one I did was a white farmer – from near here actually, from Melmoth – he was caught having relations with his house maid. He'd been convicted of it before and hadn't mended his ways. So, I gave him three years of hard labour and five lashes. The woman was a first offender – she got six months."

Anna walked up to them, carrying a tray. "What are you in a huddle about?"

"Not in a huddle, Mom, just talking about Andre's court appearance tomorrow morning. It's an Immorality case and Papa was telling us about one that he tried."

Anna froze. "Can't imagine why you'd want to talk about that," she said, deadpan. There was ice in her veins. She pulled the lapels of her coat together and avoided their eyes. "Come, Magda," she said, "help me pass these *koeksisters* around." Just then the phone in the hall rang. "I'll go and answer it," she was glad for the reprieve, "can't imagine who's calling at this time of night."

She came back into the room. "It's for you, Andre, Willie Simpson. Says he tried your house. Betsie told him that you were here."

"Ah, good old Willie," Andre got up and moved towards the door, "bet he's after some info on the case. Has a nose like a bloodhound, our Willie."

"Well, tell him to phone earlier next time."

The evening petered out and the guests left. They were getting ready for Andre's departure and Anna was in the kitchen, packing cupcakes into a tin that she wanted him to take home to his children. Andre caught Magda's eye over their mother's bent back and nodded towards the door. She followed him into the study, knowing from his face that something was wrong.

6

"How could you, Richard?"

The question stopped him in his tracks. He had just walked in through the kitchen door, with the dogs swirling around his legs, when Magda accosted him. No smiling face or welcoming kiss, just a belligerent, cross-armed stance and an implacable stare that made his blood curdle. Even the dogs stopped, and their tails stiffened. Brydon and the others had remained with the vehicles, overseeing the unpacking so that they could retrieve their belongings and load them into their own cars. Richard was grateful for that, grateful that none of them had followed him into the house. Panic welled within him. How much did she know? And how had she found out? All the way back from Mozambique, rattling along, mile after mile on dust-laden and heavily corrugated roads, he had eschewed conversation with those sitting beside him and had instead used the long silences to plan and think – much like a chess player who stares at the board in front of him, trying to anticipate his opponent's every move and so out-manoeuvre him. Always it was done from the perspective of him playing white, him making the first move. Never had he anticipated playing black and being on the defensive, playing catch-up. He felt he had been checked and wasn't sure what move he should make.

"How could I what?" He reached for her, hoping that an extravagant smile would be enough to break her concentration and induce her into his arms, "I've missed you, Mags, I really have. It's so nice to be home."

She swatted his hands away and stepped back. "Did you screw her?"

He allowed first shock then a look of grievous hurt to register on his face, while ice-cold fear clawed its way up his spine. "Screw who? What on earth are you talking about?"

"Thandi. Is that why you took her to Mozambique, so you could screw her?"

"Magda, I have no idea what you're talking about. She's a nurse, for God's sake. You know that. She came with me as she always does when I go to clinics. She helps me –"

"Answer the question. Did you screw her?"

Richard took a deep breath and stared right back at her, eye to unblinking eye. "No, I did not." The words came easily, as easy as feigned praise. Screwing her sounded horribly crude and besides, it was not true – he had made love to her.

"Where is she? You didn't bring her here, did you?"

"Of course not. She travelled with Isaac in the Ford. They should be back on the farm by now. We split up at Mposa, so we could take the back road home –"

"Never mind that, did you go to LM with her?"

"Yes." He tried to mask his unease by raising his eyebrows and rolling his eyes. "And if you must know, we took a very sick woman to hospital. Brydon was there as well. You can ask him –"

"Did you spend the night there?"

"What?"

"You heard. Did you spend the night in LM?"

Richard could feel his shirt sticking to his back and the knot was tightening in his stomach. Self-pity cruelled his thinking and right then he hated her, hated Thandi, hated himself and hated just about everything to do with the trip to the beach. It didn't help; she remained before him, resolute and unmoved. He changed weight from one foot to the other and tried again.

"Magda, what's got into you?" Out of the corner of his eye he saw someone at the sink, moving like a shadow. "This is hardly the place for this. Not in front of the servants. Let's go into the –"

"Did you? Yes or no."

"Yes."

"Did you take her to a nightclub?"

His mind was racing, looking for boltholes. He felt like a fox being pursued by hounds, at the end of its endurance and not sure which way to go. "Yes," he said, choosing words he hoped would put her off the scent, "there's nothing wrong with that, is there? We had dinner at Costa – you and I have been there, remember? Then we popped into this place where there was music playing. Just wanted somewhere to relax for a while. We'd had a hell of a day, you know, and were feeling pretty buggered. But tell me, where did you get the idea that we were at a nightclub? Where did that come from?"

"Did you dance with her?"

"Why? I don't see –"

"Richard, did you dance with her?"

"Yes. Just for a little bit. Come on, don't be silly. The music was nice and –"

"I heard that you were all over her like a cheap suit."

"Look here, Mags," he said, now furious that she had the audacity to interrogate him like this, "I've had enough of this. What a bloody awful homecoming! I don't know where you got all this or who you have been speaking to. I was not all over her like a cheap suit as you put it."

Resentment burned white hot; he wondered who she had been speaking to. Richard could feel himself shaking. He brushed past Magda and headed for the outside door.

"I was teaching her to dance. Don't suppose you were told that. Ask Brydon. Ask her if you like. And yes, when the music played slow; yes, we did dance close. Hardly a hanging offence, is it? Now, if you don't mind, I'm going to help the others get their gear."

"Did you shag that woman?"

He looked back over his shoulder at her with his face screwed tight. She thought he looked like a dog that had been run over.

"Yes. Right there on the dance floor. So, everyone could see. Now, are you satisfied?"

Magda stared at him. Her doubt began to waver. She was not sure what else she could do to extract from him what she was looking for. She was looking for a flaw in the marble of his perfectly carved persona, one that would ease her own conscience. She hesitated. In that long moment she brought all to mind, balancing gain against loss. Don't push too much anymore, she told herself, there's too much to lose. Imagine ending up being the ex-wife. Ex-wife of a doctor. Ex-wife of a wealthy doctor. Unthinkable. Her thoughts began to overpower her. She knew that Richard and Thandi were fond of each other, but would they really go that far? If not, then why the jealousy? Was it because the woman was black? Partly. Was it because she, Magda, had always called the shots and had never before been jilted or even bypassed? Possibly. Was it because she herself had succumbed to temptation and had been found wanting? Or was it simply in her stars – was it because she was a Sagittarian and could not let anything get in the way of her all-important happiness? She decided to go with that. It was like pulling a plug – tension drained from her body, leaching acrimony and indignation as it went.

"Come here, Rich," she said finally, walking up to him and placing her hands on his arms. "Please don't get cross with me. I want to believe you, honestly, I do. It's just that my brain runs away with me – can't help it, just does – I end up imagining all sorts of horrible things. So scary, I could hardly sleep these last few nights. I'm a woman, aren't I? A woman who wears her heart on her sleeve and who doesn't ever want to be hurt."

She looked up, her eyes warm now and entreating. He felt a wave of vertigo engulf him and he steadied himself by holding onto her elbows. "Just promise me that you haven't had relations with her. That's all I ask, Richard. That's all. I think I'd die if I knew that you'd been screwing a native. I won't have you back in my bed if you ever do that, not in a million years. Understand? Now tell me once and for all, you sure nothing happened?"

"Nothing. Nothing at all." He suddenly had the feeling that he was killing an animal with his bare hands – not putting it out of its misery, just killing because he wanted it dead. What surprised him was how easy it was. Loathing rose in his mouth, and he gagged.

"You remember Willie? Willie Simpson?"

The sudden change of subject snapped his head back and he stared at her.

"Yes, Andre's sidekick. We were at junior school together. What of him?"

"Well, apparently he saw you in a nightclub in LM – he was there, in that exact same nightclub. He told Andre and Andre told me. That's how I heard. Maybe he made it out to be a bigger deal than it was, I don't know. But it doesn't matter now."

He bent to kiss her and closed his eyes, concealing his relief. He told himself that if he could convince her, he could convince anyone. His voice bristled with new-found confidence.

"Nothing happened, Mags. Nothing at all. I didn't see Willie there – I'm not saying he wasn't there, but I didn't see him. Anyway, I wouldn't believe everything he says if I were you – he's a reporter and always looking for an angle. Now tell me, why on earth would I want to have a fling in LM and do something that I'd never forgive myself for? Would I be so stupid as to put it all on the line when I have all that I need, right here?"

She stood on tiptoes and kissed his lips. He wrapped his arms around her and tucked her head against the curve of his neck. "Oh, Mags," he said, nuzzling her hair and breathing in her fragrance, "trust me. Just trust me." Richard felt the quick flush of elation, as though he had escaped a bullet. Then regret set in. And disgust. He began to feel that this was all a charade – that he was performing no better than a common huckster, a dealer in stolen goods.

Suddenly she leaned back, and her hands went to her mouth. "The kids. Don't you want to see the kids? They're in the playroom."

"I'm itching to see them." He opened the door and shepherded her out. "But first, come and say hello to the others – they'll be on their way soon. I know Brydon's keen to get back to Durban before dark. Come, it'll be a quick hello and goodbye." He paused and gave her a broad smile. "They'll be wondering what we have been up to."

7

Jack returned to the farm the day after Isaac returned from the fishing trip to Mozambique – he had been at Ngwelezana, a black township just outside Empangeni, where had been overseeing the building of his retirement home. Heavy grey clouds obscured the distant skyline, and a light drizzle was falling when he drove up to the office complex. He covered his head with his hands and hurried into the workshop. Isaac was not there; he looked at his watch and realized that it was mid-morning break. He picked his way through scattered tools and the entrails of a motor that lay on the concrete floor like a disembowelled animal and made his way to Isaac's office.

"Hello, Isaac," he said, happy to find him there, "glad to see you back. We managed while you were gone – only just, I have to say – but it's nice to have you back. How did it go?"

Isaac was reading a newspaper and had a cup of tea beside him. He looked up and smiled. "Hello. Went well. We got back yesterday afternoon. Had a good trip – no mechanical problems this time. Where have you sprung from?"

"From Ngwelezana. Was sorting my house out for a couple of days. It's nearly finished and looking good."

"Want a cuppa? The kettle's still hot. Seen this?" Isaac folded the newspaper in half and passed it to Jack. "It's about a guy called Tiro who was asked to speak at the graduation ceremony at *Turfloop*. Apparently, the main cats there didn't like what he said, so they chucked him out. That's dumb, I reckon – it's a red rag to a bull, asking for trouble. Now the students are on strike and have asked other black universities to support them – says here it's the Alice Declaration, whatever that means. Students everywhere are now boycotting classes. What a bloody awful mess. Tell me, Jack, you being educated and smart – the country, it's going to pot, isn't it?"

Jack skimmed the article and tossed it back. "The government has shit for brains. It doesn't care about anything that isn't for the Whites. All this does is stir up a hornet's nest."

He poured himself a cup of tea and sat down. "Haven't heard you say this much about politics before; what's up?"

Isaac laughed. "I've always been interested but with a grandfather like my mine, it's hard to get a word in edgeways. Actually, just before

240

the fishing trip, I went to a Labour Party meeting – at the Mill – reckon there were more than a hundred people there. Heard Hendrickse speak and now I'm more confused than ever."

"Why's that?"

"Well, he's against the government but wants to work with it. So, what does that mean? He agrees with the ANC – but doesn't support the armed struggle or their call for international sanctions. So, I'm not sure what he really stands for, do you? And he's wary of the Black Consciousness movement – says that it's for pure Blacks and that we don't fit in. Said it's a case of white fears against black aspirations, and vice versa, and that we need a national convention where everyone can have their say. I don't know, Jack. Us coconuts cannot get our shit together – too much squabbling and infighting. We don't know who the hell we are or what we want."

"Well, all I know is that there is change coming, as sure as God made little apples. It's happening everywhere – the old world is falling apart, and about time too. Question is, how will it affect us? My guess is that unless the government starts talking to the ANC – and others, of course – there'll be blood in the streets – and plenty of it."

"Yah. I'm afraid you're right. We'll be the meat in the sandwich, us brownies. We'll get screwed whatever happens. Scary, isn't it?"

"Funny thing is I could have gone back to England, but I didn't. My sister Jill is still there – she has no interest in Africa at all. For some reason that I can't put my finger on, I decided to stay here. Guess I convinced myself that this is my natural home … Where I was born. But, like you, I'm neither one thing nor the other. Whites don't want me, and the Blacks don't like me. Funny, isn't it?"

"You know, *Oupa* took Mom to England to have me. He wanted me to – hey, what's wrong? Did I say something funny?"

Jack had risen quickly from his chair and gone to the window. He had his back to Isaac, and he reached into his pocket for a cigarette.

"Nothing. Nothing at all," he said, lighting his cigarette without turning round. "You were saying?"

"I was saying the Old Fella wanted me to have a British passport so that I could go back there. I have one, always have … Maybe I should cut and run – you know, maybe I should go and smell the breeze over there. Is it really as good as he says?"

Jack turned around. He leaned back and placed his elbows on the windowsill. The cigarette hung down from his lips. Isaac thought he looked old and grey. "You okay, Jack?" He asked, going over in his mind what had just been said, "Look like you've seen a ghost. Have I upset you?"

"No. Not at all. I'm fine. Everything's fine. You were telling me about Frankie. Keep going."

"I was just saying maybe I should have listened to him and gone to England. Maybe I was just too lazy. Don't know … This place is fucked – especially for people like us. Whites have everything except the numbers. Blacks have nothing except the numbers – at least, not yet."

"Yah, but we all know that's going to change –"

"But where does it leave us, hey? What's going to happen to us poor bastards? Okay for you. *Baas* Bill has built you a house in Ngwelezana – lucky you. Sure, you deserve it, but what'll happen to me and Mom if I get buggered up – you know, if I can't work anymore? We'd be in the shit. And what'll happen when I reach your age – if I'm still here – where will I end up? There's no place for Coloureds here, no Ngwelezana for us. It's probably the reason why I never got married … Can't see a future. Crazy like a daisy to bring kids into … Hey, man, why are we talking like this?"

Jack finished his cigarette and flicked the butt out of the window. He sat down and drained his cup of tea. "For what it's worth," he said, picking up a ruler on the desk and playing with it, "I reckon you should hang onto your British passport. It's gold. I still have mine. One day, you'll meet a lady and fall in love." He stabbed his finger at Isaac. "When it happens my friend, it'll blow your brains out. You'll tell the world that it can go to hell – your balls will feel so big that you'll think nothing of punching the devil on the nose. It's a hell of a feeling, believe me."

Isaac stared at him. There were sounds of people moving around outside. He stood up and went to the window. "The boys are back," he said, his mind far away, "I have to go." He stared again at Jack, a long thoughtful stare, then picked up the cups and took them to the washbasin in the corner. He put them down and then, as if in slow motion, bent forward very deliberately and gripped the enamel basin with both hands.

"He slept with her." Isaac's back was towards Jack, and it heaved.

"Who? What are you talking about?" From where he sat, he could see Isaac's knuckles gripping the sides of the basin. They were white. "Who slept with whom?"

"Richard. He slept with Thandi. That's who."

Jack jumped up from his chair and then fell back into it – like a buck that leaps into the air at the sound of a rifle shot and staggers for a few paces before realising that it has been shot. Understanding pierced his brain. He had been so blind. He found his voice and cleared his throat.

"You sure?"

"Yes." Isaac turned around like a man impaled. "She told me. But don't tell anyone, please."

Jack's mind was in overdrive. He fished for another cigarette. I'm smoking too much, he said to himself, far too much. Isaac watched him and waited. It took an eternity for the match to find the end of the cigarette. Then came the long exhale.

"You love her?"

"What?"

"You love her, don't you?"

There was a long pause as Isaac gathered his thoughts. His feelings had words in the sanctuary of his own mind but, he suspected, if he were to give them voice and air them to the world, they would come out the wrong way and sound stupid.

"Yes. Yes, I do, God help me. But for Christ's sake don't tell a soul. Promise me. She doesn't know. Ever since Miss Mary's wedding. I have tried so hard to keep them bottled up – my feelings, I mean. Didn't seem possible that she'd like me more than … well, more than just being a friend. It didn't seem right, at least not here, not in South Africa. And I'm a bit older. But we get on very nicely together, we have lots of fun, you know … And she's so kind and so pretty, it hurts … It's like I'm in a dream when I'm with her. We go to the bioscope, and we go dancing. She probably thinks of me as an older brother. I never said anything to anyone – not even to Mom or *Oupa*. I was too scared that I would frighten her off and … Well, that would be the end of the dream, wouldn't it? Why would he do this? He has a wife, and children … He has everything … Why? Why does he want more … Hasn't he got enough?"

Jack got up. He placed himself in front of Isaac and put both his hands on his shoulders.

"Tell me, Isaac, does she love him? Do you know?" He could see that Isaac was not used to questions that stripped him bare, so he dropped his hands and eased back a step or two. The sound of rain on the tin roof was loud in their ears. Jack took out his cigarettes and lit one for Isaac. "Here, have one. Good for the nerves. You think she loves him?"

"Oh, I don't know." Isaac exhaled and took another long puff, trying hard to still the tremor in his voice. "I asked her. Up at the beach. She said she didn't know – said she thought she did. Thought that love would find a way. I don't know, Jack – I really don't. She was very upset – you should have seen her, crying and all – broke my heart. She asked me what she should do."

"So, then what?" Jack waited. "What did you say?"

"I know stuff all about women – what could I say? I said she should give it a chance – hated saying it, but I said it. Said she should give her heart the benefit of the doubt –"

"Isaac, listen to me. You say being with her is like being in a dream. Well then, make it real. You know, if we don't dream, we can't fly – we simply exist in cages of our own making. Simple as that. Who wants to live like that? Don't you want to fly? So, listen. Sounds to me like she's at a crossroads, maybe even having second thoughts. Who knows what's going on in her mind? Doesn't matter. Here's your chance – grab it. Grab the bull by the horns, my boy – don't muck around. Declare yourself. You just step into the gap – be there for her."

"You think so?"

"Damn right, I do. I had a similar dream, once. Slipped through my fingers before I could get a grip on it. There's nothing worse than regret – it'll gnaw away at you. Will consume you. I was bloody lucky; I had a second go – Mavis. Thank God for her. Now, my advice is this: you don't ever want to die wondering. Go and see her. Talk. Tell her. Show her. What have you got to lose?"

"I hear you, Jack, loud and clear," he raised his arms in surrender, "but would she have me? What can I offer her, hey? I'm a bloody *goffel* for Christ's sake – no money, no future – why in God's name would she want me? After all she's been through with him, she'll probably take the safe and steady path – you know, settle for one of her own."

Jack barely heard him. An idea, propelled around his mind like a marble in a pinball machine, ricocheted its way around obstructions and hit the jackpot with lights flashing and bells ringing. Isaac was his son. Isaac needed help. He still had a bank account in England. What is more, it had money in it. He knew what he wanted to do.

"Isaac, I have an idea. But first, you must speak to Thandi –"

"No, no! Not yet."

The last thing Isaac wanted to do was make a fool of himself or, worse still, jeopardise his friendship with Thandi. "Let's see how the cookie crumbles first. Maybe then I'll have a chat to her." He'd had enough of this talk; he shrank back into his shell, angry with himself at having exposed what he always liked to keep hidden. Work. He must get back to his work – it would give him time to think. He loved to let his mind wander while his fingers worked on their own.

"I've got to go. That engine out there has to be put together. The boys are waiting for me, but thanks for the chat. See you later."

"Don't forget," Jack called after him, "you see Thandi and then come and see me."

Jack went to the window and watched Isaac drop to his knees beside the engine. Aaron, one of the shop boys, squatted down opposite Isaac and passed him a spanner. He's just like a surgeon, Jack thought, the way he takes the instrument without even looking and then inserts his hands into the belly of the engine, and there, with practiced fingers, he feels for the entrails and tightens nuts and bolts, sight unseen. Every job well done has its own beauty, he thought.

He watched for another moment before he stiffened his shoulders and ran across the yard to his own office. He shook raindrops off his clothes and closed the door. Then he went to his desk and sat down. The telephone stared at him. He picked up the handset and toyed with it for a while. Then he dialled. In the Empangeni Post Office the operator came onto the line and told him there was a half hour delay for international calls. He looked at his watch. He could wait. He booked a call to Watson, Williams and Wycliffe, his English lawyers who managed his bank account in England for him, and then sat back with his legs stretched out in front of him. What was he going to say? The rain kept falling, light fingers drumming on the tin roof, but he never heard it, so lost was he in the intricacies of intrigue.

8

As was his custom on clinic days, Richard had come home early to have tea with Magda and the children. It was nice and drowsy sitting in the afternoon sun, listening to the children play. He kept glancing at his watch and fidgeting about.

"Are you in a hurry?" Magda asked, noting his unease.

"No, not in a hurry at all – an hour to go, plenty of time. This clinic is at Cartwright's farm, you know, on the Mposa road. No, it's just that this is the first clinic since I came back from the beach and I'm wondering how many patients will be there."

That wasn't true at all. His agitation had a name. Thandi. His stomach was bunched into the old familiar knot. Thandi. She would be there. He hadn't seen her for a long time, and he felt like a cat on a hot tin roof. Immediately after their return from the beach, Thandi had asked Molly if she could take leave for three weeks. As the clinics had been closed while she and Richard had been away on their trip up the beach, Molly readily agreed, though she was surprised at the short notice. They had not seen each other since their return and in the intervening three weeks, Richard had been extremely busy catching up with the backlog at his practice and, at the hospital, had been on call for those doctors who had covered for him while he had been away. That aside, when he was at home, he made a concerted effort to court Magda with the fervour of a man on his first date, saying and doing whatever he thought was necessary to not only appease her and regain her esteem, but also to convince her that she had nothing to worry about. It wasn't so much that his feelings for his wife had cooled – though, like a well-worn pair of shoes, they had lost their newness – it was rather, that his entanglement with Thandi had somehow been predestined and was therefore wholly unavoidable. A compulsion orchestrated by forces beyond his control, he kept telling himself, forces that had led him by the nose off the beaten track into a hidden garden of forbidden fruit.

All through this period of being apart from Thandi, apprehension, like a stitch in his side after a long run, had never left him. Despite his best efforts to squash it, it leaked out everywhere. Magda saw it, just as she saw through his eagerness to please, but she never said a word. It affected his appetite – he merely picked at his food and played with it, even leaving his favourite meals half-eaten. The children noticed it as well, though they said nothing – when he read bedtime stories to them, he did so absent-mindedly, and often his voice would taper off, whispering into silence. Apprehension also affected his sleep – he'd wake in the middle of the night and would lie on his back, dead still,

245

and would stare into the fathomless void, hour after wretched hour. He wanted to see her, desperately, and then again, in cold sweats of fearfulness, he didn't.

The phone rang. Magda got up and answered it.

"It's your mother."

"Ah, Rich, you still there? Good. I want to let you know that Thandi will not be coming to clinic with me this afternoon. She's not well. Sent a message to Jack – asked him to tell me. So, I nipped up the hill to see if she was okay. Didn't see her – she was in bed – but I spoke to Busisiwe. Apparently, Thandi came back from leave yesterday and seemed fine. But today she's feeling lousy. Busisiwe said that she is feeling nauseous and is vomiting a lot. You know what? I think she's pregnant – doesn't that sound like morning sickness? Well, well – didn't know she had a man in her life! Anyway, darling, you and I can manage on our own, can't we? I'm on my way – I'll see you there."

Richard put the phone down carefully and stared at it. His blood turned to ice.

"What's wrong?"

"Nothing."

"Don't be silly. I know that look. What did she say?"

"Oh, nothing much. She just called to say that Thandi won't be at the clinic today – she's not well."

"So? What's the drama?"

"No drama. Mum asked me if I wouldn't mind popping into the farm on my way home to see if Thandi is okay."

"Honestly, Richard, that woman rules our lives. We are always at her beck and call. Surely if it was serious, she would have said something. It's probably nothing to worry about –"

"Maybe, maybe not," said Richard, choosing his words with care, "but she may need meds, Mags. The least I can do is sus it out for her. It's on my way home, so it shouldn't take long."

***

The children were bathed and having their supper when Richard returned home. He parked the car and turned off the engine, allowing the darkness to obliterate his surroundings. There was no comfort in the inky stillness – none at all. He rested his head on the steering wheel and tried once again to resolve the dilemma that had been tormenting him, ever since he had left the farm. What should he say? He couldn't say he hadn't had time to visit Thandi because obviously he had – that's why he was home later than usual. He couldn't say he had spoken to her because he hadn't – she had told Busisiwe that she did not want to see anyone, not even him. He couldn't say he did not know what was wrong with her because clearly, he did – any doctor worthy of his calling would ask those in attendance what symptoms they had observed. He couldn't concoct an ailment because, sure as apples, he'd be found out. So, if he were to grip the nettle with both hands and tell Magda that Thandi was pregnant, what would her reaction be? That question would, he knew, immediately trigger the obvious follow-up question – who's the father? Could he say he had no idea – that he was not privy to her private life? That might buy him time, but for how long, and then what? Wouldn't that just be digging the hole deeper?

Richard walked into the sitting room whistling under his breath, giving the appearance of a man who hadn't a care in the world. He paused. Magda always had such a presence. It made him catch his breath. She had showered and changed and now, fresh, and ever so pretty, was sitting on the high-backed sofa near the fireplace. She was leafing through a magazine on her lap. There was a glass of wine on the coffee table in front of her and their two dogs, lying at her feet, wagged their tails when they saw him.

"Hello, darling," he went to his wife and bent down, giving her a nuzzling kiss, "sorry I'm late." He plonked himself down beside her and began to play with the dogs. "I see the kids have nearly finished their supper. Would you like to read to them, or shall I?"

"Hello, Rich. Love it when you're home. No, it's your turn – you read to them." She pushed the magazine aside. "Drink? No, let me." She got up and headed to the cocktail cabinet. "Clinic go alright? And tell me, how's Thandi? What's her problem?"

"Clinic went well. Mum helped. Not as many patients as I expected."

"And Thandi?"

"Oh, she's fine, I think. I didn't actually see her. Was asleep. Busisiwe said she didn't want to be disturbed, so I didn't hang around."

"What's wrong with her?"

"Not sure." And then, with-spur-of-the-moment cunning, he added, "Busisiwe thinks she's pregnant."

"What?" Magda spun on her heel and nearly dropped the glass. "Pregnant? By whom?"

"How would I know? I'm not her personal confidant. I have no idea."

"You know, Richard –"

"Don't, Magda." He stabbed his finger at her, "Don't you dare. Don't go there. How many times must I tell you? That's got nothing to do with me, for Chrissake. Nothing at all, okay? When will you believe me? *If* Busisiwe is right, and *if* Thandi is pregnant, then I can tell you, hand on heart, that I have absolutely no idea who the father is – and I don't really care. Now, is that perfectly clear?"

She heard him, heard the indignation ringing in his voice but his eyes, darting back and forth and unable to hold hers, said otherwise. In that moment she knew. And decided.

"Slow down, Richard."

The enormity of this confirmation felt like a huge hand, pressing her down. She must be drowning – she had read somewhere that when someone is drowning, their life passes before their eyes – hers was flashing past right now, like celluloid film passing through the stuttering gate of a film projector. She shook herself free and came up, gasping for air.

"Slow down. It hadn't crossed my mind." She took her time, seeking off-putting words while she poured him a drink, "I believe you. Why wouldn't I?" Then she found what she was looking for and added, "I wasn't going to say anything of the sort – I was just going to suggest that we should offer her some of our baby things. You know, some of the stuff in the box room – we'll never use it again."

Richard breathed heavily through his nostrils. Magda was a little minx; she was toying with him. He knew she wanted to accuse him but now she was playing a game with him, one he was more than ready to join.

"Sorry," he shrugged his shoulders and rolled his eyes, "thought you were going to pin it on me and quite honestly, I'm sick to death of it." He threw back his arms and stretched. "You're right, that is a good idea. But first, let's wait and see if she really is pregnant." He got up and went to her. With one hand he took the drink she was holding out to him, and with the other, he fondled her bottom. "Thanks, Mags. Didn't mean to so be edgy, just now. Ah, here come the kids – story time."

He put his drink down on the coffee table and turned to the door, using his back to hide his relief. The children ran to him. Magda watched him bend down and sweep them into his arms. He thinks he's safe now, she said to herself, thinks I don't know. And then, almost unconsciously, she allowed her eyes to sweep around the room. They took in the original paintings on the walls, the polished antiques that she'd placed around the room with such loving care, the Persian carpets that she had bought in Johannesburg, and the matching curtains – all these things had a grandeur of their own, and breathed style, and elegance, and station. She knew then, knew without a shadow of a doubt what she did not want to lose. It was a moment of profound introspection in which she brought all to mind, weighing everything with the exactness of a jeweller bent over his scales. Before the night was out, she knew what she was going to do – what she needed to do, or needed to have done, in order to safeguard the world that she had created and all that she held dear.

9

Thandi of course, knew she was pregnant. Her blood now pulsed through two hearts, and love flowed with the stream. Pregnancy crystallised her thinking as could nothing else and gave her a clarity that for so long had been elusive. Guilt, self-pity, regret, fear – indeed, all the emotions that had wrapped their fingers around her thinking at one time or another, throttling her ability to reason properly and raising her anxiety to disproportionate levels, were now downplayed, stripped of both urgency and significance. Life! She was going to be a mother!

She had not been ready to see Richard when he came round on clinic day – not then, she was still adjusting to her new reality – but now she waited, knowing that it would not be long before he returned like a bee to its flower. She smiled, *izinyosi zidl' uju lwazo*. True enough, two mornings later, instead of doing a ward round – a colleague agreed to do it for him – he drove down to her house. Busisiwe, tending to Titus at the breakfast table, saw the car coming up the road. She called out to Thandi who ran to the window, saw it, and recognised it, and straightaway took her dressing gown from the cupboard and wrapped it tightly around herself. She hurried outside and waited for the car to come to a standstill.

"Hello, Thandi," Richard opened the door and was getting out of the car when she stopped him, waving him back inside. She went round to the passenger side and climbed in.

"Hello, Richard. Let's talk here. It's better in the car."

Her composure threw him – she was so calm, so self-assured, and somehow so in command that for a long moment, all he could do was gape at her.

"God, how I've missed you," he reached across to take her hand. "You're in my head all the time … I've been dying to see you … And to hold you, just to hold –"

He glanced down. She had withdrawn her hand. "I am pregnant, Richard."

He stared at her. She watched his face and saw all that she wanted to see.

"It's over, Richard. You and me, it is over."

Instead of feeling relieved – which, in a way, he had been praying for – he now felt even more burdened, abandoned in an impenetrable wilderness, lost and alone. He couldn't help himself asking the questions, knowing full well how inanely stupid they were, but he asked them anyway.

"Pregnant? Who? Me? What are we going to do?"

"Yes. I am pregnant. You know who. I want to –"

"Do you want it? I mean, I can help you –"

"Yes. I want the baby. Very much. I am looking forward to becoming a mother."

He stared at her, nonplussed by her equanimity and not quite sure how to respond. Then his feet found a well-trodden road. "Money. Do you want money?"

Thandi lifted her eyes and stared at him, searching his face. Then she began to smile.

"Another time, another place – who knows, it could have worked. It was love, was it not so?" She cupped his face with both hands. "But thank you, Richard – I do not want your money. And I am not going to embarrass you – I shall tell no one. Go back to your wife, look after her and your children. Thandi will always be your friend. Always. Maybe, sometime in the future, you can help with education or something like that ... You have given me a child, isn't that enough?"

He began to cry. Violent sobs worked their way through his body, erupting with snuffles of anguish that melted her heart. She would never know who his tears were for – were they for himself because he had failed her, for her because he had failed himself, or were they for them both because the forces lined up before them were in the end, insurmountable?

"Oh, Thandi, you are too good. You are ... I am weak ... unworthy ... Here, hold me. Please."

He moved across to her, snivelling and miserable, and laid his head on her chest. She hesitated, then reached down with her hand, and blindly, with infinite tenderness, she began to stroke the back of his head. She rocked him in her arms, as if he were a child, and let the storm run its course.

Presently, he raised his head and reached into his pocket for his handkerchief. There were tears streaming down her cheeks. Their eyes locked; hers gave him permission, so he kissed her. On her mouth; a soft, fleeting kiss, intimate, but devoid of passion; the salt of her tears burned his lips. The moment passed. She pushed him away gently.

"I must go, Richard." She smiled and prodded her stomach gently with her forefinger. "This one has a nose. It will show me where to go. I will be alright. Besides, *ngibhekwe amadlozi akithi.* You know that."

She opened the door and stepped out. "Go now. Nothing changes." He willed her to look back. She did not; the screen door closed behind the dressing gown, and she was gone.

10

They met for lunch at a nondescript eatery, in a quiet street, well back from Durban's Golden Mile. She would have much preferred the Royal Hotel on Smith Street or, if it had to be near the beach, then the Edward, but as Andre liked to remain low-key and unobtrusive – a policeman, he said, prefers to stay in the shadows – she agreed to a corner table in this rather grubby establishment. She had a phobia about men in uniforms and was pleased to see that he was in plain clothes. They ordered and settled back, toying with the ice cubes in their drinks.

"Mags, you said you were coming to town on a shopping jaunt and that you wouldn't come unless you could see me. So, out with it, what's it all about?"

Andre pushed his chair back and raised his ankle onto his knee. He lit a cigarette and his unflinching eyes, peering at her over the flame, watched her keenly. "Why all the secrecy?"

"It's about Richard," she said, leaning closer to him and starting to fiddle with the salt cellar, "he's had an affair. I know it."

"Had? Or is still having one?"

"Had. I'm pretty sure it's over."

"So?" He showed no surprise. "Happens all the time, doesn't it? I suppose though, so long as one is careful and discreet – you know, so long as one keeps it on the side … Anyway, you're hardly one to complain."

"If you're talking about Eugene, that was just a bit of fun – on the side, as you say. Didn't hurt anyone, did it? Richard never knew. Anyway, it's over now."

"So back to Richard. What's up?"

"You remember you told me what Willie Simpson saw in LM? About Richard dancing in a nightclub with a black woman?"

"Yes. With a nurse, wasn't it? You got quite angry."

"Well, I had it out with him when he got back. He said he danced with her, but that was all."

"So?"

"He lied. She's pregnant."

Andre's foot slid off his knee and he sat up. "You sure? And he's the father?"

"She's pregnant, all right – her mother said so –"

"Yes, I get that, but is he the father?"

"He's the father, alright – I'm pretty sure about it. A woman can tell these things … My husband with a black woman – makes me want to puke every time I think about it. I feel –"

"Magda, do you know what you're saying? You're quite sure about this?"

"Yes. Absolutely sure. It's … an infatuation … I'm quite sure of that. I know he's fond of her – and she of him – but not enough for him to leave me for her. No ways, hasn't the guts for that."

"Fuck me. I had no idea he was so stupid. Bad enough to crap on your own doorstep, but with a *coon*, that's madness."

The waiter brought their food. They waited in silence for the man to leave. Andre picked up the tomato sauce bottle and squeezed it, squirting sauce all over his pie and chips. Magda had a Caesar salad. She watched him put the bottle down. She didn't like tomato sauce – or pie and chips, for that matter – she considered them bad for her figure.

"You were saying?"

"I was saying he must be mad. But tell me, what are you going to do?"

"He won't leave me. I know that. Says he loves me. And the children – he's mad about them."

She picked up a fork and began to eat.

"You know," she said, between mouthfuls, "when you first told me about him mucking around with her in LM, I was pissed off – really pissed off."

"I know. Go on."

"Well, I could have cut his balls off then. And sent him packing. But now I've had time to let it sink in. Perhaps I should have done more, you know, should have made sure his eyes didn't stray."

She put her fork down and waited until he was looking her in the eye. "Andre, can you imagine if this gets out? The cops would charge him under the Immorality Act, wouldn't they? Imagine the *skande*. He'd also be blackballed from the club, I reckon. And my friends would desert me, wouldn't they – we'd be outcasts. Imagine that! And even if I bailed out, I'd be tarred by that brush, wouldn't I? No ways. I don't think I could face that. He'd lose his job, then what would we do? Where would we go? No, there's too much to lose. There's no way I'm going to piss it all against the wall – not for a *coon*. I'm going to stick by him, but she must go."

"Go? What do you mean?"

"I want her out of our lives. I'm scared that even if she goes off quietly and has her baby, she'll come back one day, looking for money. They all want money. I mean, she could blackmail us. I don't want anything that could come back and bite me in the bum."

"Is she going to have it? The baby, I mean? He's a doctor, isn't he? Richard knows how to fix things – if he wants to, that is. Have you spoken to him?"

"Yes and no. He's very touchy about it and swears that he's innocent. He would never leave me, I'm sure of that ... perhaps he thought he could have his cake and eat it, I don't know, and you know what? I don't care. Not anymore. I'm over it. Totally. Andre, listen to me. My marriage, I want to keep it. You understand? I'm not going to give it up. I'll eat humble pie if I have to, but I also want her out. She's a Christian – she'll have the baby, that's for sure. And she'll want to keep it."

She looked at her brother, working him over with her eyes.

"That's where I was hoping you could help me."

"Me? How can I help you?"

"Can't you ... Sort of give her an awful fright ... You know, scare the living daylight out of her ... You're a policeman, can't you let her know that if she ever threatens us, the law will come down hard on her like a ton of bricks – something like that?"

"Mags! I cannot break the law just to help you –"

"I'm not asking you to break the law. I'm asking you to help me find a way of getting this woman out of my life. She can have her baby. And she can keep it for all I care. But she mustn't put Richard's name on the birth certificate. I don't want anyone to ever find out. Imagine, imagine if a coffee-coloured kid walked into our house one day and said, 'I want to see my father.' It's unthinkable. Not going to happen. She must go and not come back. A clean break is what I want."

Andre stopped eating and wiped his mouth with his napkin. His sister's plight moved him, and he heard the anguish in her voice. For a moment he wondered why Richard would have a fling with a native and get himself into all sorts of strife when he was married to such a beautiful woman. And who'd be so silly as to poke a black without putting a rubber on his prick? He shook his head.

"A clean break, you say. Is that all you want?" He grinned at her and finished his beer and then unbuttoned his breast pocket and took out a notebook. "Okay, I can't promise you anything. But I'll see what I can do. Now, give me some details, please. What's her full name?"

"Thandi. Her surname is Dlamini, I think. Not a hundred percent sure."

"She's a registered nurse? Where does she reside? Any family details you can help me with?"

"Her mother worked for the Barclays for a long time. Busisiwe is her name – surname is Dlamini, it's her maiden name, I think. She's married to Titus – Titus Mkhize, he's a priest, but he's had a stroke and is a bit gaga these days. They all live on the farm. I have very little to do with them. Titus? He's Busisiwe's second husband. She had Thandi and a brother from her first husband who died in jail. The brother's name is Gordon –"

"Gordon Dlamini?" Andre looked up. "Wouldn't be a teacher by any chance, would he?"

"Yes, I think so. How did you know that?"

Andre stopped writing and snapped his notebook shut. "Leave it to me. If my hunch is right, I think I may be able to make your problem go away for you."

Magda stared at him. She found herself feeling incredibly happy; it wasn't so much that a heavy weight had been lifted from her shoulders, much more it was akin to her having picked and backed the winner of the July Handicap. She was awash with gratitude and reached over the table and took both of Andre's hands in her own, squeezing them warmly.

"Oh, Andre. You are a marvel. I knew I could count on you."

Moved even more by his lop-sided grin and the brightness in his eye, she got up and went round the table, wrapping her arms around his neck. She kissed him.

"Hold on. Let's not count our chickens before they hatch. There's a long way to go. Right now, I have to get back to work. Can you pay? Thanks."

He rose from the table and disentangled himself from her arms. His mind was already thinking of faraway things. "Don't call me about this.

Not a word to anyone. You understand? Just leave it to me." He kissed her cheek. "Have a good trip back. Bye now."

And with that, he walked out through the door and disappeared down the street.

11

Isaac was beside himself with curiosity. He had seen Richard's car leave Busisiwe's house and was curious as to what had transpired there but was unsure of whether he should go see Thandi or respect her privacy.

The knock-off bell was still ringing in his ears; it gave him the impetus he needed to make up his mind – he would go up to her house. He waited for the shop boys to leave then stood pondering – he ought to go home first and change, but that would mean having to answer questions from his mother, and he didn't feel like that. Abruptly, he turned on his heel and went inside to the washstand where he peeled his overalls off his shoulders and tied the arms around his waist. He washed his hands thoroughly and was busily splashing water over his head and chest when he heard a knock at the door.

"Ngena," he called over his shoulder, and reached for a towel to dry himself, *"Ngena."*

He was drying his hair when he heard the door open, and he turned around. It was Thandi.

"Oh! Sorry to interrupt you. I'll come back –"

"Thandi!" he struggled into his overall, "Sorry, I thought you were one of the boys. No, don't go. Come in. Please. Sit down. I was just about to come and see you."

He held a chair for her, and she sat down. Then he went behind his desk and wheeled out his chair and placed it closer to hers. They surveyed each other, each waiting for the other to speak first.

"Richard came," Thandi folded her hands in her lap, "did you see him? He came to the house."

"Yes, I saw him. Only when he came back. Didn't look very happy. What happened?"

"I am pregnant." She scrutinised his face, searching for even the tiniest hint of disapproval, "Have you heard?"

"Not directly," Isaac swallowed and looked away, he wasn't sure what the appropriate response ought to be, so he babbled on, "but when you didn't go to work, you know, there were rumours going around, here in the shop I mean. Probably that *intombazana,* the one that helps Busisiwe, maybe she spilled the beans. But I put two and two together. That's why I was going to come and see you."

"It doesn't matter. You say you wanted to see me? Why?"

Isaac began to blush. He ducked his head to hide his face. "Wanted to see if you were alright, you know – see if there was anything I could do to help. And Richard. Wanted to find out what he was doing here – none of my business I know, but –"

"It's over."

"Over?"

"Yes, I told him it is over. I wanted to tell you myself."

"You did? Thank you. Tell me, Thandi, what did he say?"

"I think he knew." She got up and walked around the room, with her hands clutched in front of her, "Knew that I was pregnant, and I think he knew that it was over. He cried … We both cried … This was a path covered in thorns – too many for my bare feet … I had to turn around and go back. And leave him there. It was my decision, and I am pleased now."

She stopped beside him and gathered her thoughts. "Until now, I was unsure what to expect. Becoming pregnant was a big shock – I should have been more careful … Not been so naïve … But the heart doesn't like to listen to the head, does it? Anyway, my pregnancy has forced the issue and it has made everything clear. And I am glad. I am not sad, Isaac, not sad at all. I have no regrets and I am not angry with him –"

"That's good of you – too good, I reckon. But what did he say?"

"Not much. It was me telling him. First, he asked if I wanted the baby, and when I said yes, he asked me if I wanted money. I said no, I don't want it."

"Money. Always comes down to money, doesn't it? It's the white man's God. Shit, if it was me, I'd have asked for plenty."

"No, you wouldn't. Not if you were me."

She patted his head with both hands and only realised what she was doing when he looked up at her with a strange look on his face.

"Sorry, didn't mean to do that," she walked round him back to her chair and sat down. It was getting dark, and she realised she should be going. Busisiwe needed her in the evenings, needed her help with Titus and the evening meal. But she dallied, feeling a compelling need for his nearness.

"What are you going to do?"

"Do? I'm going to be a mother, that's what I'm going to do."

"Yes. But what about work? Money? A place to live? Have you thought –?"

"Not yet. All in good time. But nothing changes, Isaac. I told Richard that. I'm a big girl, I can manage. Titus always says when one door closes another one opens." She paused, looking at him in a way that made his heart race. "Why, Isaac, what do you think I should do?"

Before he could answer, the door opened. It was Rosie. She stopped in the doorway and stared. Her eyes swept from one to the other. "Hello, Thandi. Sorry, I didn't know you were here." She turned to Isaac, "Didn't mean to interrupt. Thought you'd be home by now, thought something had happened. Everyone else had gone, so I thought I'd come and see."

"That's all right," Thandi stood up and moved towards the door, "I was just talking to Isaac. It's late, I must go. Goodbye, Rosie." She moved past Rosie and half turned, calling over her shoulder as she went, "Isaac, if you like, why don't you come over to our place after dinner? Come for coffee?"

Isaac leaped from his chair and rushed to the door, pushing past his mother. "Thank you. I'd like that. Very much." He glanced at the sky and reached back with his hand for the switch that turned on the outside lights. He flicked it on, illuminating Thandi in a glare of yellow light.

"It's dark, Thandi, let me walk you home."

Rosie watched him take Thandi by the arm and lead her off towards Busisiwe's house. She saw him look back and call to her, "Wait for me, Mama – wait there. I won't be long." Rosie stood staring into the night for a long time. Never before had she seen that look on her son's face. Never.

12

A few days later Thandi was in town to pick up supplies from the pharmacy that Molly had ordered. Despite the occasional bout of nausea and the need to urinate more often, she was able to resume her duties without restraint. She glanced at her fob watch and saw that she had half an hour before her rendezvous with Zachariah, the farm priest and driver of the mini-bus. He was doing his rounds in the combi, and they had agreed to meet in front of the Post Office at 4:00 pm. It was a warm day and she felt like an ice cream. She sauntered up the street to Kerr's Corner Tearoom and joined the queue at the window where non-Whites were served. When her turn came, she fronted Mrs Simmonds at the counter and ordered an ice cream cone. Mrs Simmonds knew Thandi well – she added an extra half-scoop on top and handed it over. Thandi thanked her and paid. She looked for somewhere to sit. Across the street there was a low wall that some people were sitting on, so she made her way over to it. There was a police van parked at the curb with its engine running and as she walked around it, the passenger door opened and a white policeman stepped in front of her, blocking her way.

"Are you Thandi? Thandi Dlamini?"

"Yes. Why?"

"I want to talk to you." He slammed the door shut behind him and led her towards the back of the van, out of earshot of the driver and any passers-by. "I hear you are pregnant. Is that right?"

"What?"

"Are you pregnant?"

"Who are you? Why do you ask me that?"

"Captain Jamison, based here in Empangeni. I have been asked to question you by my superiors in Durban. Now, are you pregnant?"

Thandi stared at him. She was incensed. How dare this man question her about something so private and so personal! But fear clawed its way up her spine. She kept staring at him and said nothing.

"We have reason to believe that you are pregnant and that the father may be a white man – is that right?" Thandi began to sweat. What was this all about? Why was she being interrogated by a policeman in the town's main street? Her mind was in freefall. Still, she said nothing.

"My girl, you may think that you can stand there and say nothing but be careful. Let me tell you some facts that might jog your memory and loosen your tongue. It was well known that when you were working in Ubombo that you liked to spend time with a white man. Not so? You were seen in Lorenco Marques dancing in a nightclub with this same white man. Not so, hey? You like white meat, don't you? Don't look at me like that – you are not dumb; you know what I am saying is the truth. Also, you and your family live – illegally, I might say – on a farm belonging to this man's family. Not so? And you work for his mother. Seems like you are very fond of this man – you have the hots for him, don't you? Now, I ask you again, are you pregnant and who is the father?"

"It is none of your business and I am not going to say if I am pregnant or not."

"Fine. Let me ask you another question? Is Gordon Dlamini your brother?"

"Yes." The change of question rattled her, and she took a step back.

"He is an enemy of the state."

"I do not know anything about his politics or what –"

"He's a terrorist. He lives abroad. And he writes to you regularly, doesn't he? Letters addressed to you at the hospital at Ubombo which Dr Schultz, the Superintendent there, very kindly forwards to you here on the farm. How am I doing?"

Thandi could feel her knees shaking. She kept staring at him.

"Still nothing to say? Well then, I could deduce that you are silent because you do not want to incriminate yourself, couldn't I? I could say that you are aiding and abetting an agent of a terrorist organisation."

Captain Jamison came up close to her, so close she could smell the nicotine on his breath. "Girly, here are your options. Listen very carefully. If you are pregnant and if the father is as I suspect the white man we have been talking about, then I suggest you consider getting rid of it. If you remain pig-headed and have the child, then you will not be able to keep it. In terms of the Population Registration Act of 1957, the child will be classified as 'coloured', and it will have to be put up for adoption or placed in the custody of a classified coloured family. We shall see to that. Do you hear me? And, just in case you think you can put your middle finger up at the law, think again – we are duty-bound to enforce the law to the full extent. Now, if you think your get-out-of-jail card is to publicly name and shame the father, think again – we may have to consider the question of your brother. In that instance we cannot guarantee that you and your family will not be brought in for questioning and even detained – nor, for that matter, can we guarantee that you and your family will be able to stay in that nice little house on the farm. Have I made myself absolutely clear?"

Silence crashed around them.

"Think long and hard. The ball is in your court. You can go now."

Captain Jamison climbed back into the police van and pointed to the road. The black Sergeant sitting behind the wheel engaged the gears and they drove off up the street.

Thandi watched it all the way to the stop street. It turned right towards the police station and disappeared from view. She looked down. The ice cream had melted and was dripping all over her hand. She felt sick. She walked over to a rubbish bin and threw it away. A car hooted. She turned around. It was Zachariah. He was waving at her. Heavy of heart and on feet made of lead, she made her way to the combi and climbed in.

13

Jack had just sat down in his lounge. He had a cup of tea in front of him and he settled himself to read the newspaper. There was an article about workers in Durban striking for an increase to the minimum wage that he thought would interest him. A knock on the door disturbed him and before he could respond, it burst open. Isaac and Thandi. They bustled in and stood before him, ill at ease, their faces stricken and contorted.

"Can we come in, Jack?" Isaac didn't wait for an answer.

"What's this all about?"

"Thandi was in town. Some bastard policeman gave her a hard time."

"Wouldn't it be better if Thandi told me herself?"

A short while later, their conversation became all-consuming; they heard not the insects at the windows nor the nightjar calling outside – they heard only what their beating hearts told them. It was as though they were lost in an impenetrable jungle and needed to pool their bushcraft in order to find their way out. Jack stood up and summarised it for them, noting all the signposts and the milestones they would encounter along the way. They nodded. He undertook the task of getting the ball rolling and, somewhere around midnight, both Thandi and Isaac rose, stiff and tired, and went their separate ways.

14

One sunny morning, two months later, Richard was sitting in his consulting rooms, waiting for a patient who, apparently, was a 'no-show'. He felt irritable. His world had been falling apart ever since his ill-fated fishing trip to Mozambique. Thandi. In a way she had let him off the hook but, by the same token, she had left him with a pin-pricking feeling that he had failed. Loss. It tormented him. No more Thandi in his life. It was unthinkable. How he ached for the past! He stared out the window, a prisoner in a cell of his own making, and contemplated what could have been.

His receptionist, who had been with him for a long time, read his moods like a book. She knocked on the door and brought him a coffee and biscuit to cheer him up. No sooner had she left than she called him on the phone from the waiting room, next door. She said Brydon Hamilton was on the line, should she put him through? Richard frowned. Why would Brydon be calling him at his surgery during working hours? He was about to dunk his biscuit in his coffee but thought better of it – instead, he put it down and sat back, swivelling his chair so he could look out the window. He took the call.

"Rich? It's me. Brydon."

"Hi, Brydon, what's up?"

"How's it going? We haven't chatted for a while."

"I'm fine, thank you." Richard took a sip of his coffee. "Been pretty busy, you know. Magda's in Durban for a couple of days – so I'm baching it. She's taken her mother on a shopping spree. God knows how much they'll spend."

"You okay, Rich?"

"Yes, why?"

"You sound sort of flat … flat as a tack."

"No, I'm fine. We're all fine, actually. Mags is in good form and the kids, full of the joys of spring – they're with Mum and Dad on the farm, while Mags is away … Bry, you know what? Thandi resigned a month or so ago … She's gone … That buggers things up here … Puts a big hole in Mum's clinic work. Don't know what she's going to do – Thandi, I mean. Haven't spoken to her in ages. Mum says that she has asked if they can stay on the farm. Not as easy as it sounds … And if that wasn't enough, Isaac has also resigned – remember him?"

"The coloured chap who came fishing with us?"

"Yes, that's him. Bloody good mechanic. Now he's taken the gap. Also gone. That stuffs up things on the farm pretty badly. Dad's pissed off – he and Mum were going to the Cape for a holiday – it was all booked – now he says he has to stay home and sort things out." Richard took another sip of coffee and broke a piece of biscuit off with his fingers. "I can't work these people out. We give, give, and keep giving, and what do we get? Shafted. You know, Bry, our family has been very good to him and his family – free housing, free medical attention, free rations, and a host of other benefits. And then he goes and roots us – just like that. No warning, no reason – just says he's quitting. And his mother and grandfather are moving back to Mandeni – after all these years! It's got me stuffed."

"Ah, Richard, that's what I wanted to talk to you about –"

"Everything is going to pot, Bry – everything. I feel like looking for a deserted island. You know, stop the world, I want to get off."

"Rich, have you spoken to Jack?"

"Jack?" Richard straightened up. He uncrossed his legs and slid his feet under the desk.

"Yes, Jack. That's why I'm calling you. Strictly off the record – only telling you because you're a good friend and I think you ought to know."

"Ought to know what? How come you've been speaking to Jack? I didn't know that you even knew him. What's going on?"

"Well, about six weeks ago – maybe more, I can't recall – Thandi phoned me and asked for an appointment – could I meet her at my office on a Saturday? That's because she was working during the week and couldn't get off. So, I said yes, of course. She came down with Isaac and Jack. I was surprised – didn't know they were coming. You're right, I'd never met him before, though you have told me quite a bit about him. He's quite something, isn't he – a charming man, I liked him at once. Has such a lovely English accent and such good manners – the perfect country squire. Anyway, it turns out a couple of months ago a policeman barrelled Thandi up in Empangeni – asked if she was pregnant and, if she was, he wanted to know who the father was –"

"A policeman asked her that? Why? Sounds crazy to me."

"Hang on, let me finish. Apparently, she was dumbfounded and refused to answer him. He then told her that if she had the baby and it turned out to be coloured, then he would ensure that the State would have it adopted or placed into foster care. That really blew her mind. Just to put the boot in, he said that if she had ideas of exposing the father's identity – you know, threatened to name and shame him if he didn't cough up money or play ball – then the police would bring her mother and her stepfather in for questioning –"

"This policeman said all that? Whatever for? What's going on, Bry?"

"Well, you might as well know – but I didn't tell you, remember that. Gordon. Her brother. I gather he is or was a friend of yours. This fellow Gordon – used to be a teacher – is working for the ANC abroad. He's on the wanted list –"

"Gordon's on the wanted list?"

"Yes. I represented him and some of his colleagues when they were arrested for agitating factory workers here in Durban. He's a client of mine."

"Fuck me dead. I had no idea. So why did Thandi, Isaac and Jack come and see you?"

"Isaac is taking Thandi overseas. They are leaving the country –"

"Thandi is leaving the country? With Isaac? For good? You're joking. She would have told –"

"No, Richard, she wouldn't. She made it quite clear that she has made a clean break from the past. She and Isaac are going to England to start a new life together. They want –"

"Thandi and Isaac? You sure about this?"

"Absolutely."

"All this done behind my back? That's gutless. I could puke. Bloody unbelievable."

"Hear me out, Rich. They are going to join Gordon in London. Thandi has the key to a box we're holding for him, here in our vaults. She opened it and got his contact details. Actually, she called him from here, from my office – got through straight away. I also spoke to him."

"How the hell is she going to get there? She has no money, no valid passport – she travelled to Mozambique with us on a Restricted Travel Document. And she has no job. Come on, Bry, this sounds too ludicrous for words."

"Jack's got money in London – he's financing everything, he paid for their passage."

"Jack's paying? Whatever for? What's he got to do with all this? Why's he opening his hand for them – do you know?"

"No, I don't. I asked, but he was a bit cagey about it – wouldn't be drawn. Said something about wanting to give them the same opportunity that had been given to him – by your grandfather, he said. Funny, he said that his opportunity came because his mother refused to comply with native custom – you know, the one that said the second or weaker twin should be put down at birth. Now Thandi's refusing to comply with European custom – for much the same reason."

"Well, our custom, as he put it, isn't exactly going to bump her baby off, is it?"

"No. But the prospect of being forced to put your child up for adoption is just as awful I would have thought. Anyway, to answer the rest of your questions. Isaac has a British passport. His grandfather's doing. Apparently, the old bugger always wanted Isaac to use it as a means of getting out of South Africa – you know, getting back to England where he was born. They told me they couldn't wipe the smile off the old man's face when they told him that they were going to live in England. With regard to work over there, Jack has been in touch with Phoebe – your godmother, apparently. She's delighted that they are coming, and she's already found nursing work for Thandi in London."

"Brydon, all this going on behind my back – you never breathed a word. How could you –"

"Client confidentiality, Rich – you know all that. Anyway, I fixed the paperwork, I arranged the passports. It was a bit of a sweat because as you say, Thandi didn't have one – only had a travel document that

261

you got for her trip to LM. Fortunately, we have contacts here in the relevant departments and she now has a *bona fide* South African passport."

"I'm stunned, I really am. When's all this happening – I mean, when do they leave?"

"That's why I phoned, Rich. They leave tomorrow."

"Tomorrow! For the love of Christ, Brydon! You could have told me earlier. That's bugger all notice. I'm operating all day tomorrow. I can't just –"

"I was asked not to say a word to anyone. But I saw them this morning. They're all set to go and very excited. I asked if I could go to the docks and see them off. They seemed pleased with that and agreed. Then, I asked if I could tell you and see if you wanted to come along as well. Thandi thought about it and then said, yes why not – she said it would be nice to see you one more time. So, there you are – it's an invitation. Why don't you come? I think you ought to. I mean, you can hardly refuse, can you?"

Richard hardly recognised his own voice. "Suppose not … Yes, I'll be there. What time?"

"They're travelling on the Windsor Castle. It's the sister ship to the Arundel Castle which, Isaac tells me, was the ship that took his grandfather and his mother to England in 1937. Sails at 2:00 pm. Why don't you come by the office and pick me up? Parking's awful down at the docks, so one car would be better. What time can I expect you?"

They agreed on a time and said goodbye. Richard sat like a man in a trance. After a while, he picked up the phone and spoke to his receptionist.

"Please cancel my patients for the next two days. Say I'm sick. Yes, rebook them, starting on Monday. And call the hospital. I can't operate until further notice. That's right. Tell them I'm not well and went home suddenly this afternoon. Sorry about this, but I have to go now."

Richard walked towards the carpark. The Mercedes sports car, gleaming in all its finery, was Richard's pride and joy; right now, it was as appealing as a rust-bucket on flat tyres. He lowered himself into the driving seat without closing the door and sat hunched forward, the door still wide open and his arms crossed over the steering wheel. Thandi. With Isaac. She had found a path without him. They were leaving tomorrow. He had to see her one more time. What was he going to say to Magda? He decided to phone her and tell her that Brydon had called unexpectedly and that he was wanted in Durban on a business matter – he would tell her that he was coming down in the morning, would see Brydon, and after that, would meet up with her. They could go out for dinner, and he would spend the night with her at the Royal. Satisfied, he pulled the door shut and drove home.

15

Anna and Magda paused at the top of the stairs and surveyed the ballroom that lay spread out before them. It now served as the main dining room of the Royal Hotel and with its heavy drapes and gilded woodwork, it breathed elegance and decorum – it was a grand place, a holy place the landed gentry would say, a place where people spoke in hushed tones. Magda looked around. All the men she could see were wearing suits or coats and ties, and the well-groomed women sitting beside them were artfully made up and in evening gowns – some had stoles draped across their bare shoulders. The turbaned *maître d'* was dressed in crisp whites and wore a red sash over his shoulder. He met them and escorted them to their table. Eyes looked up and followed Magda – followed her as iron filings are drawn to a magnet. She was used to it and stared straight ahead; Anna was not, she followed like an acolyte, shoulders squared and basking in the warm glow of borrowed adulation.

"You said that Richard called you?" Anna took up her menu, "Everything alright?"

"Yah. Everything's fine." Magda straightened her cutlery before looking up. "But he's coming here tomorrow. To Durban. He's going to spend the night here with us."

"Here? That's a change of plan – pretty sudden, isn't it?"

"Yes."

"What for? Why's he coming – did he say?"

"Not really. But his mother did. I called her just before we came down to find out how the kids were. She told me."

"Well?"

"Rich only said it was unexpected – that he was coming down for some business or other with Brydon. Remember him? His lawyer friend? Didn't say what it was. But Molly did. She said that he and Brydon were going to see Thandi off – Thandi and Isaac."

"Thandi and Isaac?"

"She's that nurse I've told you about. Remember? She's pregnant. Isaac is … a *Kleurling*. He worked on the farm. Was the mechanic – his family has been there for ages. Apparently, he's taken up with her and he's taking her to England –"

"To England! Whatever for?"

"They are going there to start a new life, apparently."

"A new life!"

"That's what she said."

"And pregnant!"

Magda studied her mother's face, "What's wrong with that?"

"Nothing. Nothing at all. Just seems incredible."

"But you came out here to start a new life, didn't you?"

"Yeah, but that's different."

"How come?"

"Well, I was a white person going to a white man's country, wasn't I? These two are black, aren't they? And I wasn't pregnant. But she is. Going to have her baby overseas, is she? That's not as easy as falling off a log ... Blimey, black people going to live in England ... It's unbelievable. I mean, England is so white ... Who gave them that idea?"

"I have no idea. But at least she's going. That's all that matters as far as I'm concerned. Going for good, I'm told. That makes me feel –"

"So, Richard and this Brydon chap are going to see them off, are they? What for?"

"How would I know? Brydon did the paperwork for them – got them their passports. He and Rich are going to see them off at the docks. I gather half the farm is going as well. The boys are going to dance. Yah, a *shindig* on the wharf. Can you believe it?"

"*Ek is stom geslaan.* Rich ... He must have known – why didn't he tell you?"

"Oh, I don't know, Mom." Magda felt her irritation rising. "Apparently, he only learned about it when Brydon phoned him this afternoon. Well, that's what his mother said. Thandi and Isaac didn't want anyone to know, don't ask me why. Seems Brydon asked them if he could tell Richard – why it was a secret, I have no idea. They said okay. Also, they said Richard could go with him to see them off if he wanted to. Ship leaves tomorrow afternoon. That's all I know. Brydon phoned Richard this afternoon to invite him. I guess ... I guess Rich didn't want me to know the real reason why he was really coming to town because ... You know ... Because he wanted to save my feelings."

"Save your feelings?"

"Oh, I don't know. She's pregnant. And there were these rumours going around –"

"Rumours? You're not suggesting that –"

"I really don't want to talk about that, Mom. At least, not now. Ah, here's the waiter."

The waiter went through the menu with them, and they ordered. "Cheers," said Magda, raising her wine glass, "here's to good riddance."

"Magda! That's not very kind, is it?"

"Mom, if only you knew." She lifted one eyebrow and silenced her mother with a wave of her forefinger. "Not now, Mom, not now. Let's drink to something else then ... What about to new lives?"

"I'll drink to that."

They touched glasses and drank. "Goodness gracious," said Anna, taking another sip, "this is incredible! So, what are you going to do?"

"Do? What do you mean?"

"I don't know. Just thought it might be fun to go along as well – you know, go and see her off."

"See her off? Why would I? I have no intention of seeing that woman again."

"Suit yourself, my dear. But if you want to go, I'll come with you. Come to think of it, I haven't been to the docks since … Well, since I arrived here … We don't have to go on board or anything like that –"

"You really want to go?"

"What else are we doing tomorrow afternoon? Just thought you might like to go and watch."

"I am kind of curious to see what all the fuss is about. You know, why the farm boys are turning up to see them off. I don't want to get involved or anything like that – just want to see what's happening."

"What time does the boat leave?"

"At 2:00 pm. If we don't get held up in Pinetown, we could just make it – you know, get to the docks in time to see the boat leave. We could hang back but still have a sticky beak."

Anna could not say why, but she suddenly felt rather pleased with herself. "Well, that settles it then. Must say I'm looking forward to having a sticky beak with you."

16

If it had not been for a cane trailer that had overturned on the road just before Stanger, Richard would have arrived in Durban early and would have had plenty of time to pick up Brydon and get to the docks without rushing. As it was, he arrived at Brydon's chambers late and they made a mad dash through the city traffic down to the docks. There was a long queue of vehicles at the gates. At last, it was their turn. They drove through the gates; Richard, looking around, noticed a lorry parked well back from the wharf. It looked familiar.

"Bloody hell," he said to Brydon, "that looks very much like one of our farm trucks."

Brydon said nothing; a knowing smile played on his lips. They found a parking spot and then hurried onto the wharf. There they stopped to find their bearings. The Windsor Castle, with her white bows pointing towards them and gleaming in the sun, was easy to see, so grand and imposing. She was berthed far off at the end of the quay and, shading their eyes, they could see a large crowd of well-wishers gathered around the gangplank. The hooter sounded. They grabbed their hats and began to run. Then, as they approached, they heard a booming sound, the hollowed-out sound of a cowhide drum.

Richard stopped in his tracks. "What's all that about?" he searched Brydon's face and grabbed him by the arm, holding him back, "Africans dancing on the docks? Can't be."

"Come on," Brydon pulled away and ran on, "we're late, for Chrissake. The bloody hooter has just gone. She'll be leaving just now. Come on, run."

They reached the back of the crowd and shouldered their way through to the front. Richard stopped, gobsmacked. There, right beside the hull were the dancers from the Barclay farm. And there, with his bare chest slicken with sweat, was Fanakanye, dancing out in front, like a man possessed. Then he stepped back into line. The dancers surged back and forth, holding their line all the while, and their bare feet, smacking the concrete in perfect time, rose and fell as one. The drum throbbed, the women wailed, and they danced on and on. The crowd, not used to seeing such a spectacle, stood riveted, watching in awe. Richard couldn't believe his eyes.

"Over there," Brydon was pointing to the side, "look over there."

Only then did Richard notice a small group of people standing to one side. There, watching the dancers with deep-seated intentness, were Jack and Mavis. Busisiwe was there too – beside her in a wheelchair was Titus, and behind him stood Peter, tall and as stiff as a ramrod. Next to him were Frankie and Rosie – one hand was on the back of the wheelchair and with the other, she dabbed a handkerchief at her face. Zachariah was also there – his clerical collar stood out like a white scar.

"Come," said Brydon, "Jack's waving at us."

As they walked over, Jack stepped forward. "Glad you could make it, Sir. Very glad indeed." Only then did Richard understand. He turned to Brydon who was grinning from ear to ear.

"Yes, Rich. Jack set this up. Your Mum's in on it as well. The whole farm was given the day off. My job was to get you here. The dancers wanted to say goodbye. What a wonderful send-off, don't you think?"

Jack tapped Richard on the arm. "Up there, Sir. There they are. See, near the lifeboat."

And then he saw her. She seemed to be standing right above him. He heard the dancers, but his eyes were searching her face. She smiled. He didn't know what to do, so he tried to be brave and smile back at her. He waved a half-hearted, lack-lustre wave that made him feel wretched. His eyes moved and found Isaac's eyes. He locked onto them. Isaac did not flinch. He nudged Thandi. "Go on, say something. I know you want to." Thandi looked up into his face and felt his love pouring all over her. She turned. *"Sala kahle,"* she called, and lifted her hand to her mouth. She blew Richard a kiss. It hit him like a javelin, piercing him to the core. He would have fallen had Jack not stepped quickly forward and held him.

"Thank you," he cried, as though a weight was being lifted from his shoulders. Then his voice rose, rose high above the throbbing drum and silver wings carried it across to her, *"Nkulunkulu abe nawe, sithandwa sami."* She nodded and gave a brief wave back. It was enough. It was exoneration, plain and simple. He fell to his knees and burst into tears.

The tugs nudged the ship away from the wharf. Still the dancers danced. Richard looked sideways through his tears. Busisiwe was waving a handkerchief, tears streaming down her face. Jack was waving and he too was in tears. Mavis had her arm around his waist and her face was averted. Titus, the grand old man, bowed his head and sobbed. Only Peter did not cry – he stood there resolute and watchful, like a Praetorian Guard. The hooter sounded its final blast and the ship's engines began to beat faster. Richard got up and went to the others; heedless of the tears streaming down his face, he hugged each one in turn. When he came to Titus, he bent down and put his arms around his shoulders and sobbed against the old man's head. Then he heard, almost too quiet to be sure he actually heard the words, "It is written, '*thy word is a lamp to my feet and a light to my path.*'" And he sobbed even louder.

When he looked up, the ship had cleared the harbour. The dancers had stopped, and the crowd was beginning to disperse. Brydon came up to him and put his arm around his neck.

"You okay?"

"I'm fine, thanks. Sort of hit me. You know, saying goodbye like that."

"Reckon so. Had enough? Shall we head back into town? Hey, hold on, who's this? Bit late if they're coming to say goodbye."

Jack, who was busy lighting a cigarette turned around. He saw two white women approaching. Richard looked up and gaped. The women were still some way off, but he could see they were well-dressed and in high heels. He recognised one of them immediately – recognised the full-breasted figure and the long-legged, flouncing walk – it could only be one person. Magda. Here on the docks? Then he took in the other woman. Anna. His eyes swept back and forth between them. Mother and daughter. Both of them, on the Durban docks, walking towards him. His stomach began to knot.

"Mags! What on earth are you doing here?" He stepped forward and kissed her – awkwardly, as though he was kissing a maiden aunt. Then he turned to Anna and held her at arm's length. "Hello, Mum. This is a surprise." He bent forward and kissed her cheek. "We've just come to see them off –"

"I know," said Magda behind him, "your Mom told me."

"She did?"

"Yes."

"I only heard about it yesterday, Mags, I swear. Brydon told me, didn't you, Bry? Didn't want to bother you with it, Mags, did we, Bry?"

"It's okay, Richard. It's no big deal." She stood back and pointed at her mother. "Hello, Brydon. Don't think you've met my mother, Anna Celliers."

"Sorry," said Richard, overtly regaining his composure with a gallant flourish of his hand, "I thought you knew each other." He returned his attention to Magda. "Damn traffic held me up. Nearly missed it. Didn't go on-board, though. But it was quite a send-off."

"I know. We were watching from up there." Magda pointed behind her to a smaller, raised carpark that overlooked the wharf. "We got here late as well. We were shopping. In Pinetown. Only saw the end of the dancing – a bit too far away to see properly. Why the big turn-out?"

"That was Jack's doing. He organised it all."

"Who's Jack?"

"You don't know our Jack?" Richard turned to Anna and searched her face. "Never met him? That's a surprise. I thought everyone knew Jack. He's our farm manager. Hey, Jack, where are you?"

Jack had gone back to join the others. He was talking to Mavis. Peter nudged him and pointed towards Richard. "You are wanted."

Jack walked back. "You called, Sir?"

"Yes, come and meet my mother-in-law. Anna, this is Jack."

Jack stuck his hand out and then stopped. He could feel the blood draining from his face. He shook his head and looked again. He stepped closer, crowding her, keeping his back to the others.

"Elsa." His voice was low and hoarse. "Elsa. It is you, isn't it?"

"Jack!" Her lips barely moved. "Is it really you?" Her hand was frozen in his and she stared up into his face. "Oh my God, I don't believe it."

For what seemed like an eternity, they stood like that, strangers at a crossroads, and neither of them sure what to do next. Jack recovered first. The words of his wife echoed in his mind and to reassure himself that the moment was real, he glanced back at the ship where his son was departing and smiled, first to himself and then to the woman who was lost to him – the woman he shared that son with. He had no right to burden her with more revelations – some truths he knew were too burdensome to bear – it would blow her world apart, especially now when his was complete. In that moment, Jack got the closure he so desperately craved. He stepped back and bowed his head.

"Pleased to meet you, Mrs Celliers." His voice was crisp and matter-of-fact but his eyes, moist from the sight of her and the joy he felt, lingered on her upturned face, lovingly. But only for a moment. "Now if you'll excuse me, Sir," he said turning back to Richard, "I have to get the boys onto the truck and get them out of here."

A feeling of vertigo overcame Anna. She swayed and nearly fell. Magda steadied her. They watched Jack go – square of shoulder, they noted, and firm of step.

"You all right, Mom?"

"Tired, that's all. Just a bit tired. Need to sit down, I think. Can we go now?" Richard came up and put his arm round Magda's waist.

"Here, let me help you." Richard moved around to Anna's other side and took her arm. "Come on," he called to the others, "let's go. Mum's a bit tired."

They formed a line and walked abreast, arm-in-arm. They made their way back down the wharf, past the arching cranes and frontend loaders that scurried like crabs around them – they walked slowly, heedless of their surroundings, all the way to where Magda had parked her car. Brydon watched Richard help Anna into the passenger seat. He thought she had suddenly aged – she seemed to teeter as though her feet had suddenly shrunk in her high-heeled shoes. He climbed into the car and closed the door. It was hot and stifling. He opened the window just as Richard slid into the driver's seat. The ship, as though released from a bow, was arrowing out to sea.

"Instruments of precision," Richard said, almost to himself. He slipped into his seat and pulled the door shut.

"Instruments of precision? What's that all about?"

"Ah. It's a quote from a book we did at school, that's all. A short story by Lionel Thrilling, if I'm not mistaken." He leaned his elbow on the steering wheel and pointed at the ship. "It reminds of that quote. Don't know why, it just does. The ship – see, it sails with precision, knows exactly where it's going, doesn't it? I mean, there are no tracks for it to follow, are there? No path, no road, nothing like that. Just follows something unseen, doesn't it? But it gets to its destination. Very precisely, and on time. Same with Thandi and Isaac … they don't have a path, do they? Just a destination – they know where they're going, don't they?" Richard started the engine. He drove out of the parking lot and onto the road that led away from the docks and the departing ship. He followed it unconsciously, back into the city. "Strange, isn't it? The things we follow … blindly, most of the time … but in the end we all find our way."

THE END.

GLOSSARY

Aangename kennis (Afrikaans) – Pleased to meet you.

Ad hoc (Latin) – When necessary/needed.

Afrikaans (Afrikaans) – An official language of South Africa, derived from Dutch.

AmaBhunu (Zulu) – A collective word for Afrikaners.

Amadlozi (Zulu) – Ancestral spirits who watched over the living and provided guidance on how to live a good life.

ANC – African National Congress.

Apartheid – A policy/system of segregation and discrimination on the basis of race

Azikwelwa (Zulu) – The name of the bus boycott (We will not ride) launched in Alexandria – at its height, 70,000 Africans refused to ride local buses to and from work when owners, PUTCO, increased the fare from 4d to 5d. The boycott was successful – PUTCO reduced the fare after six months.

Baas (Afrikaans) – Boss.

Baba omusha (Zulu) – Stepfather.

Bain-Marie – A utensil used for cooking, that contains heated water in which food in smaller pots can be cooked.

Bantu – Relating to a group of sub-Sahara languages that are spoken in central, eastern and southern Africa, such as IsiZulu.

Bantu Education Act – The Bantu Education Act (1953) governed the education of non-white South African children – it sanctioned racial segregation and was aimed at training non-white children for manual labour and those menial jobs that the government deemed suitable for those of their race. Furthermore, teaching was to take place in the student's native tongue, though syllabi included classes in English and Afrikaans.

Betogers (Afrikaans) – A *betoger* is a demonstrator, an agent provocateur.

Bheshu (Zulu) – Loin cloth made from softly tanned cowhide worn by males – it has a short front piece and a larger skirt-like piece at the back.

Bhosha (Zulu) – To pass excrement.

Biltong (Afrikaans) – Lean meat is cut into strips, seasoned with salt and spices, and hung to dry – it is a South African delicacy.

Blackjacks – In essence, black municipal 'bobbies on the beat' in the city centre.

Blankes (Afrikaans) – Whites.

BOAC Comet – British Overseas Airways Corporation.

Boers (Afrikaans) – Afrikaans speaking South Africans, the word is derived from '*boer*' meaning farmer.

Boer War – Also referred to as the Anglo-Boer War (1899-1902) was a conflict between the two Boer Republics (The South African Republic and the Orange Free State) and the British Empire.

Boetie/ Boet (Afrikaans) – Brother.

Bomvu (Zulu) – Red.

Bulalani abathakathi (Zulu) – Kill the wizards.

Bushveld – A region in the hot, dry north-east of South Africa.

Cane – From 1944 onwards, the use of the cat-o'-nine-tails was restricted to the Supreme Court only – its application then declined.

Cape Corps – The Cape Corps and its predecessor units were the main military organisations in which the coloured members of South Africa's population served – 146,000 whites, 83,000 blacks and 2,500 Coloureds and Asians served in World War One.

Coconuts – Slang for non-whites who behave like whites – 'brown on the outside, white on the inside'.

Chorbs – Slang for acne, teenage pimples.

Ciskei – A Bantustan located in south-eastern South Africa, made up of largely Xhosa people – was a fiction of the Apartheid-era government.

Congo – refers to African nationalists in the Belgian Congo who agitated for independence which they achieved on 30 June 1960.

Commies – Communists.

Coolies – Derogatory term used for low waged/unskilled labourers, usually of Indian or Chinese descent.

Coons – Offensive slur for a black African.

Corporal punishment – In 1947, the Lansdown Commission (Smuts government) in reviewing the country's penal policies, recommended that corporal punishment be retained because such punishment was a deterrent of 'special efficacy' for Africans, who the Commission noted, had not yet emerged from an 'uncivilized state.'

Dadewethu (Zulu) – My sister.

DCM – The Distinguished Conduct Medal is the oldest British award for gallantry by (mostly) non-commissioned officers and was a second level military decoration, ranking below the Victoria Cross.

Deduka (Zulu) – Move out of the way.

Defiance Campaign – The Defiance Campaign against Unjust Laws was presented by the African National Congress (ANC) at a conference held in Bloemfontein, South Africa in December 1951. The Campaign had roots in events leading up the conference. The demonstrations, taking place in 1952 were the first 'large-scale, multi-racial political mobilization against apartheid laws under a common leadership.'

Dingaan – Zulu king who succeeded the legendary king Shaka and who confronted the *Boers* when they trekked into Natal in the 1830s.

Div – Abbreviation of Sir de Villiers Graaf, leader of the UP and Leader of the Opposition.

Doketela (Zulu) – Doctor.

Dompas – The Natives (Urban Areas) Act, 1923 deemed urban areas in South Africa as 'white' and required all black African men in cities and towns to carry permits called 'passes' at all times. Anyone found without a pass would be arrested immediately and sent to a rural area. The Pass Laws Act, 1952 made it compulsory for all black South Africans over the age of 16 to carry a 'passbook' at all times within white areas. The law stipulated where, when, and for how long a person could remain. This pass was also known as a *dompas*.

Dr Banda – Dr Hastings Banda left Nyasaland (Malawi) to study in the US and UK. Was away 42 years and returned to the country, became Prime Minister in 1963 and President in 1966.

Dunn – John Dunn was an English hunter/trader who became a confidant of the Cetshwayo, the Zulu king. Dunn married Catherine Pierce in 1853 but, over a period of time, accumulated 49 Zulu wives as well. After the Zulu war (1879) the victorious British divided Zululand into 13 'principalities' and awarded the largest to John Dunn who had assisted them, after the disaster at Isandlwana.

Dutchman's – English South Africans sometimes referred to their Afrikaner countrymen as Dutchmen because their forebears were mostly of Dutch origin – a supercilious and somewhat derogatory term (The Dutch East India Co occupied the Cape of Good Hope 1562-1795. Britain took over in 1806)

Ek is stom geslaan (Afrikaans) – I am dumbstruck.

Farm police boys – Many farms had 'police boys' who wore uniforms, carried large sticks and were provisioned with handcuffs. Their role was to assist the indunas and maintain/enforce law and order, especially in the compounds.

Father Cosmas Desmond – Was an Irish Catholic priest – when he came to South Africa, he witnessed the forced removal of black residents under the Group Areas.

Feet with no nose (From the Zulu idiom *Unyaw' alunampumulo*) – Because of the absence of a nose, the feet are unable to smell their way – as a result, they may land the owner into places which he would like to avoid. This echoes Robert Frost's poem 'The Road Not Taken.'

Fundekela (Zulu) –Molest.

Gesondheid (Afrikaans) – Good health.

Gevaar (Afrikaans) – Danger.

Ging – Shortened for Gingindlovu, a farming town about 30 miles south of Empangeni.

Goffel – South African slang – a demeaning and often offensive term for a person of mixed race (usually white and black)

Gwalagwala – Knysna Loerie, a beautiful bird of the evergreen forests which, in flight, displays magnificent red underwings.

Hendrickse – Rev Allan Hendrickse, a founding leader of the Labour Party (1969) that represented Coloured people on the Coloured Peoples' Representative Council.

Hluzo/ihluzo (Zulu) – Is a woven beer strainer, used in the preparation millet beer to separate the grain from the liquid.

Hlyana (Zulu) – Mad-man, a lunatic.

House arrest – In terms of the 'Suppression of Communism Act' detainees were confined to their homes where strict conditions (restricting their movements and who they could associate with) were applied to them.

Ilanga – Ilanga lase Natal is a Zulu newspaper founded in 1903 by Dr John Dube (1871-1946) who was the founding president of the South African Native National Congress (SANNC) which became the African National Congress in 1923.

Imidibi (Zulu) – Young boys carried the sleeping mats, cooking utensils and other paraphernalia for the warriors going into battle.

Immorality Act – Immorality Act was the title of two acts of Parliament which prohibited, amongst other things, sexual relations between white people and people of other races. The first Immorality Act of 1927 prohibited sex between whites and blacks, until amended in 1950 to prohibit sex between whites and all non-whites – up to 5 years in goal for the male and up to 4 years for the female. The second Immorality Act, of 1957, continued this prohibition and also dealt with many other sex offences.

Impupu (Zulu) – Corn meal porridge, a staple diet.

In flagrante delicto (Latin) – In the act of wrongdoing, especially along the lines of sexual misconduct

In lumine tuo videbimus lumen (Latin) – In your light we shall see the light.

Indabazabantu – Department of Bantu Affairs.

Induna (Zulu) – An induna is a headman or senior advisor to a chief. In workforce parlance, an induna was a foreman (*indunas* plural)

Ingcino (Zulu) – Glue.

Inkhosana Lichad (Zulu) – Master Richard. There is no 'r' in Zulu. In words beginning with 'r,' the 'r' is elided and is typically replaced by 'l' which is easier to pronounce.

Inkhosazana Meli (Zulu) – Mistress Mary There is no 'r' in Zulu. In words beginning with 'r,' the 'r' is elided and is typically replaced by 'l' which is easier to pronounce.

Inkone (Zulu) – Patterned.

Inkosi/Nkosi (Zulu) – Literally means chief but is a common form of address to an employer and shows respect in the sense of 'Sir'.

Intombazana (Zulu) – Is a young (unmarried) girl.

Inyanga (Zulu) – A herbalist, a healer and practitioner of traditional medicine, fulfilling deep-seated societal needs.

Isibindi (Zulu) – Literally liver, but here it means fortitude or character.

Isifebe (Zulu) – Whore.

Isicoco (Zulu) – This head ring symbolised that the wearer was an elder and was therefore highly regarded and well-respected in his community.

Isihlilingi (Zulu) – A catapult – the word is from the English word 'sling'.

Izikelemu (Zulu) – Vagabonds.

Izinyosi zidl' uju lwazo (Zulu) – The bees eat their honey – has two meanings (1) that one subsists on that which one has laid by for oneself (having prepared a bed for oneself, one must lie on it), and (2) it can also describe an unwise act which is calculated to harm or diminish the doer.

Izithunzi (Zulu) – The 'shades' or living dead, ancestral spirits.

Jabulisa inhliziyo yami (Zulu) – Makes my heart happy.

July Handicap – South Africa's premier thoroughbred horse race, held annually on the first Saturday in July since 1897 at Greyville in Durban.

Kaffirs – A highly derogative term for a black African

Katanga Secession – In 1960, the province of Katanga under the leadership of Moise Tshombe broke away from the Congo state and proclaimed its independence, precipitating a long bloody war and widespread civil unrest in central Africa.

Khaya (Zulu) – Home, dwelling.

Khosikazi /Inkosikazi (Zulu) – A term of respect that used to be conferred on the wife of a chief, but now said to any married woman.

Kikoi (Swahili) – A colourful piece of cloth, commonly worn wrapped around the waist by African men.

Klaar (Afrikaans*)* – Finished.
Kleurling (Afrikaans) – A coloured person, a person of mixed race.
Koeksisters (Afrikaans) – Sweet dumplings soaked in syrup and pleated into strips, eaten with coffee or as a dessert.
Knobkerrie (Afrikaans) – It is a fighting stick with a knob on its end – most African men used to carry one when they went out and about.
Kraal (Afrikaans) – A traditional African village of huts, usually enclosed by a fence.
Krauts (Kraut singular) – Is a derogatory term for German people.
Kudu – An African antelope.

Laager – (Afrikaans) means a camp or encampment (derived from ox wagons drawn into a defensive circle for protection)
Lekker – (Afrikaans) Nice.
Liberté, égalité and fraternité (French) – A cry from the French Revolution (1789) that ever since has echoed right around the world. Freedom, Equality and Fraternity.
LM – *Lorenco Marques.*
Lobola (Zulu) – A traditional dowry of sorts, usually cattle, paid by the groom to the bride's father.

Maas (Zulu) – Curdled or thick sour milk, often eaten with *putu*, an African maize meal.
Makoti (Zulu) – A term of endearment, literally means 'my wife.'
Mali/ imali (Zulu) – Commonly used word for money.
Marula (*Sclerocarya birrea*) – One of the great trees of Africa, valued for its fruit and its shade.
Met wortel en tak (Afrikaans) – Thoroughly, by root and branch.
Mkhulu (Zulu) – Literally grandparent, but here it is a term of respect afforded to a tribal elder.
Mlungu /Abelungu (Zulu) – White person/European person.
Munt – A disdainful slang word, sometimes used by whites when referring to black people (from the Zulu *Umuntu* meaning person)
Muthi/Umuthi (Zulu) – Medicine; in some contexts, can have a magical connotation, capable of casting evil spells.
My magtig/ Magtig (Afrikaans expletive) – Good gracious!

Nats – Members of the National Party, also known as the Nationalist Party (founded in 1914) originally promoted Afrikaner interests and first came into power in 1924, but then governed South Africa continuously from 1948 until 1994, during which period it implemented and enforced its policy of racial segregation (Apartheid) and separate development.
Nchebe (Zulu) – Arthur Barclay's Zulu nickname, meaning 'The Beard'.

Ngancelisa ebelini 'kama (Zulu) – I suckled it from my mother's breast.
Ngena (Zulu) – Enter.
Ngibhekwe amadlozi akithi (Zulu) – I am watched over by the spirits of my family.
Ngicela niphathele obhiya ababili. Shesha! (Zulu) – Please bring two beers. Hurry!
Ngiyanibingelela (Zulu) – I salute you.
Ngizokweqa (Zulu) – I will jump (the border).
Nguni – Classification of related Bantu groups from South Africa.
Nie Blankes (Afrikaans) – Non-Whites.
Niks is verkeerd nie (Afrikaans) – Nothing's wrong.
Nkosana (Zulu) – Literally, heir to a chief, but commonly used as a term of respect.
Nkonkoni (Zulu) – Blue Wildebeest.
Nkulunkulu abe nawe, sithandwa sami (Zulu) – God be with you, my love.
Nsundu (Zulu) – Brown.
Nukela. Nukela kabi (Zulu) – (This) smells. Smells badly.
NUSAS – National Union of South African Students.
Nxambalela – These are sandal-like shoes, made from old car tyres.

Ossewabrandwag – A secret anti-British organisation (founded in 1938 on the centenary of the Great Trek) that conducted acts of sabotage against South Africa during World War One. Vorster rose in its rank to be a general in its paramilitary wing and was detained in 1942.
Ou Baas (Afrikaans) – Old boss.
Oupa (Afrikaans) – A term of respect/affection for a grandfather or elderly man.

PAC – Pan African Congress.
Pad-kos (Afrikaans) – Literally means 'road food' describes provisions for a journey.
Pas op vir die kleintjie, Esther. Dankie (Afrikaans) – Look out for the little one, Esther. Thank you.
Plig teenoor koning en land (Afrikaans) – Duty to king and country.
Pondoland – A region in South Africa on the coast of the Indian Ocean – this territory is the homeland of the *amaPondo* people.
Popola – A theodolite.
Por favor (Portuguese) – Please.
Pork and Beans – A disparaging and churlish reference to Portuguese people.
POW – Prisoner of War.
PP/Progressive Party – In 1959, 11 dissatisfied UP members, broke away to form the more liberal Progressive Party which advocated a

qualified franchise for all South Africans, irrespective of race, colour or creed.

Progs – Members of the Progressive Party of South Africa.

Qhikiza (Zulu) – A female, qualified by age and experience, appointed by the community to oversee the rights of passage of the young girls growing up in her charge – she is like a godmother who ensures that all the customs are properly observed as these young girls grow up, until they are married.

Qhotho (Zulu) – Whiplash.

Qonda phambili (Zulu) – Steer or point straight ahead.

Rand – Short for Witwatersrand (Ridge of White Waters), a 56 km gold-bearing escarpment upon which the city of Johannesburg is built. The Durban Riots (January 1949) saw racial tension - primarily between the Zulu and Indian and African communities - erupt into chaos and bloody confrontation. Killed: 142 (87 Africans, 50 Indians, 1 White); Injured: 1,087 (541 Africans, 503 Indians, 11 Coloureds).; Buildings destroyed: 306 (1 factory, 58 stores, and 247 dwellings).; Buildings damaged: 1,939 (2 factories, 652 stores, 1,285 dwellings)

Reduced majority – In 1972 the government increased the number of seats in the House of Assembly from 166 to 171, a move widely seen to benefit it but still had a reduced majority in parliament.

Regmaaker (Afrikaans) – A pick-me-up.

Rivonia Trial – The trial in which Nelson Mandela and others were sentenced to life imprisonment.

RMS Arundel Castle – Royal Mail Ship

Rooinek – Taken from Afrikaans, a **Rooinek** is an English speaking South African, usually of British decent. The name literally means 'red neck' and comes from the sun burnt necks of the British Army soldiers who wore pith helmets on campaign in South Africa. The helmets often did not afford enough protection from the sun which resulted in the sun burn.

Sala kahle (Zulu) – Stay well, goodbye.

Sangoma/Isangoma (Zulu) – A witchdoctor or diviner, someone in communication with the ancestral spirits.

Sawubona (Zulu) – Literally means 'we see you' but here means hello.

Shaka – King Shaka was a military genius who founded the mighty Zulu nation in the early nineteenth century – it was feared far and wide.

Sharpeville – Police at Sharpeville fire on a crowd of black people who were protesting against the Government's pass laws, killing 67 (20 Mach 1960)

Skande (Afrikaans) – Shame.

Seker niks pla nie (Afrikaans) – You sure nothing is bothering you?

Sekonyela – This vassal chief had apparently stolen cattle from Dingaan who asked Retief to recover them for him. The cattle were recovered and Sekonyela was punished.

Shangaan – The Shangaan tribe, of the Tsonga people in South Eastern Mozambique, was generally held in contempt by the Zulus.

Shades – Ancestral spirits who watch over one.

Shenge – Chief Mangosuthu Buthelezi's title as head of the Buthelezi tribe.

Sizobonana (Zulu) – We will see one another, or more loosely, Until we meet again.

Smuts – Field Marshal Jan Christian Smuts, OM, CH, ED, KC, FRS (1870-1950) was a prominent South African and Commonwealth statesman, military leader, and philosopher. He served as a *Boer* General during the *Boer War*, a British General during the First World War, and was appointed Field Marshal by King George VI during the Second World War. In addition to various cabinet appointments, he served as Prime Minister of the Union of South Africa from 1919 until 1924 and from 1939 until 1948.

So gaaf en bedagsaam (Afrikaans) – So kind and thoughtful

Sobukwe – Robert Sobukwe launched the Pan African Congress (PAC) when the ANC refused to challenge the 'pass laws' directly.

Stoep (Afrikaans) – Common South African word for veranda (borrowed from Afrikaans)

Sy hou te veel van hom. Sy kan my nie flous nie (Afrikaans) – She likes him too much. She can't fool me.

Thakathi (Zulu verb or noun) – Witchcraft, brought about by a sorcerer or witchdoctor.

Trousseau – A bride's bottom drawer.

Tshaneni – Battle of Tshaneni (1884) in which paramount chief Dinizulu of the Usutu faction who, with the help of the *Boers,* defeated chief Zipephu of the Mandlakazi faction, thereby securing the Zulu throne.

Tsotsi – South African term of Zulu origin for a black gangster or young urban criminal, especially one from an urban township.

Train crash, the one at Harrow and Wealdstone – Multiple train crash (8/10/52) in which 112 died and 340 were injured.

Turfloop – University of the North, for non-white students. Abram Tiro, the outspoken SRC President was expelled on 3 May 1972.

UCT – University of Cape Town.

Uitlander (Afrikaans) – Outlander, hence outsider.

Ukhandi (Zulu) – A throwing sick, favoured by herding boys to strike partridge or guinea fowl on the wing.

Ukubuyisa (Zulu) – The bringing back home ceremony is a religious act practiced by both Christians and traditional believers – it is an invitation to the dead to make their presence in the midst of the family.

Ulundi – The Battle of Ulundi, the final battle in the Anglo-Zulu War, saw the defeat of King Cetshwayo and the annihilation of the Zulu army – Ulundi, the royal *kraal*, was burnt to the ground and the king was forced into exile. This re-established British authority over the Zulu kingdom and made up for the disastrous defeat that the British had suffered at the hands of Zulu warriors at Isandlwana where 1,300 British troops lost their lives.

Umfaan (Zulu) – A youth who has gone through initiation into adulthood but who is not yet married – a colloquial term for 'boy'.

Umfundisi (Zulu) – Is a minister of religion, and in this case means Reverend.

Umgodoyi (Zulu) – A stray or pariah dog.

Umhlaba ujikile (Zulu) – The world has changed (those days are over).

uMkhonto we Sizwe – Spear of the Nation – was the (underground) militant wing of the African National Congress (ANC) that took up arms in the liberation struggle. Was founded by Nelson Mandela in 1961 after the Sharpeville Massacre and was disbanded in 1991.

Umsimbithi (*Androstachys johnsonii*) – Ironwood.

UN – United Nations.

Unayaw' alunampumulo (Zulu idiom) – The foot has no nose. With no nose, the feet cannot smell their way.

Ungayigcina imfihlo – (Zulu) means 'Can you keep a secret?'

UP – United Party, the official Opposition in the South African Parliament to the ruling National Party.

Verboten – Something not allowed/permitted, it is forbidden.

Vorster – B. J. Vorster, Minister of Police and Prisons, succeeded the assassinated Hendrik Verwoerd as Prime Minister in 1966. Resigned in 1978.

Wildebeest – Antelopes that are native to Eastern and Southern Africa.

Winds of Change – This refers to British Prime Minister Harold Macmillan's 'Winds of change' speech that he gave to the South African Parliament in Cape Town (3 February 1960)

Wogs – In the context of this book, refers to people who are not white.

Yebo (Zulu) – Yes.

ABOUT THE AUTHOR

David Butler was born and raised in Zululand where his maternal grandparents were pioneer sugar farmers. He grew up on their farm, learned to speak Zulu quite well and developed a lifelong appreciation of and interest in the Zulu people and their customs. His parents, vehemently opposed to apartheid, taught him to see past colour, creed and race – they afforded him what was then considered to be a liberal education and he grew up keenly aware of injustice, inequality, and racial discrimination.

He married his wife Sonja in 1973 and, disillusioned with South African politics and unable to see a future for his children in the country of his birth, immigrated with his entire family (23 members in all) to Australia in 1977-78, where he has lived ever since.

He always wanted to write a book about South Africa that was interesting, authentic and based upon fact. This historical fiction is David's first novel and was ten years in the making.

David is retired and lives happily on the Sunshine Coast in Queensland where he indulges his passion for writing, doing what he can for conservation – especially the rainforests of Far North Queensland – and regaling his grandchildren with stories of a bygone era.

www.ingramcontent.com/pod-product-compliance
Lightning Source LLC
Chambersburg PA
CBHW051335020726
47501CB00007B/2096